Solomon's 

A Typological Portrait of Solomon and the Shulamite Woman

by Mark Aho

The Solomon's Bride Series:

Down from His Glory

The Shepherd King

The Stone and the Seal

Virgo Rising

The Bridegroom Cometh!

Available from
secretwineonline.com

Solomon's Bride:
Virgo Rising

Published by Secret Wine

ISBN 978-1516832491

Copyediting by Suzanne Brooks, Margaret Ball, Anton Liachovic, and Cheryl Clayville.
Formatting by Sharon Solutions.

All Bible quotations are from
the King James Version of the Bible

Secret Wine

Home of the World's Best Christian Reading
www.secretwineonline.com

Solomon's Bride

A Typological Portrait of Solomon and the Shulamite woman

Book 4

Virgo Rising

The full Solomon's Bride Series:

Down from His Glory

The Shepherd King

The Stone and the Seal

Virgo Rising

The Bridegroom Cometh!

Order books from:

www.secretwineonline.com

Chapter 1

Many daughters have done virtuously, but thou excellest them all. Favour is deceitful, and beauty is vain: but a woman that feareth the LORD, she shall be praised.

Proverbs 31:29-30

The wisest of men once said, "There is nothing new under the sun." Following each his own pathway, men turn like stones in a great mixer, a mass of shuffling bits, combining and recombining, comparing shade to shade, producing infinite variations, yet nothing truly new. Though time erases names, the heart of man remains consistent, and new characters replay the same drama as their predecessors.

This we observe in the little Israelite town of our fiction, for with slight variations, all of the imagined drama in Shunem could be found in any town, in any nation, at any time. The town of our story is unusual only in the vividness of its drama, for in this narrative, a secret visit by the king drove to the surface hidden forces, revealing plainly things that normally operate in the background.

The maiden, Abishag, whom we have allowed to be the bride of the king, and then left to turn and shuffle in the drum, soon found her person lined up next to others with various results. Some of her associates were revealed to be of like nature to her, some of contrasting nature, and some a combination. But the secret she carried exposed hearts. Such was the king's genius from the start, for the demands of justice are not so much decreed as they are revealed when a heart is truly exposed. Let us enter our story.

Following the departure of the king, drama began without delay. Abishag soon found herself in the company of a person she had not had much contact with for several years, the maiden Dinah. The two maidens found themselves thrust together unexpectedly, pursuing a cure for the swamp fever in the heat of the baker's oven room, the very first morning after the king's escape.

Abishag, flushed red and moist with sweat, wiped aside a black strand of hair from her face as she sat on the stone bench across from the oven. She fingered her water flask, looking thoughtfully at Dinah whose turn it was to tend the fire. Abishag scooted farther down the bench as Dinah's small white hand reached for the oven door handle. It was wise to stay as far back as possible when the oven door was opened, for the blast of heat that rushed out made the already sweltering room almost intolerable. Abishag smiled as she watched Dinah. She was pleasantly surprised to find this former acquaintance in the oven room when she arrived early that morning to begin a week of exposure to the hot, dry air as Solomon had instructed her.

Dinah, while surprised to find herself joined by Abishag, was not immediately sure if it was a pleasant surprise, and might have said so if not for the fact that she had already endured the heat alone for four days. She was grudgingly happy for another person to complain to, even if it was a person with whom she was not completely comfortable.

For Abishag, the requirement to sit and do nothing was rare, but welcome. After the dizzying events of the previous day—indeed, the previous weeks—her mind accepted gladly the sudden intermission, seizing a much-needed chance to reflect upon the surprising turn that her life had taken. The previous night, she and Huram, her newly-found and instantly loved brother, had huddled around a late burning lamp, relating to their mother, Abelah, the story of the king's questioning before the elders, his turning the tables on his accusers, and his remarkable escape. Abelah had listened with rapt wonder.

When these astonishing revelations were concluded, Abishag informed her brother and mother of her other secret: that she had contracted the swamp fever and was to begin treatment in the baker's oven room the very next morning. Huram, though pressed with urgent business on many fronts, volunteered to stay with Abelah for the week Abishag would be gone.

"What business can be more important than the care of my own mother?" he had asked.

Abelah gratefully agreed, and Abishag felt more comfortable being absent, knowing that her mother was not home alone.

Abishag watched Dinah work. Dinah moved quickly and efficiently. Dinah seemed to do everything fast. She could speak fast, think fast, talk fast, draw fast, and, when working, her hands moved fast. Dinah had opened the oven door and whirled, stoking it with dry logs quickly, holding her face back from the heat, and then slamming it shut as much in anger as in haste. Abishag held up the water flask to the pretty, dark-haired girl she had known in the past as a fellow disciple under the tutelage of Shammai. In recent years, Dinah had drifted away, giving herself instead to employment in her father's drinking room, a seamy occupation that Abishag sadly watched Dinah enter. Dinah took the flask and savored a deep drink, and then sat down next to Abishag on the bench.

"I never should have agreed to this in the first place," she complained, giving Abishag an irritated glance and then taking another drink. Abishag smiled at her silently, panting from the heat.

"What I really don't understand, Abishag, is why *you* are here—my father has forced me. He insisted that I try this free treatment before paying at Jockshan's healing room for a treatment that will actually work. I am his little 'experiment.'" She cackled in dour humor. "You may think you are unfortunate to not have a father, but at least an orphan like you, is free."

Abishag smiled at her and remained silent.

"What? Why do you look at me that way? Or have you been listening to those fools who believe this absurd treatment actually works?"

Abishag replied with silence.

"You have! You think I am actually being cured by this two-week vacation in Gehenna! Well, you are not going to convince me. I don't care how much you talk. This is pure insanity!"

Abishag answered her with more silence.

"I'm headed there anyway. It's only fitting that I get acclimated to it now," Dinah muttered to herself.

"Can I see it now?" Abishag asked, indicating some papers on the bench next to Dinah.

Dinah had brought her drawing instruments into the oven room to pass the time practicing her art, but quickly having run out of things to draw in the dark little space, offered to portrait Abishag.

"Oh, it's not finished, and certainly not my best, but consider the circumstances."

She handed the sheet to Abishag, who studied it for a moment thoughtfully, then shook her head.

"I don't understand how you do this so easily, Dinah. If I had hours to work I could not produce a likeness half as good as you have in just a few minutes."

"That? Oh, that's nothing."

"You are very talented, you know."

Dinah cackled out loud.

"Oh, yes, me the talented little wine server, Dinah! How I

rank among the great artists of the world! No, my late night scratchings are of no use beyond self-amusement, drawing lines to erase memories of all those long hours tending my father's drunken losers. You should see some of the stuff I draw some nights—it's downright crazy."

"If it is as good as this, it is an accurate rendering of crazy," Abishag replied. "Although you are much too generous to me in this one. I'm afraid your accuracy has given way to flattery."

Dinah looked up sharply with disgusted skepticism.

"Abishag, you only say that because you have never owned a mirror. Do you know how much money a girl like you could make for any of these owners? Men would stay and drink until morning just so they could stare at you."

Abishag chuckled.

"I don't think any man would stare at a veil that long, and even less if they could see the plain face behind it."

"Ha!" Dinah exclaimed high and sharp. "You amaze me Abishag. You always have, you know. Do you even *know* what you look like? That drawing isn't perfect, but it isn't flattery. Either you are hopelessly ignorant, or maddeningly modest—hiding behind that silly veil all these years. How do you ever expect to get married if you never show a man your face?"

"How many offers have you received in the years since you abandoned your veil?" Abishag replied.

For the first time, Dinah hesitated, staring twitchingly at the calm girl before her. She stood up quickly and paced a step or two, then sat back down.

"I could ask the same question of you," she muttered, folding her arms in front of her and flitting a sideways glance at Abishag. "Besides, I receive an offer almost every night."

"They must be incredible offers."

Dinah glared at her. Abishag smiled back.

"Will you stop doing that?!"

Abishag truly did like the maiden, Dinah, and had been very disappointed when she had abandoned the veil of the virgin, ceding to her father's wishes. The two had drifted apart in the years since that time, but these hours alone in the fire room were rekindling Abishag's affection for her, even if they were as different in personality as they were in choices.

Abishag attempted to casually toss a question in the direction her curiosity had been wandering.

"Dinah, what are the men in the drinking rooms saying about the things that have transpired in our town recently?"

Dinah looked over.

"You mean with the stranger?"

Abishag nodded.

"All kinds of things, I suppose. A lot of people seemed to like him, for one reason or another, others were afraid. Some I think were just plain jealous. The maidens wondered if he was married. He wasn't."

"How would you know that?"

Dinah chuckled.

"I just know. You don't spend as many years as I have serving men without developing a sense about these things. Oh, he maybe had some wives somewhere—I mean, he was wealthy— but that is a different kind of marriage. He was an unsatisfied heart. I saw it right away."

"You met him?"

Dinah's expression grew distant.

"Only once, and he told me something I haven't been able to stop thinking about . . ." her voice trailed off.

Abishag's lips curled up into a knowing smile. If she had had any doubt that they were speaking about the same person, Dinah's reaction removed it.

"He came into the inn one night . . ." Dinah continued reflectively. Then she shook her head, snapping out of her reverie.

"But I don't suppose there is any sense in thinking about it now."

"Well, whatever he told you, it appears it was the truth."

Dinah stared at her. Then her eyes got wide as though she was struck with an idea. Abishag smiled at the interesting reaction.

"Do you want to know what he told me Abishag? Oh! You are going to love this!"

"What?"

"He asked me a question. He said, 'If the saloonkeeper loves every drunk, why is his daughter wed to none of them?'"

She paused and looked at Abishag.

"Good question," Abishag said.

"Yes . . . I thought about that for a long time."

Abishag smiled at her. Dinah noticed.

"And YOU have been sitting here saying the same thing every day, you little mind reader!"

"But I haven't said anything."

Dinah pursed her lips.

"Abishag, you are so ignorant. How are you so wise and so naïve at the same time? You are *always* saying something. Even when you just sit there, you are saying something. How can a person so smart be so dumb?—so blind and so perceptive? You are so . . . so everything! Let me tell you something. You have communicated more in this town with your silence, than all the elders at the city gate could pack into a year of their bickering arguments. I don't know how you do it. You sit there like that, and you just . . . and you reveal my every thought—my every want, my every . . . you just . . . I just . . . I can't even talk sense to you! Why do I always end up telling *everything* to you?"

"Why *is* the saloonkeeper's daughter wed to none of them?" Abishag asked.

Dinah stared at Abishag for a moment, then her eyes seemed to glisten more than the flush and sweat could account for. She shook her head, and turned away, looking down. Abishag regarded her with compassion.

"I did not mean to offend you," Abishag said.

Dinah looked up with the sober expression of a person resigned to honesty.

"You were right, Abishag. From the very start you were right. I should have listened to you. My father never intended to marry me away; he just wanted to use me to profit his business. I've been so blind—why did I not see it sooner? After all the money I have made him. I see him playing this cruel game with my very life—sending me in here to perhaps save a few shekels when he has the money to afford Jockshan's treatments. Can you believe that!? What father would take such a risk with his own daughter? He worships money. He's never going to marry me away. I should never have abandoned the veil. But it's done now."

One thing that Abishag had always admired about Dinah was her honesty. Even when the truth was most unflattering, Dinah was forthright. She lived her life without pretense.

"Dinah," Abishag said gently, "the veil can be put back on."

Dinah gushed out a half laugh, half cry.

"For me? Oh, that would be a joke—a real talker in this town. After all I have done—putting the virgin's veil back on? What a mockery."

"Your reputation cannot be worse than mine," Abishag replied.

"Ha!" Dinah chuckled. "Sadly true, but I deserve my reputation. You don't. And not everyone believes what is said about you. They play along with it because they are afraid of the elders, but they don't believe it. But me? It's only fitting that I should perish from the swamp fever in this hot hole. I deserve it. You don't."

Abishag sighed and looked at her with empathy.

"So what the man told you was the truth?"

"Truth of a pretty high kind, for not even knowing me," Dinah muttered.

"Where do you suppose he got that kind of wisdom?"

"I have no idea."

"I do."

Abishag paused. Dinah fidgeted. The fire crackled in silence in the hot room.

"All right already! I'll ask! Now are you going to tell me or are you going to just sit there and toy with me, making me expose myself even worse?!"

"Dinah, I would very much be honored to tell you, but the answer comes with cost attached. You may be required to start planning for the future, and preparing to wear the veil with me again, rather than preparing to die in this 'hot hole.' Fire can destroy, but it can also purify. Wherever Jedidiah found the wisdom to put his finger on the heart of your dilemma, from that same source, he obtained the knowledge that this treatment, uncomfortable as it is, cures the swamp fever while Jockshan's makes it worse."

Dinah's eyes got wide, and she inhaled in surprise.

"That same man designed this treatment?!"

Abishag nodded.

"And also the balm that makes it tolerable," she added, pointing to the flask of medicine in the corner. "And I can assure you that both you and I will walk out of here completely whole in a week."

Dinah was staring at her.

"Do you doubt me?" Abishag asked.

"But . . . but, where will I go? How will I live, support myself? There is only one occupation available for a young maiden with no skills who leaves her father's house unmarried. I'm not doing that, I still have *some* pride."

Abishag smiled.

"Sounds like the words of one who intends to live and, and that with a new occupation."

Dinah blinked.

"How did you do that? I never decided that! Are you putting words in my mouth?"

"No, I am responding to them. You asked how you will live, how you will support yourself. *You* said that, not me. If you will take the veil with me, and live again as Shammai taught us, I promise you, you will not be in want. You can move in with me, to begin with."

Dinah sighed.

"I don't know how you made me say that. The veil is so uncomfortable."

"Medicine is not designed for its comfort, but for its effect. Jockshan's treatments give relief, but they cost you your life. This treatment causes discomfort, but results in your cure. So it is with many things in life. Consider not the comfort, but the results. Are you happy with the results you have obtained doing things your way?"

Dinah hesitated under the weight of the question. In the past, such questions were evaded by avoiding the one who posed them. Dinah would brush quickly past Abishag in the street with a friendly greeting and a place to hurry off to, never allowing her former mentor to get close enough to ask such questions, afraid that her own honesty could not contend with them. But there was no escaping them here. Dinah looked up with dark sincere eyes.

"Abishag, if I could change places with you, I would do it in a second. If I could go back in time, you have no idea how much heartache I could save myself."

"Then you simply need compare the discomfort of the veil with the pain of the heartache of living without it. Which is worse?"

"Hm, I don't have to think much about that one."

"Truly, and if you spend too much time thinking about your

past, you will poison your future. The past is beyond reach, but the future is a picture not yet drawn—like this blank sheet here." Abishag held up one of Dinah's art sheets. "Dinah, your future is like this sheet. It is blank. What is drawn there is entirely up to you. You can continue to draw the same old things you have in the past, but I am seeing something different. I am imagining a beautiful picture, and you have the power to put it there."

Dinah's eyes traveled down.

"You don't want to know what I had to do to get that papyrus. It's expensive, and my father would not buy it for me."

"Well since we are talking about the future and not the past, I won't ask."

Dinah sighed.

"Do you truly believe it is not too late for me?"

Abishag was still holding the blank page.

"Is it too late for this page?"

Dinah looked at the page, and back at Abishag, studying her.

"Why are you doing this?" she finally asked.

"Selfish motivations, I am afraid."

"What!? You? Oh. Oh, no."

"Dinah, you are my friend and I need your help."

Dinah was surprised.

"You need *my* help? What?—help with your vineyard?"

Abishag shook her head.

"No, not that kind of help Dinah. I have missed you. I need . . . I need *you*."

Dinah, the lost sheep, humbled and honored, unable to doubt the deep sincerity in Abishag's appeal, even if she felt unworthy of it, turned away briefly to hide her welling eyes.

"What could *you* ever need from *me*?"

"We have much to talk about Dinah, much."

Dinah searched Abishag's face in wonder. Suddenly there were voices in the hall. For the first time, Abishag was the one moving quickly, as she hastily began donning her veil.

Chapter 2

The pattering rain reached the young soldier distantly, even when it trickled off his hood and onto his nose. Soon the young guard with the amber locks was running, tripping, and stumbling down the muddy road to Jezreel, his battle attire rattling along clumsily as if protesting a poor decision. How did he make the decision to go this way rather than turn back and report the escaped prisoner as any sane guard would do? He did not know. His feet seemed to have made the decision on their own, leaving his mind to puzzle at their unexpected vector. In his mind's eye, a face loomed before him, as did one behind him. Two different faces, but somehow they seemed connected. Behind loomed the strange prisoner with his mysterious aura, ominous words, and miraculous escape. Ahead, in Jezreel, his sister, a puzzling person with whom his relationship had been strained of late. But, suddenly and inexplicably, there was no one else to whom he was more desperate to speak.

How had he come to be traveling this way? The day had spun in a direction far removed from its beginnings. He had received an order to escort a certain fugitive to trial. He had received the mission with excitement and hopes of putting some of his newly developed skills into practice—something real, not just another training exercise. Yet, when the man began to speak to him, his steely "soldier face" had melted, as a shadow fleeing the light. He found himself mesmerized as much by the man's voice and manner, as by his words. The prisoner had an incredible aura. Benaiah had melted before him, and he knew it. His mind flashed back as he stumbled down the road in the rain. How had the man done it? How had he been so utterly convincing, so quickly? And how, when under examination, had this apparent fugitive so effortlessly risen above the highest authorities Benaiah had ever known, escaping from their grasp as easily as an eagle from a nest of rats?

Doubts chased him as he ran breathlessly along—distant doubts—unable to match his pace. Somehow, he knew his feet were correct. Reporting the escape was the wrong response. Duty and orders pulled in different directions, and the voice of duty called louder. The man was innocent, Benaiah was sure. But he was observing something in himself now more akin to madness than duty: suspicions that this strange prisoner was actually King Solomon. Madness! Yet his feet told him he believed it!

Behind him in Shunem, his benefactor in the militia was a young man named Lotan. This unlikely friend was a relative of Hamon, and might even now be hearing reports of the escape from the other guards. Benaiah's absence would be noted. Thoughts of Lotan brought back a swirl of mixed emotions. Benaiah remembered how he had come to his present station. Lotan had offered Benaiah a position in the militia after Benaiah's father lost his land in one of Hamon's buyouts. Benaiah's father, a displaced farmer struggling to support a family of three children while working out of a trade as a metalworker, urged Benaiah to accept, which he did. None in the family knew then that this man, Lotan, expected something in return: Benaiah's support when he proposed marriage to his sister. But the maiden had flatly denied Lotan. Despite Benaiah's best attempts to sway her, she denied him. His father's attempts fell just as flat. The unsavory result of her stubbornness was the loss of a much-needed dowry, and an uncomfortable strain on Benaiah's relationship with Lotan—a relationship that was unequal to begin with.

So why, under the burden of his recently acquired intelligence, could the young guard think of no one more fit to confide in than his sister? It was inexplicable, but undeniable. His feet kept moving, taking him southward toward Jezreel, as though pulled by an invisible rope.

When the young farmer turned soldier reached the city, the rain had finally subsided. That rain puzzled him too. A strange rain! In what was normally the hottest, driest season in Israel, any rain at all was usually no more than a passing shower, but this sudden storm had raged on unabated for several hours and seemed made to order for the prisoner's escape.

Ahead, the high brick walls of his family's residence in Jezreel appeared through the mist. The building was not a house, just an apartment above a street shop. Benaiah wanted to avoid his parents, hoping some way to engage his sister alone. He was relieved at the sound of pipe music drifting down from her street-side window. He hurried up to the building and stared at the closed shutter from which the music floated. He momentarily wavered in doubt that it was in fact his sister playing the pipe, for the skill of the musician exceeded his memory of her ability, but quickly dismissed the thought. Who else would be playing a pipe in his sister's room? He found a small stone and threw it up at the shutter. The pipe music stopped and the shutter opened a crack.

"Jemimah!" he whispered loudly.

The auburn-haired girl peered down through the mist at a dark form.

"Who is there?"

"It is I, Benaiah!"

"Benaiah?" she called out loud.

"Quietly! I need to talk to you."

"Benaiah? What is wrong?"

"Something has happened. I need to talk to you—just you. Can you come down? Alone?"

Jemimah discerned the urgency in her brother's voice, studying his breathless manner and disheveled soldier's gear. After a moment of curious hesitation, she agreed. Benaiah went to the door and a few moments later the latch turned and Jemimah stepped out.

She looked at her brother curiously, noticing right away an even greater urgency in his expression than his voice had revealed.

"Benaiah, what is it?"

"Jemimah, something has happened, something very strange! I don't know what to do or what it means, but I think perhaps you were right. Father should not be supporting the Brotherhood."

Both children knew that their father had contributed funds to the Brotherhood, but secretly, so as to avoid disfavor with Hamon. It was a delicate situation. The fact that Benaiah was in the militia signaled that the family was favorable to Hamon, a signal they did not want to contradict openly. But secretly, they were supporting the Brotherhood hoping it would succeed this year and become stronger, so that in a future year, they could be a part of another buyout with less risk.

Jemimah studied her brother curiously, noting his ominous expression and manner. He seemed afraid.

"Benaiah. What has happened?"

Benaiah briefly and haltingly explained to her all the events of the day, and his experience with the strange prisoner who had escaped, while Jemimah listened fascinated.

"Who was this man?" she finally interjected, when he seemed to be repeating himself.

"I think he was . . . well, you know who it *looks* like he was, but he went by the name Jedidiah."

Jemimah inhaled sharply in surprise and her eyes became wide, as she threw her hand over her mouth.

"I know this man!"

"You do?"

"I do! When we visited Abishag's farm a week ago, he was there. He talked to us, it was incredible."

"Yes! Yes! It was Abishag's farm where we were sent to arrest him, but he met us on the road down. It was raining and he gave me this hood." Jemimah looked at the hood then peered curiously down at the lower left corner of it. He noticed and followed her eyes.

"What is that on the hood?" she asked.

He lowered his chin to try and see where her eyes were focusing, then ripped off the hood to get a better look. The two peered down at the spot. There, in the corner, burned into the fine leather was a tiny replica of the Seal of Solomon. Their eyes met in silent wonder.

"Jemimah!"

The voice called from upstairs. Jemimah blinked and turned.

"Yes, father?"

"What are you doing down there? It's getting dark."

She looked quickly back at her brother.

"I better come in," Benaiah suggested.

"It's Benaiah! He is here!" she called back up the stairs.

The two heard his mother's voice excitedly repeat his name from inside.

"We'll talk more later," Benaiah said to his sister quickly.

The pair went upstairs.

For the rest of the evening, Benaiah and his sister suffered impatiently through the obligatory rites of an only son's surprise visit: a long dinner, a longer after-dinner period in which the same questions were asked and then re-asked and re-answered. Benaiah nobly tried to satisfy his parents that all was well. His commission was secure. He had simply struck an unexpected day off and he was still in good graces with Lotan and Hamon. He assured his parents the Brotherhood would succeed and they would all someday move back to the family farm which Benaiah would assume as his inheritance. Still something in the son's manner left the parents less than satisfied. Finally, long after dark, the informal gathering was adjourned. After Benaiah had endured another agonizing wait to be satisfied that the house was in the quiet of sleep, he stole into Jemimah's room to finish their interrupted conversation. Jemimah told all she knew about the stranger, Jedidiah, and confessed that though she understood him to be well-known to Abishag, Abishag had said nothing about the man actually being King Solomon! After much discussion, they determined that the best thing to do would be to speak to Abishag directly, and together they made plans to visit her the following day. At the very least, something strange was going on, at most, something incredible.

Chapter 3

All the labor of man is for his mouth, and yet the soul is not satisfied.

Ecclesiastes 6:7

Early the next morning Hamon paced anxiously in his private quarters. He had slept very little. He was not sure what to make of the strange story the two returning guards had so shrilly imparted to him the previous evening. The fact that Jedidiah had escaped was disaster enough, but that he had received help doing it changed the equation uncomfortably. If a man who possessed such a tremendous ability to defend himself alone, also had the benefit of unknown aid, he was an adversary much more formidable than Hamon had anticipated.

This peculiar man who had appeared out of nowhere only weeks ago somehow always seemed to be one step ahead of him. The trial intended to neatly put him away had actually backfired and implicated Hamon himself. Now, he was on damage control. His first priority had been to capture and report the "accidental death" of the prisoner. The tragic death of a fleeing prisoner on a wilderness trail far from the city could be both neatly arranged and believably defended. But to say that the search had been unsuccessful was an understatement. Not only did the party fail to find the escapee on the road to Tyre, as expected that rainy night, they had even failed to locate any recognizable trail to follow. In the mud this should have been a simple visual matter, but when no tracks were found on the main road, the posse concluded that the man must have cut through the brush country avoiding the road. After a long and arduous night criss-crossing the wilderness, no trail—and no escaped prisoner—was anywhere to be found. The man seemed to have vanished into thin air, just as he had appeared in town to begin with

Hamon flushed with anger at the thought, an emotion that frequently recurred lately. He knew the man had outsmarted him at every turn, and, to add insult to injury, had stolen his planned trophy wife, Abishag, right from under his nose! His initial rage, left without an object on which to vent, was now receding into a dark and calculating anger. He reached for the arm of a nearby chair and stiffly sat down rubbing his eyes with his fingers. He was used to getting his way, and as his mind rehearsed the series of events that had unraveled all his plans, his rage returned again. Suddenly he arose from his chair and screamed for his assistant.

"Yes, my lord."

"Get me those guards again!"

Hamon again listened, twitching his finger nervously as they recounted the escape of the prisoner. It sounded just as strange on a third hearing as it had on the first and second. Either it was the product of a very disciplined and coordinated fabrication, or it was the truth. Having found no evidence of the escapee, there was a growing sense of suspicion both in Hamon, and among certain elders, that the guards were not being completely forthright with their story. Could it be that there was a defector among them, or had there been some collaborative effort to hide the prisoner in town allowing him to slip away later? Whatever the case, Hamon now worried that the stranger had made a deeper impact on the psyche of the local population than was previously known. The man had sown the seeds of hope—though a strange and wild hope. Such hope was dangerous; it gave men the courage to do things they normally would not. If the man had escaped alive and word of this leaked out, dangerous hopes were fed. Hamon needed the man dead—if not actually dead, at least *reported* dead. But he also needed him dead for other reasons—personal reasons—reasons that pertained to a certain peasant girl who was proving most difficult to manage. On that score, a reported death—after those reports reached the maiden—could serve his purposes almost as well.

"It is hard enough to account for the lack of a single set of tracks, let alone *three* sets," Hamon objected, after the report of the two guards descended into wearisome repetition.

"As we said, we did not actually see them leave the city," one explained.

"You mean, 'him'," Hamon corrected.

The guards exchanged a glance.

"No, we mean 'them' and we did not see which way they went."

"That troubles me also. For trained guards, you did not seem to see much at all, beyond the ghosts you thought were chasing you. Scared rabbits!—that is what you were! Is this how you were trained to respond to an attack?"

"Those men were real!" the guard objected. "I tell you, we were lucky to escape with our lives! I don't know where they came from, but it was incredible. I don't know a man in the valley who could have fought them off."

"But no single man was required to according to your wild story. There were *four* of you. I for one find it quite marvelous how the four of you could be so quickly and fully overcome by only two, no matter how frightening the ghosts that challenged you."

"But there were only three of us," the guard protested.

"That is worse. You could not even keep your *own* forces together, let alone keep track of a single prisoner. Where pray tell did the fourth guard go?"

"I honestly do not know. He was with us, and then, he was gone. Perhaps he was killed or . . ."

"No body was found," Hamon snapped.

"Or he was taken captive, or . . ."

"Leaving *four* sets of tracks to be dragged through the wilderness? I don't think so."

"Or perhaps he turned back . . ."

"Without your notice? If that is the case I have cause to seriously question your attentiveness to your duty. More likely, that fourth guard did not want to lend his support to your unlikely story, and had honor enough to hide rather than face the council with a lie, but not courage enough to face them with the truth. I wager that when, or *if* he returns, the story he tells will be vastly different from yours."

"But it would be, if he did not see anything."

"It would be if he saw everything! Your creativity is marvelous, but I fear it is the *only* thing in your favor! You should have thought this through more carefully before agreeing on a lie that would so insult your competence to have four armed men put to flight by two. But if you are truly that inept, I, for one, find it more likely that you were somehow outfoxed by the prisoner himself. He slipped through your fingers and then hid somewhere until the chase was over. Either that or you assisted him yourselves. Do you know what the sentence is for treason? Have either of you ever been in prison?"

"Lord Hamon, we did not assist him."

"Yes, so you say. You did not assist him, nor did he escape you through craftiness, which eliminates the two most likely possibilities. So you are left standing before the board of inquiry—and one will certainly be called—with nothing but this wildly unlikely third option. I wouldn't give a shekel for your chances of getting acquitted with that crazy story. All I can suggest if you persist in this nonsense is to prepare your wrists for the chains. There is a lot of grain in this valley yet to be ground into flour. Each of you will have your place at the wheel—*if* you are allowed to live at all."

The guards stared at him in stunned silence.

"Lord Hamon . . ." the younger of the two began.

"Frightens you, does it? It should. There will be little mercy in prison for a guard who is convicted of aiding and abetting the very man he was charged with keeping, especially one who is a known murderer."

The guards cast their eyes to the ground, unable to find a response to Hamon's objections and feeling silly themselves at how unlikely their explanation sounded.

"Unless . . ." Hamon said, tantalizingly.

The guards looked up.

"It was rather dark that evening, and misty, as I recall. I suppose it would have been hard to have a very clear view of things, would it not?"

"What is your meaning, my lord?"

Hamon gave him a look somewhat between compassion and disdain.

"Look. I know you boys are new to the soldier's life; you have not had enough training to perform like true warriors. Some day you may attain to that if you remain in the militia. But it would be a shame to see young lives such as yours thrown away for an innocent mistake. Perhaps, something else happened in that dark tunnel. To be sure, anything that happened there would have been difficult to discern. It was murky and dim, was it not?"

"Well, yes, and rainy, and. . ."

"Exactly. I don't suppose the guards in back would have had much if any view of the guards ahead. Looking through that shadowy tunnel, it would be almost impossible to determine in a glance the identity of a person on the other side. Perhaps, *this* is what happened: When you entered the tunnel, some diversion occurred, some sound, some unexpected surprise that caused a moment of confusion. In that moment, the prisoner bolted away from you and ran. You were startled, and turned, perhaps slipped and fell. You perhaps pulled swords, and looking through the tunnel, you each saw two dark shapes with drawn swords on the other side. In that split second you did not recognize that it was each other you were seeing. Then you remembered your duty. You chased the man, but he had slipped away into the city, perhaps hopping over a wall or fence to hide, and you ran by unawares. Not finding him, you went directly back to the elders to report the escaped prisoner. Do you know why I think it happened this way?"

The guards were staring at him in curious confusion.

Hamon leaned forward, as if giving out a secret.

"Because—and this has not been reported yet—we *did* find him in the chase. We located his trail, far off the main road. We were all fanned out. Those who found the trail did not have time to round up the others, so just a few of us chased him and eventually caught up with him, running and alone. There was a struggle, and when it was over, he was dead."

The guards scowled at Hamon's strange tale.

"Do you know why I think it happened this way?" Hamon asked.

They were silent.

"Two reasons. One, I personally was there, and when we caught him, he was alone. And second, because *this* way, you stay out of prison. You neither defected, nor did you fail in your duty. You simply mistook what you saw. But no harm was done, the prisoner was caught due to your prudent and prompt report of his escape and the matter is resolved. Is it possible it happened this way?"

The guards shuffled their feet, exchanging a nervous glance.

"It is possible, I suppose," one of them muttered.

His companion looked at him skeptically.

"It was *dark* there!" he protested. "Dark—don't you remember?!"

"That's right," Hamon agreed, "Quite dark. *Anything* could have happened there. Don't you think?"

"I suppose it is possible . . ."

"It needs to be more than just *possible*, it needs to be what actually happened," Hamon said.

Hamon suddenly leaned back in his chair and put his hands behind his head, striking a different tone.

"Tell me, boys, do your fathers have the funds they need to redeem their land?"

The guards stared back at him.

"Because if what we have recounted here today is actually true, I can assure you that the funds they need are available to them. Do you understand my meaning?"

The implication of his question hit them momentarily and their eyes widened.

"I do, my lord," one of them whispered.

"Good," Hamon said, "Let us make sure we understand each other on this matter from now on. Because if that fourth guard ever returns—and he might—and presumes to give a different testimony, it is important that he be outnumbered. Are you committed to this version of events? You need to be quite certain about this, for in it lies not only your honorable acquittal of any wrongdoing, but also the redemption of your land. But in your first version—" he shook his head, "in that lies only the hard recompense of traitorous soldiers who failed in their duty."

The guards were dismissed. They departed with the clear understanding that Hamon was doing them a favor—a favor that was hard to reject for a silly sounding truth. With a combination of relief and faintly contained excitement, they assured Hamon of their certainty of his version of events. Then, with the relief of men who have narrowly escaped the gallows, they hurried home to inform their families of their unexpected good fortune.

Chapter 4

Sleep fled from Jemimah early. Normally, her mornings were spent helping her father, Laban, with various tasks related to his metal shop, such as pounding soft, hot metal into thin sheets. Those sheets could then be cut into strips, and the strips bent into rings to make chain links. Not having been raised a metal smith, Laban had difficulty competing with the quality of other craftsmen, and tried to make up in volume for what he lacked in quality. Jemimah knew that her father depended on her. She tried to bend up a good number of rings before the sun had risen, since she and Benaiah would be traveling that day. She also knew it might be difficult to explain to her parents the sudden need to visit Abishag.

There was a soft knock on her door.

"Jemimah?"

It was Benaiah.

"I am awake."

He opened the door.

"What shall we say to father?" he asked.

"I was just thinking about that, we can not lie to him, of course."

Benaiah pursed his lips. His sister's habitual honesty was sometimes inconvenient.

"I will tell him I need your help today," Benaiah offered.

"Doing what?"

"I don't know, I'll think of something. Maybe I'll tell him I'm moving into a new place," he suggested, thinking in the back of his mind that there might be some truth to the statement. Depending upon what they would learn from Abishag that day, returning to Lotan's house and service in the militia could be a thing of the past.

Jemimah looked at him skeptically.

"But I will pay you for the day so he will not have to worry about the lost work hours," he added.

"That would help, but I was thinking about something else, Ben. I think we should tell Aijeleth also."

Aijeleth, the oldest sister in the family, had been away tending to a sick relative and was not expected to return until later in the day.

"You may have to tell her yourself, Jem. I may not be coming back here, tonight," Benaiah said ominously.

"But . . . where will you go?"

"Depends on what we learn from Abishag. I may not have a home now. If that man actually is the king, and they are against him, I cannot stay in the militia. But this house is too small; I couldn't come back here either."

Jemimah searched her brother's eyes.

The family gathered for an early breakfast, and both Jemimah and Benaiah were surprised at how little resistance they encountered to Benaiah's proposal to take Jemimah to Shunem for the day. Their parents, Laban and Jael, saw their youngest two children to the door, and after it had safely closed, exchanged a knowing glance.

"Perhaps Benaiah has finally convinced her to accept Lotan's proposal," Jael said hopefully.

Benaiah and Jemimah traveled first to Abishag's farm, and were surprised to learn from Abelah that Abishag was not present. Knowing harvest time was in full swing, they were even more surprised at the reason. Neither had yet heard much about the unusual treatment for the swamp fever other than what Benaiah had heard at Jedidiah's hearing. He explained it to his sister on the way into town. The fact that Abishag was pursuing this unusual treatment rather than the services of a doctor was telling to Jemimah.

"She would not do this without good reason," she said.

"Well, soon she can explain it to us . . . and a whole lot of other things."

****

Dinah noticed Abishag's hasty arranging of her veil at the sound of the approaching visitors.

"You don't even know who is coming."

"That is why I am putting it on," Abishag replied.

Dinah sighed and shook her head, realizing she might be seeing in Abishag's actions a preview of things she herself would soon be doing, if that persistent little inner voice that had been urging her to heed Abishag prevailed.

"Someone here to see you, girls," the baker's voice called into the room.

Abishag was hastily finishing her veil when Jemimah entered the room. Abishag's eyes widened in surprise and excitement at the appearance of her friend.

"Jemimah! Oh my dearest friend! How did you find me here?" she called, stepping forward to greet her. Then she saw the man behind her and squinted trying to recognize him in the dark.

"Abishag, you remember my brother, Benaiah?"

"Yes, of course, at your service, my lord," Abishag said, bowing humbly to Benaiah.

After all due greetings were exchanged, the room fell silent for a moment before Dinah broke it.

"Well, if there are going to be this many of us in here we're going to need to set some ground rules. I sit over here, farthest from the oven. You newcomers sit over there. I've already suffered in here for four days, and I'm not inclined to make allowances for fresh fish!"

"Dinah!" Abishag protested.

"We are not here to stay," Benaiah said. "We just came to speak to Abishag. Something has happened and we need to know what is going on. Jemimah thought maybe Abishag could enlighten us."

"Oh! Well, carry on then. Don't mind me. I'll just be over here in my studio," Dinah said sarcastically.

"It is a pleasure to see you too, Dinah," Jemimah said kindly, "It's just, we did not know you were in here."

"Yes, well, the plague is blind to justice. It attacks the righteous and sinner alike. Abishag is as good a person to die with as anyone."

Abishag smiled at her.

"I'm not dying, Dinah, and neither are you."

"Oh right. Here we just enjoy the torment of hell without the release of death," Dinah muttered.

"Abishag, does this treatment really work?" Jemimah asked, "We heard you were sick, and if you can't afford a doctor, we could perhaps raise some money."

"I am here by choice, Jemimah. This treatment not only works, it is the only thing that does work."

Benaiah was nodding.

"You know that for a fact?" he asked.

Abishag nodded.

"There are few things of which I am more sure. Do you know from where this treatment came? Jemimah, do you remember my friend that was staying with us for a while?"

"Staying with you!!?? He was staying with you? You never told me *that!*" Dinah exclaimed.

Abishag looked over.

"I said we had a *lot* to talk about, Dinah. Yes, he was staying at our farm—in the guest hut. People thought he was my brother, but he was not. Anyway, he is the one who designed this treatment, and many are already cured by it—as will we also be."

"If we don't die of the heat first," Dinah objected.

Abishag glanced at her and sighed.

"It is a fair bit hot in here," Benaiah said, loosening his clothing. "But I can vouch for you on the origin of the treatment. I heard the man admit to it himself at a recent hearing before the city elders."

"You were there, Benaiah?" Abishag asked.

"Yes, I had an assignment there. Were you?'

"I was."

"I was appointed to guard the prisoner," Benaiah explained. "And I heard how they ruled for you, Abishag. I never believed it—what people said about you. You should know that."

Abishag was touched.

"Prisoner?" Dinah asked.

Abishag looked over.

"Jedidiah was taken in for questioning. Hamon felt threatened by him."

"Really," Dinah said, with a curious frown. "Well, anyone

who could threaten Hamon would find friends in this town."

"And enemies," Benaiah said.

"And you were assigned to guard him?" Abishag queried. "Was that on the way to the hearing, or from it?"

Benaiah fidgeted.

"Both."

Jemimah looked directly at Abishag.

"Abishag, some strange things have happened recently concerning Jedidiah. My brother came to tell me of them last night, and we . . . we don't know what is going on. We thought perhaps you could tell us if you know anything more about this man. He was . . . is . . . unusual."

Abishag stared at her friend a bit longer than expected. Her trust in Jemimah was complete; but her brother, Benaiah, she knew, had been seen lately among Hamon's associates. If he had been guarding Jedidiah, he would have been there to witness his escape, something Abishag herself had not seen. Nor did she know how the guards had explained their loss of the prisoner to Hamon and the elders. Was Benaiah now to be trusted? Jemimah was treating him like he was. And to his credit, he *had* been forthright so far and was not acting like he was beholden to Hamon.

"Benaiah," Abishag queried him, "It is known that the man escaped somehow. You were there, did you see it happen?"

Benaiah shot a suspicious glance at Dinah.

"I might have."

"Abishag," Jemimah said lowly, "he saw the whole thing. He told me about it, and some other things about that man that are strange. Jedidiah was not alone. Other guards came—out of nowhere—and overcame them all. But they left everyone unharmed. He said other things, too. Abishag, did Jedidiah have. . . . another name?"

Abishag glanced at her and the other two, then rose to her

feet and paced a step or two, while Dinah studied her curiously. Abishag looked over at Dinah, then back at Jemimah, and her brother.

"I want you to know I trust you—all of you," she said, looking over carefully to assure Dinah she was included in the statement. The three looked at each other in turn and back at Abishag.

"This man, Jedidiah . . . he was not who people thought he was. He was not even who I thought he was. Until just a few days ago, I thought he was a man from the courts of the king, sent to investigate injustice in this area. But I learned that he is actually more than that. He does go by another name, but he did not use it in this area. In other places, he goes by . . . Solomon."

Jemimah and Benaiah's eyes widened. Dinah glanced around innocently.

"Oh, you mean like the king's name, King Solomon, he has the king's name?"

All three remained silent. Suddenly the implication hit her.

"Oh. Oh! Wait a minute! You don't mean . . ."

Abishag gave her a knowing look.

Dinah stared at her in shock. Then she looked over at the brother and sister, seeing in their eyes the same ominous expression. She suddenly felt like she had stepped into a dream.

"Oh. Oh, come now."

Abishag replied with one of her most expressive silent replies yet.

"Oh! You are crazy," she said, whirling her hand by her ear. "You are crazy." "She is crazy," she said to the other two, at the same time noticing their reverent expressions had not waned.

"Oh, don't tell me, *you* believe it too? I knew you girls were going around the bend a bit with those crazy teachings you study up there, but this is rich. This is too much. You actually believe that man was the king? Now I know you are crazy. I am stuck in this hot hole dying with a bunch of lunatics!" she yelled, looking up at the ceiling.

"Am I crazy too?" Benaiah asked.

Dinah's head shot around and she looked at him narrowly.

"I never followed any of that stuff they study up there. But I'm not basing anything on that. You know me, Dinah. I'm not righteous; I'm as rough as the rest of them that meet in your father's place every night. But I *saw* something that night. I spoke to the man. He told me things, and he gave me this," he said, holding out the hood with the emblem on it.

Abishag caught her breath.

"The hooded one . . ." she whispered.

Jemimah glanced at her curiously.

"You were a safe distance away when his men met him in the tunnel were you not, Benaiah?" Abishag asked.

"Come to think of it, I was, but I don't know why. How do you know about the tunnel—the men?"

"His guards were instructed not to harm the hooded one—when they overcame you in the tunnel."

"How do you know about that?" Benaiah asked, bewildered.

"Well . . . you see, I . . ." Abishag broke off, groping for words. "He had it all planned in advance—how he would escape."

Dinah looked at Abishag and back at Benaiah, and then snatched the hood from him and began examining the spot he had pointed to.

"So he really is the king," Jemimah mused in wonder.

"Think about it," Benaiah said, "it all makes sense. The way he came into this town out of nowhere. The gold he had—the wisdom, the way he was able to threaten Hamon and intimidate even the elders who sit at the gates."

"And the wisdom, when he talked to us that night? It was

amazing," Jemimah added.

"And beyond all of that, I have the testimony from his own lips," Abishag said. "He proved it to me in ways that are beyond question. He gave me many infallible proofs. He left me his . . ." she broke off.

Dinah was still probing the emblem on the hood.

"Just because he had this hood does not prove he was the king. It's just a miniature of his seal. Any artist could do this. Even I could do this."

Abishag reached into her clothing, and removed her hand in a closed fist.

"The Lion of Judah is a common piece of artwork," Abishag agreed, speaking carefully, "But an uncommon medium can render a normal thing strange."

"What do you mean?"

Abishag held out her closed hand before Dinah, then turned it.

"I believe this is also the same picture."

Dinah inhaled a gasp and her eyes went wide.

Benaiah and Jemimah stepped forward to see the strange object.

"Go ahead," Abishag nudged.

Dinah tentatively reached down and poked the gold earrings, leaning in to see the artwork inscribed on them.

"That is gold!" she exclaimed in awe. "How did you get these?"

"Yes," Abishag agreed. "How could I, a peasant girl, have such as this? The value of this gold could buy a small farm. Where did I get them? A very wealthy man gave them to me—so wealthy that the purchase of a farm is such a small matter that he could give away a trinket of greater value without any strain on his means. He gave them to me though I am of all women most unworthy."

Dinah was at a loss to answer, shaking her head.

"Abishag," Jemimah said, "these are incredible, but why? Why would he give you this?"

Abishag looked at her pointedly.

"Jemimah. Do you remember when we studied with Shammai—of the story of Abraham, and his son, and Eliezer—do you remember the earrings?"

Jemimah's eyes looked away in thought as she recalled the story, then filled with recognition and her mouth opened in a silent "Ohhh."

"What?!" Dinah asked sharply. "What story? What earrings?"

Jemimah was staring at Abishag in wonder, as though she had never seen her before. Benaiah was as confused as Dinah.

"You missed an *important* meeting, Dinah," Jemimah informed her.

"I can see that!" she snapped. "But what? What are you not telling us!?"

"Dinah, the gold of these earrings proves this was no ordinary man. But, here is another question for you, could you, as an artist, make an imprint of the real seal?" Abishag asked.

"The Seal of Solomon? I think that would be just a teensy bit illegal, dear," Dinah protested.

"But could you do it? Just, theoretically."

"I'm not crazy enough to try, but it would be very hard to get it exactly right. You have to take something flat and project it back onto something curved. Not to mention it would have to be carved, so not just the lines, the depths would have to be exactly right. It's three diensional. Plus it's stone. If you chip a little bit too much out, you can't put it back. On top of that, there are trained experts that can find the smallest difference. I wouldn't risk my neck trying to get away with it, I'll tell you that."

Jemimah was looking intently at Abishag.

"Abishag, what did he leave with you?" Jemimah asked barely

restraining her excitement.

Everyone looked at Abishag but she hesitated.

"He left me his . . . seal," she finally replied. "But you mustn't tell," she added quickly.

The room was silent.

"Excuse me, dearest, he what?" Dinah asked, fluttering her eyelids at Abishag with exaggerated disbelief.

Abishag sighed.

"We are going to have a lot to talk about, Dinah," she said.

"Oh. Yes. I can see that we certainly do. Perhaps we ought to start at the beginning now, shall we? This man—your friend—is actually King Solomon and he stayed at your farm for weeks, and he knows you and you and you and, oh, by the way, he gave you golden earrings worth a small fortune, and his seal!—for good measure, and a hood to keep *you* dry on a wet day, and oh, sure, he threw in a cure for the plague, of course. Oh yes, there might be a thing or two to talk about. But, oh no, we must not tell, we must not tell! Oh! This is crazy! What are you going to tell me next—that he picked you to be his queen!? Oh yes, let's just have a nice little talk now, shall we?!"

"Dinah, I have already declared my trust in you, but now I ask: do you trust me?" Abishag queried directly.

Dinah studied her with something between awe and confusion, while Abishag held her gaze with steady sincerity.

"Have I ever lied to you?" Abishag asked softly.

Dinah was the first to blink. She looked away and gushed out a sigh, putting her hands to her head and looking up at the ceiling.

"So, why is his daughter wed to none of them?" Abishag asked gently.

Dinah continued to vex, shaking her head and looking anywhere but at Abishag.

"How did I ever get into this?" she muttered to herself. "It's true, isn't it? *I'm* crazy. I'm as crazy as all of you."

Chapter 5

Abelah looked up at a sound outside. She had already received several unexpected guests as the day wore on, and so was not surprised to hear noises outside yet again. Her son, Huram, had spent the first part of the morning at the farm, but then left to make a trip to the thresher's mound, promising to be home before dark. Since that time, there had been a strange parade of visitors. The earliest to arrive were known to her, the maiden, Jemimah, and her brother, Benaiah. As surprised as she was to see Jemimah, she was more surprised to see her brother and realized that for the pair to have arrived at the farm at such an early hour, they would have had to leave Jezreel at first light. It was clear that they had not come for social reasons but were indistinct about their real purpose. Seeming not inclined to go beyond small talk with her when they learned that Abishag was in the oven room at the baker's shop, they made an abrupt and hasty departure.

Since that time, several groups and individuals had come to the farm asking about medicine that Abishag was said to have available for them. Abelah truly did not know what to answer them, and gathered from various conversations that Solomon had developed medicine for swamp fever—a fact which she had had some vague awareness. That he had charged Abishag in the distribution of it, she had not known. Being quite unaware of the dosage or to whom the medicine was to be given, she determined to discuss this with Abishag when she returned for the night, before hazarding guesses on something potentially dangerous. She politely but firmly informed them that they would have to return the next day before she could help them.

She was busy about the house trying to anticipate what Abishag would need when she returned. She truly was not certain in what condition she would get her daughter back. Would she be hungry, or tired, or thirsty, or in need of a bath, or some unknown service? Reaching up to retrieve a pot, she attempted to scoot aside the jar in which Abishag saved the silver. It did not move. Curious, she took it down, surprised to find it heavy enough to require both hands and a vigorous effort. She lowered it down onto the table, and lifted the lid. To her surprise, it was filled to the top, with silver. She stared at it in wonder, more wealth than she had seen in many years, all it one place, and in Abishag's jar!

"Solomon," she whispered, putting her hands over her lips while her eyes roamed.

Suddenly she heard the snort of a horse outside. She quickly put the lid back on the jar and with considerable effort got it back onto the shelf. The presence of a horse heralded the arrival of a different class of visitor than the common folk and beggars who had thus far arrived. She quickly went to the lattice to peek out and was quite surprised to see a company of six men on horseback dressed in official attire, and armed with swords. The horses were trotting through the yard and would soon be upon the house itself. She smoothed her garment and stepped out curiously to meet the strange contingent.

"Abelah, mother of Abishag," the man in front greeted her from atop his horse.

"How may I serve you, my lord?"

"I, and this company, have been sent by the elders to take charge of your daughter. She is wanted for questioning. Is she present in the house?"

Abelah stared at him in surprised alarm.

"Questioning? Questioning for what?"

"The nature of the inquiry is determined by the elders who have sent for her. I am not at liberty to give you any more particulars than that. Will you kindly bring her forth?"

"Is this related to the hearing that took place yesterday?"

"Dear madam, our orders are to return with the maiden, not to stand here and satisfy your curiosity. If you do not bring her forth, we are authorized to enter and take her, by force if necessary."

Abelah was indignant.

"My daughter has committed no crime. You have no right to treat her like a criminal."

"If she is innocent, then you have nothing to fear from her being questioned. Stand aside now, please."

He approached and leaned forward to call into the door. "Abishag, the Shunnamite, you are under orders by the elders to come with us for questioning. Step forward at once!"

Suddenly there was a sound to the right, and Abelah and the whole party turned to see an unknown man standing calmly nearby.

"I would expect the elders of any Israelite city to be aware that any demands that are placed upon a household must first be declared to the head of that household. If you wish to speak to this woman, or her daughter, you will direct your comments to me," Huram said.

The entire party looked him up and down. The poised princely looking man met their gazes, holding himself in such a way that made them feel as though they were caught in a crime.

The speaking soldier scowled at him, noticing the large roll of paper the elegantly dressed man was holding in his right hand. The roll was too large to be a legal document, and paper too expensive for any recreational use. His casual possession of it added to their puzzlement.

"Or are you unaware of this protocol?" Huram said, to their lingering silence.

"Ahh . . . of course we are aware of it, but who . . . are you?"

"I am the rightful charge of this property, and the woman you seek. I am Huram, son of Abelah, and brother of Abishag."

"Brother?" the man asked, confused.

There was rustling behind him. The spokesman turned, and exchanged a few hushed sentences with a couple of his men. He turned back to Huram, who had moved to the center, and guided Abelah to stand behind him.

"It is known among this party," the man said, "that Abishag has been collecting unknown . . . brothers, of late."

"Do you question my stated identity?"

"Your presence here does surprise us, for the brothers of Abishag are all known to us. Yes, I would say we have reason to doubt it."

"Then I will present official testimony before you. Mother?" he said to Abelah. "Please tell these kind lords to whom they speak."

Abelah stepped forward.

"This is my blood son, born of a legal marriage before I was married to Genubath. He is exactly what he says."

"Thank you, mother," Huram turned back to them.

"You now have testimony that you must contradict with evidence. As I am sure you are aware, the testimony of the mother outweighs all others with respect to parentage. Unlike a father, the mother must be present at the birth. Since both my testimony and hers have been declared, legal responsibilities have come into effect. If you would question this testimony, I am sure you are aware it must be challenged through legal processes—and this before any other demand can be honored. For, as you have admitted, the head of a household must be first informed of any legal demand. I will expect, therefore, that you will provide me with an officially sealed document from the chief elders calling me to a hearing for a determination of my parentage. Then, and only then, will I speak to you of my sister. Until then, I bid you, shalom."

He turned, guiding Abelah toward the door.

"Wait!"

Huram turned.

"Have you a recorder among you?" Huram asked, "Because we are now speaking of matters of legal import. If you continue to ask questions of this nature, the record of them must be available for future proceedings."

The guard stared at him then looked back around. Another man began hastily preparing to take down some notes. Huram waited until the man seemed prepared, then said,

"Tell Hamon, that the brother of the accused claims 'Right of Head of Household.' I expect to see your charges against her in writing, before I deliver my sister to you."

The man scribbled down his statement.

This time Huram turned from them in truth, and taking Abelah with him, shut the door behind him, leaving the stunned contingent staring at a closed door.

Huram went calmly to a seat at the table, while Abelah looked at him in awe.

"Are you going to leave it like that?" she asked.

"Yes, for the time being. Unless I am much mistaken, they will depart shortly."

After some discussion, the party outside concluded that, under the circumstances, the doubts that they were authorized to enter and take the maiden were valid enough to prevent further action. They wheeled their horses and trotted back out of the yard, disappearing over the hill.

Abelah was visibly impressed with her son, as though seeing him for the first time, quite taken aback by his bold and very effective actions. He answered her silent question.

"These provincial politics can be a nuisance," he commented with a sigh.

Abelah curiously observed the calm and confident disposition of her son. The authenticity of his outward serenity, well evidenced by his placid observation, was offered as though the matter held no personal significance to him whatsoever. She formed a question.

"I do not presume to doubt you, dear son, but I should perhaps mention that you employed a legal argument—a very effective one, it seems—for now. But those men were sent by Hamon, not by the elders. I am sure you realize that he will not be deterred by legal technicalities."

Huram nodded, and removed his turban, running his hand across the side of his head, smoothing his thick black hair. The movement caught her attention, and her mind traveled back decades in an instant. She remembered that his father had had the exact same gesture.

"You are quite correct, of course," he agreed. "But I did not have much time to devise a response to them. My purpose in presenting this argument was simply to gain us some time and to keep them from knowing the whereabouts of Abishag, at least for now. They will probably return, and having believed she was in here all along, will expect to find her. But they will not."

"They will not?"

He shook his head.

"This man Hamon is every bit as dangerous as you have declared—and more so. But it is not widely known where Abishag is just now. She is not here, nor is she in her vineyard, and she is not seen in the city. It occurs to me that her place in the oven room is a very safe place to hide, for the time being. I believe we ought to advise her to stay there—for the present."

"Stay there? Overnight?"

He nodded.

"I think it would be prudent. If you will assemble some supplies for her, I will make a trip down to deliver them and explain the situation. It may be that if she remains hidden for a week, they will assume she has left the area."

"But she has not left the area. She will be out again in a week. Then what will happen?"

He smiled at her quizzically.

She found it a strange thing to smile about, but was finding herself strengthened by his calm confidence.

"Mother, the king *did* advise us that things could get complicated," he said gently.

"Yes, he did."

"But he also assured us, that we, his family, will be together in Jerusalem, and Abishag will be his queen—whatever happens between now and then not withstanding. I have not just met this king yesterday. I, for one, have confidence that if he has declared it, it will be so, just as he has said."

"What do you think they wanted her for?" Abelah asked.

"It is quite clear to me that they are trying to find their escaped prisoner. They think Abishag might have some idea of his whereabouts."

"She does," Abelah said.

"Yes, she does, but they have already rejected the answer she has for them. And no lie is too implausible for men who are not satisfied with the truth."

"But we did not lie to them—nor will we."

"No, fortunately for us, lies are not necessary. Such men invent their own lies to believe," Huram replied.

Abelah pondered.

"That sounds like something Solomon would say."

"I have been awarded such compliments before. One cannot

spend the hours that I have with this king without absorbing some of his manner. You find yourself starting to sound like him, think like him and react like him."

"It is a blessed model you have found to follow, dear son. I could not imagine a better answer to my prayers," she said reverently.

"Knowing this king has been the greatest blessing of my life," he agreed, placing his roll of papers on the table.

She looked down at it curiously.

"Would you like to see something else the king has decreed?" he asked.

"Something else?"

He smiled at her and began unrolling the paper.

"What is represented here is an abstract of something that will exist in the very near future. Though we cannot yet see it, the king has decreed it so it is as good as done. This is what will stand on the thresher's mound at this time next year."

Abelah watched the roll slowly open and caught her breath at the immense and highly detailed but curious structure it revealed.

"You drew that all today?" she asked, realizing that not only was the structure represented, but the surrounding terrain and hillside with great accuracy.

"It is rough, I admit. But I expect to improve it in the next couple of days. All of the measurements and scale must be correct, for we will be fashioning many of its components off-site."

She was still studying the picture.

"Mother," he said, more seriously.

She glanced up.

"As you may know, every building project has challenges and obstacles that may deter or slow the process, or increase its cost. Between the drawing of this picture and the actual structure standing, there spans a vast array of unknowns."

Abelah sensed that he was trying to communicate something to her beyond the uncertain nature of construction projects.

"Yes, I suppose that would be true."

"And so it is with your daughter and my sister, Abishag. Her destiny is already recorded. But between this time and the realization of that destiny, there lies a period of time in which unforeseen setbacks and many challenges will arise. But we are not to be disheartened by them. In the end, they all will be forgotten; and the structure will replace the picture. Do you understand?"

She was nodding, fingers over her lips.

"Do not fear for your daughter, whatever may happen. She is under the protection of the king now—as are you. You may rest in that. Even if she is taken by Hamon or the elders, such as they desired to do today, they can no more harm her than they can prevent this structure from standing on the thresher's mound."

"You speak wisely."

He patted her hand.

"And you receive wisely, though I understand it is much to absorb, all so suddenly. But, it grows late. I should be preparing to go see Abishag."

"Oh!" she said suddenly, rising up, "I so owe you an apology, my son. It has been an unusual day. With all the visitors who came today, I have not yet had time to prepare anything for you!"

"Visitors?"

Abelah explained how she had received a parade of sick townsfolk seeking medicine. He was intrigued, not having known, as Abelah had not, that Abishag was charged to distribute the medicine.

"In that case, I had better hasten to speak with my sister. If she is not coming home tonight, she will need to advise us what we can prescribe for the sick who return tomorrow."

Huram insisted that he would be able to find something to eat in town if Abelah would hasten to get Abishag's things together straightaway, which she hurried to do. Before the sun set, Abelah was watching her newly recovered son, Huram, leave the yard to deliver his package, and his message, to his beloved sister in the baker's fire room.

****

"But there was a *man* there," the chief guard protested to Hamon, who sat with his head down, rubbing his forehead at the revelation that the guards had not returned with Abishag as instructed. His brother, Caleh, and their nephew, Lotan, had been in a meeting with Hamon when the guards returned, and now listened curiously to the unexpected announcement.

"A man? A single man? Were there not SIX of you?"

"Well yes, but he presented us with a legal argument. We were not sure of our authority . . ."

"What legal argument could an unrelated stranger present that would prevent you from taking a widow's daughter for questioning? Am I truly surrounded by such incompetence that you withered at such slight resistance?"

"But, my lord. He claimed right of Head of Household. He claimed to be her brother."

Hamon looked up.

"Here we go again," Caleh snickered.

Hamon's head snapped around, and Caleh's smile vanished.

"Brother?? You know as well as I do that Abishag has no other brothers than those we know. And they have claimed no such right. What could he have said to so quickly convince you of such an outrageous claim?"

"Well, for one thing, the mother testified to it also, and for another . . ." the man hesitated.

"Yes?"

"He was . . . quite convincing, my lord."

Hamon groaned. Caleh and Lotan looked at each other.

"Did you see the maiden? Was she there?" Hamon asked, great weariness in his voice.

"We did not see her, but we did not enter the house."

"Ahhh. Then she *was* there, they were hiding her."

"Perhaps."

"Have you seen this man before?"

"Never. He appeared quite . . . well, princely I would say, well dressed, articulate . . ."

"Yes, yes, I get the picture, another smart, clever, articulate, and a completely-unknown-to-everyone 'brother' of Abishag. I know the type. Did you get his name?"

"He said it was Huram."

"Oh, that tells us a lot. There are perhaps a hundred with that name from here to Tyre."

"There are not a hundred of this type of man," the guard objected, then added, "My lord," when Hamon gave him an irritated look.

"Maybe we should launch a formal inquiry with the elders—find out if he is actually head of household," Caleh suggested.

Hamon looked over.

"Since this is obviously exactly what they want, I find your idea to be, what shall I say—the *opposite* of astute. Of course, he wants to tie us up in all this legal nonsense, and once we emerge from it, even if the man is proven false, the trail of our escapee will have grown hopelessly cold. No, we don't want the elders involved in this. We must find a means to draw the maiden out of her own will."

Hamon looked back at the guard.

"Dismissed, for now."

The guard bowed and left. Hamon looked over at Caleh and Lotan.

"I do not believe the two of you have sufficient respect for the intelligence of the people we are dealing with. They are clever. Just because this maiden farms a vineyard on the hill, we cannot assume her to be stupid. She has apparently secured some unknown aid, first, from the man who escaped, and now by this man. This man knows exactly where our escapee fled—I have no doubt, as does the maiden."

"But how do we get her to tell us, especially if we cannot even talk to her?" Caleh asked.

"The first part is difficult, I admit. But compelling her to talk to us—that we can arrange," Hamon declared.

"But what if she is not at the farm? What if she left with the prisoner when he fled?"

"In that case, a large part of our problem is already solved, for she is the one thing he may be willing to return for. If he already has her, he would be a fool to come back to this town, knowing he is a wanted man. But if he does not have her . . ."

"He'll try to sneak back in and get her," Lotan finished, casting a glance from Hamon to Caleh.

"Most likely. And we can't have that. We can't report him dead and then have him traipsing back into town."

"Perhaps we ought to spy the farm for a few days, see if the maiden is around?" Caleh suggested.

"Now that, I can agree to," Hamon said. "But we need to keep the guards on alert. If she is seen apart from that so-called brother, in town or anywhere, she should be taken immediately. Let him lodge his complaint when she is already in our possession. Then *he* can endure all the legal nonsense of getting her back. Most likely, he won't bother."

Hamon looked over at Lotan.

"Any word about that other guard that failed to return?"

"Benaiah? No, he has not come home, neither last night nor today. Nor has he been seen that I am aware of."

"That is suspicious," Hamon said. "I want him brought in as soon as he is fool enough to be seen. Can you do that?"

"He is of no use to me any more," Lotan said coldly. "As soon as I have him, you have him."

"He didn't get you that little blossom you wanted, eh?" Hamon jabbed.

Lotan flushed, but remained silent.

"His family is in Jezreel, right?" Hamon asked.

"Yes, that's right."

"Well then, since I am sure you know the exact house, I want you to go there. Chances are that little guard ran home to his mother. Take one of the other guards with you. See if you can get him to see things their way. If not, bring him to me."

Lotan agreed.

After dismissing his accomplices to their tasks, Hamon changed clothes and made his way down to his favorite drinking room as had been his habit recently. The demise of the high priest had brought a curious parade of visitors into town: criminals, or presumed criminals, men without families—or honor—and most importantly, without money. Asa-Barak, whom Hamon was sure he would never see again, had apparently passed the word among his associates that Hamon could perhaps provide work for them.

The day was getting on toward evening, and Hamon wanted to be visible. Such men, it seemed, were always able to find him, if he simply stayed in public places in his off hours. He did not quite know what use he could make of this willing and unprincipled undercover army, but he was always willing to meet them and learn what resources might be at his disposal—should the need arise.

****

The extraordinary discussion that was taking place in the baker's oven room continued throughout the day. So riveting did it become and so mesmerized were they all, that the sweltering temperature was pushed to the back of their notice. The enormity of the secret excited a sense of wonder. Abishag hesitated to tell the greatest of all her secrets, other than what she had hinted to Jemimah, leaving that for another conversation. Instead, the discussion revolved around the immense political implications of the king's clandestine presence in their town, and his charge to Abishag to use his Seal to set things aright. As wild as the prospect was, it was so saturated in detail and sprinkled with easily verifiable facts that even Dinah was forced to admit the truth of what was being purported. They each, by turns, admitted amazement to be speaking so plainly about something so incredible, but as the discussion took its course, it became clear that the situation deserved frank discussion. No matter how incredible the subject, timidity would hinder more than honor it. A royal sense of duty descended upon them like a cloud, filling the room with a somber, almost reverent aura.

As evening approached, Dinah began to cast glances toward the door, knowing she must soon leave to work in her father's drinking room. She was uncertain how she could bear to work as usual, bearing the burden of such an incredible secret. But her hesitation was born of more than that, for in the hours spent with Abishag, she had caught a whiff of wild hope; hope that her life could actually be different—a kind of hope she had long since despaired of ever feeling. The intriguing sensation pulled at strong cross-purposes to her normal occupation, and as unlikely as she found it, she could not deny a twinge of regret that she was leaving the sweltering room of which she had so recently complained so vehemently. She was not fully conscious of it, but the mysterious sensation deep in her soul was whispering that somehow, somewhere, in the past few hours, her life had passed a turning point—a junction only passable in one direction. From this time on, she somehow knew, things would be different.

As Abishag and the others prepared to leave, their movements were suddenly interrupted by the entry of a fifth person—a person surprising to everyone, save Abishag. The man who entered was astonishing in his attire and manner, apparent wealth, dignity, and commanding presence. But exciting more shock than all of this, was that Abishag greeted him with an embrace! It was unprecedented to see Abishag acting so commonly with a man. So incredulous were her companions that when Abishag pulled away from him, she found them staring in stunned silence. Abishag looked around at her friends and immediately discerned the source of their astonishment.

"My dear friends," she explained with a warm smile. "May I present to you, the blood son of my mother and father, my brother, Huram."

"Well *that's* nothing but the truth," Dinah finally said, with an expression that went way beyond her words.

The others chuckled nervously with relief. Abishag introduced her friends to Huram, assuring her brother that these were friends he could fully trust, and that they knew about the king."

"It is my humble pleasure to make your acquaintance," Huram said with a bow. "May I be of as worthy service to you as you have been to my sister."

As the foursome admired the elegant dignity of the man, Jemimah began to notice a strong family resemblance between the two. Standing next to her brother, Abishag seemed suddenly elevated to the princely stature that he exuded, as though hidden nobility she possessed all along was suddenly brought into manifestation.

"I trust I can speak freely among these?" Huram asked Abishag.

She nodded.

"We have been speaking freely all afternoon." Sensing, as she said it, that he had come for some purpose.

"There was a party of men at the farm earlier today. They were looking for you. I did not reveal your whereabouts, but it seems you have become a person of interest because of your association with Solomon. If they find you, they will take you in for questioning. It is the doing of Hamon, of course."

Abishag listened carefully to the news.

"But I have committed no crime."

"None but the crime of being associated with one whom Hamon finds threatening. I have brought you some supplies. I recommend that you stay here for the night. You will not be seen nor found here."

Benaiah was quickly discerning something in this news that possibly affected himself.

"Lord, Huram. I believe I might be associated with him also. I was there, when he escaped. I did not return—nor have I yet. Would they be looking for me also?"

"Most definitely," Huram said quickly. "If you have not clearly declared yourself on Hamon's side, he will consider you an enemy."

Jemimah looked at her brother worriedly.

"What ought we to do?" she asked.

"I would advise staying away—perhaps even out of town for a time."

"You can come back home with us," Jemimah said to Benaiah. "We live in Jezreel," she explained to Huram.

"No," Benaiah said firmly. "I will not go back to father's house under the circumstances. He will ask questions. He will wonder why I have not returned to Lotan's house for two straight nights. I cannot explain any of this to him yet."

"But . . . where will you go? You heard what lord Huram said—you can't go back to Lotan now," Jemimah said.

"Guess I'm homeless then. Homeless, and unemployed, and wanted by the law."

"Oh, the blessings of meeting the king," Dinah observed sweetly.

Benaiah scowled at her.

"Huram, why don't you take Benaiah back to the farm? He can stay with you in the guest hut for now," Abishag asked.

"I suppose that would do, for tonight, but it is not too safe a place to hide. The farm is the very place where they will return looking for you."

"I've got nothing to hide," Benaiah said, "let them find me. I'll tell them the truth—all of it."

"That is not recommended, son. They will destroy you for this truth," Huram warned. "We must find a better option for you—and soon. Tonight, you stay with me."

Huram then brought up the issue of the sick who had come to the farm looking for medicine.

"How many came?" Abishag asked.

"Mother said they were showing up all day long."

Abishag studied the floor.

"Strange . . . so many seeking medicine, but only two of us here, in the fire room."

The others exchanged a glance. Suddenly Dinah clapped her hands together sharply.

"They want the medicine without the treatment! You can't give it to them, Abishag. It won't heal them, it will just make them feel better, but it won't cure them!"

Abishag continued to ponder.

"But it is not mine to deny them. It is the relief of the medicine that convinces some to have confidence in the treatment. No, I cannot deny it to them. But I must make clear its purpose—how it is to be used."

"I could explain it to them," Huram said, "but the king charged you with this, not me. It really should be you."

"But . . . how can I if I am hiding in here?"

"Perhaps you could write it," Jemimah suggested.

Abishag looked up at her.

"I could write a prescription . . . I suppose that would suffice, for the present. But it may take some time to tell all I know of it. Are you pressed to return right away?" she asked Huram.

"I do want to return to the farm soon, in case the men come back. I do not want mother to face them alone. It is unlikely that they will come again tonight—but perhaps."

Dinah was suddenly whirling around, and gathering up a stylus and some paper from her art supplies.

"Then get to it, dear," she ordered, thrusting the papers at Abishag.

Huram found himself smiling at the suddenly energetic girl.

"She's an efficient one, isn't she?" Huram commented.

"No one gets things done quite like my friend, Dinah," Abishag replied, sitting down and preparing to write.

The faint sound of a dog barking caused Dinah to look up quickly.

"Oh, I must be going! Father will need me at the inn. His losers will be arriving soon ready to exchange their pockets full of silver and dry throats for cheap wine. Well, this has all been a joy, but I really must be on my way. Have a heavenly night here Abishag—you poor dear. I shall mop you up in the morning. Friends, lord Huram, shalom!" Dinah said, whirling to get her things together for a hasty departure.

The rest of the party bid their farewells to the quickly departing maiden who left a calm silence in her wake. Abishag gave Jemimah a knowing glance.

"Be prepared to see more of Dinah from now on," she told her, which news Jemimah received with silent joy.

Huram appeared ready to leave, and Benaiah rose.

"So . . . how am I going to get back to Jezreel this late without you?" Jemimah asked Benaiah.

Abishag looked up from her writing.

"Jemmy, you are not walking back home alone. Stay at the farm tonight. We will find a way to get you home tomorrow."

"I will see that you are safely delivered to Jezreel in the morning," Huram promised.

"And what am I going to tell father?" she mused to herself.

Benaiah nodded.

"You can't lie to him, Jem," he taunted.

"No, but in this case, a lie would be much more believable than the truth."

"Then tell Aijeleth," he replied. "She deserves to know even more than I do."

After a few minutes, Abishag had finished her writing, and bidding goodbye to her friends and her brother, found herself all alone for the first time that day—alone, weary, and sweaty—in the dark, quiet oven room.

Chapter 6

As the maiden Dinah walked the few short blocks from the baker's oven room to her father's inn, she felt as though she was truly seeing for the first time. Every common sight, every familiar landmark lied to her by appearing as it always had, when the presence of the king had turned the whole town new. The warm, tingly feeling that played upon her nerves was more than could be accounted for by a day in the heat. It was a kneading, deep in her soul, stirring up currents that she had long forgotten existed.

Purpose—that is what it was. For the first time in many years she felt a sense of purpose, a sense of noble duty, a faith in the existence of order and justice in a world that inspired and rewarded cynicism and resentment. Hope—it was that also. Not hope in the sense of hoping for a desired object, but hope on a deeper level. Hope as a child hopes—the hope of unspoiled confidence, virgin faith, and unwavering expectation that the hope will find an answer fitted to it. Though her mind continued to throw up objections to the day's stunning revelations, there was a quiet current moving deeper—a current strong enough to scorn her doubts as frivolous, and not worth answering. The town, all of its inhabitants, and all of their doings, had fallen under the eye of the king. That alone, changed everything. Even now he was working in the midst of it all, and had released hidden forces that would lead to an overturning of every wicked plot. She believed it. Against every objection that her quick mind and life-hardened cynicism could heave up, she still believed it.

The darkening sky cast the rough stone buildings into silhouettes behind the torch lights that lined the streets as she made her way past the changing guard of day traffic to night, to a particular building up ahead. Its door was open to the street, out of which a familiar glow and sound oozed. That atmosphere, so familiar to her, was somehow unwelcome and distant tonight as though her reality and her dreams had traded places. She turned down an alley to enter the building from the rear where she could change and clean up before facing her father who would certainly be expecting her.

Jalaam had been watching the progress of his daughter's treatment with eager anticipation, hoping for enough improvement to send her out on the floor again. Heretofore, she had been relegated to cleaning up in the back, lest her telltale cough frighten away customers.

For two days, Dinah had been noticing what appeared to be an improvement in her condition. She had dismissed it as a pleasant anomaly yesterday. Today, however, it was the certain promise of full recovery. She believed Abishag. She always had believed her, even when she had chosen a different path for herself. Abishag simply radiated truth. On Abishag's word alone, Dinah knew she would soon be in full health.

Dinah entered the door, and turned quickly to bend over the basin that was mounted on the side wall. Not quickly enough. Her father soon appeared in the other doorway, leaning against its post, nervously stroking his beard as he looked her up and down.

"Lots of men in early," he said, omitting any kind of greeting. "Heavy traffic for a Tuesday. Thirsty men, some unknowns. Can you make it through the night without coughing yet?"

She continued washing, rubbing her face in the damp towel that hung over the basin. Even through it, she could already smell the alcohol that wafted from the room behind him, along with the sound of men's voices.

"Is there a caravan in town?" she asked, avoiding her father's question.

"None that I know of. Just, some new men around. Might have money. I need you out there, Dinah."

It occurred to Dinah that he pressed her as though her recovery were a simple matter of will, as if her health had a duty to respond to the needs of the inn. She finished with the towel on her face, and began rubbing her arms up to the shoulders, slipping off her outer tunic.

"'Din, you're a sweaty mess!"

"Should I go home and change?"

"No time. Just go sleeveless, put the apron on."

She knew what he wanted. Without the top part of her tunic, the apron covered her, but not sufficiently to keep men's leering eyes from following her about the room more than they already did. She tried to fake a cough. It came out sounding unrealistic. He looked at her skeptically.

"What was that? You're better—I can see it. You're going out there tonight."

"I can work the floor, but I'm not wearing the apron," she said, meeting his eyes for the first time.

His head snapped up and his eyes narrowed. He opened his mouth to reply, but suddenly there was the sound of a crash of dishes and a curse through the door behind him. Jalaam turned quickly and went to investigate. Dinah breathed a sigh of relief.

"Thank you, God," she whispered.

She finished cleaning up, put the tunic back on, and then the apron over it.

The night did prove to be unusually busy, as Jalaam had predicted. He soon noticed her failure to accede to his demands concerning her attire, but being quite pressed himself, was able to do nothing more than toss an occasional low angry comment to her in passing. Still, Dinah was able to remain busy enough to avoid going to the changing room again until closing time.

Dinah had noticed, in her years in this occupation, that each night of business was like a mini-drama of its own, and if one looked back upon the whole of it, a structure could be observed, an ebb and flow. On this particular night, the "climax" of the drama was without question the entrance of Hamon. It was not uncommon to see him in her father's inn, and his entrance was normally met with a slight dimming of conversation as he went to his favorite place in a corner near the fire. It was a place which allowed a view of the whole room, but was secluded enough to engage in private conversation. Regulars knew to keep the spot open until midnight, after which it was unlikely he would appear. Hamon spent several hours in the inn that night, not drinking much, as was typical for him.

On this particular night, Dinah curiously observed him entertaining several unknown men, not together, but independently, and in succession. Hamon dutifully saw that their mugs were kept filled, while he kept his own mind clear—another of his tactics.

Dinah, in contrast to many maidens her age, had long ago ceased being overly impressed with Hamon, having herself enough experience with men to be beyond the blush and gawk of more innocent girls. But it was impossible not to feel a healthy respect for his position. He never spoke to her much, but they were on first-name familiarity, and she had noticed that his eyes followed her around the room as much as any other man's. She wondered from time to time what it would be like if he, by some miracle, were to make her an offer, and in her own private game, she enjoyed imagining the sport of turning him down. However, until tonight, she never could quite bring herself to believe she actually *would* turn him down. To deny him would be foolish, and in more ways than the sacrifice of the financial rewards he could offer. A maiden would have to be either extraordinarily brave or extremely ignorant to do so.

But tonight, this grudging respect she had for him, this habit of mind, was beneath its usual strength. On this night, she curiously regarded him not as the largest man in the world in which she lived, but the smallest man in a much larger world. She wondered, in the back of her mind, if he by some sense would be able to detect that he was commanding in her a diminished respect.

He wants to find Abishag, but I know where she is!

She felt empowered by the secret, for once having the advantage over him in some small way. When he rose to leave, she met him at the desk to receive his payment, as usual. As he stood before her poking his finger into the silver in his hand, he commented, "Dressed up for the cold tonight, eh, Dinah?"

"I don't think so."

"Yes, well, you're thinking too much."

"And you're not drinking enough," she shot back without thinking.

He snorted a laugh.

"Someday that sassy little tongue of yours is going to get you in trouble."

"Could happen to anyone," she replied without smiling.

He looked at her with a curious smirk, then dropped the silver and a modest tip into her hand and went out. There was not a soul in the room that did not privately note his departure.

Dinah awakened early the next morning with only one thought. Even though she had toiled late into the night, endured a harsh lecture from her father after the doors had closed, and drawn sketches in her room for at least an hour to erase the memories of the night from her mind, she awoke early. She desperately wanted to see Abishag again. Strangely, the discomfort of enduring another day in the heat was far outweighed by the pull to be with her rediscovered friend. And strangely, the prospect of parading again before the men in her father's inn held no appeal. Their wandering eyes and flirtatious comments, from which in the past she had drawn personal validation, suddenly seemed shameful and unbecoming.

Chapter 7

Benaiah and Jemimah rounded the last corner and saw their father's house ahead. They had departed Abishag's farm early, but both were sure their father, mother, and older sister were already hard at work. Benaiah, after sharing the guest hut with Huram at Abishag's farm, had changed his mind. Finding it uncomfortable to hide as if he were some kind of criminal, and inappropriate to delay informing his father about the king, Benaiah escorted his sister to Jezreel. Duty would not allow him to leave his sister to deliver the secret alone.

Also, it had occurred to both of them, since leaving the day before in search of Abishag, that the reason for their parent's easy agreement with their time away could be none other than presumption that the journey was proof that Jemimah had agreed to marry Lotan. The thought of abandoning Jemimah to deliver displeasing news alone, coupled with the added burden of her speaking only the truth to them, was too much for Benaiah's sense of honor to allow.

Jemimah knew that Benaiah was not always clever, his world consisted of simple black and white, but once sure which was which, it never occurred to him to do anything other than what he believed was right. She imagined, and then derived from some of his conversations, that this had been a source of friction between him and Lotan, who seemed born to finesse every situation to his favor. Benaiah's blunt—and to Lotan, naïve—forthrightness in both word and deed, irritated Lotan.

That forthrightness was now propelling the young farmer-turned-soldier toward a plain and open conversation with his father in which he expected to tell everything, no matter how outrageous it might sound. He was confident the truth would be believed simply because it was the truth. Jemimah was more sensibly nervous about this, at once realizing that the truth must be told, but not entirely trusting Benaiah's ability to declare it graciously, nor in a credible way. Nonetheless, she privately conceded that having him with her was better than facing the family with these implausible secrets alone.

"We are going to talk to Aijeleth first, right?" she nudged, as they neared the door.

"I might," he replied. "No sense delaying it though. Father needs to know what happened, why I am back. All this has to be told when it comes up."

Jemimah was not encouraged. It seemed likely to her that it would "all come up" right away—as soon as the family found Benaiah unexpectedly returned again.

"No one is going to be here, you know," she said, quickly, "they are all down at the shop. Maybe I could go there now and check in on them?" she suggested, thinking she might at least get a few words with Aijeleth before Benaiah showed up.

"Go ahead. I'm going to drop off our things first."

Jemimah hurried down the street and around the corner, while Benaiah tromped up the stairs. The smallness of the place pressed upon him again as he squeezed around the furniture to try and tuck the travel sacks into a corner.

How can I possibly move back in here? But where else can I go?

Jemimah's father, Laban, rose from his stooped position carefully and not without the pang of pain in his lower back that had become all too familiar over the past few years, to face his disappointed customer. Lifting a chain from the ground is never easy, even less so when it is one that has failed in its purpose and brought dishonor upon its fashioner.

"I am sorry, my lord, I will repair it at once," Laban apologized to the man who had nearly lost his donkey in the swamp by reason of Laban's failed chain.

"I don't doubt you will," the large man replied, "but in the meantime what will I use for a chain? I still have deliveries to make this day."

Laban chanced a glance behind him, into the shop, hoping to see his wife and eldest daughter back from their trip to the well and at work fashioning another chain, but knew they were not. Jael had gone to help carry the water in Jemimah's absence. The need to cool hot metal brought double the demand for water normal to a family of their size.

"I expect to have another chain finished this afternoon, my lord," Laban explained, still rubbing his lower back.

Laban had toiled his entire life, first as a farmer, and in his later years as a metal worker, but had never been comfortable in physical labor. A man of small stature and thoughtful nature, he had for many years looked forward to the day when he could retire—give the farm over to his only son and take his place with the elders at the city gate. He loved study and discourse, and had privately fancied himself an able scholar though he had no formal training. At this late season of life, he had always expected he would be winding down, preparing for his rest, but instead, he found himself working harder than ever with not much hope of relief in sight.

"Perhaps I will wait while you repair this one now," the man suggested, irritated.

"You could wait for this chain, but I really would recommend taking a new one. I want to fully examine this one before sending it with you again. It may be weak for having been cooled too quickly."

With some difficulty, the man was convinced to take a rope instead to finish his day's work, giving Laban time to finish a replacement chain. He was turning to take the broken one into the shop, when he saw two men approaching to examine his wares, and beyond them, his daughter Jemimah approaching. At once, wanting to speak with her, and needing to tend to his potential customers, he resorted to a quick greeting.

"Jemimah, we have been so awaiting your return! I am sure you have news?" he asked her, even while drifting toward the men who stepped up to examine his hanging wares.

After greeting her father, Jemimah, unthinking, admitted that she did in fact have important news, and only after having released the words to her father's hearing, realized that the news he expected was vastly different than the news she actually had to give.

"Pardon me, dear," he said with a twinkle, "I am sure your mother and sister will want to hear it too. They will be back shortly."

He hurried to engage his customers. Moments later, Jemimah saw her sister, Aijeleth, and mother, Jael, appear down the block, each bearing a pot of water on her head. Laban finished his transaction and turned to address the approaching women.

"Jemimah is returned. She has news!" he whispered, with only faintly concealed excitement.

Jael hurriedly lowered her pot and went to greet her daughter, while Aijeleth looked curiously at Jemimah. Jemimah tried to communicate distress in a glance to her sister. Before Jemimah could object, her father and mother had herded her into the back room where they all sat down and focused their full attention toward hearing her "important news".

"What do you have to tell us, dear?" her mother asked.

Jemimah looked uncertainly at her parents and back at Aijeleth.

"Well. We did have a fruitful journey together, Benaiah and I, and we . . ."

"Yes?" her mother nudged.

"Yes, well, we did find Abishag," she said, casting a glance at her sister.

Both her parents frowned.

"Abishag?" They asked together.

"I did not know you were going up to her farm, I thought you would be with Benaiah and Lotan. Where did you stay?" her mother asked.

"We stayed with Abishag, Benaiah and I, and yes, I am helping him move, even still, for it seems, he has even returned with me. He . . ."

"He what?"

"He will be here shortly."

"Benaiah? Returned here?" her father asked. "Why?"

The four heard a noise in the shop beyond, and moments later, Benaiah himself strode into the room.

"Benaiah!" his parents called in unison, standing up to greet their unexpected son, while Jemimah again silently pleaded with Aijeleth for aid.

"Has Jemimah told you already?" Benaiah asked, when the greetings were finished.

"Told us what?" her father asked.

Lotan and Janis, an attendant guard with Benaiah, were spying on Laban's shop. Janis, who had reported the escaped prisoner, was brought here by Lotan in order to help convince Benaiah—if he were found—to accept his version of the "escape." Suddenly the two saw a maiden approaching alone.

"Jemimah," Lotan said.

"That's Jemimah?" Janis asked, then let out a whistle of

admiration as he watched her. "I can see why you wanted her."

Lotan glared at him.

"I've seen better," Lotan said, turning back to stare disdainfully at the approaching maiden.

"Where is the brother?" Janis asked.

"Right. She's alone. That accounts for the whole family, except for Benaiah. Maybe he didn't come back to Jezreel after all."

"How long do we wait?"

While the two were deliberating, suddenly Benaiah himself was spotted approaching the shop! Janis was about to step forward, when Lotan restrained him.

"Not now, you fool! We need to get him alone, away from his family."

"About the king!" Benaiah replied to his father. "Jemimah, you have not told them about the king yet?"

"The king?" his parents asked. All eyes turned upon the son.

For the next three minutes, Benaiah gave an urgent, passionate, and not too orderly account of all that had happened, including the presence of King Solomon in their area unknown for six weeks, his trial, his escape, his guards, his commission to Abishag, and finishing with the declaration that he himself was now a wanted man, had certainly lost his commission, and would need to move back home temporarily. When he concluded, the room was painfully silent. The parents studied curiously their strangely behaving son while Jemimah looked helplessly on, several times drawing a breath to try and say something, and several times reconsidering.

"Wait a minute," Laban replied thoughtfully breaking the silence, holding up a finger. "You are saying this man stood on trial the day before yesterday?" He looked over at his wife. "This must be the man the merchants were speaking of this morning. The report is in the city already. Benaiah," he looked back at his son. "This man is dead. He was chased and killed in a struggle. It is known throughout the city."

"No, he wasn't. He's not dead. He escaped. I was there. And there's not thirty men together in this town who could have overcome those two guards he had. There's no way he's dead. He went back to Jerusalem, and he's coming back later to redeem all the land. Now we just have to wait and stay on his side, and he will get our farm back for us."

Laban and Jael gasped in unison exchanging a confused glance.

"What!? Have you lost your senses? Not thirty men together?" Laban stammered.

"I saw it myself."

"Benaiah, be reasonable, you must have seen—I don't know what you saw—but you must have mistaken something. There were other guards there, what are they saying?"

"I have no idea what they are saying—I just know what I saw."

His father looked at him skeptically.

"What? You don't believe me? This is the truth. Jemimah knows. Tell them Jemimah. We talked to Abisha—"

"Abishag! What could she know about any of this? What could the king want with her? This is . . . this is . . . Benaiah, this is madness!"

"I know it all sounds strange, but perhaps I could explain better about how . . ." Jemimah began.

"No! Daughter, you be quiet now. Benaiah, you are on the verge of losing all you have gained, do you realize that? You haven't even seen Lotan in two days? They will think you have abandoned your duty. You are liable to lose your commission, your favor with Hamon, everything! You have to return at once, talk to them. Compare notes with the other guards. Find out what *really* happened."

Benaiah stood up quickly in anger, as his chair toppled to the ground behind him.

"What *really* happened? I just told you what really happened!"

Jael threw her hand over her mouth while Aijeleth reached out to Benaiah consolingly, looking back and forth between her brother and father.

"I know what you think you saw, son, but . . ."

"What I *think* I saw? What do you think I am, a blubbering fool? I know what I saw!" Benaiah declared passionately, his red cheeks glowing in anger. He was now beyond the consolation of either mother or sisters, and turned to leave the room.

A moment later Jemimah ran out after him, leaving the three remaining to look at each other in curious confusion.

Lotan and Janis saw Benaiah exit the shop and were about to follow when the sight of his sister quickly chasing after him restrained them.

"Aren't you going to follow him?" Janis asked Lotan, who appeared to be hesitating.

Lotan looked thoughtful.

"No, he is in town now. He will be easy to find if we are patient. Wait for the right moment. But just now another idea occurs to me."

Lotan suddenly rose and began sauntering toward Laban's metal works. Janis looked after him curiously, then followed.

Laban and his wife and daughter heard the sound of tinkling steel through the door informing them that someone was examining their hanging wares.

"We'll talk about this later," Laban said, still flushed with emotion, rising to meet his customers.

Lotan feigned complete fascination with the string of iron nails he was examining as Laban approached. Laban opened his mouth to speak to him, but then recognized Lotan.

"Lotan? Is it you? What are you doing here?"

Lotan turned, and looked surprised.

"My lord, Laban? Excuse me, is this your shop? I had no idea. Some fine work you have here. Jemimah told me you were a metal smith, but did not relate to me the high quality of your work. Good to see you."

"And you. Jemimah is back, you know, she was in Shunem yesterday, I suppose maybe you saw her . . ."

"Really? No brother, I did not, or I surely would have made certain she was properly hosted. I am actually here in search of Benaiah. He has not yet claimed his reward, and I have not seen him for a couple of days."

"Reward?"

"Well, yes, of course," Lotan said. "The bravery of all of the guards of the prisoner the other day is being rewarded. Is that not right, Janis?"

"It is quite generous," Janis agreed.

"Benaiah has a fair bit of silver awaiting him, when he returns. It's not like him to be gone like this, but I am sure he must have a good reason."

Jael now came to the scene and duly gushed and greeted Lotan, asking him for the second time if he had seen Jemimah the previous day.

"I did not have the good fortune," he said humbly. "But if Benaiah is with you, tell him there is a reward awaiting him. It was very brave how he and the others stood up to that prisoner. A lot of people were fooled by him—going around telling crazy stories. But our guards are better trained than to be taken in by such nonsense. I would like to shake his hand myself."

"Well, he is in the city," Laban stammered, not knowing quite what to reply.

"Is he? Good, well, I will find him—I don't want to keep you from your work. I'll be back to purchase some of these later," he said, indicating Laban's wares.

Laban and Jael bowed and bade farewell, as Lotan and Janis walked away.

The conversation around the evening table that night was stilted, punctuated with uncomfortable silence, followed by more silence. Benaiah had wandered for a good while before his sister caught up with him and convinced him to come home for dinner.

"Look at it from their perspective," she counseled. "How outrageous it must sound."

"Look at it from my perspective," he replied.

She realized that her brother was not angry, he was hurt.

No one felt the impact of the tension in the family more acutely than Aijeleth who, as bridge between parents and children, felt personally the quiet turmoil boiling in both. Father and son seemed to be in a deadlock of silence, each wanting to speak, but neither able to conceive a sensible way to broach the subject again, while the daughters and mother made tentative attempts at small talk.

"It was a fine trip to Dothan we had last year," Jael finally tried desperately.

Something in the statement jogged Laban's memory and he let out a truncated sniff that revealed he was thinking about something.

"What is it father?" Aijeleth asked, hoping to draw out something other than stiff silence.

He leaned back and dropped a fig into his mouth.

"You weren't with us, son," he said to Benaiah, "We were treated to a surprise on that trip, weren't we?" he said to the others.

"What? Oh . . ." Jael replied remembering.

"Yes," he continued, "we did not know the king would be passing through town with his royal caravan while we were there. My, that was a sight, wasn't it? How the whole town was weeks in preparation for his arrival? They swept the streets, the gutters, even the back alleys. And the banners they hung, everyone dressed up in their finest—and the food! You have never seen anything like it. I believe there were probably fifty—maybe sixty men in that royal caravan—don't you think so dear?—plus the women and servants? Maybe over two hundred in all, horses, everything."

Benaiah was silent, seemingly fascinated with the food in his dish, which he moved from place to place but seldom took a bite.

"Yes, well I am glad we were able to take a trip at all," Aijeleth said quickly. "It seems we don't get away that much . . . anymore."

"It is very tight these days," Laban admitted shaking his head, "very tight, some months. I don't know if we are even going to be able to keep this place, humble as it is. There's another flat two doors down from us coming available, I hear. Another, oh, at least a third bigger than this one, and closer to the shop. Not so many stairs to climb. Say . . ." he said suddenly, as if he had lit upon an idea.

No one bit on his invitation. Benaiah continued staring down.

"I was thinking of something that young fellow said this afternoon."

"Lotan?" Jael asked.

Benaiah and Jemimah both looked up sharply.

"Lotan was here?" Jemimah asked.

"He came by the shop with another man while you were out," Jael explained.

Benaiah and Jemimah exchanged a glance.

"He was looking for me," Benaiah said seriously.

Laban adjusted in his seat, fingering his beard.

"Yes, yes, son, he was looking for you. It seems there is a bit of silver for you waiting to be claimed. All the guards who were employed that day are being rewarded—for bravery. A fair amount, I dare say—or so the other guard claimed."

Benaiah's eyes narrowed.

"The other guard? Was it Janis?"

"I believe that was his name."

"Did you tell them I was here?"

Laban paused.

"Well, of course I did, son—I told them you were in the city, not here at this house, but in the city. Why would I not?"

"Because I told you they were looking for me!" Benaiah cried. "I am a wanted man, I *told* you that. Don't you see? They are trying to draw me out with this!"

He looked quickly at Jemimah and began to rise.

"I have to be going—right away. They will be back!"

"Now, son, sit down, this is not what you think it is. There is an answer to our prayers in that bravery reward, and you deserve it, son, you deserve it. Don't be hasty. Look at this place. Look at your mother, and sisters, squeezed into this little crack day after day. The long hours of work they put in—it's not right for a woman, especially one your mother's age. That silver could put us in a better flat. It could go toward redeeming our land back. It's *your* inheritance son, do not forget. You had better think very carefully about all of this, lest you make a hasty mistake."

Benaiah looked pleadingly at Jemimah and then at Aijeleth.

"Father. Our *complete* inheritance is on its way back to us.

Don't you understand? Not just a little bag of silver, but a full redemption—everything! I know how hard it is for you and mother, for Aijeleth, believe me I do, and it is not right. The king knows it's not right, that's why he came. But if I go back to Lotan now, it could be my life!"

"If you don't go back to Lotan, it will be your job—and right now that *is* your life. I'm telling you son, if you do this, if you go away and don't get back to your duty soon—tomorrow even—you will lose any chance at your inheritance, it will be bought by another."

Benaiah stared at him in complete vexation.

"Father. If I go back, there will be no inheritance to claim—for this family line will die with me. I've got to go— now!"

He turned to leave. His mother jumped up to follow him into the other room.

"But where, son? Where will you go?"

"I don't know! I don't know where to go! I can't go back to Lotan, and now I can't stay here, I can't go back to Abishag's farm either, I will have to just find something . . . somewhere!"

In barely more than a moment, he had taken up his hastily loaded travel bag and was rumbling down the stairs, leaving the sound of the slamming door ringing in the ears of his family, as they looked at one another in silence.

For the rest of that week, Jemimah pleaded with her sister, Aijeleth, to accompany her on a trip back to Shunem to see Abishag again. Aijeleth firmly resisted, arguing that their father could not possibly spare to have both of them gone, for even one day. In desperation, Jemimah even requested that her father allow her to travel alone, which he flatly denied. But on the next Sabbath, after morning prayers, Aijeleth was finally prevailed upon to suggest a day trip for the daughters, since the family was not working anyway. She and Jemimah convinced their father to agree, on the reasoning that Abishag might at least know the whereabouts of Benaiah, who had not been seen nor heard from since the day he left.

Laban and Jael had spent the week that had begun so promising in painful despondency, lamenting their shocking misfortune. Not only did they see the possibility of the favorable marriage of their daughter to Lotan evaporate—together with the dowry that it promised—they believed they had witnessed the quick and senseless destruction of their only son's career, removing a key support from their already failing hopes—and all while on the cusp of a financial windfall in the form of a reward for bravery. They could not have imagined a worse combination of results from the trip to Shunem. Beyond that, their youngest daughter seemed hopelessly captivated by the wild conspiracy the stranger had left in his wake, and all efforts at reasoning with her proved as fruitless as they had been with their son. The parents were in a state of distress bordering depression, and the comparatively levelheaded attitude of their eldest daughter was not enough to lift them from it.

On the walk to Shunem, Jemimah liberally and repeatedly thanked her sister for agreeing to come, and assured her that once she spoke to Abishag, she would find the result more than worth the effort. Jemimah had noticed, however, that throughout the week, Aijeleth had been politely noncommittal in response to her reports that Abishag's unusual friend was in fact King Solomon, and remained so when the topic came up between their parents. Jemimah was anxious to win her sister's full belief and support, in hope that the three siblings could muster enough credibility to sway their parents.

Chapter 8

Hamon sat ominously still as he listened to the reports of his brother and nephew concerning their assigned tasks. The angry Hamon was to be avoided, but this quiet sinister version was unsettling.

"So you did not see Abishag? Not at all?" he asked Caleh.

"No. Not even once, she is not there, I'm sure of it. And if you want to know, it was boring up there, staring at that little farmhouse all day—until the visitors started showing up."

"Visitors? What visitors?"

"All kinds of people. Toward the end of the day they started showing up, coming in twos and threes, stayed for a short while and then left. The other man that says he's her brother—he is gone during the day, but he comes back in the evening, and he meets people in that little room for the farm help, then they go their way."

"The one they call *Huram*," Hamon mused.

"Yes."

"Where does he go during the day?"

Caleh thought a moment.

"He seems to head north, on the hill trail."

"And you haven't followed him?"

Caleh looked embarrassed.

"We were looking for the maiden, not— "

"I *know* we are looking for the maiden, as a means to find her lover who is escaped! And this man who is connected with both of them, goes north on the hill trail every day. Has it ever occurred to you that this man's fugitive friend might be camped out up there somewhere, and he is going up there to consult and supply him? If so, the maiden is likely up there also."

"I'll follow him next time," Caleh said blushing.

"Yes, brother, I am sure you will, and no doubt they have moved on by now, and you will find a lot of nothing! Why do I have to do all the thinking?"

Hamon looked over at Lotan.

"What did you find? Is the boy guard in Jezreel?"

"Yes, we saw him once, but he is not staying with the family. He is around somewhere. I'm sure they know where he is though. We sent a message to him through the family."

"What kind of message?"

"We let the father know there is a reward waiting for the guards, for bravery."

Hamon looked over at his brother Caleh.

"Are you listening Caleh? Are you paying attention here? Lotan used his brain. He used subtlety—not force. You have been with me a lot longer than Lotan has, but he is beating you to every trick. He did not just stomp in there and start making threats. He threw out some bait, showed some money to the family. That little guard will feel the pressure indirectly—from his own family, rather than from us. Good plan. Let it work. In the meantime, we can increase the financial pressure on that family. Soon that boy will think it is his *duty* to go along with us."

"Suppose I could offer some special relief to that family too?" Lotan asked casually.

Hamon gave him a warning look.

"You still want that little maiden, eh? You're a fool. No man should ever let himself get that attached to one maiden. It will ruin you. But your strategy for getting the brother is a good one. Yes, if your plan brings us the boy, you can have what you need to draw the sister—but I don't recommend it. I don't know a single maiden in this whole valley that is worth *that* much effort."

Hamon's council was attended by an inner tweak. There was a particular maiden that continued to vex him in spite of his best efforts. He loathed to admit how much power she held over him. But now he was about to embark on another plan, a plan that, if effective, could yield results on that score as well as the problem of the escapee. He looked at Caleh again.

"You do understand that this maiden we are looking for can be drawn out by her strong sense of duty. She feels a debt of responsibility to her mother—to keep that little vineyard."

"Does she?"

"Of course she does! Do you even know anything about the person you are supposed to be finding? Find out what motivates a person, and you can lead them anywhere you want—like tossing grain before a duck. She is bound by duty and honor. Even if she is gone away, she won't abandon her mother. Do you realize the opportunity inherent in this?"

"Well, not really— "

"It means, that we can find out if she is really gone for good—or if she has some other connection to this place. Think about it, if the man was wealthy—and it appears that he was—why would she go away by herself and leave her mother here alone? She would take her mother with her. No—there is something else going on, something connected with this area, otherwise they all would have disappeared. Abishag can't be far away, and we can draw her back. Do you know how?"

Caleh thought a moment then he said, "Are you going to go

after her vineyard?"

Hamon scowled at him in frustration.

"Me? No, but her brothers are."

"What? Why would they take their own sister's vineyard?"

"Yes. Why. Why indeed. Would you like to see why?"

Caleh did not answer.

Hamon leaned his head toward the door, and called for an aid. Sylva appeared.

"Send him in now," he ordered, then leaned back in his chair and waited while his brother and nephew watched curiously.

A few moments later, Hemanah, the presumed brother of Abishag who had single-handedly destroyed Hamon's strategy in the inquiry against the stranger, entered the room. Following that debacle, Hamon had demoted Hemanah to hard field labor. There was presently no man in the valley whom Hamon held in greater contempt. The very thought of him made him furious.

Hemanah entered the room sweaty and disheveled, wearing a work tunic, apparently summoned straight from the field. He looked at Hamon worriedly while noticing the presence of the other two men. Hamon let the silence hang for a long moment, while he stared at Hemanah.

"Is something wrong, my lord?" Hemanah asked.

"How is the harvest proceeding on the south hill Hemanah?"

Hemanah cleared his throat.

"The harvest? Well. We are about a third done, my lord. Why?"

Hamon looked up sharply and his eyes narrowed.

"A third done? Is that all? Most of the other work groups are more than half done already. Who is working with you up there?"

"My brothers, of course, you said we could . . ."

Hamon was shaking his head in disgust. Then he looked over

at Caleh.

"It must be a family weakness, don't you think, Caleh? Put the three of them together and their efficiency drops to less than one man alone. You know," he said looking back at the nervous man, "you are becoming a real problem for me, Hemanah—and not just for me, for my brother here, and nephew. You are becoming a drag on this whole estate. We only agreed to sharecrop with you on the condition that you could continue to produce, maintain the land. At this rate, most of it is going to wither on the vine before you ever get to it. I am afraid I made a mistake in signing you on. We need to make some changes."

"What kind of changes?"

"As of today, the sharecrop agreement is off. You obviously can't keep your end of the bargain. I'm taking the land back. Caleh—can you get some men over there to take over for Hemanah and his brothers by this afternoon?"

"Shouldn't be a problem," Caleh said.

Hemanah was stunned, then he began to tremble.

"My lord! Please! We can do better—let us continue! We'll start earlier, work later. I know we can catch up."

Hamon was shaking his head.

"We're way past that Hemanah—way past that. I'm stepping in, before it's too late. That's my harvest too, you know. I'll bring it in—all the rest of it."

"All the harvest? All the land? You have to leave us something! How will we survive?"

"What do you mean—'all the harvest'? Are you saying you haven't even started yet? Oh, this is too much. You haven't even brought in that first third yet. You haven't even started! On top of everything else, you lie to me. It's over, Hemanah."

"But, how will we survive?"

"Survive? I'm not taking all your land, I'm just repossessing what we sharecropped. You will survive just fine."

"But that is all we have!"

"Is it?" Hamon asked.

Hemanah scowled in fright and worry.

"Well . . . my sister has that little vineyard . . . but other than that . . ."

"Exactly! So quit accusing me! Think a little bit before you start with your self-righteous accusations! Me taking all your land. I wouldn't do that, it's against the Law. I'm only enforcing what we agreed to in contract. You have other land, go use that."

"But . . . we . . ."

"You should have thought of that before you frittered away half the season. There is a two-week window to bring in the harvest, that's all there is, and you are acting as though you have all year to bring it in. We're taking over as of now. Now get out."

Hemanah hesitated.

"I said get out!" he yelled, and started to rise. Hemanah stumbled toward the door, and went down the hall in a daze.

Hamon looked back at his partners in perfect calm.

"So now *he* repossesses from his sister. See? And after he does, I believe we will see that maiden back to tend to her dispossessed mother very soon—if she is coming back at all."

Hemanah left Hamon's tower in a daze. Following his swift demotion and subsequent harsh treatment by Hamon, he had all but given up hope of ever making a position for himself in the estate, but he never dreamed he would lose even the right to farm his own inheritance land. He stumbled out of the city with unseeing eyes, wondering how he would break the news to his brothers, what he would put his hand to now, and how they would all survive. Fortunately, one third of the harvest had already been weighed and loaded for export. He expected that he would at least be entitled to half of that, even if Hamon took all the rest.

Strangely, even amid the swirling turmoil, he became aware of a new unexpected sensation: relief. Even though he had lost everything, was facing an uncertain future and a severe shortage of sustenance for the winter, the final break with Hamon—for that it truly seemed to be—carried with it a feeling of release, as though a burden long carried had been lifted off him.

Chapter 9

Dinah was back with Abishag at last. As encouraging as it was to Dinah to have a friend like Abishag to spend everyday with for the rest of their week together in the oven room, Dinah was, unbeknownst to herself, bestowing her own blessing upon the maiden she was growing to admire so greatly. Abishag, awestruck and overwhelmed by the surreal events of the past six weeks, was finding in Dinah the perfect audience upon whom to unburden her heart. Her friend's attentive ear, quick mind, and absolute trust were just the right combination to draw from Abishag the thoughts that allowed her to process her own feelings.

Dinah heard all, by turns in awe and admiration, as Abishag humbly and honestly explained all, starting with how she had been summoned to Jerusalem to serve King David years ago, how she had fled after Adonijah played her as a political gambit for the throne, and how she had returned home resigned to a lonely life of singleness. Then the extraordinary surprise: how the king had first come to her, how she had grown to both admire and fear him for his wisdom and kindness, how she had run away, and finally the greatest secret of all, how he had proposed marriage to her—and that he loved her, and she him. And Dinah believed every word. If any maiden in the world were worthy of such an honor, Dinah had no doubt that Abishag was that one. And at the end of each incredible day, Dinah felt even less disposed to return to her nightly occupation than the day before. The two maidens, different as they were, found themselves drawing closer in heart than either would have thought possible.

"He is the king of peace—it is his anointing," Abishag explained, "The aura of his presence lingers and reconciles, even after he has gone away. So it has been with you and me, Dinah, and I have tasted no sweeter reconciliation than to have you as my friend again."

Dinah was humbled, and continued to listen to and grow in love for her rediscovered friend.

Two days before the maidens were to finish their appointed term, a man joined them in the oven room, and to Dinah's amazement, Abishag finished her final two days in the sweltering heat in full veil! Dinah was even more impressed when she remembered Abishag was in the hot room both night and day while Dinah was at least relieved of it at night. The added inconvenience of the veil, coupled with the presence of a third person before whom they could not speak openly, only intensified the two maiden's anxious desire to finish their term so they could be alone together and savor their newly-formed heart bond. Still, Abishag gave polite attention to the man, patiently explaining the need for the treatment in addition to the medicine, and promising him that recovery was sure. Dinah always tried to stretch her stay to the last moment, so she would have a few private moments with Abishag after the man left.

On the evening of the day before the Sabbath, when Dinah and Abishag were enjoying one such precious moment alone, Huram visited once again. This time he explained that he had received an urgent message from Tyre and was required to leave Shunem a day earlier than expected. Dinah openly worried that it would not be safe for Abishag to be seen, that Hamon might still be searching for her, but was refuted by Abishag herself, who insisted that Hamon could do nothing to harm her even if he found her. To this Huram added that no additional messengers had been to the farm, suggesting that perhaps the matter had been dropped. He did inform them of one precaution he had taken before departing.

"I have ordered my own certified copy of the transcript."

"Of the hearing?—where they questioned Solomon?" Abishag asked.

"I could never be at ease knowing there was no copy other than the one kept here in Shunem with all the implicating evidence that transcript contains. I paid the scribe to begin yesterday; I will take it with me before I depart for Tyre," he explained.

Abishag wanted to know if Huram had news of Benaiah and Jemimah, to which he explained that neither had been back to the farm, and he supposed them to be back in Jezreel.

Abishag and Dinah imparted their heartfelt farewells to Huram who was not sure when exactly he would return, but promised them it would be as soon as possible. His absence, even though he was not quite gone yet, created an immediate vacuum that they both felt.

But anticipation was also growing. The completion of their treatment was now close at hand when they would walk out of the fire room together, as Abishag had predicted, completely whole. Neither had coughed in over a day. Dinah had already determined that the day they left in full health would be the day on which she would don the veil and begin her new life, for she had agreed to move in with Abishag. That day, fittingly, would be a Sabbath.

Dinah, needing to speak with her father and pack her modest belongings, suggested that they make an exit in the morning, rather than spending the full day in the oven room, so they could arrive at the farm in the daylight. Since the baker's oven did not need to be heated on the Sabbath and both maidens were clearly cured, Abishag agreed knowing that she herself had already put in much more time than was necessary. Though no complaint had crossed her lips, privately Abishag had never yearned more for a bath and a change of clothing in her life.

The cool air that met Abishag's face and lungs was uncommonly delicious on that clear morning of the sixth month, Elul, the month preceding the fall feasts of Trumpets, Atonement, and Tabernacles. It was the last month of harvest, after which Israelites, the land over, would be free to travel to Jerusalem for worship. It so happened that it was also a New Moon, making it a High Sabbath, requiring even greater devotion.

The morning was bright, as the two maidens exited the fire room in hope. Though merely a week had passed, Abishag immediately noticed a strong whiff of the approaching winter in the air. For how many years had she tasted that familiar air at just this season? The smell excited strong associations in her memory, admonishing her that she ought to be bringing in her harvest. But Abishag, for the first time since her return from Jerusalem six years ago, had no harvest to bring in; her vineyard had been charged to her neighbor, Barkos.

The plan was to proceed to Dinah's home first where she would inform her father of her change of occupation, as well as residence. Dinah suspected her father was aware that something unusual was afoot, for she had noticed him watching her with puzzled expressions as she drew back from her normal brash and clever verbal jousting with the men she served. She was more gentle and reserved in recent days, serving quietly, and speaking little. In preparing to confront her father with news she doubted he would receive favorably, Dinah at first declared that she must speak with her father alone. Shortly after this, she insisted that Abishag be with her the whole time, followed by instructions that she enter alone first with Abishag entering after a few minutes time, and finally insisting that Abishag not come in at all. After observing these painful gyrations, Abishag simply informed Dinah that she would be coming in to help her pack her things, and if a conversation with her father was to be had, she would be present for it. Dinah agreed, realizing that all her tactical shuffling had not resulted in confidence in any one strategy over another.

They walked leisurely, breathing the cool air. As they passed the market square, it was refreshingly quiet; the majority of merchants, devout Sabbath observers. Only a few scattered traders had set up booths to sell their wares to non-Israelites, or to Israelites to whom the seventh day inspired no special reverence. Along the east side of the square stretched a line of wagons upon which the harvested crops were being loaded daily to be carted to Jezreel for sale. The wagons were heavily laden with grain, figs, olives, flasks of oil, and of course, many large barrels of wine. Abishag's head turned as her eyes stretched down the train, even as they walked away from it.

"It will be a strong harvest—if it fills all of those wagons," she commented.

The streets, like the square, were also appropriately quiet, except for the occasional passing of worshippers traveling to or from morning prayers. As the maidens approached Dinah's home, Dinah slowed to a stop, pausing as if to say something, and the two stood on a street corner. The sun was high and bright. Dinah opened her mouth to speak, but hesitated, noticing Abishag looking intently into the distance behind them. Dinah followed her gaze.

"What is it?" Dinah asked.

"That woman . . ." Abishag replied, ". . . she was at the square . . ."

Dinah looked around. Down the street, and on the other side, an elderly woman stood facing them, finely dressed, apparently wealthy. She appeared to have been following them, but was now hesitating under Abishag's gaze. It seemed apparent, even over the distance between them that she was staring quite intently at Abishag.

"I wonder what she wants," Dinah mused.

The woman took a hesitant step forward, as Abishag continued to look curiously in her direction. Suddenly the sound of hoof beats echoing off the shop walls announced the approach of a chariot beyond the corner, and the two maidens instinctively stepped back from the street. A moment later, the chariot itself, drawn by horses, rounded the corner at a speed not fitted to the tranquility of the morning. The shouts of its driver echoed from nearby buildings as the chariot took the corner sharply, and the maidens stepped back even farther.

"Watch what you're doing!" Dinah snapped angrily at the driver, "You could run someone over like that!"

The driver who was accompanied in the wagon by several other men glared at her and was about to hurry on by when someone behind him grabbed him by the shoulder. He suddenly brought the horses to a quick halt.

"Hamon's men," Dinah said. "They have no respect for the Sabbath—don't you know what day it is!?" she yelled at them.

"That's her!" someone shouted.

Suddenly, several men bolted from the wagon and were headed right toward them. Abishag, startled, took a step back. Three men came at them briskly and Dinah stepped forward to continue her scolding, but they brushed past her and ran to Abishag, grabbing her roughly.

"This is her!" one of them said. "This is Abishag."

"Are you sure?"

"Yes, I know it!"

Dinah turned about.

"What do you think you're doing, Ethan!?" she demanded, walking briskly up to them, curling her fists on her hips.

"Dinah? What are you doing with the likes of her? Never mind—it's none of your concern. This maiden is wanted for questioning."

"You are coming with us," the man said to Abishag.

"What do you mean she's coming with you? She is not going with you, she is coming with me! Get your filthy hands off of her now!" Dinah snapped, stepping forward to yell right in the man's face.

"Dinah, it's alright," Abishag said, "I can answer their questions."

The men began pulling Abishag back toward the wagon, while Dinah followed and tried to get in their way.

"NO! You have no right! She has committed no crime! Now let her go!"

Across the street, a crowd comprised of well-dressed citizens returning from morning prayers began to notice the spectacle. Abishag continued to cooperate, while Dinah continued to get ever more shrill, attempting at one point to physically remove one of the men who was holding Abishag. The man suddenly turned and repelled her with a swift backhand, sending her to the ground. The watching crowd gasped.

Dinah did not stay down long. In a moment, she was up and back at the man screaming protests into his face. He raised his hand again, but this time Dinah darted away, and his swing struck Abishag smartly on the side of the face. She reached for her eye, and her veil began to loosen. The men hurried more urgently to get Abishag into the wagon to escape the emerging scene, and also her feisty and persistent companion who seemed quite intent on having her way. With some difficulty, Abishag was raised to the wagon, but not without Dinah getting a sharp kick into the shin of one of the men who yelped in pain.

In the confusion, Abishag's veil, which she had worn in public for all the years since coming of age, was ripped completely from her face and fell to the ground. Now up on the wagon with full face exposed, she covered her injured eye with her hand. Then, noticing the watching crowd, she turned away. The group gawked wide-eyed at the spectacle. Several in the group pointed and whispered to each other.

Immediately, the horses were whipped and the chariot was off and running, leaving the screaming, and now crying maiden, Dinah, to follow for a few steps until she was clearly outpaced. She screamed and kicked the street, staring after the wagon, spinning in a complete circle in waving protest, as the wagon disappeared around a corner. She found herself staring uselessly at an empty street and stood there for some time vexing in fury. There was nothing else to do. Finally, she turned. Suddenly she stopped, seeing Abishag's veil on the ground. She knelt down and picked it up, holding it before her in her hands. Some of the crowd crossed over and were standing over her. A trickle of blood ran from the corner of her mouth.

"That was Abishag?" a man asked, in wonder.

"Yes. Abishag. The most honorable maiden in the valley. Carried off by those swine, like some criminal!"

"The most beautiful maiden, anyway," someone commented.

"Her face was not disfigured at all," said another, "It was always said she had been burned in fire—for harlotry."

Dinah glared up at the speaker.

"If you ever believed that, you are a fool."

Eventually, the crowd disbursed, talking quietly among themselves about the spectacle they had just witnessed.

"Have you ever seen a lovelier woman?" was a frequent comment.

When all were gone, Dinah was left kneeling alone in the street for longer than she knew, holding the purple, grape-stained veil of Abishag. She fingered it gently and reverently, as though it were a holy artifact, too stunned and angry to think of what to do next.

We could not even get out of the city! Those swine—those arrogant swine!

Gradually, her anger gave way to concern for her friend. Her plans for the day now violently overturned by circumstance, she began to realize if anything was to be done for Abishag, the responsibility was hers.

Where would those men take her?

She glanced ahead. Her father's house stood tall and forbidding, just a short distance down the block. She stared at it, and then back down at the veil, the contrast between the two objects striking deeply on her soul. Never before had two things seemed so opposite in all they represented.

Her father's house appeared a strange and foreign place. A single week under the gentle yet precise counsel of Abishag had dislodged what years of dwelling in her father's house had instilled in her. She shook her head, pursing her lips in resolve. Then, with a surge of resolution, she turned sharply to walk in the opposite direction, casting off her father's house and all it represented.

With a resolve surprising in its power and a heart anxious yet relieved, she walked out of the city to the northwest, ignoring the fear, ignoring the nervous voice that warned against abandonment of all that had meant security, ignoring even the lump in her throat which lied to her that she had not the strength to pursue this course. Her heart set itself of its own accord toward a destination she had not visited in years. Her soul, it seemed, had already leaped ahead, pulling her body along behind as if towed by a string. On to that place—that simple farm, unassuming in appearance, yet so packed with meaning. It was more than a house, it was the past itself—a fork in the road long ago passed, where a grievous choice resulting in nothing but regret had been made. She knew she must return to that fork, and take the other road, and she must do it now.

Abishag's veil traveled with her every step, testifying to her even in its silence. She remembered, shamefully, that she had mocked the virgin's veil unmercifully in days not long past. Now the very thing she had mocked, she felt unworthy even to touch and hold. She placed it reverently around her neck, wiping tears from her eyes. Abishag's violent displacement from the veil of her chastity seemed an atrocity, a violation, a boorish and shameful disgracing of the greater by the lesser. The thought of donning it herself in a private show of respect for her friend crossed her mind, but she quickly dismissed it as unbecoming.

She cannot wear it, because it was ripped from her, but I cannot, because I am not worthy of it.

Another veil, she could perhaps put on, but not *this* one. She paused at the top of a rise, seeing the small vineyard and house—memories flooding her mind. Then she walked on. Abelah, the mother of Abishag, who in past days had been as a mother to Dinah would be there. If she could not speak to Abishag, she would speak to her mother, for she knew the same spirit was in both. Abelah would know what to do.

Abelah had been informed that her daughter was nurturing a growing friendship with the maiden Dinah, and was expecting them both that day. When Dinah appeared in the door looking distressed, Abelah was not surprised to see her, but was surprised to see her alone.

Dinah collapsed at the table putting her face in her hands unable to speak for some moments. Abelah put her hand on the maiden's shoulder.

"She's gone. Hamon's men—they took her," she finally choked, looking up at the mother of her friend with tear-filled eyes, and then explained all.

Abelah sat down without comment, while Dinah waited for some response, surprised at Abelah's calm reception of the news. When Abelah did speak she was gentle in voice, and orderly in thoughts. After discerning that Dinah did in fact know Abishag's greatest secret, Abelah suggested that the best thing in their power to do would be to alert others who could bear the matter with them. Abelah suggested that Dinah travel to Jezreel to alert Abishag's friends, Aijeleth, Jemimah, and Mahaleth, while she herself went to inform Shammai. Dinah, strengthened by this calm response, agreed to go instantly without argument and departed without delay.

Abelah, watching this friend of her daughter hasten out of the yard, perceived that Dinah was not a soul given to half measures. Her love for Abishag was evident, and she would not be satisfied until all that could be done to help her had been done. If it had been a message to the ends of the earth that required delivery, Abelah doubted not that Dinah would have embarked thence without a moments' delay.

****

Jemimah tugged at her sister's sleeve. The road she and Aijeleth traveled from Jezreel to Shunem had been constructed, with some difficulty, right through the center of the marshy lowlands. In the dry season it was a passable road, but in the rainy season, it was little more than a soft mound of earth, difficult for loaded carts to negotiate, and surrounded by murky water and patches of reeds. Due to the recent and unexpected rain storm, standing water already rested in the lower portions of the swamp—and much earlier in the year than usual. Merchants and travelers hoped that the road would be dry enough for the wagons when the train carrying harvested produce would travel from Shunem to Jezreel to be sold in the coming weeks.

The two maidens, Jemimah and Aijeleth, chose a path that tended toward the center and most firm portion of the mound. For Jemimah, Aijeleth was not walking nearly fast enough. Having been consumed with a pressing desire see Abishag for a week, a desire that was heightened by her sister's quiet reception of her urgent disclosures, the leisurely pace was difficult to submit to. She quickened her steps, hoping to pull Aijeleth into a faster tempo.

The sun had passed the third watch of the day, and was now dropping toward the horizon, stretching the shadows of the sparkling auburn-haired girl and her tall older sister across the ditch to their right, from which cool, moist air wafted up on the evening breeze. There were not many travelers on the road at this time of day on a Sabbath, but presently, the maidens became aware of a small figure ahead, alone, and traveling in their direction.

With some distance yet between them, Jemimah identified the figure as the maiden, Dinah, and grabbing her sister's sleeve, excitedly began pulling her forward.

"It's Dinah—she was there! She knows everything too."

"Dinah?" Aijeleth said with a tone of curious skepticism.

When Dinah recognized them, she came to a halt in the road, ready to unburden her sad news.

"Aijeleth, Jemimah. I was just coming to see you, something has happened . . ." Dinah began with a sigh.

"I know! I know!" Jemimah exclaimed, "I have been explaining it to Aijeleth all week. My brother—he is gone away, they are looking for him—I know they are, and my father and mother, they do not understand. We were coming to see Abishag—Aijeleth needs to see her."

"Jemimah! Listen to me. It's about Abishag. We left the fire room this morning. We were supposed to wait until evening and it was all my fault—I suggested we leave early. But we went out in the daytime. I am so sorry, it was awful what happened, just awful. The injustice!—you won't believe what they did to her! I told Abelah and she sent me to tell you—I was on my way to you just now."

"Did to Abishag?" Aijeleth asked.

"Yes. They arrested her! Can you believe that? Abishag, of all people. We were in the city; I was going to my father's house when Hamon's men came suddenly. They did not explain or anything, they just grabbed her, took her away."

"They took Abishag?" Jemimah asked wide-eyed, "Where?"

"I don't know where. They were in a chariot. They took her away. They said she was wanted for questioning."

"Questioning? What kind of questioning?" Aijeleth asked.

"Aijeleth," Dinah said, "You have no idea what has happened here these past weeks. They think she knows where an escaped criminal is hiding. But he is not a criminal. He is actually the king—Solomon! Abishag knows this. Now they think they can find him if they question her!"

Aijeleth frowned at the ground. "This is all very strange . . ."

"Isn't it?! The insanity of thinking they can find him that way—as if they could do anything to him if they did. They are insane—all of them. They only want him because he was a threat to them. And now Abishag!" Dinah said.

"And now Abishag," Aijeleth said.

Jemimah caught something in her tone and looked up at her sister.

Aijeleth glanced at her, and back at Dinah.

"Does it all not seem very strange to you, Dinah?" Aijeleth

asked.

"Aijeleth!" Jemimah exclaimed.

"No—please, listen to me. I have been thinking about this all week. My brother has lost his commission, and now is hiding—who knows where? You, Jemimah, have not been yourself all week. Now Abishag is arrested. This doesn't seem right. Think about it—is this how the king of Israel would conduct his business? Everyone who gets close to this seems to be getting into trouble."

"Trouble from the enemies of Israel!" Jemimah exclaimed. "Because Abishag is going to set things right. The king told her to—"

"Yes, I have heard all of this, Jemimah. The king gave Abishag his Seal and told her to . . . redeem the land. He told her to do it while he is away in Jerusalem, and he will return in the spring. Yes, I have listened to this and thought about it, more than you know. Jemimah. I love Abishag, she has been a dearest friend to me, but, I am thinking just now, how best can I be a friend to her? Is it possible she mistook the situation, and is putting herself in needless danger? Why would the king of Israel give such a charge to a peasant maiden, and then abandon her? Now she is arrested. He brings all this trouble on her, and he is nowhere to be found! Why would he not just redeem the land himself? It's not making sense, Jemimah."

"The king will defend her!" Jemimah answered.

"Then where is he?"

Aijeleth's question hung in the air. Jemimah studied her sister's face worriedly then looked over at Dinah.

Dinah looked back and forth at the two sisters.

"Aijeleth," Dinah said. "It does look strange at the moment, but it can all be explained. Abishag can explain it. I can understand your questioning your little sister. But, you know me—I am not from a quiet family like yours, I have been among the rough men, heard and seen things that a girl should not, and I don't believe a story easily—especially one this incredible. But I spent all week with Abishag, we discussed these things thoroughly. She proved it. The king has a plan—and we are all a part of it. Nothing is going to happen to Abishag."

"Then why are you rushing over to tell us she was arrested?"

"So we can . . . so we can . . . pray! Get the word out—support her. I don't know what we can do, but she is our friend—we have to get her out of there!"

"That's just the problem, Dinah, *we* have to get her out of there. Don't you see how backward this is? She is the bride-to-be of the king, and *we* have to protect her. It just isn't right." Aijeleth looked over at her sister.

"Jemimah—we better be getting home. It looks like we are not going to see Abishag today. I'm sorry, Dinah."

"Go home?! How can we go home?! What about Abishag?"

"And just what do you think you are going to do for her, Jemimah—break in there and rescue her? There's nothing you can do—this is in the hands of the law now. We should be getting back; it's the only right thing to do under the circumstances."

"But I can't go back! I have to see her! *You* have to see her—you have to talk to her. Come, let's go on—we'll find her, somewhere!"

"Jemimah, you are going to get yourself in as much trouble as she is!" Aijeleth said, raising her voice. "Our father needs us in the morning—more than I think you realize. We can't let ourselves get caught up in this crazy sham! I can understand Benaiah believing this—but you have more sense, Jemimah—you should know better!"

"Crazy sham?! How can you say that? I can understand Benaiah *not* believing—but not you, Aijeleth. You know Abishag. She is not foolish, she is careful—exceedingly careful. You know she would not fall for some silly hoax. You have to talk to her—at the very least. You *owe* her that much."

"No, Jemimah. As much as I owe Abishag, I owe my father more—and so do you. Our place is back home. I am going now, and so are you. Father will be waiting."

"But . . ."

"Come, sister," she ordered, and took a step.

Jemimah hesitated. Then her eyes began to well.

"I can't, Aijeleth. Aijeleth. Please. We will still come back tonight, but Dinah came all the way here—we have to help her. I can't go back now."

"What do you mean, you can't come back? You know you are charged to obey me—just as you are charged to obey father. I am responsible for you. You are coming."

Jemimah stared at her, and then slowly began shaking her head.

"Aijeleth. I can't. As bound as I am to obey father, I have another duty, to the Lord, and to the kingdom. If it comes to that, I must serve Him . . . first."

"Aijeleth," Dinah broke in, "there is a solution. I will bring Jemimah home tonight—just as she promised. But she is right. If Abishag is being held in the city—and you will see that what Jemimah has told you is all true—we have to at least make some attempt to find her, let her know she is not alone, that we are supporting her. God knows how much strength she has imparted to others over the years."

"Support from you, Dinah? How much support do you think you have given her, since you left the veil?" Aijeleth asked.

Dinah searched her face, then her eyes began to mist.

"You don't know what it has meant—Aijeleth," she said, her voice cracking, "How I was so blind, for so long, but Abishag—she spoke to me all week, she . . . she wants me to move out of my father's house, and in with her. I know I have been unworthy, but she is not. I can't abandon her . . . not now."

Aijeleth stared at her, her lower lip quivering.

"I appreciate that Dinah, truly I do, but I must support my father—and protect my sister. Let's go, Jemimah," she whispered, and turned, taking her sister by the sleeve.

"There are times when supporting your father is the wrong choice," Dinah replied softly. "I would know."

Aijeleth froze, staring at the ground momentarily.

"My father is not like yours, Dinah."

Aijeleth resumed moving. Suddenly, Jemimah pulled away and started walking briskly in the opposite direction.

"Jemimah! Come back here at once!" her sister cried.

Dinah gave Aijeleth a look of hurt pity, then turned and followed Jemimah. Jemimah kept walking.

"How can you abandon father like this!?"

"How can you abandon Abishag?" Jemimah called back, her words choking almost unintelligible.

Dinah caught up with her and took her arm and the two continued on together. Aijeleth helplessly watched the two figures recede until it was plain nothing more could be said or done. She finally turned, wiping her eyes in grief, and started slowly back toward Jezreel, wondering just how she could face her already distraught father with such disastrous news.

Chapter 10

For as the crackling of thorns under a pot, so is the laughter of the fool.

Ecclesiastes 7:6

The campfire sent out a spray of sparks that curled up and away in the breeze as Hamon stoked it with a stick. The smoke drifted to the north carried by the warm, moist wind that whipped up from the valley. Lotan was watching.

"Perhaps the former rains are coming early this year," he commented.

The residents of the area knew the local economy depended upon the rain watering the newly planted crops for a good spring harvest, but the west wind, which brought rain clouds from the sea, normally did not blow until after Yom Kippur which was still several weeks away. The recent weather, especially the unexpected early rainstorm, had been a local curiosity.

Hamon and his associates, not having much interest in Sabbath prayers, had spent the weekend hunting wild mountain roe in the unfarmed hills northeast of Shunem—a yearly tradition for them upon entering harvest time. Hamon sat down on a rock and loosened the string on his bow, then began rubbing olive oil into the wood.

"And the roe are late," Caleh replied disgustedly.

Hamon looked up and snorted.

"You are too impatient brother. You think if your game doesn't wander right by you in the first hour, it's not there." He looked out over the twilight darkening hills. "No, the roe are out there," he mused, a moment later adding ominously, ". . . as is everything we seek."

Lotan caught his tone.

"You mean that maiden—and her lover."

Hamon looked at him narrowly.

"I wouldn't call him that but, yes, any good hunter knows his game is there, even when he does not see it. It's just a matter of patience, learning the habits and ways of the prey—teasing it out."

Caleh dropped his chin into his hands.

"No deer—bad weather—should-a' brought some girls with us."

"Oh, that would make for a successful hunt," Hamon said. "Scare off every roe from here to the Chinnerith. No—if you'd keep your mind on your business, for once, we may yet have success. There will be plenty of time when we get home for . . . other hunts."

The party planned to spend one more night in the hills, try an early morning hunt, and then make the two-hour ride back to Shunem the following day. The heaviest week of harvest was just ahead.

"You don't suppose she left permanently, do you?" Lotan asked.

Hamon shook his head.

"You don't know her."

"And you do?"

"Well enough. Her harvest still on the vine, her mother still at home?—she's around—count on it."

The men fell silent. Hamon had both considered and dismissed the possibility that Abishag had gone with the escaped man permanently, as much as he would have liked it to be the case. That would ensure that the only person proven to be a real threat to him would have no reason to ever return. But another possibility had since occurred to him. The man would also not return if there were no maiden to return to. How indeed could that be arranged? Of course, she could not be killed outright—that would be too obvious. But it was possible, he reasoned, that Abishag could be exposed to forces that would lead to an innocent and tragic end.

Suddenly, the men raised their heads at a faint rumbling sound.

"Thunder?" Caleh suggested.

Hamon stood slowly, dropping his mouth slightly open to facilitate better hearing.

"No," he replied carefully, "horsemen."

Hamon and his partners stood to meet the approaching riders whose horses were sweaty and breathing hard from a long run. Even from a distance, Hamon had recognized them as his own men. The three riders pulled up just outside the ring of the camp.

"We have news, my lord," the lead rider said quickly, dismounting and limping toward Hamon, shooting a quick glance at Caleh and Lotan. "We thought you would want to know right away. The maiden you have been looking for—she is found."

"Is that right?" Hamon said, calmly.

"She is in detainment even now, my lord."

Hamon nodded, glanced at Caleh.

"Like I told you, eh brother? A good hunter knows. Well

boys, best start packing up."

Caleh blinked.

"What? We're going—right now? I thought we were going to stay another night."

Hamon shook his head at his brother.

"A minute ago you couldn't wait to get home. Now you want to stay. He's a piece of work, isn't he?" he said to Lotan, then to the messenger, "Where did you find her?"

"Right in the city. She wasn't hiding or anything, just walking along with that other maiden . . . that maiden, oh—what is her name? She's—oh, everybody knows her—I ought to remember her name with this lump on my knee she gave me. I swear one of these days I am going to forget my own name. The maiden—that little plaything who works at Jalaam's inn—Jalaam's daughter."

"You mean Dinah?" Caleh said.

"Yes, Dinah—that's it."

Hamon frowned.

"Abishag was with Dinah?"

"Yes, yes—spunky little rascal too, I haven't been kicked that hard since I tried to toetrim my sick mule. Anyway, in the morning, right after prayers, there they were just walking in the city—no particular hurry. We went right in and took her."

"After morning prayers? Did anyone see?"

"It was over very quickly, my lord," another of the men broke in suddenly.

Hamon began to fall into the ominous silence that meant trouble to those who knew him.

"You made a scene, didn't you?"

"My lord," the man explained. "We did everything you said. We got her in that cell—the lower one, with the window, where the cold wind comes in right off the swamp. Her veil is off now—oh, when that came off, you never saw a crowd get so quiet!" He whistled. "What a beauty!—not disfigured at all. I haven't seen a girl like that since, well, I've *never* seen a girl like that."

"Wait a minute." Hamon broke in, "What crowd? What people?"

The men looked at one another.

"The people who were in the city for morning prayers…"

"You took her veil off in the city?!! People saw her??!!"

"My lord, you *said* to take it away, get her in that cold cell by the window . . ."

"I said to remove it *after* she was in the cell you fool! How many people were there? Did it make a scene? How many people saw?!"

"My lord—it was that maiden Dinah—she made the scene, we were quick about it, but with all her carrying on . . ."

"How many people??!"

The men paused.

"Oh, I suppose, maybe a dozen . . . or two."

Hamon's face grew red. Then with a groan, he turned sharply away and stared out at the hills, his finger on his chin, his eyes darting back and forth, while the men stood nervously by. Then he looked around.

"Break camp. We are leaving. Now!"

****

The prison where the Shunamites detained such petty criminals that wandered through their town was actually a converted grain silo. It stood dark and silent, silhouetted against the far hills that rose beyond the swampy lowlands to the south, from which a steady moist wind swept up. Torches were seldom lit at the prison's location at the edge of town, and foot traffic rarely wandered by.

Inside, its single inhabitant rocked back and forth holding her bare arms while sitting on the stone floor of the small, dark room. Leaning against the wall with her knees curled under her, Abishag shivered in her thin, sweat-dampened garment. The men had not only taken her veil, but also her woolen tunic, leaving her with only a thin, sleeveless slipover made of a rough fabric scarcely finer than sackcloth. Through the barred window, through which the damp wind entered, the pale light from the rising moon was just beginning to glow against the stone walls, reflecting from her large, dark eyes and long, tangled, sweat-matted hair. The wind made a low constant and mesmerizing tone as it traveled through the tower like a pipe. The cool air, which had initially felt so delicious to Abishag after a week in the sweltering heat of the fire room, had now completely lost its appeal. She was cold.

But Abishag had retained two small treasures, kept hidden even through the rough treatment of the men who had deposited her into the care of the key-keeper. Around her neck still hung the seal of Solomon. And curled up in her fist, were the golden earrings that bore his insignia. Noticing the glow that was entering the window, she extended her arm into its light and opened her hand, seeing the glint of moonlight on gold. She stared at them for a long moment, studying the fine and tiny artwork, her mind going back to the moment when he had given them to her, and her lips spread into a misty smile. Realizing she was alone and no one would see her, she hung them from her lobes for only the second time since she had received them, letting her fingers stroke down to feel their soft, cool weight. A queen incarcerated. A princess in prison. She chuckled to herself at the irony of it.

The men said she was wanted for questioning, but no interrogators arrived. She had been asked nothing at all, neither was she told anything. Neither accused, nor questioned, she was left to ponder curiously the purpose for which she was in this place, how long she would remain, and what he, whoever he was who ordered her to be put here, expected to accomplish by it.

She looked over toward the door next to which the key-keeper had left a jug of water and a partial loaf of old barley bread as her only provisions for the night. She shivered again. A blanket, at least, would have been humane, and she had waited for several hours expecting someone, anyone, to return with either some word or provision for her. But at this late hour, she was now resigned that whatever she now possessed would have to suffice for the night. She rolled over to lie on her side on the cold stone floor, leaning her back against the wall and staying curled up as much as possible. The stone floor felt cold against her bare arm which supported her head, while her hair spilled onto the dirty floor. It would be difficult to sleep here. She was cold and lonely, but not downhearted—curious and confused, but not despondent. She would try, at least, to sleep.

The night proved to be a long, difficult affair. Yet no matter how persistently the cool swamp air filtered through her thin, damp garment, she coughed, not at all.

When dawn finally broke, it broke slowly, gradually filling the dank cell with secondary light. The lock turned. Abishag had been sitting up for several hours already, finding leaning against the wall more conducive to rest than any attempt to sleep on the floor. The face of the fat, old key-keeper with his long, straggled gray hair peered through the gate.

"They never sleep much that first night," he said gruffly.

She smiled at him shyly.

"I hope I was not too much of a burden."

His head snapped up from looking down at the key he was fiddling with and snorted a laugh.

"Still have a bit of humor in you, eh? Well, that doesn't last long either here," he replied, at the same time noticing that there was nothing in her eyes but sincerity.

She gracefully stood up from where she was seated at the wall, causing his eyes to widen at the ravishing beauty he had not had much chance to observe in the activity of the previous day.

"I brought you food," he said, with inadvertent kindness.

"I still have plenty remaining from your kindness yesterday, my lord, but there are a couple of other things I am lacking."

"Ahh, yes. The demands begin right away of course. Prisoners here seem to think I am their personal butler. I only honor one request a day—*if* I have the time—and I am already providing you with this food. That should suffice for today."

She studied him curiously.

"Only one request?"

He stared at her, taken aback at her gracious gentleness, artfully joined to incomparable beauty.

"Yes . . ." he mused, staring at his unusual prisoner.

Abishag put two fingers over her lips and considered, looking down in thought. Abishag had meant to ask for a blanket, but as the night wore on, sleeping little, she had become consumed with concern for Dinah, wondering how she fared with her father without her support. She looked up at the key-keeper.

"If it is true that only one request can be honored, please forgive my rudeness in asking that instead of this food you have generously provided, you provide me with something to write on, and an inkhorn."

He scowled.

"An inkhorn?"

"I wish to write letters today, for I do not know when I will next see my friends."

He stared at her, stroking his straggly beard.

"You are a strange one," he answered, continuing to study her curiously.

He turned and taking the plate of food with him, closed the gate and shuffled away. Abishag quickly stepped forward and placed her hands on the bars, looking after him.

"I can pay you for the paper, my lord."

He paused without turning, then shaking his head, continued

on.

****

“Jemimah!” Dinah whispered.

Jemimah’s lids fluttered and opened.

“I am sure your father will need you today; you can yet be home by daylight.”

“Yes,” Jemimah croaked, stretching. “And Abishag!—you must be about finding Abishag!” she added, her worry from the previous night quickly returning.

Dinah had not yet detected any light through the shuttered window, but the sounds of travelers on the street outside informed her that dawn was near.

Jemimah could scarcely remember a time when she had felt so torn between two competing sets of obligations. They had not found Abishag. What few elders the maidens could find on that Sabbath day seemed to have no knowledge of the arrest of Abishag, and both Hamon and his senior assistants were apparently out of town. No one who answered at any of his gates had any information.

Jemimah was not yet prepared to give up the search. Pleading the darkness on the road to Jezreel, she begged Dinah to let her stay the night in the city. Against her better judgment, Dinah agreed, and after another couple of hours of fruitless searching, the maidens turned in for the night at the house of Dinah’s father, who was away on business purchasing supplies for the inn. Dinah did not expect her father to return until the following afternoon, at which time she knew he would expect her to help him unload and cache his supplies and prep the inn for its nightly business.

As dawn approached, the two maidens quickly prepared themselves to leave the house and stepped out onto the cobbled street where they were greeted by the cool, dark morning. Laborers and merchants preparing for a day of work in the harvest fields were already on the shadowy streets, moving with their animals like strange dark shapes en route to their destinations.

"There is one place we did not try," Dinah mused, as they made their way toward the southern gate to the Jezreel road. "I will look there once I have delivered you back home."

Jemimah perked.

"Where?"

"They said Abishag was wanted for questioning, but obviously no questioning took place yesterday, at least not in any of the normal places. It may be that they put her in the old tower for the night."

"In prison?!" Jemimah asked, aghast.

"I know, I know, it's unthinkable. But all the other possibilities led us nowhere. When they took her, it did seem as though they considered her a criminal."

"Oh my soul," Jemimah replied. "Poor Abishag!"

After a few moments of walking in silence, she added.

"It *is* on the way . . ."

Dinah glanced over at her companion and sighed, seeing the urgency in her eyes. She pursed her lips.

"We will need to be quick about it."

"Oh yes, very," Jemimah quickly agreed.

Upon reaching the edge of town, the maidens turned to the east where the silo of the old grain tower could be seen poking up like the mast of a sinking ship, on the edge of the marshy low lands, beyond which the eastern sky blushed red. They hurried toward it. After applying at the key-keeper's lodge and learning that a prisoner fitting Abishag's description was in fact detained in tower, the maidens urged and cajoled from him permission to see their friend and obtained vague directions to the cell in which they might find her.

Creeping and feeling their way tentatively through the damp

gloomy passageway, the maidens approached the cell. The sight that greeted them upon arriving caused them to gasp in unison. As surprised as they were at the sight of Abishag, calmly occupied with writing as she squatted against the stone wall of the tiny cell, more surprising, and unsettling, was the obvious neglect of her basic needs. Her face and hands were dirty from sleeping on the stone floor, and there was a deep black bruise around her right eye. Her unveiled head was covered with a mass of matted stringy hair, owing to a week of sweat in the fire room. She was unbecomingly attired in only her rough sleeveless slipover, and scrunched in a dismal dirty little room that appeared to have no furnishings, little light, and lacking even the most primitive comforts. She appeared to have been reduced to an object of pointless abuse.

"Abishag!" Jemimah gasped, putting her hand over her mouth.

Abishag looked up and her eyes widened and she smiled.

"Jemimah! . . . and Dinah! Oh, thank the Lord I have been so worried about you! How have you been? Have you moved in and settled? Have you spoken to your father? I feel so badly for having abandoned you! I did not know when I would be able to speak to you again."

"Oh, Abishag," Jemimah croaked tearing up. "How could they do this to you?"

"They have no right," Dinah seethed.

"What, this? Oh, they just want me for questioning. I am sure I will be out soon, but Dinah, you don't know how I suffered for you last night. Did you speak with your father? Did it go well? How did he receive it?"

"Abishag . . . I did not see him, I went to your mother's house, and then we spent the whole day looking for you. He was gone when I—we arrived home."

Abishag looked over at Jemimah.

"We? Jemimah, are you staying in the city? What about your father? Your work?"

"I stayed with Dinah last night. We came to see you yesterday . . . Aijeleth and I. But when Dinah told us what happened, she went back home. Abishag, my sister doesn't believe us—neither Benaiah nor me."

"Benaiah—is he well?"

"I have not seen him for several days, he must be hiding somewhere."

"Oh, Lord help him," Abishag said worriedly.

"Abishag, my father did not believe him, and now Aijeleth—she does not understand," she said as her voice cracked.

Abishag looked at her compassionately.

"Oh, Jemimah. Do not despair. You must realize how strange it must sound to them. I am sure I would struggle to believe it too, in their position."

"Abishag!" Dinah said, "We are going to get you out of here! This is appalling."

"We? Dinah, I don't understand. Jemimah, you have not left home permanently have you?"

"I had to find you Abishag—I just had to," Jemimah pleaded. "When Dinah told me what happened, Aijeleth tried to make me go back with her, but how could I? How could I not help look for you?"

"Oh, Jemimah, you truly are blessed with a tender heart. But you worry needlessly over me. I am in no danger. And truly, what could you do for me anyway? They will ask me their questions, and I will be out. But what of you? Your father—does he even know where you are?"

"No . . . he doesn't, and I . . . I wonder if I should even go back home at all . . . now."

"Not go back?! Oh, Jemimah, no, no, that is not the way at all. You certainly must return home, your father is depending on you. He has probably worried over you all night long. Just because your family does not believe you is no reason to abandon them. You must not do that. Go home, Jemimah. They will learn the truth in time, but you must not sin by disobeying your father."

"Abishag . . . I thought you needed help, I felt—feel so compelled to support you!"

"No—Jemimah, your responsibility is to your father, not to me. I insist that you return home at once, apologize for being away, and promise me you will not do any such thing again. It will certainly make neither your father nor Aijeleth favorable to believe you if you are acting this way. Dinah—"

"Yes?"

"You said you were up to my mother's house. My brother, Huram, is gone. Is anyone distributing the medicine?"

Dinah blinked.

"Well, I suppose, I have no idea . . ."

"You must return there and see to it, right away. I will rewrite the prescription. We can't leave people without the medicine, they are suffering."

"Abishag! YOU are suffering! We have to get you out of here!"

"And your father—you must speak to him of course. Is he in the city?"

"I expect him back this afternoon, but Abishag . . ."

"Back? Where did he go?"

"Every week he goes to Jezreel for supplies, he will return with a wagon that I normally help him unload, I will not see him until then. But Abishag, who? Who is responsible for putting you in here?? When are they going to ask you these questions? They took your veil! You have nothing to wash with—not even a mat or chair. No lamp. And where is your tunic? You must have nearly frozen in here last night. This is deplorable in every way!"

Abishag appeared thoughtful, then she looked up at Dinah, noticing one of her own veils draped around Dinah's neck.

"Dinah, I recall you told me that the Sabbath would be the

day you took the veil again, why are you not wearing it?"

Dinah looked down.

"This is *your* veil, Abishag."

Abishag stood silently with an expression of disappointment that Dinah noticed.

"I truly do not need a veil in here," Abishag commented. "You ought to be wearing it."

"Me? Abishag, it's yours—I brought it here for *you*. You need it for warmth if for nothing else—you will freeze in here! Here, take it!" She held it out, through the bars.

Abishag did not reach for it, but stepped back out of reach.

"And you need it for holiness, Dinah. Which is more important, my warmth or your holiness? Put it on, please, as we agreed. You may bring me another, if you have occasion to visit me again."

Dinah was still holding it out.

"Take it, Abishag. Please!"

Abishag shook her head.

"You told me you would take the veil again, Dinah. You wish me to wear a veil, in here? No, I will not take a veil in here, until you are wearing one . . . out there."

Dinah blinked at her.

"Abishag . . ." she began in frustration.

Abishag did not move.

Finally Dinah retracted her hand and, for the first time in six years, began to don the virgin's veil. Jemimah was watching the exchange in wonder.

"I don't know how you do this to me," Dinah muttered, sniffing, and wiping her eyes. Then she looked up at Abishag.

"There. How do I look?"

"You look much better Dinah—like a righteous virgin. And

from this day on, that is what you are. You will wear this from now on, until you are married? As you promised me?"

"Yes," Dinah replied, shaking her head in resigned amazement.

"You are a true friend to me, Dinah, more than I could ever be worthy of. And if you have made a promise you intend to keep, if you wish, you may bring me another veil—after you have helped your father unload the wagon."

"What?!"

"You told me he is expecting you. You have always helped him in the past, and you did not have the chance to speak with him about moving out. You cannot abandon him in such an abrupt way. The transition must happen sensibly, with respect to his needs, or he will always resent your decision."

Abishag glanced toward the high window, noticing the glow of the morning light.

"You need to hurry along now, Jemimah," she nudged.

Jemimah, nodded, choking up.

"Don't worry about me, Jemmy. I am truly fine and comfortable here. We will speak again after I am out. I so want to see Aijeleth. Please send her my love."

"Yes . . ."

"And give my deepest respects to your father and mother, and Benaiah, if you should see him. I worry about him so."

Jemimah reached her hand through the bars, and took Abishag's who squeezed it and gave her a smile.

"Shalom, now."

Jemimah said her goodbyes and quickly left in tears, leaving Abishag and Dinah alone. The two friends looked at each other for a silent moment.

"Abishag, you shame me with idleness in the face of your suffering. Is there truly *nothing* I can do for you?"

"Dinah—my dearest friend. You have already done so much more for me than I deserve, and there are those who are *truly* suffering that must be helped. What you do for them, you do for me. But, if you must, I could perhaps do with a little something, perhaps an apple from the market, if it is not too much trouble, or . . ."

"You have no food?!"

"I do—they supply me well here, it's just that I traded my morning meal for writing implements. I was preparing letters—one for you, for Jemimah, and for my mother, but now that I have spoken to you, you can convey my messages in person. Assure everyone that I am well, adequately supplied. No use in people worrying needlessly about me. I will write the prescription—you may take it when you return with the apple—I will pay you for it—and then, perhaps later, after you have gone to my mother's house, you might remember my book of Psalms. My mother knows where it is—please be careful with it. Also a blanket, perhaps a change of clothes, if it is not too much of a burden. But if it is all too much to carry, just bring the Psalms."

Dinah's pity for Abishag was merging into a deep seething rage.

"I am going to find out who is responsible for this Abishag. I am going to get you out of here," she said, her cheeks tingeing red.

"Dinah, the Lord is responsible for my being here. His will brought me in, and it will bring me out. All I need from you, truly, is the few things I mentioned. Please promise me that you will speak with your father about leaving, as soon as you can do it honorably."

"I will, Abishag. I will do anything you ask of me. Anything."

Abishag blushed, and smiled humbly.

"You are too kind to me."

"No, Abishag, I am not worthy of you."

The friends said their goodbyes, and Abishag sat down to

continue her letters. Dinah walked away from the tower to begin her assigned errands in a quiet seething rage. She resolved to not rest until she had secured the release of her noble friend, at any cost.

****

Barkos and Jared had been toiling hard for several days to bring in the harvest from Abishag's vineyard with the help of a few beggars whom Abishag had instructed them to hire. It was a small vineyard, but it produced an exceptional harvest, and it was all the two lame men and their helpers could do to keep the grapes from growing soft and falling to the ground before they could get to them. They were resting in the shade near midday after a morning of hard work, when Hemanah, the brother of Abishag, arrived wearing an ominous expression. He looked at them oddly, surprised to see them there.

"Is Abishag here?" he asked, frowning at the fruit-laden baskets resting near the men.

Barkos glanced at Jared, realizing that the brother did not know about the current arrangement.

"No, Hemanah, she has not been here in some days. You may not be aware, but your sister left us to tend to this harvest."

"She hired you?" he asked, looking confused.

Barkos and Jared looked at each other. How to explain?

"Hemanah, I guess you are not aware of this, but Abishag—she gave us this harvest—after mine was destroyed by the foxes and the lack of tending," Barkos said.

Hemanah scowled.

"You are aware that my vineyard was destroyed in that debacle with the foxes, aren't you?" Barkos asked.

"Well, I guess I heard," Hemanah said, "but what is this that Abishag is doing? How can she give you this?"

"Well, I suppose maybe she could best explain it to you, but she has come into some . . . resources. By the way, what are you doing here, Hemanah? Don't you have a harvest you ought to be bringing in?" asked Barkos.

"I did have, but Hamon . . ." he broke off.

"Oh, so he got you too, did he? All that time he was playing you and me against each other with that fox trap nonsense. I thought I came out on the short end, but that's Hamon for you. He managed to destroy us both. How did he get your field?" asked Barkos.

Hemanah was irritated by Barkos' forthright manner.

"That's none of your concern, Barkos. I lost my fields . . . temporarily. I'll get them back."

"Oh you will? Oh sure, when will that be, next year?"

"I hope so," Hemanah said.

Barkos had been kidding, but his eyes narrowed realizing Hemanah actually had lost his current harvest.

"He took your harvest too?" Jared asked.

"Most of it, I'm afraid. I just came up here to assess what is left of the estate. That's why I need to talk to Abishag, right away."

The real meaning of Hemanah's visit suddenly dawned upon Barkos and Jared.

"You're thinking about *this* vineyard!" Barkos suddenly exclaimed.

Hemanah pursed his lips.

"Now look. Things are not as simple as they used to be. I don't know what Abishag is doing, or how she thinks she can just give all of this away, but there's been a serious shift in our family holdings. We are going to have to talk about this . . . all of this."

Barkos was studying him, stroking his beard.

"Isn't that a surprise," Barkos finally commented, not

sounding surprised at all.

"What do you mean?"

"Hemanah, look at the situation. Why now? Why do you think Hamon is doing this to you right now? He's using you—just like he did me with the foxes. It's his way. He plays people like game pieces. He probably even plays his own brother against his nephew. He gets people all fighting with each other, and then he comes in and picks up the scraps. Hemanah, Hamon doesn't want your field, he wants *this* one. Either that or he doesn't want Abishag to have it for some reason. So he's making you take it from her—he's playing you against your own sister, don't you see?"

"If he is or not, I don't know, but one thing I do know, our family no longer has enough for the winter. I've got two brothers and a mother, with Abishag and her mother, that's six people, and all we have to sustain us is this little vineyard."

"You may have more than that, Hemanah," Jared said.

"What are you talking about?"

"Like we said, Abishag has come into resources. You need to speak with her."

"That's what I have been saying, where is she?!"

"Hemanah," Jared said, "I will tell you where she is, but first, tell me honestly, are you finished with Hamon? Have you had enough?"

"He's had enough of me, anyway. But where is my sister?"

"She's been taken," Barkos said.

"What? Taken? Where?"

"We got the news yesterday. She was arrested in the city. They say they want her for questioning, but really, they are after Jedidiah. They won't get anything from her. They can't hurt her," Jared said.

Hemanah was shaking his head in confusion.

"What is going on here? Everyone knows that that man was

killed. And my sister has money all of a sudden? And now she is arrested? I think you two have been out in the sun too long."

"If you believe he was killed, you are listening to the wrong people again, Hemanah. That's what Hamon wants you to believe, but think!—if Jedidiah were really dead, then why would Hamon want Abishag for questioning? On the other hand, if he were alive wouldn't it make sense that Hamon would want to find him? And what would be the best way to find him? By putting pressure on you and your sister at the same time—getting you to repossess what is hers. Don't you see? He is trying to play you against her, but it doesn't have to work—not this time."

Hemanah was silent, thinking hard. He did not relish the thought of taking his own sister's vineyard, but under the circumstances, he did not have much choice, unless there really was something to all of this. But then, what of the other issue: Abishag arrested? How strange. If she really was in trouble with the law, could he be certain she would be coming back at all? He suddenly had absolutely no idea how to proceed.

"I'm going to have to look into all of this—consult with my brothers," he said, finally. "In the meantime, I trust you will not let any of this harvest be wasted. It may be all I have left."

"Don't worry about the harvest Hemanah. If it's yours, it will all be loaded for sale in a couple of weeks. Until then, we are treating it as our own, so we're not going to neglect it," Jared explained.

"Yes," Hemanah said thoughtfully, looking at the baskets. "I can see that."

After he left, Barkos and Jared exchanged a knowing look.

"Even if he does take the vineyard back, Abishag has resources," Jared said.

Barkos nodded.

Hemanah, however, departed in search of a place to think. So much that was taking place around him made no sense. Should he go speak to his sister as they had advised? He was suddenly hesitant to do so. Why was he always finding out important information concerning himself after it was too late. It was frustrating. Why was Hamon detaining Abishag—even imprisoning her? What could his miserable little sister have of interest to Hamon? But if she had fallen into his disfavor, Hemanah would have to be careful. He could not afford to incur any more of Hamon's wrath. If it was now directed at his sister, he would have to distance himself from her.

****

Hamon had arrived back in town, but found it easier to return to town than to discern the exact course he ought to take once there—now that Abishag had been captured. Originally, he designed to question her in hopes of finding the whereabouts of Jedidiah, but a whole week had since passed. At present, with the story of the escaped prisoner's death being spread for that full term, it was difficult to imagine a cause for Abishag's detainment that could be convincingly defended. But such a cause he very much needed to find—at least one that would allow him to keep her detained long enough to make it probable she would contract the swamp fever. Any way he shuffled his case, it seemed weak. If he released her now, when would he have such an opportunity again? But he could not inform the elders of her arrest without any clear rationale to give them. In the end, he decided that perhaps knowledge of her capture could be kept to a minimum—at least long enough to learn from her where her "brother" ran off to.

****

Abishag stared at the ceiling, fingering her stylus, her paper curled open on her lap. She had passed the days writing letters, praying, and journaling, recording her memories of Jedidiah, and all he had done for her. She found his phrases returning to her mind, and she quickly committed them to writing, the power and the wisdom of them accompanying each memory. Such thoughts nearly made the cell around her disappear, as her soul was caught up to soar on the wings of revelation and love.

She heard a noise and peered up from her writing through the bars into the dark hallway beyond. It appeared empty. Had she heard something? She looked back down. A moment later a form emerged out of the darkness approaching slowly forward toward the bars. Abishag strained to see and arose.

"Who is there?"

Tentatively, the form in the hallway stepped nearer yet, allowing the light from the high window in Abishag's cell to fall across its face. Puzzled, Abishag found herself under the inquisitive stare of a well-dressed and dignified looking elderly woman, who regarded her with pensive silence.

"You are Abishag," the woman said, in a clear but melodic voice that reverberated in the still chamber.

"Yes, my lady. May I be of service?"

The woman continued to study her up and down in silence, allowing Abishag's question to hang unanswered. The woman's mouth pursed.

"You are dirty."

Abishag looked down at herself.

"I am sorry if my appearance offends, my lady."

"You do not recognize me."

"I . . . it is dark, my lady," Abishag explained.

"I am Hildah, wife of Simeon, of the chief elders."

Abishag suddenly recognized her as the same woman who had been following her on the day she had been arrested.

"Forgive me, my lady," she replied, "May I serve you in some way?"

The woman's chest heaved slightly, after which emitted from her mouth the tell-tale cough, which she tried to restrain and covered her mouth with her hand. Abishag's eyes widened in recognition.

"You have the swamp fever."

The woman shot a sideways glance at her, keeping her head turned while clearing her throat for some moments, and then turned back.

"I have heard of you," the woman said, in a carefully recovered voice. "And not always well spoken of."

"I am deserving of no compliments."

"But . . ." the woman continued, as if not finished, "I have cause to wonder. Recently . . . I have had cause . . . to wonder."

Abishag remained silent this time.

"At times it seems that the men of this village believe that truth is theirs to determine, by majority vote," Hildah mused.

Abishag nodded slowly, putting her finger to her lip, pondering.

"Did you know the woman, Orpha?" the woman asked abruptly.

"Orpha? Yes, a dear and loved woman of our village, who recently met with a tragic end."

The woman's eyes narrowed.

"So they say . . . a tragic . . . end, but . . ."

Abishag waited.

". . . I knew her also . . . better than most. Orpha—she lived on our estate, in a small house. For many years she lived there. She kept the garden for me . . ."

Abishag took a slow step forward.

"And she spoke to me . . ." she continued, holding Abishag under poignant and solemn stare.

". . . of the cure."

"Of the cure," Abishag repeated softly.

The woman coughed again, looked down at her side, where a fine handbag dangled from her left hand.

"And now, I am required . . . to face a question I did not expect to face. Orpha, it seemed, was recovering, before she met her . . . tragic . . . end."

Abishag regarded her visitor thoughtfully.

She is here in desperation!

The woman's eyes wandered upward, searching her memory.

"I observed Orpha for three years, as she faithfully pursued Jockshan's treatments, and yet, her condition worsened. But, then, suddenly, in a few short weeks, all of her symptoms vanished. I noticed. I wondered . . . why."

Hildah appeared lost in thought for a moment. Then she looked directly at Abishag.

"I inquired of Orpha, and she spoke to me. The day before her death, in fact. She spoke to me . . . of the man, and of the medicine, and . . . of you."

"My lady," Abishag said softly, "There *is* a true cure."

"I . . . think . . . perhaps . . . so. But the elders . . . my husband . . . they claim that such is to be found only in Jockshan's steam room. My husband has provided me with the means for six months treatments. I am to apply there at once . . . so he has instructed me." She glanced down at her bag, and then slowly lowered it to the ground in front of her.

Abishag followed her glance down and back, then her eyes widened.

"Oh, my lady, you are most kind, but you do not understand, you cannot buy the treatment with this . . ."

"I can bring more," the woman said quickly.

"No, my lady, what I mean to tell you is, the medicine . . . is free."

The woman blinked at her.

"Free?"

"It is a gift of God to the suffering, and no price can rightly be charged for a gift of God. However, the medicine does not cure you, it only relieves you. To be cured, there is a therapy that must be engaged."

"Therapy? What kind of therapy?"

"Hot air, my lady. You must breath hot, dry air, such as is in the baker's oven room, consistently for several weeks. That is where the healing is accomplished."

The woman frowned at her, leaning back and turning her head to the side.

"The baker's oven room?"

"Yes."

She glanced down in thought.

"Is it dirty?"

"Well . . . I suppose, it is dark and sooty, and . . ." she broke off noticing the woman's dour expression.

Hildah continued to scowl, while her eyes moved back and forth. She looked up.

"You are bold, maiden. You presume to suggest that a lady such as I would subject myself to a smoky dark grotto for weeks? Jockshan's healing room is clean and comfortable, you are aware."

"If you wish to die comfortably, my lady, then you may freely attend Jockshan's steam room, but if you wish to live, you must go through the fire. All who would be cured must, there is no other way."

The woman pursed her lips.

"And this is the counsel of a dirty, despised peasant girl in a dark prison?"

"I am all of that and more, my lady, but the healing power of the cure is not hindered by my many faults."

Hildah studied her in silence.

"Why should I believe you?"

"Surely unbelief did not draw you here, my lady," Abishag replied softly.

The lady looked puzzled, studying the curiously confident yet gentle peasant girl she faced through prison bars.

"Dear maiden—I perceive you are clever, but I am afraid a girl like you would have no way to understand the delicacies of someone in my position. If I were to do as you suggest, and my husband discovered—if it was told I had abandoned Jockshan's treatments, and was partaking of the treatment of the pitiable, fatherless girl and her runaway lover . . ." she shook her head. "It could be uncomfortable, in many ways."

"I understand," Abishag replied softly. "Your dilemma is clear: You must choose to be uncomfortable, and alive, or comfortable, and dead."

The woman scowled. Then smirked.

"Comfortable and dead! You have a teasing tongue maiden. Do you consider me a toy for your entertainment? Your answer is quick and clever, but falls short of sense. Do not trifle with me. Why can you not just give me a stronger dose? I can pay you handsomely."

"You are most kind, my lady, but I can give you no stronger dose than the truth. A stronger dose of medicine that cures you not, still leaves you sick. I know of what I speak. I myself have been through the fire, and am cured. So much so that in this cold room where I sleep, though I lack pillow or blanket, I am in no danger."

Hildah looked past Abishag into the cell, searched the floor.

"You have no blanket?"

Abishag shook her head, "I meant no complaint," she added quickly.

"And no food or water, no mat, no lamp . . ."

"I am in want of nothing, my lady."

"And you will take no money."

"My every need is supplied, my lady."

The woman stared at her amazedly.

"This is not right. Ignorant peasant girl or not, you are not an animal. My husband . . . would not suffer this."

The direction of the woman's mind was apparent on her face.

"My lady, I did not intend to invoke your pity. I make no complaint. But I would inform you that the medicine is available at my farm. Your condition is serious. If you will make your way there, this afternoon, and speak to the maiden, Dinah, she will provide what you need. But you must not delay going through the fire. Your condition will worsen rapidly."

Hildah looked back sharply from her thoughts.

"Of that, I am not yet certain, Abishag, but of this I am. If I partake of your medicine, I will *not* be in your debt. You must be paid in some way. My husband will hear of this," she gestured up at the prison around them.

"That is truly not necessary, my lady."

"Do you not see your own condition?"

"I could ask the same of you, my lady," Abishag replied softly.

The woman looked sharply back at her, then let out a stilted laugh of incredulity, which turned into a cough. Covering her mouth, she turned her head to the side and continued to strive with the spasm for some moments, until she overcame it. Then she looked back at Abishag, who had observed the whole of it in silence.

"For *your* condition, my lady, is clear . . . to me."

The woman stared at her until her eyes moistened. Abruptly, she turned and began walking away, down the dark passageway.

"May the Lord bless you," Abishag called after her, the echo of her voice reverberating up into the cool, dark tower.

Chapter 11

For the rest of the day, Abishag waited in vain for the expected questioning. Shortly after Hildah left, Dinah returned to Abishag's cell with food and supplies, but she had not yet been to the farm. Abishag gave Dinah the prescription as planned. After helping her father unload the wagon, Dinah was barely able to squeeze in a quick trip to the farm and returned with the items Abishag had requested. Though she brought a veil for Abishag—a warm one—the key keeper strictly and inexplicably disallowed it. The maidens puzzled over this, and Dinah seethed. But Abishag artfully and persistently moved the conversation away from herself and onto Dinah and her present challenges.

How could Dinah move out now? She strongly objected to moving up to the farm as long as Abishag was in prison, and insisted on spending her nights in town to be nearby. After some deliberation, Abishag agreed it would be best if Dinah continued to help her father in the inn until a replacement could be found. So as Abishag continued in prison, writing letters and waiting for the questioning that never seemed to come, Dinah spent her days on the farm and her nights at the inn, serving medicine to the sick by day and alcohol to coarse men by night.

Abelah visited the tower and informed Abishag that she had passed the word to everyone that might be able to help. Shammai, the livestock farmer from around the north hill, promised to take up the matter with some of the elders he was acquainted with, but admitted that his rank among them did not make him a likely candidate for favors.

Dinah returned to the cell often. Every spare moment she could glean, Dinah remained at the door of Abishag's cell ready to tend to any need she might learn of, only to be continually guided by her mentor back to the farm for the distribution of medicine. Day after day, her frustration built, a frustration heightened by the fact that her business allowed so little time to pursue the one problem that vexed her most: Abishag's release.

One morning, as she was distributing medicine to applicants from the guest hut on Abishag's farm, Dinah, now regularly wearing the veil in public, was recognized, and was not in the mood to answer probing questions.

"Hey—aren't you the girl who serves in Jalaam's drinking room?" the man asked. "Why the veil?"

"What's it to you?"

"Nothing to me, just seems like kind of strange sideline for you."

"Ah. Right. Well, I serve the complete package now—medicine by day and poison by night. And don't think you're getting any of this concoction without promising to obey the rules. I want to see that flask again tomorrow to make sure you didn't take too much. I'll half-glass you and cut you off early tonight if you cheat."

She ladled a few spoonfuls of medicine into the flask.

"That's all?"

"I'm not giving you more than twenty-four hours worth because you can't handle it. You can drink yourself silly tonight, but this medicine is not cheap wine, it is dangerous—too much of it will kill you. Come back tomorrow and I'll give you more."

"Can't I pay you for a weeks worth?"

"No you can't. We don't charge for this, it's free. And no gratuities either—house rules. The price of service is to follow instructions.

"What about tonight?"

"You can tip me all you want there, but what happens there makes no difference here. Count on it!"

The man started to protest, but she shoved the flask in his chest and looked over his shoulder calling for the next person in line. The man hung his head and went out sheepishly. The next person that stood before Dinah surprised her. She hesitated, finding herself facing a dignified looking woman who, though appearing earnest, also appeared uncertain.

"You have not been here before," Dinah noted.

"No. And I am not certain I will return."

She coughed. Dinah peered at her.

"That's because you have not tried it yet. But I must inform you that this medicine does nothing for the disease itself. For that you must breathe . . ."

"Hot air—yes, Abishag explained the process."

"You spoke to her? You saw her?"

"I did indeed. And though I do not understand the reason for her current . . . habitation, I find the conditions there less than adequate."

"You don't have to tell *me* that," Dinah replied in sudden anger. "Abishag is absolutely innocent, and they are abusing her like some convicted criminal!"

"They? Perhaps you could tell me who 'they' are. I would like to know who is responsible for her state."

"I don't know who is responsible, but I know who took her in. I was there. It was Baal Hamon's men."

The woman nodded knowingly.

Dinah gave her a small supply, and after explaining again how to properly dose, encouraged her to attend the fire room without delay.

"There will be at least one delay, dear maiden," Hildah explained. "For you have given me intelligence that I must pass on to my husband, before anything else."

*****

Several days later, after her morning prayers, Abishag became aware of the approach of yet another visitor. A well-dressed, middle-aged man suddenly stood before her cell and introduced himself as Dakenath, the town clerk. Abishag stood respectfully, asking how she might serve him.

"There is no service to be offered to me, maiden," the man replied, "Only to identify yourself. I have been sent here to deliver a message to Abishag, daughter of the widow Abelah, of the estate on the north hill."

Abishag looked down to see an official looking scroll in the man's hand.

"Yes, it is I, my lord."

"This message is delivered to you on behalf of the changers of money. You are to be informed that gold has been allocated to you from the account of Simeon of the chief elders."

Abishag hesitated.

"Gold, my lord?"

He unrolled the document he was holding, and glanced down, and back up at her.

"Would you like me to read to you the orders of this document, maiden?"

"I . . . will read it myself, if you please, my lord."

He studied her curiously, then handed her the document.

She unrolled it, and he saw her eyes widen as they traveled right to left over the text. She gasped and put her hand over her mouth.

"Oh, my lord. There has been a terrible mistake. I cannot accept this. This gold is payment for something that I have in no wise sold."

"I was already advised that you may object in this way, maiden. I have not come to ask you if you will receive this gold, but to inform you that the account has already been opened with the money-changers in your name. The gold is there, whether you take possession of it or not."

"But, my lord! This is not right—I assure you I have not delivered any merchandise to answer for this gold! You must return this at once!"

"I am afraid that is impossible, maiden. This gold is neither mine to accept, nor to return, but yours. I have only come to inform you that it is there."

"But . . ."

Abruptly, the man turned and left the cell without further comment. Abishag looked back down at the document in wonder.

****

When a man's ways please the LORD, he maketh even his enemies to be at peace with him.

Proverbs 16:7

The night was especially cold. Abishag shivered violently in the dark cell in the hours past midnight. Dinah had returned that day and supplied her generously as always. Late in the evening, the key-keeper had allowed her to bathe and change in the adjacent room, in which there was a basin. She bathed, then washed her tunic also. Then, without explanation, he removed all her supplies before shutting her in for the night, leaving her not only with wet clothing and no blanket, but facing the cold wind, damp from bathing and her long, black hair hanging wet.

When she had politely asked him the reason for this, he shunned to meet her eyes, declared that he had received "orders," and then shuffled quickly away, not looking back. Hours later, she huddled in a corner, sleep being impossible. Suddenly, she started at the sight of a quick and pensive movement.

"Abishag!" a voice whispered urgently.

She strained to identify its source.

"It's me, Benaiah!"

Benaiah stepped up to the bars, looking nervously back in the direction he had come.

"Benaiah! Is it you? Where have you been these past days?"

"I've been hiding away. I saw Jemimah yesterday—she told me you were here. Abishag, I'm getting you out of here!"

She saw an urgent glint in his eye and steely resolve on his face.

"Benaiah? No—you mustn't."

"I'm tired of this! All of this. I am tired of running, of hiding! We have the truth on our side, let's move with it!"

She saw him fumbling with something.

"Benaiah what are you doing?"

He looked up at her quickly and back down, and she saw the glint of metal.

"These are from my father's shop," he said.

"Benaiah no!"

He placed an iron wedge behind the bolt that held the door. Then he lifted a hammer.

"Benaiah! No! Stop!"

The hammer struck the wedge, echoing up into the chamber

like the gong of a bell. He looked up wildly, then with increased urgency, began hammering on the wedge filling the entire tower with the impact and hum of his blows. Abishag's protests were lost in the sound that filled the chamber. After a dozen or so blows, the bolt snapped free, and the gate swung open as the echo lingered and died away.

"Come—let's run, now!"

"No, Benaiah, listen to me!"

Suddenly there were noises down the hall.

"Abishag! Hurry!"

Abishag stepped back farther into the cell, while he continued to urge her to come. Instead, she moved until her back was pressed against the wall under the high window, then she sunk to the floor.

"Benaiah—this will not accomplish anything! I am innocent now, but if I do this, the law will pursue me with reason! I cannot go! I am not going!"

"Abishag!"

The sounds were getting louder, then a voice called out.

Benaiah's head snapped around toward the sound then back to Abishag. He panicked.

"Is there another way out?"

"No—I don't know. I don't think so!"

He looked around in fright, and then bolted down the hall away from the sound.

The flickering light of a torch illuminated the hallway, and the key-keeper appeared at the far end of it dressed in bedclothes. When he saw the barred door standing open, he gasped, and shuffled quickly forward. Abishag was sitting against the far wall, her knees tucked up to her chest.

She heard the man shuffling down the hall, moaning and muttering to himself in urgent panic. He appeared in front of the open cell with a look of terror. Then his eyes traveled down and spotted the woman on the ground at the back of the cell. His eyes widened.

"What! Ho! What? You are still here?"

"Yes, my lord. Do not be afraid, I would not leave this place without your permission."

"Without my permission?! Without my per . . ." he broke off and was shaking his head from side to side violently.

"No, my lord. I do not wish to escape. Such would be a great calamity for you."

He stared at her in wonder, then looked over at the wide-open cell door.

"How did this happen?"

She smiled timidly.

"I have some overly zealous friends. I am so sorry for the damage—I tried to stop them but . . ." she lifted her shoulders in a shrug.

He studied the calm, beautiful, maiden up and down.

"You could have escaped. You could have escaped! Why? What is wrong with you, maiden!? Freezing and suffering in here like this! An old gray-beard like me would never have been able to catch up with you in the night! Even now you could . . ." he broke off looking at the open door.

"I assure you I am not leaving, my lord."

He looked back down at her.

"But I am a bit . . . cold."

The man pursed his lips in anger, as his face turned deep red.

"I am not going to suffer this any longer. You stay right there!"

"Uhh . . . yes, my lord."

He turned and shuffled back down the hall muttering to himself. A few minutes later, he returned to find Abishag exactly where he left her in the back of a wide-open cell. He had brought with him all of Abishag's provisions, which had been removed, plus a mat, a pillow, and several more blankets. He was still muttering to himself.

"I don't care *what* Hamon says. I'm a key-keeper, not a torturer. He can let someone else do his dirty work from now on."

"I am most grateful to you, my lord."

"Yes. Well. I may have to come take these things away—in the daytime, you understand," he grumbled.

"It is not my place to disclose your doings, my lord," she replied, and gave him a kind smile.

He could not resist it. For the first time, Abishag saw the old key-keeper smile, a gruff old smile, with most of the teeth missing. He fought it off, and returned to feigned gruffness.

"But don't expect any more favors from me."

"Oh, certainly not my lord."

He swung the door of the cell shut.

It bounced off the broken latch and swung back open, causing him to lurch in surprise. Abishag laughed out loud and covered her mouth. He looked back at her suspiciously.

"Whether the door locks or not, I am not leaving, my lord. I would stay in this place on your orders alone, if there were not only no door, but no walls."

"Yes . . . I can see that. Very well then . . . you stay in there!"

"Right."

He carefully swung the door back to the shut position, and removed his hand. It stayed in place.

"I believe I will sleep now," Abishag said, and opened a blanket and curled up into it.

"Yes. Well. Good night then."

"Goodnight, my lord."

The man stared at her in amazement for a few seconds, and then shuffled back down the hallway, muttering to himself. Moments later, the wind through the window caused the barred cell door to move. The hinges creaked, and it swung completely open, leaving Abishag incarcerated in a wide-open cell.

A quarter-hour passed in silence. Benaiah reappeared in the open door of the cell, looking sheepish. Abishag heard him and looked around. He stared at her a moment.

"You are really not going to leave, are you?"

She shook her head.

"No. But your offer to rescue me is most kind. I am only thankful that you did not succeed. Do you believe it would be possible for you to repair this lock?"

He looked over at the gate latch.

"I suppose I *could* do it—I don't have the tools right now."

He glanced back at her.

"As if you *need* a cell with a lock. Why Abishag? You could be free. We could be all the way to Jezreel by morning . . . and beyond."

"Benaiah, I *am* free. My king has charged me to stay in this village, and that is where I am. If I run with you, I would have to keep running, right out of the safety of his will. It is not the lock that holds me in here, but his commandment. In that, I am already free—free from all wrongdoing, free from any breach of conscience, safely in the will of my king. But if I were to escape unlawfully, I *would* be in prison—forever locked in a prison of my own making from which I could never escape."

"And I thought I was helping you."

She gave him a kind smile.

"How have you been surviving these past days, Benaiah?"

"I have been camping in the hills, across the valley. But I am tired of it Abishag. It isn't right; I should be home where I belong, living in my own house, farming my own land. Why should I have to live on the run like a criminal?"

"And you will have all of those things, Benaiah, but I can understand your not wanting to hide. The Lord surely has a place for you to live."

"Yes . . ." Benaiah said while staring at the floor looking unconvinced. He looked up. "Until then, is there truly nothing I can do to help you, Abishag?"

Abishag looked at him thoughtfully.

"There *may* be. . . . "

"What is it, Abishag. Just tell me."

"In fact . . . there may be two things . . ." she added thoughtfully, and looked up at him. "You are in contact with Jemimah?"

"I see her at night only. The rest of them, Aijeleth, my father, they think I should report back to the militia. I only go to her window."

"Well then, here is one thing you can do." Abishag reached down and picked up some documents. "I have written letters that you may deliver. Will you?"

"Well, sure. I could get this one to Jemimah yet tonight."

"I would be most grateful."

"What is the other thing?" Benaiah asked.

Abishag looked down at the rolled document she was holding. Benaiah glanced at it curiously.

"Benaiah, do you know the man, Simeon, of the chief elders?"

"I do know of the man, but I don't think he knows me."

"Yes, well, you might think this strange, but I believe there is a place for you to live, on his estate."

Benaiah blinked.

"On his . . . what are you talking about?"

"Benaiah, go to his estate. Go in the daytime, when Simeon sits at the city gate. Do not go through Shunem, but go around, so you are not seen. Inquire at his home for his wife, a woman called Hildah. Tell her you have come to rent the gardeners' house that has recently come available."

"But I have no money."

Abishag extended her hand, in which she held a small rolled document.

"Present her with this. Tell her, it is payment. It should more than suffice."

Benaiah took the document and unrolled it. His eyes widened.

"Abishag! How did you get this?"

"Never mind that. I am quite sure that the woman will receive you. And . . . one other thing . . ."

Benaiah was looking at her mystified.

"Benaiah, you were never born to be a soldier, or a metalworker. You were born to be a farmer. You have a talent for making things grow. I would know. If you want to do something for me, do this: promise me that this woman will have the best kept garden in the entire valley. Can you do this for me?"

Benaiah gushed out a laugh.

"Of course!" he said, "Of course, I could!"

Chapter 12

Dinah brushed by a man ignoring his comment. She was getting used to wearing the veil while working, though the men who knew her were baffled.

Hamon appeared in the door of the inn and glided casually to his usual place, an entrance noted by everyone in the room, but by none with greater apprehension than Dinah. Upon the very sight of him, her pulse quickened, this time not with hopes of some flattering attention or a generous tip, but with deeply held and barely contained fury. She was certain that Hamon was responsible for the incarceration of Abishag, a fact that made her required service of him almost intolerable.

Hamon did a double take upon seeing Dinah approach in full veil, only after hearing her voice ascertaining that it was indeed she. She answered him curtly and shortly, spending barely enough time to know the sense of his order, and departed without courtesy, not looking back. Hamon, puzzled, leaned over to someone nearby and queried, gesturing in Dinah's direction.

Wherever Dinah traveled that night, her mind was on Hamon, though her eyes avoided him. She was barely succeeding by stilted treatment to restrain a boiling reservoir of rage—a rage that seemed to intensify as the evening progressed. Spending minimal time in Hamon's area, she trusted herself to make no comment to him at all, and allowed not so much as a single glance in his direction when passing by.

To Hamon, being ignored was far more intolerable than almost any affront, and in her frequent passings, he began to toss out baiting comments designed to provoke some reaction, each of which Dinah, with great effort, ignored. However, when it was time for her to refill his mug, interaction could not be avoided. Hamon peered up at the ashen girl who poured wine into his mug without meeting his eyes, this time noticing something about her attire that he had not previously.

"Say, Dinah, isn't that Abishag's veil?"

That got her attention, and her eyes met his sharply, and shot quickly back down, but she remained silent.

"I thought so. Since when did *you* start wearing a veil?"

"Why shouldn't I wear one?"

He smirked.

"Yes. Why indeed. We all know that veils are worn by both virgins and prostitutes. If you can't wear it for one reason, perhaps you can for the other."

Her cheeks tinged red, but she restrained herself, barely.

Hamon was puzzled. The Dinah he knew thrived on dark flattery. She would normally have wrung some clever banter out of such a comment—responded in kind with a quick evocative comeback, but she seemed strangely different tonight. Then he remembered that Abishag was seen with Dinah on the day she was captured.

"You have been spending some time with Abishag, I understand."

"My company is my business."

"Ahh. Yes. Everyone knows that Abishag always wears the veil, but it's not been your habit, Dinah. Is that where you got it from? From Abishag? Did she teach you that?"

"I might have learned a few things from her."

"That's good, Dinah, I hope you listen and learn well. A girl like you could learn a lot from a girl like Abishag."

She hesitated under the compliment.

"Thank you," she replied, and began to turn. She was almost out of range to hear the ill-advised comment he uttered a second later. Almost—but not quite.

"Takes a good harlot to train a good harlot."

The fateful words floated, drifted, and connected. Dinah froze.

In most occasions in life, the mind considers and then instructs the body how to act. But in other rare moments, mind and body are in such harmony, that thought and action are simultaneous. For Dinah, this became just such a moment. Her slight hesitation at that instant was not born of indecision, but could more aptly be compared to a viper measuring for a strike.

She quickly snatched the pitcher of wine from the tray, and before he could move, violently thrust its entire contents full into his face. Hamon sputtered, wiping his eyes, and after recovering from shock, leaped to his feet and began shouting curses in her face, none of which she heard by virtue of the fact that she had stepped toe to toe with him and was launching a verbal barrage of her own. It was not long before she was outpacing his invectives with her own volley of insults by a two to one margin, and at a higher volume.

Every conversation in the inn suddenly stopped as the occupants gaped at the sudden spectacle. Hamon was never more eloquent than when angry, but nonetheless was quickly becoming frustrated by the feisty girl's ability to connect with a second and third insult before he was able to respond to the first. He raised his hand in aggravation, but Dinah, who had had recent experience with such a maneuver, quickly stepped back out of his range while connecting with yet another sharp verbal gibe. While Hamon's verbal arrows tangled in his bow, Dinah was just starting to gain momentum.

"*You* would dare call *her* that? Oh—sure—let the rat accuse the lion of cowardice, you arrogant rat! Let the snake instruct the eagle how to fly, the likes of you insulting her is that ridiculous! A waste of good wine!—a bucket of manure would have been more appropriate—but it surely would have lamented the misfortune of contacting your face, you pompous, self-important scab! The trail of slime that follows you is so rancid that dung flies would shun to come near it! Prig! Insolent snob! That you would have the gall to say such a thing about the most righteous virgin this valley has ever seen, you are either the most ignorant or the most arrogant man who has ever lived—and I suspect you are the runaway winner of both awards! You are a cruel, conceited, self-centered, egotistical snake! A vain-glorious, swell-headed, broker of lies!"

She turned to the gaping room.

"Do you know what he has done? He has falsely arrested an innocent maiden—the most beautiful, most innocent maiden this land has ever seen and even now she rots in prison, without food, without water, without a blanket or pillow, and without any accusation made against her! I know it was you!—I was there!—It was *your* men that accosted her! The elders know nothing of it! There! See the fear on his face? He knows it is true! You think because you control the land you can buy everyone out with money, but you can't!—not everyone. And there are some people your filthy gold will never move. The Israelites of this valley were born to be free, and soon this whole house of straw that you have built is going to come crashing down on your head—and I for one will savor the day!"

"Don't look at me like that! You think your worn out lies still retain a believing audience in this town? Your duplicity is so transparent that even the blindest fool would have to shield his eyes from the glare. You are so pompous you don't even have *false* modesty! You are so swell-headed you'd have to deflate to fit through a city gate! You are so full of yourself that you could starve to death without feeling a single hunger pang. You are packed so tight with lies that the tiniest sliver of truth would snap trying to squeeze in! When you get out of bed the sun weeps for spoiling its morning, and the streets brace for the stench that will attend your goings! The very grass that has the misfortune of falling under your gaze wilts and dies! You think I should fear you? You think I should cower like one of your paid girls? Let me tell you something, but for hired affections not a girl in the kingdom would come near you. They would cover the eyes that had the misfortune of seeing your face, and clean out with soap the ears that heard your voice! They would loath to even sit in the chair that once held you. They would shun the very path you once walked for the stink of it! They would burn as unclean everything you touched! They would sow to salt the ground on which your shadow passed! The rotting carcass of a swine could not be less kosher! I would call you a despicable pig but the species does not deserve the insult!"

Dinah's volley of revilements continued to inflict one direct hit after another until her father forcibly ushered her out the back door, even as she hurled well-aimed parting shots over her shoulder upon the seething Hamon. The stunned spectators, not wanting to reveal anything that would incur the wrath of Hamon, nonetheless contained a fair number who had silently applauded every word of Dinah's diatribe, and believed its target guilty of every invective and more.

Hamon, with as little grace and art as could be expected of a man who had just endured such a barrage, suddenly lost his taste for the night life, and clumsily made his way to the door, actually tripping over his feet on the way out, to stilted snickers.

The conversation in the inn rose from stunned murmurings to exaggerated jabbering following Hamon's clumsy departure.

"Do you suppose it is true, that he really has imprisoned an innocent maiden? Can he have stooped that far?"

"Not just innocent—beautiful, stunning—staggering! And all those rumors about her disfigurement, you never heard such lies. I *saw* her."

"So did I!"

"But did you see Hamon's face?!"

"That had to be the best tell-off I have ever seen."

"And the most deserved."

"She shamed us—that little wine server did—made cowards of us all. There's not a one of us that has not dreamed for years of doing what she just did."

In the back alley, where Jalaam had forced his daughter with a strong grip on her upper arm, a different kind of discussion ensued.

"Dinah! What in Goshen has gotten in to you?! Are you trying to destroy me!? I knew something was wrong with you, but you have completely lost your senses! Do you realize you are destroying everything we depend on for survival? I have poured my life into this inn—my life! Like it or not this establishment is my *only* sustenance—and yours! Do you think this kind of success just happens? I have sacrificed for this—for years!—the toil, the investment—building clientele, creating atmosphere, fanning habits, persuading the wealthy to make our place their favorite? This inn has been *years* in the making, and you are on the verge of destroying it in one night! I would like to know by what madness you picked the most influential man in town to insult in the face of everyone! I don't know what has gotten in to you, but you were more useful when you had the swamp fever! And that stupid, asinine, childish joke of a veil! You haven't worn that in years—why do you insist on taking it now? It's ridiculous! It's absurd, it's pathetic, it's laughable, and it's making us the mockery of the town!"

"It's *holiness*, father, and I ought never to have abandoned it in first place. As for Hamon, he deserved every word of that and more. You know it, I know it, and everyone in that room knows it!"

"It's not about what he deserves, it's about how we are going to survive in this town! We don't have land! We aren't going to get land, so we have no choice but to survive on the prosperity of this inn! Destroy that, and both you and I become beggars in a year!"

"Better a beggar than a coward."

Jalaam opened his mouth, and then hesitated.

"Are you saying, I . . ." he began, his face reddening, as he searched for a response.

Dinah began to tear up, staring at her father's angry face. Suddenly, in a moment as surreal as it was unexpected, she perceived him anew. For the first time in her life, she regarded him with more pity than fear.

Dinah was bold and brash with others, but had always been submissive to her father. For years she had placated his temper, never having fully made the transition from subordinate child to young woman with both the right and responsibility to make her own choices. As the only child in a motherless family, a strong sense of obligation had always held her firmly in her father's sway. But that sense of responsibility had now been trumped by a greater one, and her new duty was attended by an unexpected strength, which now welled up within her for the first time. It flowed as deep and quiet as the ocean, strong and serene. Strong—so surprisingly strong! Could she now defy even her own father?—the one person who's will had always over-ridden her own?—and that peacefully, with pity rather than anger?

Her father stood before her, but for the first time, she saw him not as her father. She saw him as a man—just a lonely sonless widower who had long ago traded his inheritance land for a city building. A man—just another desperate man in a difficult situation, as were so many in this town.

"I am sorry father," she said in a choked whisper. "I just cannot do what you want any more."

She held his gaze. He stared at her in amazed frustration.

"Get out Dinah. Get your things and get out. I don't know who you are any more, and I can't risk having you back in there again. This is it. You made your choice—you find your own house, make your own way from now on. Then maybe you will understand how hard it is. I'll *hire* a girl who will do what needs to be done."

"Is that the way you want it, father?"

"That is the way *you* want it, Dinah, you've made it painfully clear."

For all of Dinah's recent eloquence, her tongue suddenly could not find a single word as she stared at him mistily, a lump in her throat. He turned from her abruptly and stormed back into the inn, slamming the door behind him.

"I love you, father . . ." she whispered, standing in the quiet alley, staring at the door that had been closed upon her. Closed, it seemed, for the last time.

She looked down. Her veil hung awkwardly on her shoulder, half removed. She patiently adjusted it, carefully correcting its dishevelment. The door to her father's inn beckoned no more. Setting her face and her bearing to the east, she turned toward the one person in the world she had left to turn to.

****

Hatred stirreth up strifes: but love covereth all sins.

Proverbs 10:12

Hamon was not long in deliberation. Even while smarting under the lingering after-sting of the feisty girl's attack, and the embarrassment of enduring it without rebuttal, his powers of calculation failed him not. He was running out of time to extract the information he needed from Abishag. This night, he knew, may be his last chance. He threw the cheap clay vase he had been nervously toying with to the floor violently, causing it to shatter in all directions, and stormed out of his quarters, making his way with deliberate resolve to the east, toward the edge of town. The scenery that met his eyes on that clear, cool night may as well have been on the other side of the world, so consumed was he with a mental vision of a certain maiden in a dark cell in the base of a gloomy old tower.

Abishag looked up and saw Dinah, instantly reading more in her expression than any word she could have uttered.

"Dinah," she whispered.

Dinah sniffed.

"It's over, Abishag. It's all over now. I will never serve my father again."

"You quit the inn?"

"No, I did not quit. My father sent me away—for good. He does not want me any more."

"Dinah. Tell me. Tell me."

Dinah sat down cross-legged on the cool stone floor facing the bars, while Abishag took the same position across from her within, and dutifully began to relate the entire episode.

Hamon approached the tower in as much desperation as anger, and as much uncertainty of what he would do, as certainty that something must be done. His mind had already weighed several possible strategies for deriving from the frustrating maiden his needed intelligence, but could settle upon no one idea over another. He slowed as he neared the entrance, turning aside to walk around it, and rubbed his head violently as if by such a movement he could expel from it a workable idea. It was then that he heard voices, soft voices, feminine voices, wafting out of the high window near him. He glanced up, and stepped closer. His pulse raced when he identified first one, and then both of the speakers.

With barely contained emotion, he listened silently while the window declared a full account of his recent humiliation, in the voice of the very one who had showered it upon him. Though softly spoken this time, it was not without residue of the same anger that had accompanied its first delivery. After Dinah's account was finished, a silky silence lingered. Then, the voice of the other maiden was heard, soft, melodic, calm, and purely without guile.

"I feel for him."

The response was soft and muffled.

"I do. I truly do, Dinah."

Silence.

A long sigh.

"I don't understand. Abishag, I just don't understand. I don't understand you—I don't understand . . . anything! How can you feel that way? After what he said—after all he has done to you—to me—to this whole town? Is there not a hint of righteous indignation in you?"

"There is every kind of evil in me—this I admit. But Dinah, you must understand what spirit we are of. This is not the season of justice, but of restoration, repentance. Justice will come, in its time. But Hamon, like everyone else, is being given a space to repent. He is not an evil man—no, don't look at me that way—he is not, he is just in need of a turn of heart. He has been my friend—for many years he has been my friend. No one in this village has known him longer than I. I have seen good in him—it is there yet—just suppressed, drowned out, buried under the cares of life. I do not allow that the heart of any man is beyond restoration. But I fear that what you have done will hinder him. If only there were some way you could apologize—make it right with him."

"Apologize?! Abishag! I can't. How can I? How can you? Oh—I know *you* could—but I'm not you! No one is you. I am just so angry I could explode—I *did* explode—and there is not a word I said to him but it was the truth."

"You just make it harder for him, Dinah—but it is over now. I can't hold it against you, any more than I can hold it against him. You are both my friends. I would that I could see *all* of us reconciled. But I know it cannot be that way. Sadly, some will not turn, no matter what grace is shown to them."

"Well Hamon is one such. If there ever was one such, it is

he."

"Of that I am not certain, Dinah. I don't give up on a friend that quickly. But of this I am sure, you are correct about your father. You have served him for the last time."

Hamon's countenance darkened under the weight of his own unexpected uncertainty. He slumped to the ground with his back against the tower, one hand on top of his head. The tongue of his gentle nemesis was as incomprehensible as a foreign language. There he remained—long after the maidens finished their conversation. Alone in the dark he continued in fruitless contemplation, brooding upon the unearthly creature who's presence so near in space, yet so far in spirit, unknowingly vexed him just a few short cubits away on the other side of the stone wall. He saw the dark form of the maiden, Dinah, appear on the road and then disappear into the night. His former resolve to enter the tower had fled from him, and he could not find the arc of its passing. His violent plans wrecked by the irresistible intrusion of wonder, he stewed in the moist grass, remaining there until the cool night mist brushed a wisp of its fragile dust onto his clothing and hair, chilling the back of his neck. Finally, he stood, straightened, and made his way home.

****

The talk that was in general circulation in the streets of Shunem the following day tickled the ears of everyone who heard it—everyone, that is, save one, who's ears, rather, burned as conversations fell into silence at Hamon's passing, giving way to snickering and pointing thereafter.

That night in the inn, Jalaam was forced to endure with frustration the continuous gaffes of a new maidservant-in-training, on what was by far the busiest night his inn had ever seen. In droves they came, in train upon miraculous train to visit his suddenly famous establishment, from ragged servants, to dignified rabbis and elders, and parishioners from a class he had long abandoned any hope of attracting. But to each and all, in tedious repetition, he was forced to apologize and explain that the star they had come in hopes of seeing—his daughter—was not present.

Hamon, meanwhile, was paid a surprise visit from Simeon, one of the chief elders of the city, who challenged him with direct questions about Abishag. Having dissembled these as best he could, he then mentally prepared himself to appear before a most undesired audience. Hamon had always striven to avoid creating circumstances that would require his standing before this particular counselor. Embarrassing as it was, he knew the situation had now deteriorated far enough to require submitting to this particular advisor. Responding to an unexpected summons, he went up to hear the counsel of his dying father.

Chapter 13

Hamon sat in the dark room, leaning forward with his head in his hands. The rasping sound assured him that his father was indeed awake, and had heard his last comment, though the silence lingered. In earlier days, such moments spent waiting for his father's response would have been shrouded in a silence of the most unsettling kind. But the inhuman sound that emanated from his father's disease-ravaged lungs that filled the room as he brooded was perhaps even worse.

The air felt sultry. The dark, velvet curtains that surrounded the deathbed of Baal Hamon, the elder, seemed to radiate heat. Even so, the deteriorating man was mounded with blankets, one of the demands of the disease that was slowly draining his life away. It was not the swamp fever, it was something far worse.

Hamon was tired of being stared at by the imposing collection of Amalekite gods that surrounded his father's bed, so kept his head down and waited. On this particular day, Hamon's father was alert, and communicating better than normal. He had demanded a full account of Hamon's recent dealings, an account that Hamon knew better than to lie about. If bad enough word had reached his father's ears to result in a summons, Hamon knew his father all too well to think he would be fooled by a softened version. So he told all, as humbling as it was.

"And you now fear this man may return," the elder broke the silence.

Hamon flushed. As much as he disliked his father's use of the word 'fear,' enduring subtle jabs such as this were necessary for hearing his father's always astute, if not pleasant, advice.

"Dead men do not return," he replied.

The elder rasped a sigh.

"There is a difference between actually dead, and politically dead. You are confusing one for the other."

Hamon almost said, *you would know*, but restrained himself. Instead he said, "It is possible that what has been published could be made a reality."

His father snorted.

"Stupid suggestions such as that are proof to me how little you have learned. Do you want to get out of this mess, or are you determined to turn a minor problem into a major disaster? It was your attempt to destroy this man that got you into this fix in the first place. Continue on the same path and you are liable to precede even *me* to Gehenna."

"I *had* at first attempted to enlist the man," Hamon protested.

"Yes, and when that failed, your good sense was as short as your patience. You tried to build your house on an unfinished foundation. You thought that because you had the favor of a few selected elders, the rest of the town was won, and you could convict an innocent man without cause. If you couldn't even sway this man, what made you think you could destroy him? You followed up a minor blunder with a major one, and nearly destroyed yourself. But this was obviously no local farmhand—such as you are used to dealing with. You ran into another class. Fool! Have I not warned you for years how fragile our position is here? They know we are foreigners; they are just too stupid to do anything about it. But *this* man was different. Next time you *will* be destroyed, if you don't improve your base of support. It's only on the goodwill of the population that we have survived here. Controlling the economy is not enough. The favor of the powerful few is not enough. The masses are a latent force. If you are not loved by them—not accepted, *loved*—they will turn on you the first chance they get. Count on it!"

It was a speech that the son had heard many times from the lips of his father. He had expected that he would have to endure it again. He braced himself for the rest of the lecture, but the older man said no more. The speech was shorter than Hamon was used to, perhaps owing to his father's difficulty in speaking.

"What about the woman?" the elder instead asked.

"Abishag?"

"No! Chavah, the queen, you fool! Of course, Abishag."

Hamon hesitated.

"She has been in prison for questioning."

This was answered by one of his father's more troubling monologues of silence.

"What kind of a fool have I raised," he muttered, barely audible.

Hamon heard.

"Am I forced to endure—on my dying bed—that not only is my son poised to lose everything I worked for, he is to do it with such a burst of idiocy that my memory is forever to be besmirched by the mere association? Oh, brilliant son, brilliant. Do you actually believe the harassment of innocent peasant girls will win you graces in this community? You have let your personal feelings for that little harlot cloud your judgment. She will have won the sympathy of every family in the valley by the time you are finished with her. You better find a way to get her out of prison quick."

"I only thought to find through her the location of her lover."

"Yes, I know, so you can murder him too. And not because

of the legal threat he represents, but because of the *personal* one."

Hamon's gut knotted. His father amazed him. How could a man who spent every hour of every day rasping away behind dark curtains have such an accurate read on the situation outside?

"I know *you* son," he answered his son's silent query, "I *know* you."

Hamon wanted to protest. He wanted to explain how Abishag should have been rightfully his. True, it was not an actual engagement, but there had been an understanding of sorts. But he realized that defenses of this sort would only serve to prove his father's case.

His father sighed. Hamon looked up.

"I was in a similar position once, you know," the elder said. "When I was younger, newly come into this area—I truly did not understand these Israelites. I was prospering—close it seemed to achieving my full goal, but did not know that I was even closer to losing everything. I was spared—barely—and only by a strategy of the most humbling kind."

"What was that?" Hamon asked.

"I converted."

Hamon frowned and stared at the ground in thought, well aware of the Amalekite idols that even now stared down upon him. The father noticed his son's silence.

"Does this puzzle you? These Israelites, they are a rare breed. No matter how wicked they are in every other way, they compromise not in confessions about their 'god.' They freely mock him with their conduct, but they will never abide a foreigner to do so. And conversely, if a foreigner such as I—or you—even make the appearance of accepting their god—a few well-published confessions—it will do more to win their favor than a thousand acts of charity. Yes—yes, it was a highly visible repentance, and not a moment too soon either. Another week and my barns would have been raided bare, and I would either be dead, or running for my life."

"You did not *truly* convert," Hamon observed after a silent pause.

The father let his eyes wander about the room.

"It is not a question of *if* I converted, but *where.* Once I converted out *there*, it was not necessary to do so in *here.*"

Hamon was thinking deeply. Many times he had been reminded of his father's 'turning point' when he had opened his barns to the needy. But he had not realized until now there was a religious connotation in it—and a strong one.

His father went on. "No, no, son, it is not because I opened my barns to them that they accepted me, though that was necessary to authenticate my conversion in the minds of some. It was because I began to openly confess their god. Circumcision, for a grown man, is a nightmare you cannot possibly imagine. But had I not gone through with it, even a restoration of the land would not have saved me."

"Then why did you not have me circumcised as an infant?"

His father chuckled.

"Because I thought you might need this one day. I did you a favor."

Hamon looked sullen.

Don't do me any more, he was thinking, but also realized that his father was right . . . painfully right.

"So you became an Israelite, and now, I must also," Hamon concluded.

His father snorted.

"You can't become an Israelite. It is impossible. You can only become accepted by them—that's all you can hope for."

The son was thinking.

Perhaps it is not impossible . . .

Though Hamon respected his father's cunning, he believed he had struck on an idea that would take him farther than his father ever dreamed possible. His father had made great gains for his time, but those were past gains. Hamon wanted more. His father believed, in typical fashion of the prior generation, that Israelite doctrines could not change. But Hamon had been raised in Israel and had come to perceive more latitude in its religion than his father knew of. True, the book itself would not change, but Hamon had observed a wide range in the interpretation of that book. Through that avenue could flow just about any doctrine that became expedient, if introduced in small stages.

He realized it would be impossible for his father to understand or support at this late hour in his life the case Hamon had been slowly building for several years, or the fruit it could bear. So he kept his council private. Instead, he baited a well-worn argument instead.

"I could just relocate back to Philistia."

His father's head snapped around.

"Philistia does not *exist* anymore—a fact that you of all people should be keeping foremost in mind. The Israelite king has a chokehold on the entire area. It may never again be sovereign. No, you are stuck here."

"But this king is much more peaceful than David. Perhaps the land can be taken back."

The elder shook his head.

"You understand nothing at all. Which is harder, to take the land by the sword, or to keep it without ever unsheathing a blade? This young king is either terribly lucky or frightfully astute to maintain such a large kingdom in peace. Think of it!—preempting wars before they even begin, allowing his enemies nothing to work with—even winning favor among them, turning his adversaries into willing, even adoring servants. It's the most amazing political coup this region has ever seen!—and I would never have believed it had I not seen it. You give him too little respect."

"I saw it coming years ago. We fought against Saul and won, but when I encountered David—the loyalty he inspired! He was like a wild ox in his strength. I knew our days were numbered. My brethren back in the homeland, where are they now? Carrying stones in the king's slave-labor force. They mocked me then, but not any more. This young king—he is a quiet genius—much more dangerous than the father ever was. Whatever you do, don't attract his attention."

"What could he ever care about this area? He has no reason to come here."

"Keep it that way."

Hamon was not in full agreement, for his theory was that Solomon's early success was really owing to a well executed bluff perpetrated by some astute and experienced carryovers from David's administration—a bluff that temporarily intimidated potential enemies into acquiescence. His knowledge that Asa Barak had stood before the king and escaped was proof to him that the reports of the king's wisdom were exaggerated. But once again he elected to not contradict his father, which could only serve to derail the conversation away from his own intentions.

"Do you still hear tidings from them?" Hamon asked.

"Our kinfolk? Not in some time, but I still do have debts to pay—to those who helped me escape, and others. The generals who served before me, they died by assassination. I took the position by the same means. On any given night I could have lain down in my tent never to raise again, my head paraded away on the staff of some disgruntled footman who, with the help of one of my close aids, pinned me to the ground with my own spear. It was impossible to know who to trust any more; so I escaped with my take. I have kept in contact with those who helped me, and they have pressed me for a return of the favor, more so these past years, as the enemy king has seized their land. I owe them, and so do you."

"Why should the son be saddled with the father's debts?" Hamon sulked.

"Hmph! For the same reason he enjoys the father's prosperity. But lest you think this mere charity, you err again; there is an opportunity in it for you. You will always be an outsider in Israel, but these men, they are your kinfolk. You can have an understanding with them that you never will with these Israelites—even if you sojourn among them for a thousand years."

"But they are far away, what could our people possibly do to . . ." Hamon's voice trailed off as his father's meaning dawned on him. "The Brotherhood is bankrupt you know, there is little need of outside help now."

"I have never feared this Brotherhood. It was doomed before it even was formed. But what you ought to be asking is, why did it arise in the first place? Whatever seeds sprouted into this weed are still in the soil. There will be another, and another, and eventually, one will succeed. Do you know what those seeds are?"

Hamon thought for a moment.

"What are they thirsting for?" his father hinted.

"Land ownership."

"Exactly. And that thirst is heightened by the fact that they take a percentage of profits out of the fields, rather than just wages. After working the same soil year after year, they come to feel attached to it, as if it is their own. They know too much—too much about how much profit is made on it, and too much about your take. We have used sharecropping thus far, but it is the sharecropping system that resulted in this wretched Brotherhood. It must be replaced with waged laborers."

"And you suppose our Amalekite brothers would work for wages?"

"No! No, you fool, no! When will you ever learn? They will *manage* the Israelites who work for wages. But, unlike these Israelites, they will do so without believing they are entitled to own the land. And believe me, they will think you a hero if you make a place for them here."

Hamon sifted the possibilities. His father's plan was not without merit, but incorporating his own ideas into it, it could perhaps be even more successful.

"Perhaps I should take a trip down there."

The elder looked pleased. For years he had tried to form in his son some regard for his own people. Now, he finally seemed to be getting through.

"I will tell you who to contact, and how to find them."

Both men were silent for a few moments as the afternoon heat wafted through the window, moving the velvet curtains hardly at all. The old man's breathing changed. Hamon worried that his father might sleep before he could ask the one question that troubled him the most.

"Do you suppose he will return?" Hamon asked.

His father jolted, and looked over, inhaling sharply.

"Return? The man who was always one step ahead of you, revealed you for the ignorant shepherd boy you are?—you worry that he is not finished humiliating you? I'll give you this, at least you have learned from this episode to recognize a threat."

"But do you think he will return?"

"You called him Abishag's lover—was that his testimony or hers?"

"Hers. She said they were engaged."

"Would she lie?"

Hamon blew out a disgusted laugh.

"Never!"

"Would she be deceived?"

"About love? She is untouchable. She would never promise herself for a lie."

"Then you have your answer. He will be back, and if you are lucky, it will be for her only, and not you."

Hamon silently seethed, but realized that his father was right again, *painfully* right.

Chapter 14

Say not thou, I will recompense evil; but wait on the LORD, and he shall save thee.

Proverbs 20:22

Lotan and Ono approached the old grain tower, a queasy knot in their stomachs. The urgent tone with which Hamon had dispatched them was still ringing in their ears, making the approaching assignment even more daunting. Lotan was not unaware of the importance of this situation to Hamon, and the fact that he had been entrusted to address it evidenced his rising status in the administration. "You acted shrewdly, with the young guard's family in Jezreel. Perhaps you can draw from the maiden her secret," Hamon had told him. "I would do it myself, but I am prevented by circumstance. Don't fail me!"

He also reminded him that the girl could no longer be detained and would certainly be straightaway released regardless of what she confessed, but *she* had no awareness of that—ignorance which could be played to great advantage. With this advice, and an admonition that this may be their last and only chance to derive any intelligence from her, Lotan was released to his own judgment, a tribute he found both honoring and ominous. With the full strategy in his hands, if he failed, he would fail alone.

The key-keeper shuffled down the hall to Abishag's cell, leading his two visitors, and Abishag heard their voices echoing in the chamber long before she saw them.

"She's right down this way," his hoarse, old voice echoed. "Between you and me, I can't imagine what the elders think she's guilty of—the sweetest little songbird I ever saw, I tell you. I hope you can clear this up and get her released. A spring meadow flower would look dirty standing next to her."

"That's what we have come for," said a young man's voice. "We intend to clear this up, and get her out of here at once—if she will but cooperate."

The key-keeper snorted.

"Cooperate? She'd dress a waller-hog in a silk suit, if I asked her to—and then apologize when it got muddy."

The key-keeper and the two men stopped before the cell. Abishag looked up curiously.

"Well, here she is; I'll leave you to your business."

He shuffled off.

Abishag found herself under the curious gaze of a strangely matched pair of men: a young prince, and standing next to him, a tall, balding older man, peering at her through the bars. As she stood, their eyes widened.

"May I serve you, lords?"

The young man cleared his throat, gaping at the gentle and beautiful woman.

"Yes. You are Abishag—well, of course, you would know who you are, but, do you know who I am?"

"I do not believe I do, my lord," Abishag replied, although

both men looked familiar.

"My name is Lotan, and this is Ono, recorder for Baal Hamon's estate. We were told we would find you here. We are not here to harm you; we have come to intervene on your behalf. Word has reached Baal Hamon, that you have been wrongly imprisoned. He has not taken the hearing of this well. Since the moment he learned of it, he has been taking actions to secure your release. He speaks very highly of you."

"Your maidservant deserves not the kind notice of a man as great as he."

"Yes, well, you should know that after much effort, the noble lord just may have found a way to help you. It is not a certainty, but there is a chance. He sent us here to counsel you on what you can do to secure your release from this wrongful imprisonment."

"Wrongful? How so?"

Lotan looked puzzled.

"Well, if not wrongful, then certainly, uncomfortable. What you have suffered here has been unpleasant, I am sure."

"I have had very few visitors, my lords. How is it that Hamon has come to know my state?"

Lotan inhaled then hesitated.

"Well . . . certainly you know of the keen perception of the noble lord," he said quickly. "However he came upon this knowledge, I can inform you that Hamon has prevailed upon the elders to declare their conditions for your immediate release—conditions that you may well be able to meet. Obtaining this concession was no easy task, you must understand, for there are those among the elders who believe you to be guilty of many crimes, along with the prisoner who recently escaped. But since you have not been proven guilty of anything, Hamon believes it quite improper to keep you incarcerated."

Abishag looked back and forth between the odd pair curiously. Noticing her glance, Lotan then explained.

"This man, Ono, the recorder, has come that your testimony

might be properly documented."

"Ahh, I see. You wish testimony of me. Well. I am quite willing to declare to you such things as I am in a position to know. What testimony do you require?"

Lotan looked down, and shook his head looking grave. He spoke lowly.

"Dear maiden. I hope and trust that you do not find the testimony that would release you hard to bear. You have been imprisoned here, simply because many have presumed you guilty of crimes committed by another. But Baal Hamon has searched out a way in which you can be exonerated, so that you will no longer be implicated in that other man's crimes. If you will but cooperate with us, and do one and only one thing, we can help you. If Hamon's strategy is successful, no man, even among the elders, will have grounds to detain you any longer. But you must cooperate, no matter how difficult it may be. Will you cooperate?"

Abishag leaned forward, and lowered her voice, mimicking his grave manner.

"Cooperate? With the law? I could do no less."

"This is a great relief to us, dear maiden. Very well then—if you will answer a few simple questions: It is known that you were associated with the man called Jedidiah."

"It would be the greatest of honors for me to confess even the slightest association with him."

Lotan's eyes widened and he gave Ono a nod, at which he produced instruments of writing, and prepared to use them.

"You would be willing to go on the record and answer our questions concerning him then?"

"But of course, my lord, anything I could say that would be of help to you, and the elders, would be my most humble and rightful service."

"I see. Well then. The issue that is of greatest concern to the cause of justice is the location of the escaped man."

"I quite agree with you my lord."

Her statement was met with momentary silence.

"You do? That is . . . good—that's very good. And perhaps you are aware that it is believed that you, because of your . . . 'association' with this man, would know where he is hiding. Now surely you understand that the needs of the law must prevail above the sentiments of any one individual. Whatever your relationship with this man, the law now requires that you lay all aside and declare what you know of his present location."

Abishag was silent. Lotan gave a quick glance at Ono, said, "Do not hesitate now, maiden."

"Was it for this question that I was brought to this place?" Abishag asked.

"It was, in the main. And I assure you, your release depends upon a forthright answer."

"Oh, my dear lords. I am so sorry for the misunderstanding. If I had known the elders desired this, I surely would have reported to them straightaway, rather than causing all the inconvenience of searching for me, and then detaining me these past days. Please forgive me this oversight, for I would be happy to tell you the exact location of the man you seek."

Lotan glanced at Ono quickly, and then back at Abishag.

"You would tell?"

"Why yes, certainly, of course!"

Ono prepared to record.

"All right then, we will take your testimony now. This man Jedidiah—he is believed to be in the area still—as I am sure you know. But, the elders want that you would lead us to his place of hiding—in secret, so that he may be captured without opportunity to escape. Can you do this?"

"My dear lords. I am afraid there is no chance of doing that. For the man you seek is not hiding. He is not in this area at all. He is in fact in Jerusalem."

Ono was scribbling. Lotan frowned.

"Jerusalem?"

"Yes, I am quite certain of it."

"Why . . ." he broke off, thinking carefully, "why do you say he is in Jerusalem?"

"Because that is where he is. You may take this as my sworn testimony, and bring it to the elders in confidence. If those who seek him will but go to Jerusalem, they will surely find him. He is quite visible there."

Lotan was stroking his well-kept beard, trying to get a read on the situation.

"Jerusalem. All right. So, you are saying that this man, after leaving here, went north to Tyre, and then after that, came back here and told you he was going to Jerusalem? Is that how it happened?"

"No, my lord. He went directly to Jerusalem from here. He did not go to Tyre."

"He told you this? After the hearing?"

"Oh no, he told me this *before* the hearing, days before, to be truthful. He was to be leaving on that day regardless of the hearing."

Lotan frowned. Ono continued to scribble.

"I . . . am not certain I understand."

"Is some part of my testimony unclear to you?" Abishag asked.

"No . . . no, not unclear, quite clear."

"Then I have provided for you the one thing the elders wanted of me."

"The one thing?"

"Yes, the one thing. You very kindly informed me that this one thing—my testimony on this question—was all that the elders required."

"Yes . . . but . . ."

"So I can now expect that the elders will send their notice of my release to the key-keeper, correct?"

Lotan looked back up at her from his puzzling.

"Jerusalem?"

She nodded.

"Yes."

He was silent.

"Shall I prepare to depart this place now?" she asked.

"What? Oh, yes, with your testimony, as I said, you may now . . . go."

"And the sealed notice of release from the elders, you have it?" she asked.

"Sealed release? Oh, no, you misunderstand, maiden. Now that you have offered sworn testimony, the elders' requirement is met. In this case, actually, *we* have been authorized to release you."

"You? You release me? How can *you* release me? Surely there must come some official notice from the elders. I would not want anything to be done improperly; it would be unfair to the key-keeper, for I am sure he requires proper documentation. And I would like to have it myself as well—in case this question ever comes up again."

"Oh, no. No, no, you err, dear maiden. I assure you that this is not necessary at all. The elders have already agreed that if we obtained your sworn testimony, we would be authorized to release you at that very moment. I will instruct the key-keeper to unlock your cell and you are free to go, at once."

Abishag looked thoughtful.

"That will not be necessary, my lord," she said slowly, "for my cell . . . is already unlocked."

Lotan glanced down at the bolt, his eyebrows going up in

surprise to find it broken. Then he reached up and tugged the barred gate and it swung toward him a short distance.

"Does the key-keeper know of this?" he asked, aghast.

"Oh yes, he knows. The lock has been broken for some time. But he also knows I will not depart illegally. I must leave legally, or not at all. You may open the gate if you like, but I would never presume to pass through a gate merely because it is open. I am detained by the law, not by the gate. I will remain here, until you bring the sealed statement from the elders, authorizing my release."

Lotan cleared his throat.

"Abishag. You are complicating this unnecessarily. The elders do not need to be bothered with another document. Please, come forth at once, you are free to go home. Surely you are eager to leave this place."

"Oh no, I am quite comfortable here. To wait for the proper document is no trouble. No doubt if you depart now, you could return from the elders in less than an hour. Go to them at once. I simply must be certain this is done properly."

"Abishag!" Lotan said flustered, "You misread the situation, and do not appreciate how delicate your position is! Do you realize how difficult it was for Hamon to derive this concession from the elders? If you tempt them with these complications, they may retract their offer! I urge you, leave at once! You are free! Abishag—please! Go home!"

Abishag shook her head solemnly.

"I could never do that, my lord. I simply must have the signed release. I insist. I will not leave this cell until I do."

"But . . ." Lotan began, shaking his head in amazement at her.

Abishag turned from him, went to the corner, and sat down, taking up her pen and inkhorn. Lotan was speechless. The two men looked at one another.

"You will return shortly then?" she asked, not looking up from her writing.

"I . . . Well. I suppose I . . . will need to explore . . . exactly what the procedure is . . . under the circumstances."

"That would be most kind."

Lotan scratched his head, and, after staring in silence for some time, turned and the two men left down the hall, Lotan trudging numbly on, as Ono followed with his tablet.

Hamon stood before the window lattice in stillness, the flexing of his jaw muscles the only evidence that he was more than a statue.

"And she will not leave?"

"No. She was quite insistent. Until I return with a sealed release from the elders, I am quite sure she will remain incarcerated . . . in an unlocked cell."

Hamon muttered a curse.

Lotan sat behind him, nervously fingering the edge of his sleeve while Hamon brooded. He opened his mouth with the thought of offering a comment in his own defense on several occasions, but then reconsidered.

"How did she look?" Hamon asked the window.

Lotan blinked.

"Excuse me? Oh. Well, she was a fair prize to look at . . . if I may understate—well, more than that even, I suppose, she is . . ."

"No, not to look *at,* you fool! Did she appear healthy? Did she cough or anything?"

Lotan thought a moment.

"Well, as a matter of fact . . . no, she did not. In fact, I would say she appeared the picture of perfect health—the picture of perfect . . . well . . . *everything.*"

Hamon reddened. He turned his head quickly to the side.

"Not even a sniffle, some slight clearing of throat? A shiver, anything?"

Lotan was almost afraid to answer now.

"Perhaps you ought to go see for yourself, my lord."

"Ignorant female," Hamon muttered. "First we could not get her in, now we can't get her out. If I did not know better I would think she was toying with me. Can she really be that clever?"

"If she was designing this deliberately, my lord, it certainly did not appear so. She seemed just—innocent."

"As do the shrewdest of all," Hamon replied.

"So what do we do now? The talk in the streets is against us, the elders could become involved at any moment, some action must be taken."

Hamon left the window, and began pacing the room. Lotan followed him with his eyes. Hamon turned and inhaled, but then paced again, rubbing his chin beard with two fingers.

"A letter," he declared.

"My lord?"

"A letter to the elders. We must explain that the order to capture and question her was issued immediately—after the prisoner escaped. But, by some oversight, was never canceled after the man was killed in the chase. The militia caught her in the village some days later, and brought her to the tower. We have only just recently learned she was being held there, and now a document is needed authorizing her release."

Hamon looked over with an expression that seemed to invite an opinion. Lotan nodded.

"Under the circumstances, I suppose that is about the best we can do. Although, if any serious inquiry is made into this, it will be difficult to prove our ignorance."

"I know that," Hamon snapped. "But I do not believe this woman has advocates interested enough to press an inquiry on her behalf."

"Perhaps she would press it herself," Lotan suggested.

Hamon shot him a glance.

"That is one thing I am confident will not happen. You do not know her like I do. She would give her life to save a worthless beggar, but would never lift a finger in her own defense."

Lotan looked confused.

"Strange woman."

"You don't know the half of it," Hamon spat.

"Well. If she is as you say, then the only risk is that she may have an advocate that we do not know of."

"Yes," Hamon said, collapsing down behind his desk. "She does appear to be surprisingly resourceful. But what choice have we?"

Lotan had no response, watching his lord descend into silence.

Hamon's brooding resulted in the revelation that Abishag was sending him a message, a very direct and personal message. She was informing him that she knew he was responsible for her incarceration, and that she was not afraid of it. His blood boiled at the thought, but his hands were tied. How could a single peasant maiden in the back of a dark cell so fully sway everything in her favor in spite of his best efforts? It was nonsensical. Mysterious, confusing, baffling . . . and terribly irritating.

Abishag was becoming an unwelcome obsession. In spite of himself, Hamon found her invading his thoughts, her kind and gentle manner and innocent purity almost mocking him. Add to that, her incomparable beauty—frustratingly untouchable beauty. She killed him softly, without a hint of guile. Beyond that, she threatened to destroy all his well laid plans, all with hardly any effort, or so it appeared. Powerless to dismiss her from his thoughts, his soul churned of its own in a devilish brew of love and hate.

As for the strange testimony of the escapee being in Jerusalem, that Hamon doubted, but did not doubt that Abishag believed it. He did not believe her capable of a lie. If she testified he was out of the area, it was because she believed it so. Which solved one of his problems: The dangerous man was safely away. *And if she is not in contact with him . . .* he mused, his mind wandering, sifting the possibilities. *The woman is shrewd, but I have another lot to cast into this game—one that may outplay even her.* Hamon became aware of Lotan's pensive stare, and looked up.

"Sylva!" he called out the door. A woman's voice answered.

"Get me a writer!"

Hamon, though fuming, dictated the letter to the elders, and dispatched it with a messenger. He glanced at Lotan, who stared back blankly.

"With any luck we will get that maiden *out* of that cell."

As Abishag waited in an open cell for the letter that would release her and implicate the one who incarcerated her in the process, she received one more unexpected visitor. She looked up to see her eldest brother, Hemanah, looking confusedly back and forth between her and the open door. Abishag immediately felt a stab of pity for him. There seemed to be no man in the valley more often left in abject confusion lately than her brother, Hemanah.

"How blessed of you to come, my brother. I have been so missing you."

He scowled.

"Abishag, why is this gate open? And why have you been put in here?"

"Hemanah, the gate is open rightly, because I am on my way out. I am expecting to be released soon. I was wrongly detained here—it was a mix-up. But I could ask the same question of you. Why are you here, have you some news for me? How is it with Hamon, and the harvest?"

Hemanah glared at her sharply.

"Abishag. Things have changed. I am no longer working with Hamon."

"Truly? You are taking all of it then? How did you manage that?"

"I am taking none of it. Except half of what I had harvested until . . . until Hamon and I agreed to modify the share-crop. Now I am reassessing our whole estate. I understand you gave away your harvest—to those beggars. I don't know what you think you are doing, Abishag, but you should be consulting me! Everything is different now. You have no right to give away what rightfully belongs to me. Besides, you have to think about your own survival, and the support of your mother. Or did you think that you would just live off of my harvest?"

"No, my lord, and your maidservant would just as soon give the harvest to you as to them, but I was not aware you had need of it, your fields are so laden. But now, am I to understand that you have ceased from sharecropping with Hamon?"

"Abishag. I told those beggars of yours to hold off. I need to assess what remains to us, and how to best manage it. There has been a change of plan. That vineyard you have been tending—it may need to be invested."

"Invested? How so?"

"You would not understand Abishag. It's men's business, but there are some men pooling their resources to redeem their lands using this year's harvest as the means. With your . . . my upper vineyard added, there may be enough in the pool to get all of our lands back once and for all. That's why I quit Hamon."

"Ahh. So that is why you quit. You are very astute, my brother. And though it is not mine to question your judgment, I am sure you have already considered the unlikelihood of the harvest from one small vineyard raising enough funds to redeem lands ten times the size, in one year."

Hemanah hesitated.

"Of course I have thought of that! But this is all answered in the terms I negotiate with the Brotherhood. With the right kind of bargaining, we could end up with a greater return than you think."

"I see. Well, I am quite blessed to be under the care of a master as astute as you, and I am sure whatever agreement you reach will be most profitable for the family, as have been all of your past dealings. But as for myself, I would not be at all offended if we just kept the remaining harvest and shared it among the family. We can get by on it for one winter. In fact, my mother and I have savings enough to take us through already; we would not burden you at all. You and your mother and brothers can have all of what remains on the vines. Then, next year, perhaps we can begin planning for a redemption right from seed time."

Hemanah scowled.

"But I have already been planning right from seedtime, Abishag. It just was not necessary to tell you about it until now. I am certain we have quite enough to redeem the rest of our land. That is why I called off the sharecrop with Hamon. That was why I have been so concerned about your not giving so much away to beggars. Are you starting to understand now?"

Abishag nodded slowly.

"I believe I am, my brother. And I support your wisdom in this matter. But be assured there is no impatience on my part; next year will be more than soon enough for me. And remember, you only have four to feed, not six. I can even share some of my savings with you—if you do not have enough."

Hemanah looked irritated.

"We have *more* than enough Abishag, far more than enough! Besides, your few shekels would fall far short of covering our enormous lack. That is why we *must* invest in the Brotherhood! Don't you see? It's our last and only hope now that my fields are gone! That is why I have been planning this from the start, to put us in the strong position we are in now. We are about to lose everything! You worry far too much. But I don't suppose I should expect a woman to understand these things."

"I doubt I ever could."

He looked over at the gate.

"So you are getting out soon, you say?"

"This very day, it is my true belief."

"Well then. Be prepared to see me in your vineyard later—and be prepared to work. I don't know what you did to get put in here, but try to stay out of trouble from now on. Your reputation around here is not the best, you know."

"I will do my best, my brother."

Shortly after Hemanah left, the awaited letter arrived. After paying deep respects to Nebo, the key-keeper, promising to pay for the broken cell latch, and apologizing for being such a troublesome prisoner, Abishag left the grounds, freely, and legally. As Nebo watched her walk away, he was overcome with an uncommon feeling of melancholy, a wave of remorse sinking in his gut. He was sure he had never had such a pleasant prisoner in his forty years as jailer.

Chapter 15

Because sentence against an evil work is not executed speedily, therefore the heart of the sons of men is fully set in them to do evil

Ecclesiastes 8:11

The morning was bright. The sounds of voices in the bustling market square drifted out to greet approachers well before the square itself was in view. The largest caravan fair of the year was scheduled to convene in Jezreel the following day, a market to which the residents of Shunem brought their produce every year, with great fanfare. The crops were transported a day in advance of the event itself, allowing plenty of time for the produce to be inspected and sampled before trading began. This was to be the day—that distinctive day known as "Departure Day"—when the fruit of many months of toil would be released with prayers into the hands of God, to pass before the discriminating eyes of traveling merchants, and to be tested against the larger markets of the world.

Abishag and Dinah had traveled down from Abishag's

hillside farm, where Dinah now lived, and were strolling before the rows of wagons watching as workmen loaded the last of the grain bundles, baskets of figs, barrels of wine and olive oil, and tied down the loads, checking and rechecking their riggings. Two men were fussing over a loose wagon wheel, while others hitched the animals that would draw the wagons.

Of all the produce lined up for export to Jezreel, one particular train held greater interest for most of the residents of Shunem, than any other. In fact, it excited greater angst than any harvest train had in many years. For this train was to bear the collected produce of the Brotherhood, the profits from which they hoped would redeem a large portion of inheritance land. The hopes and prayers of many an Israelite lay upon those wagons, hopes and prayers that the quantity and prices its products commanded would be sufficient to complete the bold and risky plan to redeem the land, led by the physician, Jockshan.

Abishag and Dinah invested no hopes in that train, nor did Jared and Barkos, who wandered together beyond the maidens, pointing and talking. But Hemanah did. Against the advice of all four, Hemanah chose to throw all that was left in his control—the harvest from Abishag's vineyard—into the pool with the Brotherhood. Abishag and the others had come down to see the harvest off in as much support of Hemanah as they did in respect for years of habit. Departure Day was an event not to be missed in Shunem, even if one had nothing invested in it.

After being released from prison, Abishag was warmly received by friends and family. The week following her return had been uneventful, except for the curious report of a lamp fire in the Hall of Records building, which destroyed the sealed records of some recent hearings.

After Hemanah repossessed Abishag's harvest, the silver which Abelah had found in the house was brought forward as sufficient means to sustain them through the winter, in spite of the loss. Barkos and Jared thankfully received this charity and prepared their shared house for the winter, while Jared's young daughter, Abihail, was overjoyed with the unexpected treat of frequent company with the older young maidens to whom she was now a neighbor.

Those same maidens now thoughtfully observed Hemanah, as he mixed among the crowd. The eldest brother of Abishag, responsible in full for the management of the family estate, was exciting more sympathy in his younger sister than he knew, and even if he had known, would not have appreciated its value. She watched him as he basked in sudden popularity, warmly greeted by the members of the Brotherhood. Abishag knew her brother had doubts about the arrangement, and they were real and deep, but they were momentarily lost under the sweet balm of brotherly acceptance. She doubted he would be able to discern that it was not personal acceptance that he was receiving, but an acceptance born of desperation.

The nervousness had reached such a pitch among investing families in recent days that no fault could be found with any man who threw his means in with them, no matter how questionable his character. Abishag knew Hemanah was more uncertain of his mind than he admitted. Being a blunt and simple man, wrestling with the complex decisions that his position demanded was a mantle uncomfortable to him—even more so now, with the stakes so very high. His solitary brooding and hours in the company of wine and loud friends informed her that he was still fighting his own doubts, no matter how bold his confessions. She knew the quiet voice of his doubts would be inaudible here—lost under the thanks that were being showered upon him. His decision to invest, though ill-advised from Abishag's perspective, could not be blamed, for to all outward evidence, the Brotherhood did hold the next best hope for a man who had fallen into Hamon's disfavor.

Abishag, along with Dinah, Jared, and Barkos, had crept up to the edge of full disclosure with Hemanah, but none were able to find the right combination of receptive spirit and fitting moment to fully enlighten him on the real situation. It was he that shrank from these conversations as they neared the climax, descending to baser arguments. Still she yearned for him, inwardly pulled for him, that he would somehow catch a whisper of rugged light, soar above his blunt and plain nature, and receive the strong and wild hope that she and her associates were living before him. Thus far, he had not.

As the first of the wagons rumbled and turned out of the square toward Jezreel, the people cheered. Curiously absent on this festive day, Abishag noted, was Hamon himself. Jockshan had arrived, of course, and was bustling about nervously attending to last minute details, as the Brotherhood train, which would be both the longest and last to depart, was receiving its final preparations. Many farmers, young and old, together with their wives and families stepped forward to speak with the doctor, to give—or to receive—some word of encouragement.

Eventually, only the Brotherhood train remained, the men working on the loose wagon wheel finally resigned to replace it altogether. Jockshan climbed onto the back of a wagon to speak to the people.

"I owe you all a great debt—a great debt," he declared heartily to the remaining group in the suddenly quiet square. "This time, this day, and the vision that has brought us to this day has been the dream of many. Though we have struggled, and encountered many setbacks along the way, God has confirmed the wisdom of our plan in recent days. The returns that are being reported in early sales are higher than we anticipated—much higher. Every year since Solomon has become king, more and wealthier merchants have been coming to our fair driving up prices. Meanwhile, our creditors, surprisingly, have given us the grace to continue until harvest, even when we were short on funds. And, some last minute additions to our pool have come in. We are thankful to our brother, Hemanah, who over the past two days, has added to our wagons wine of a quality that surpasses any we had yet obtained. Though not great in volume, it will be surely useful to distribute among our potential buyers as a sample of our quality."

The crowd glanced over at Hemanah who was smiling proudly.

"But above all, we take confidence in the fact that this venture has been bathed in prayer—in fact, it does not escape my notice that many of you slept very little last night. No doubt you were in prayer—as was I. I very much expect the Lord to reward this sacrifice, even as he has rewarded us with a strong harvest, in spite of the recent fox plague. With these confirmations, we can be assured that we are in the center of His will, and after this plan succeeds, we will enjoy greater confidence among the larger population, to accomplish even more next year. You are the brave few who mustered the faith to step out, risking your livelihoods to restore what is right, and this day, the Lord will reward that faith."

Abishag became aware of a person slipping up beside her as the crowd stood listening. Glancing over, she recognized the woman Hildah, who quietly greeted her with a warmth Abishag had not previously observed in her.

"I would like to speak with you, dear maiden."

Abishag brightened at the sight of her, observing the woman's clear eyes and easy breathing.

"My lady! You find my cure more credible now."

"I do."

Jockshan finished with his comments, finally bowing his head and leading the group in the sincerest of prayers, after which, the last harvest train, laden heavily with the dreams of many, lurched into motion—the prior wagons having long before departed.

"Abishag," Hildah said, as the people disbursed, "I no longer have the luxury of a mere opinion of your medicine, for I am no longer sick. Your cure works. But, I have some things to ask you—other things. I would be most honored if you could find leave to join me at my home, for noon meal."

"I assure you, you owe me nothing, my lady."

The woman shook her head.

"I have learned, maiden, that however much I may disagree with you on that point, it is fruitless to try and reward you. No—I only wish to speak with you. Will you come?"

Abishag looked over at Dinah—who shrugged.

"I will tend to the medicine at the farm," Dinah offered.

"Yes, well, it would be an honor, my lady," Abishag agreed.

The room in which Abishag found herself entertained by the woman Hildah and her servants was of a level of opulence that inspired awkward timidity in the peasant girl. She adjusted herself in the soft couch several times, sitting on the edge of it, as though offending by touching it.

The small talk in which Hildah conversed so fluently was an unfamiliar language to Abishag, and she responded in awkward economy, wondering just why it was that this woman of rank had invited her here. She had not long to wonder, for the woman suddenly came to the point, as though the predetermined period of preliminaries demanded by convention had been fulfilled.

"Abishag," Hildah said abruptly, putting down her chalice on the low table in front of her, and looking at her guest directly. "I have not yet thanked you for the boy you sent to me."

"Benaiah? I am so thankful you were able to take him in—he was without a situation. Has he served you well here?"

"He has served me better as a volunteer than some of my hired help have for pay. A very well mannered boy—and hard working! You ought to see what he has done with the yard in the short time he has been here."

"Benaiah is a talented gardener." Abishag agreed.

"Yes he is, talented, and . . . plain spoken, I would add, quite . . . forthright with his thoughts."

Abishag took a deep breath.

"I have noted that quality in him my lady. He has been . . . speaking with you?"

"Yes. He has. He has told me many things. Odd things." Hildah looked directly at Abishag, "*Extraordinary* things. Things that are . . . difficult to believe."

Abishag nodded slowly.

"I am sure you have found them nearly as difficult to believe, my lady, as the fact that a home remedy distributed by a peasant girl can heal in a few weeks what an excellent doctor has been unable to cure in years."

Hildah cocked her head curiously.

"You puzzle me, maiden. You lack so much, in art, but somehow, all of it you seem to restore, in sensiblity. Quite so, his tales are that difficult to believe . . . and more."

"Truth is not always determined by what is easily believed, my lady."

Hildah looked thoughtful.

"But what is truth . . . can we not expect to flow in some continuity with what has always been true?"

"It may be that what has always been assumed true is out of continuity with what has actually been true," Abishag replied.

Hildah put her finger on her lip and leaned back in her chair, studying her strange guest. Abishag looked at her innocently, then lowered her eyes.

"Do you find me entertaining, maiden? For your comments smack of sport."

"My dearest lady. I have not asked you to believe anything, or to place any confidence in my own word. My word will fail, but truth abides of its own. It soars higher than the one who professes it. Just because truth is found on my lips—if it be found on such unworthy lips—does not make me its source. If what my friend has told you is true, it matters not what I say. The truth will seed its own testimony, in time—like the medicine, and the cure that followed. When that happens, it will not be necessary to accept truth on the word of another, but to receive truth on its own merit. So it is with all truth."

Hildah stared at her.

"You speak well, for one so young. How have you come by such eloquence?"

"If I do speak well, it is surely to the credit of worthy instructors, who have drawn from me more than my station should allow."

"Worthy instructors! So you do not deny what this boy alleges then? You admit it to be true?" Hildah asked.

"Truth is no more mine to deny than it is mine to create."

"Is it not possible, maiden, that you have been cleverly deceived?"

"I know myself capable of great folly. But if I be deceived, what did the deceiver gain from it?"

The question hung in the air, the elder woman finding no instant answer to it.

"Abishag. If you will forgive my forthrightness—you are allowing that the king—King Solomon himself—lived in our village—unknown, for six weeks! Quite a copious proposition, do you not think? Surely . . . *surely* . . . the king of Israel would have come forth in some official way that the elders could know and submit to his wisdom."

"Perhaps it is the will of the king to allow his wisdom to attract followers on its own merit—independent of the grandeur of his office."

"But your boy informs me the king was not here merely to improve conditions in the local economy."

"The king wisely combines his purposes. Perhaps he sought a similar attraction, in a maiden."

Hildah chuckled out loud.

"This is your pronouncement on the matter?"

Abishag was silent. Hildah waited also.

"My lady. I am here on your invitation. I have not come to make pronouncements to you. But if you constrain me with direct questions, what am I to do? What has befallen me over the past six weeks was none of my choosing, and I am of all maidens the least deserving of it. I volunteer no claim before you, but nor can I deny the truth of what you ask. If you find my answers fanciful, I respectfully request leave to enjoy my private folly in silence."

Hildah studied the girl for a long moment. Abishag lowered her eyes to the floor. Hildah savored a deep puzzled sigh, studying the beautiful, gentle, and confident girl who sat before her.

"Well," she said at last. "You are a very fine girl Abishag, that much is obvious, and I owe you a great debt for my healing. I even find myself growing fond of you, though I am not quite sure why. It is clear that you will not take any recompense from me, so I am left with no way to reward your kindness, other than to perhaps enlighten you on matters that would be beyond the expected understanding of a peasant girl. If my council spares you some folly, let that serve as my thanks. Suppose that it were true, that the king, for his own inscrutable purposes, did design to go throughout the land unknown, in search of a maiden worthy of special honor. So be it. Now, there is a maiden, Asenath by name, eldest daughter of one of the chief elders in Jezreel. Perhaps you have heard of her. She is highly spoken of by all, born of an esteemed family, raised with every advantage. She can sing, play instruments, draw, and converse equitably, even with educated men. It is even reported that she can read and write. And none see her but once than that they thereafter declare that our valley has never seen a fairer face. When queen Chavah visited our area recently, Asenath was seated near to her, and I dare say our local princess outshone even her royal highness. If a maiden in our area possessed the graces to rise to queen status, it would surely be one such as she."

"My dear lady, I deny none of what you say. Who could dream that a lowly maidservant such as I could approach the esteem of such a glorious virgin? It would be great folly for me to even imagine such. But it cannot be doubted that the king already has available to him many maidens that compare to and perhaps even surpass the magnificent Asenath. However, if the king intended to honor the common Israelite girl, of plain face and untrained speech, what better means than to choose the plainest and lowliest of them all? And on that score, I am surely the champion," Abishag replied.

"Champion?" Hildah laughed out loud, shaking her head. "Champion of the plain and lowly! Are you truly that naïve? I am not certain *what* you are, but I am certain you are not that! You are so . . . so . . . so . . . " she broke off.

"I have been told that before my lady."

"Exactly! I am sure you are told such all the time. I have never seen a girl so high in natural graces, so low in self-regard. Very well then, maiden. Let us pretend it is as you say. If the king did design to go throughout the land dressed as a sheepherder to find for himself among the peasant girls a maiden worthy to be his queen—and I do not mean to concede that he did—but *if* he did, I am constrained to believe he did not miss his target . . . with you. You are extraordinary—and I hope, not extraordinarily naive. If, for the sake of discussion, every known convention is temporarily put aside, and we imagine you offered for the king's review, with nothing but the merit of your person to recommend you . . . I can understand why a king would desire such as you. Kings are known to collect rare treasures, and he would likely find very few of your species."

Abishag flushed at the compliment.

"Thank you my lady."

"And for your sake, I hope you are correct," Hildah added. "You will forgive me if I yet find this difficult to accept. There remain puzzling questions, such as why a king would abandon his chosen bride to all this suffering, even prison, without his knowledge or protection. It is to Simeon, absent the king's help, that you owe your release, and it was I who intervened with him on your behalf. So much the more difficult it would be for my husband to believe your tale, for how, after it was necessary that he come to your aid, is he to believe that you were under the protection of the king?"

"No doubt the lord Simeon is a great and wise man. It is only meet that he should doubt such a fantastic story. And the king's purposes may be difficult to discern. However, your cure certainly does not escape his notice. Does your husband also find it difficult to accept that you are made whole so quickly?"

Hildah shot her a quick glance, and hesitated.

"Is he not yet aware of the treatment that produced your cure?" Abishag asked.

Hildah leaned in and took a confidential tone.

"Abishag. You must understand. Simeon would not take well the knowledge that I declined Jockshan's treatments, in favor of yours."

"A most fair reaction, for one in his position. Yet he certainly takes well your recovery and no doubt credits it to treatments that are killing the wives of other men. With your cure, my lady, comes a responsibility."

"You are direct, maiden."

"People are dying, my lady. Surely my frankness is justified. Would you deny, for your own convenience, the cure which snatched you from the grave, but leave them to die in ignorance?"

"But I have denied nothing."

Abishag nodded slowly.

"When there is so much to deny, my lady. If per chance, some day, our whole village stands before the king, will you want it to be said, on that day, that you were cured by his wisdom, while others died under Jockshan's? Yet, you denied nothing?"

Hildah opened her mouth, but spoke not. Abishag held her gaze. Then, Hildah looked down, and smoothed her garment nervously.

Suddenly, urgent voices were heard approaching the house. Hildah and Abishag looked toward the sound. Moments later, two men entered the house, the first being Simeon, of the chief elders, who walked briskly with his head down, while behind him entered Jockshan the physician, talking as he walked behind him, his face ashen.

"How was I to know?" Jockshan demanded, "Who could have predicted this? No mortal can be held responsible for what

God alone could foresee. Our plans were not flawed, they were sabotaged!"

Simeon circled to pace the room as Jockshan followed behind him.

"It was a wild and risky scheme from the start Jockshan!" Simeon retorted, whirling to face him. "I told you that from the start and I tell you again. Only now, it is much too late for you to heed my counsel. Cooperation with Hamon has kept us in peace these years. Patience is the answer, not confrontation. Hamon is young—his father was once young and brash as he—but time, *time* is what will reform him, not baiting his ego with challenges, such as this reckless attempt to buy him out. Now you appeal to the elders to rescue you from your self-inflicted disaster! This is your affair not ours. What do you expect council would be able to do?"

Being absorbed in their discussion, the two men had not at first noticed the women who sat wide-eyed in a corner of the room, but now saw them as they turned. Hildah arose.

"Simeon. What has happened?" she husked.

The chief elder looked over at her and back, rubbing the back of his neck, then collapsed in a chair, rubbing his eyes with his palms.

"The harvest is lost," he muttered bitterly.

"Of the Brotherhood?" Hildah gaped.

"Yes."

"How?"

"We were attacked on the road to Jezreel," Jockshan explained, trembling. "There was no chance for us, no chance! They came from both ends, as we crossed the bog. We could not turn, we could not run, and we could not fight. We were sorely outnumbered. We were lucky to escape with our lives—and the capture of one attacker who chanced to slip into the swamp. But the harvest—all of it—is gone. Carried off, spilled, or cast into the water."

The eyes of Hildah and Abishag grew wide.

"By whom? Who did this?!" Hildah exclaimed.

"They wore Hittite armor—battle armor, and full face helmets. Twenty of them at least. They were well organized, ten coming from each direction. It was a planned raid."

"Hittites!" Hildah exclaimed. "We have not had a Hittite raid in this area since . . . since Solomon took the throne!"

Simeon looked up at his wife painfully, glancing over at the other maiden whom he vaguely recognized.

"Simeon," Jockshan began again, "Hamon will repossess. He will repossess everything! The council must stop him—you must have one voice!"

"Stop him?! How will we stop him? He has a legally sealed covenant! Sealed by you—and every member of your wretched Brotherhood! We have no grounds to stop him!"

"But you must resist him—pressure him! Pledge repayment, bind yourselves to an oath, vow to find other options, but do not let this repossession go forward!"

"It is not a repossession Jockshan. It is retention of possession. Hamon owns the land, you were attempting to buy it back."

"But it is not his land, it is God's land!" Jockshan shouted.

"And God wrote the laws by which it now stands in Hamon's control! We have no power to rewrite them!"

"No Simeon! No! I do not charge the Almighty with this iniquity! It is *your* cowardice that allowed it to fall into Hamon's control. Cowardice! A council of cowards!"

"Jockshan! You are not a lawyer, you are a doctor. You simply are not trained to understand these things. Do you not think that elders who have spent their entire lives examining the law would have found another way if there was one to be found? But your recklessness has turned the dreams of hundreds of innocent families into a nightmare! You have a fine talent, doctor, but it is not law. You have cured my wife—and that is the *only* thing I have to thank you for. Stick with doctoring from now on."

Jockshan blinked, and looked over at Hildah, confused. Hildah froze and paled. Simeon noticed the strange reaction in his wife, and frowned. Abishag carefully leaned forward on her seat.

"Simeon," Hildah whispered, her eyes watering.

Jockshan looked afresh at the maiden who sat silently on the couch behind Hildah, and recognition came over his face, after which he fell into a deep stunned silence. Simeon looked back and forth between his wife and Jockshan confused.

"She is cured, is she not?" Simeon asked Jockshan, suddenly uncertain.

"I cannot rightly testify to the truth of that fact, Simeon." Jockshan replied evenly, "For I have not examined her."

"Not exa . . ." Simeon began.

"Nor have I treated her. But perhaps . . . someone has," he added, casting a glance past Hildah to Abishag.

"Simeon," Hildah said. "I *am* whole—*completely* whole! But not by the treatments of the doctor. I have secured for myself, another remedy."

Simeon's eyes widened.

"Hildah! You have not partaken of that which brought death upon Orpha!?"

"My lord!" Hildah said, "It has healed me! I am perfectly cured! That which Abishag has given me has . . ." She broke off, covering her mouth.

Simeon looked narrowly at Abishag, and his face reddened.

"What have you done? What have you done to her?!"

"She has done nothing, my lord!" Hildah broke in. "My recovery began from the first day and now . . . "

"Orpha recovered at first too! And then she died!"

"Simeon!" Jockshan broke in. "There may be yet time to save her. If she is brought to my healing room at once, perhaps we can sweat the poison out of her!"

Simeon hesitated in shock. Then turned quickly.

"Go! Go at once!"

"I will take her and go," Jockshan replied quickly. "But you—you must call the elders! Call an emergency meeting, speak to the council! Please, do this for me, for I cannot prevail upon them and save the life of your wife at the same time!"

"Yes . . ." Simeon said, dazed, "yes . . . I will speak to them for you . . ."

"Thank you my lord," Jockshan replied, stepping forward to take Hildah by the arm, "I will be forever in your debt."

He forcibly ushered the protesting Hildah out the door. Abishag found herself oddly alone with Simeon, the chief elder, who leaned forward in his chair, rubbing his eyes. When he raised his head, his eyes fell upon the maiden seated on the couch across the room from him. His face twisted into a scowl.

"What kind of demon are you?" he hissed. "I intervened for you, at my wife's request, and this is how you reward me?"

Slowly, Abishag arose, took two steps toward him, and then dropped to her knees, bowing her face to the ground before him.

"My lord," he heard her say softly, her voice muffled into the carpet. "I am not worthy even to set foot in your house, let alone to address you. But you have asked me a question. If your great kindness will suffer me space to respond, I will speak truly."

Simeon stared at the woman on the floor. Abishag moved not, remaining prostrate, and silent. A long and painful silence ensued, until Simeon realized the maiden was neither going to move nor speak again, but at his command.

"Maiden," he hissed, "you are dismissed from my house."

Abishag silently arose, keeping her head down, and moved

quickly toward the door. She was nearly upon it, when Simeon made a noise, causing her to hesitate.

"Unless . . . he said, "you can impart some knowledge of how the poison you have given my wife, can be neutralized."

Abishag turned, looking at the tortured man with compassion, then lowered her eyes once again.

"I would only advise my lord of this: The medicine which your wife has taken, is more than two weeks in her system. No amount of bathing will remove it from her now. If your wife survives, you will know by this that the treatments of the doctor did not save her from my medicine, but that my medicine saved her from the disease."

Simeon trembled.

"Get out!"

Abishag quickly turned, and left the room.

Chapter 16

It is better to hear the rebuke of the wise, than for a man to hear the song of fools.

Ecclesiastes 7:5

As Abishag made her way out of the city and up the hill trail toward her home, her thoughts a-swirl with the shocking news of the destruction of the Brotherhood harvest, word of it was also spreading via runners from farm to farm, pulling a dark blanket of despair over every hill and vale. Never had a day so bright in hope been rendered so dark in spirit.

The harvest is lost!

Abishag's hand reached up and clutched the royal seal of Solomon that hung about her neck, knowing that in it lay the answer to every man's destroyed dreams. One day she would wield it. Was that day now upon her?

Presently, she became aware of footsteps approaching behind her, and turned to see a gangly tall man, out of breath, stumbling desperately toward her.

"Abishag!" he cried.

"Hemanah."

"Abishag! Something dreadful has happened!" he choked, stumbling up to her, out of breath. "You must return, with me, in all haste! There has been a catastrophe, a disaster worse than you could ever imagine."

"I know of the attack Hemanah."

"You do? You do! Oh, Abishag, but you don't understand! All is lost! All the harvest—and with it, all the land! Oh, God have mercy upon us!—Hamon is going to repossess everything! All I have—and all that *you* have Abishag! My fields, your vineyard, the house, everything!—I pledged it all! Nothing will be left to us!" he wrenched, staggering in a circle. "Come back with me Abishag—everyone must come, as many people as possible! Jockshan is going to entreat the counsel. We must all go. We must prevail upon them to intervene, save us from this disaster! We must . . . "

"Hemanah!"

He looked sharply over at her, stunned and surprised. Never in his life could he remember his sister speaking to him—or anyone—in such a crisp tone.

"Have faith in God," she said softly, looking directly at him. "It is, after all, *His* land."

He stared at her wide-eyed, as though beholding some kind of apparition.

"And do not fear, brother," she added, before he could find breath to respond, sounding as unafraid as her counsel, "do not fear."

"How . . . can . . . you speak such?"

"I can speak no other and be true. No matter how dark the hour, the end will not be calamity, but restoration. I will go with you, as you have said, but not to beg. A boy once stood before a giant, and victory came to him through faith in God. Even so is it today. The wisdom of the king covers the land as a blanket. There is no injustice so dark that the light of His eye cannot expose it, and no crime so distant that the arm of His justice cannot reach. Such a land has not room for fear."

Hemanah gaped at the strange apparition that stood before him. A sphere of peace seemed to emanate out from her, enfolding him like a warm cloak, an island of calm in an overpowering storm. No words equal to her counsel were found in him. Inhaling to retort and hesitating, he instead let out the telltale cough, and was tossed in the grip of it for some moments.

Abishag's eyes misted, beholding her confused, desperate, despairing, and now, sick brother.

"And no dreadful disease safe from his cures," she added softly. "Stay with me, Hemanah, and I promise you, all will be well."

She reached out her hand, projecting warmth into his tormented eyes. With a shudder, he melted before the gentle confident creature that beckoned him with her warm entreaty. Trembling and speechless, he found his hand reaching for hers, as a falling man reaches for a rope, and felt in it the strength of a sure rescue. She pulled him close, and he wept. Together they turned and walked. The sniffing, confused, wavering brother was supported more by Abishag's mysterious strength than by his own feet. Shamelessly, Hemanah leaned on her, both surprised and thankful to find in his long under-valued sister a strong pillar, in a storm.

****

The room was sultry. With each new party that entered the place where the hastily assembled council was wrestling with the shocking news, the pressure mounted, threatening it seemed to bulge the very walls. If brick and stone could tremble with human anxiety, this building surely would.

At first, only a few senior members of the council had convened, their low terse conversations frequently interrupted by hurriedly arriving members, for whom the state of things was rehearsed. It was early evening when Jockshan himself arrived, leaving the wife of Simeon in the steam-bath, under close watch of his apprentice. His entrance was met with a foreboding hush. In his desperation, the shrewd doctor had dispatched messengers to all quarters, summoning farmers, peasants, and stakeholders, any and all who would, to come make their appeals to the council in person. Soon these were entering, passing freely by doormen with a determination the latter were not equal to resist. Young and old, trembling work-hardened farmers, together with their weeping wives, children in tow, continued to stream in, filling the room, standing in aisles and around the back, raising the temperature, even as they raised the stakes high and clear before those who had the power to intervene in the economic avalanche that hung waiting to break, when news of the lost harvest reached Baal Hamon.

Abishag and Hemanah found themselves barely able to enter for the crowd, the sister unable to see anything, until Hemanah pushed to the room's corner, leading her to where they were both able to glimpse the proceedings. A farmer was standing before the council making an urgent appeal for intervention. The faces of the council were deeply furrowed with lines of anxiety. Their usual argumentative style, born of years of theoretical wranglings, was wholly ill-suited to the frantic appeals of their desperate countrymen. Rhetorical tactics honed in debates over trivia fell uselessly before men whose whole appeal was born of emotion. Simeon wiped perspiration from his brow as he looked up to meet the despairing eyes of yet another distraught farmer, standing with his wife and children to plead, beg, and add his most earnest appeal for intervention.

Once again, Abishag found herself in the company of another, only this time, Hildah, coming up from behind, took her arm, and stood resolutely. Abishag's eyes widened in surprise.

"Hildah! How are you away from the steam bath!?"

"It would take a larger boy than Jockshan left me with to

detain me in that cauldron of death. It must not be thought that those treatments saved me. Besides, the fate of many Israelites hangs in the balance here today, and I have reason to believe you may have hidden means to sway the results. I am here to support that means—and you. As you have rightly instructed me, certain responsibilities have recently befallen me, which I cannot neglect."

Abishag studied the woman's eyes.

"The Lord reward you, my lady."

Hildah nodded and squeezed her hand.

The council turned and spoke lowly with one another, aware of the host of peering eyes and ears that strained to hear any uttered word. Frank and candid deliberations were impossible under the stares. Simeon glanced up at the approach of Jockshan, and immediately bid him to come near. The two men spoke lowly for some moments, and Simeon nodded with relief, as the doctor assured him of the care of his wife. Then another query ensued. The council wanted to know the exact amount of the shortfall, and what amount would meet the difference lost by the harvest. Jockshan gave them the figure, which was met with moans of disgust, followed by somber head shaking. An elder at the end of the table stood up.

"Jockshan—surely you know there is not man in the valley who can raise such a sum. Who has funds equal to the collected harvest of all of these farmers—other than Hamon himself? The figure is beyond reason for our area—and would surely strain the coffers of the richest in Israel. Where do you suppose such gold is to be suddenly found—conjured up out of the dust by some magic spell?"

"It is not necessary to cover the entire shortfall all at once—but simply secure a pledge until next harvest where we will make up the difference," Jockshan replied.

Another elder replied to him.

"By what madness do you expect to make up two years of harvest in a single year? You will not retain even half of those who are invested with you now. No, this is wholly untenable. You will never raise the funds in one year."

The crowd which had pressed forward, protested and chorused an appeal. Jockshan stilled them with his hand.

"With the clear and open support of the council to strengthen them, every investor will return—and more will enlist. And if we do not attain what is needed in one year, then we will in two—or three or four! Only keep the agreement with Hamon alive through negotiated payments until the buyout is fully achieved. It can be done, I tell you! It *must* be done."

The crowd agreed.

"Jockshan—all of our means combined could not raise that much money!"

"But given proper terms, and land offered in surety, there is enough. This I say: negotiate a manageable payment, but by no means project to Hamon the appearance of any lack. He has the heart of a bloodhound; he will pounce like a dog smelling fear. But his hand can be stayed with firm assurance—and a unanimous voice. Pool your resources. Secure a delay. We will address the source of the funds at a later time."

An elder at the end of the bench who had thus far remained quiet suddenly stood.

"Address funds after our land is pledged!?—just as it was with this first failed attempt!? You would have us bind ourselves to a sinking ship, and then hope we can repair it! It is this foolish policy of deferring to later times that raised the axe that is now poised above your own neck! Half the valley is poised to default to Hamon—leaving no resources remaining to seed redemption for at least a generation. Under your plan, *both* halves of the valley will fall. One does not stay an avalanche by diving into it. The elders have a duty to protect those who still have something left to protect—who were not carried away with your folly."

"It was not folly, it was tragedy! An intrusion by forces beyond our control—an act of God! Our plan was working! No man could have predicted this outcome!"

This time Simeon replied.

"You have called it an act of God, Jockshan, and rightly so. Clearly God has spoken. To proceed in kind next year would be the same risk bound to greater stakes. The Almighty has revealed the foolishness of this scheme plainly before us all. Any man with a hint of prudence will heed Him, and not repeat this folly."

As the course of the discussion became clear, observers' faces went ashen, and hearts fell.

"This will not stand." Abishag heard a man near her seething to his neighbor. "We will fight. We have remained passive too long. Our fathers died for this land—it is rightfully ours. Hamon will have a war on his hands."

His neighbor shook his head.

"He controls the militia, he is supported by the elders, and he has a legal covenant. There are no grounds for armed resistance, and no chance of defeating him in such a battle."

"I would rather die on the side of right than live on the side of wrong," the man spat. "I will no longer live as a slave on my own land."

Several around him seemed to be in agreement with his sentiments, and Abishag noticed a wild gleam forming in Hemanah's eye, as he stared in the direction of the instigator.

Jockshan and the elders seemed to have fallen into a sulking silence, each staring at the other, with nothing left to say. The room felt stiflingly hot.

Abishag sensed Hildah drawing near.

"Daughter," she said lowly, "if you have something to bring to bear on this situation, know that I will support you, if you step forth now."

Abishag moved not, a deep, most impenetrable air about her. A tinge of doubt crept over Hildah's face, as she studied the motionless maiden curiously.

"I am not certain it is the time, my lady," Abishag whispered.

"If this is not the time, what is? Use the seal. Step forth and declare now—if you truly have means to declare."

Abishag began to lean forward almost imperceptibly, but then held once again.

"Well then . . . ," Simeon began, clearing his throat to address the crowd.

Suddenly, all heads turned at the sound of a noise to the side. Appearing in the doorway was Ono, accountant for Hamon's estate, holding in his hand a sealed scroll on which small printed text was visible. The crowd gasped at the recognition of him, realizing his presence portended the immediate entrance of Hamon behind him. A tense moment of silence passed, as every eye watched the door, but looking beyond Ono, none other was seen. A curious glance passed between the elders.

Then a strange and unidentifiable noise echoed from beyond the door. A moment later two servants passed the threshold, bearing poles on their shoulders, and behind them, two more servants bearing the other end of the same poles. Between the servants, and suspended from the poles, hung a chair, and in the chair hunched a man. As surprising as the entrance of the strange entourage was, the man in the chair claimed immediate attention from all present, by reason of the fact that he appeared to be in open anguish, and that to a degree sufficient to bring a collective gasp from everyone in the room. The servants continued to bear their charge directly into the center of room, where they ceased and lowered him, and the man winced as the chair contacted the floor.

Hamon raised his eyes gingerly, keeping his whitened hands on the chair rails for support. His face was contorted, his forehead covered with perspiration, as his eyes raised upon a room full of shocked, wide-eyed faces. Jockshan took a slow step forward, hesitating before the agonizing man.

"Baal Hamon," Simeon said, astounded.

Hamon turned slightly at the sound, wincing and turning back again. Gripping one rail of his chair more firmly, he gingerly raised the other hand in greeting.

"Blessings, my brothers," he husked, in a tortured voice.

No one moved, all were staring.

"Please forgive my rude intrusion. I confess, my intention on this of all days was to remain on my couch, tending to my healing, but news of the recent disaster being told to me, I could not but appear before you. Anything less, would be unworthy of you."

The humility of his greeting, uttered as it was in such manifest pain, caused the already quieted room to congeal into a stunned hush, as many leaned forward to see and hear. A servant wiped Hamon's forehead and held a mug of water before him, which he took and drank. Then he raised his eyes again.

"This recent news, of the loss of your harvest," he began, "I may have received with delight, only a few short days ago. This I admit to my great shame. But what has befallen me between then and now has so reversed my thoughts that I can no longer conceive of a man who would receive this unspeakable tragedy with anything but distress— Blessed be the name of the Lord."

A few in the room exchanged curious glances with one another.

"Much in the way of explanation is due you, my brothers, if you will bear it," he added.

Many in the room murmured, and Simeon raised his hand for silence, and then gestured for Hamon to continue. Hamon leaned forward, and began to speak, huffing lowly, and slowly in an ominous tone.

"Brothers, I will not delay revealing to you the meaning of my strange address before you today. The night before last, shortly after midnight, I was asleep, in the dreams of the night, when suddenly, I was awakened by a horrible noise, a noise of such unearthly resonance that the very room, it seemed, trembled in its echoes."

Hamon paused and looked around, all were listening.

"I opened my eyes to behold a strange and brilliant apparition, a light from heaven, hovering over me, close enough to touch, yet blinding as the noonday sun. I shielded my face from its paralyzing glare. So terrified was I at the sight, that I thought my heart would fail me. Then . . . it spoke. Yes, truly, the holy light did speak to me—a voice from the light, and in an oracle so dreadful, so appalling, that I loathed even life itself. The divine voice that emanated from that awful light, charged me, convicted me, and sentenced me. I became as dead. My sins lay before me, as the light hovered over me and I trembled beneath it, my bedcovers insufficient to hide me from its terrible stare. Then, with a parting word, it left me in silence, with one final word: 'Unless thou repent,' it said. The room went dark and silent as death itself. I could not move nor speak for hours. I clung to my bed in terror, praying for dawn, that I might find a priest, lest my life sink into the dread pit of Sheol as a heathen forever—guilty, judged, and sentenced, as those who shun holy circumcision rightly deserve."

There were gasps and murmurings in the room.

"Yes. Yes, my brothers and sisters, Israelites who honor our fathers Moses, and Abraham, I was constrained by that light, and that voice instructed that I have been weighed in the balance and have fallen dreadfully short in the scales of the Almighty. It is not enough for me to live among the family of Israel, for Israel must be the throb of my heart, as it is for you. It shames me to learn at such a late hour in life the depth of my depravity, but I am grateful beyond expression that the God of our fathers has found the grace to reveal to me my dreadful error, and allowed me space to repent, before executing his righteous judgment. Short of that grace, I would be of all men most rightfully condemned."

Hamon paused, and the servant wiped his forehead again.

"Hamon—you have been circumcised?" Simeon asked.

"It is done, as of this very morning."

There were murmurings in the room.

"And though I find the experience unspeakably rude in body, I would repeat it a thousand times for the ecstasy it has brought to my heart, and the blindness it has lifted from my eyes. Now, I see plainly the treasure that has dwelt before me continually: the family of Israel, the desire of the nations, the hope of the world. And I now understand that it is through the chosen family of Israel, and through it alone, that peace and equity can flow out to the rest of the world. To think that I lived among you for so long, and never comprehended this—it shames and embarrasses me! But though I am of all men most unworthy, your God, in his infinite grace, has received my repentance, and accepted me as His love slave. His ways, from this time forth, are my ways."

"When I heard of the loss of your harvest, I knew instantly what I must do. The accountant of my estate, Ono, has with him the covenant between myself and the Brotherhood, and the record of your payments to date in your noble attempt to redeem your land."

At that, Hamon's mouth soured, and he shook his head in self-disgust. "As though a man's rightful land ever should be in need of redemption. For it is his always." He spoke sullenly, as if speaking a great insult. "Ono, please allow me the instrument."

Hamon weakly lifted an open hand. Ono placed a rolled document in it.

"Brothers, this very hour, I make an official restoration of all that is true and right, and I loathe to delay it a minute longer. In this scroll is my legal title to that which is yours. Oh! *My* right to what is *yours*. The very *terms* are anathema! Only a madman could dream such insanity—and such a madman was I. But no longer. As an Israelite brother, I retain neither the right nor the desire to keep for myself the property of my kinsmen. Family cannot oppress family."

Hamon started to unroll the scroll, pursing his lips as his eyes traveled over the contents, shaking his head.

"Abomination," he said bitterly. "This abomination must be destroyed. This holy land was never my possession. Nor was it my father's. It is only by your great charity that I have been allowed to share a single scrap of this bounteous land that God has laid to your charge, and to live among you. Harvest or no harvest, this land—every cubit of it—must be restored to its rightful ownership. Ono, please remove this abomination from my sight. It sickens me."

He held the roll up by the end. Ono took it.

"Burn it! Burn it now, before us all!"

Ono lifted the scroll to a nearby torch, held one end into the flame, and then held the burning scroll out before him by the end, while Hamon continued speaking to the stunned and trembling crowd.

"This is just the first of many amends that I intend to make before you my brothers, and before all my kinsmen in this city."

Ono dropped the burning scroll to the ground, as the flame consumed it, leaving a smoldering pile of black ashes.

Hamon lifted his eyes to the people.

"My dear brothers," he said, "the land, is yours."

One can only imagine the stunned silence that followed such a performance at such a place, in such a moment. From elder to peasant and everyone in between, not a breath could be found to answer the scene just witnessed, as wide eyes beheld the man on the chair, and then looked to one another, as if in search of evidence that it was not a mere dream that just passed.

"It's a miracle!" someone finally whispered, and many among the crowd began to tremble and weep. The marvel that lay before them began to be rehearsed throughout the room in halting terms that barely broke the plane of stunned tongue-tied silence. The rustling continued, building in momentum to include more overt corporate sighs of relief, followed by open rejoicing, as the reality sunk into collective consciousness. Hamon lowered his face into his hands, and began to tremble, heave, and weep before them all.

Those near enough instinctively stepped forward to comfort the sobbing man, hesitating at the last moment to comfort him gently in respect for his condition. Women wept, and men never good friends embraced and hugged. The amazed exultation reflected in the faces, voices, eyes, and manner, of each and every person in the room. Every, that is, save one. Abishag, the Shunnamite, remained still and thoughtful, even as Hildah and Hemanah embraced her from either side—an island of doubt, in a sea of belief.

Chapter 17

And through his policy also he shall cause craft to prosper in his hand; and he shall magnify himself in his heart, and by peace shall destroy many: he shall also stand up against the Prince of princes; but he shall be broken without hand.

Daniel 8:25

Over the course of the week that followed Hamon's miraculous turnaround, the elders and the Brotherhood held a series of meetings with the young lord to arrange for the orderly repatriation of the land, even as the news of his astonishing conversion spread to neighboring towns. In all of these meetings, Hamon faltered not to maintain his initial contrition, garnishing it with a humility of manner that descended so deeply in meekness that members of the council began to advise him that he was being too harsh on himself. All of these forays Hamon resisted; there was not a remark concerning his past behavior low enough that he could not plunge beneath it in his own self-evaluations. What a terrifying vision that must have been!—to so fully turn such a depraved man. And the authenticity of his conversion was clearly proven by his relentless insistence on the immediate restoration of all of his land to the Israelites in the Brotherhood. As astonishing as it was, the miracle was undeniable.

So vigorous was Hamon's divestiture that the elders began to worry that he was acting too hastily—that he would leave himself with no way to make a living, owning no rightful inheritance of his own. With some difficulty, Hamon was convinced to retain, for the time being, the lands not included in the Brotherhood buyout, to allow himself time to transition to another means of employment.

It was in the course of these events, that it came to be observed that Hamon, more than any other, had accurately foreseen the vulnerability of the area to attack. However oppressive his economic principles had been, he was manifestly correct when it came to the importance of maintaining a local army. In private meetings, the elders began to sound the idea that Hamon could perhaps make a useful contribution to the community, by continuing to lead and strengthen the militia.

"He certainly has leadership skills, and his cunning cannot be doubted. What man is more fit to be the watchdog of our protection?" —was the common thought. In a follow-up meeting, the possibility was put to Hamon himself, who, after expressing great surprise that he would be considered for such a role, declined quickly, and fell into stunned silence. He was, however, coaxed into offering an opinion on the matter, after being advised that it was his duty, if he saw any weaknesses through which an enemy could damage his countrymen, to reveal them.

"Since you have urged me to comment," Hamon replied, "and though my unworthiness to even sit among you weighs heavily upon me, if per chance through my observations the security of our region could be improved, perhaps through this I could atone for some small portion of my many sins. I categorically deny that my counsel is deserving of even the slightest esteem, but since you have prevailed upon me to reply, I would direct attention to the following: in recent days, there was a stranger among us, who, if you will recollect, succeeded in weakening us through our own disunity. Surely a great weakness was revealed among us, for if a single man could so easily dissemble us, what could a real enemy do? It seemed, in that case, that we were all cleverly played against each other—the elders, the Brotherhood, and myself, by this cunning man. I do not presume to instruct, but if our security is to be improved, I cannot but think this breach must be addressed first. There are too many divergent voices among us; we could never act quickly and decisively, such as would be needed when under attack. To remedy this, perhaps it would be more efficient, if we could unify these three groups into a single panel, with representatives from them all. A council—say, a "Council of Kinsmen"—consisting of two from each party: two from the Elders, two from my estate and the militia, and two from the Brotherhood. These could convene to make decisions for all."

Hamon's council was thoughtfully heard, and seemed to contain a fair bit of sense in the wake of the recent Hittite raid, the one flaw being that six members of a voting panel could be locked three to three. The meeting was adjourned, and the matter delayed pending further consideration, but in the next gathering, one of the elders put forth a bold and daring solution: if Hamon himself were added as a seventh member, such a deadlock could be avoided. One can only imagine the shock and dismay with which Hamon received this proposal, but the gentle urging of the council and others softened him, and he was gradually convinced to accept the post. So it was that Baal Hamon became the official chair of the "Council of Kinsmen," a new form of city government, charged to preserve and protect the security of all the people of Shunem. Owing to the recent attack, the Council of Kinsmen was urged to convene quickly, and bolster the city's defenses, lest another like tragedy befall them. This they did, and began to take steps at once.

The first order of business for the new council was to formulate a response to the recent attack. Toward that end, it was clear that the one Hittite raider who had been captured, Pildash, who was being held in prison, must be questioned. Hamon, who had not known until that time that there had been a captured raider, surprised the council with an instant and vigorous response. He was suddenly focused, serious, and direct—much more than his meek manner thus far would have portended. He immediately insisted he should be given full responsibility for the interrogation.

"I have been a foreigner—I know how they think. I will best be able to derive from the captured Hittite the information we need, if there is any to be gained. He will tell me things that he would never tell any of you."

Faced with such direct and confident advice, the six members gave Hamon leave to handle the situation as he deemed best, believing they were already seeing the value of having such a man as Hamon as an ally.

Chapter 18

The mouth of a righteous man is a well of life: but violence covereth the mouth of the wicked.

Proverbs 10:11

Abishag was in her vineyard. Habits a lifetime in making are not easily broken. Having invested so many years among her vineyard rows, she now found herself drawn to them more for solace than necessity. With such large portions of her life in transition, the vines that were the backdrop of her private reverie for so long afforded the comfort of familiarity. The harvest now complete, the next task was to check and secure the vine tyings, and make sure everything was in order for the winter.

Barkos and Jared had already finished most of the work, but she could not pass by the vineyard, as she now was doing almost daily, without finding her eyes pulled in its direction, and she had noticed a couple of things that could be improved. At work at those tasks now, in the very nest in which her love was birthed, memories of her beloved rushed upon her. The aching she felt for him seemed to grow in intensity as she lingered there. He was near her, moving among the vines. His melodic voice was in the rustling leaves; the aura of his presence floating up from the very earth as it were, sending her on a rapturous swirl between dream and daydream.

Then, suddenly she did see him! Tall and elegant, seated on a large rock, by the trail at the far end of the row she now worked. She caught her breath and her pulse quickened as she stared, stunned. Her basket of tools tumbled from her hand, and she hastened down the row toward him.

She was not far along when the whole world suddenly whirled around in the opposite direction and she recognized the tall man on the rock as not Solomon, but Hamon. He looked up at her approach and raised his hand. She hesitated, but then continued on, her rapture fading, and her apprehension rising.

Hamon did not rise, but remained on the rock. When she reached the trail, it also became apparent that he was alone. She knew he seldom traveled unaccompanied, and that would have been strange enough, but something else caught her attention. His expression revealed great agony restrained, and frailty, as though if he were to leave the rock, he could scarcely stand. Her empathy stirred.

"Hamon! Are you in need of service?"

He nodded an acknowledgement at her approach, and attempted something like a courteous smile.

"Abishag. You are kind as always, but I am afraid there is no help for the ailment from which I now suffer."

"You are here alone," she observed, looking around behind him.

"I am."

He fell to silence, causing her to puzzle, looking again at and beyond him for any clue of his purpose.

"Well—may I assist you in some way?"

"Abishag. My dear old friend. It would be well if you could, but the task that stands before me cannot be aided by another. I am neither sick nor injured, as you suppose, though for many years I have been worse than either. But now, though I am physically afflicted, my soul is finally at peace. I have come to speak to you of this, and, to offer you my repentance, and to make amends for all of my offenses toward you."

She studied him warily, trying to discern his words, draped as they were with humble manner and physical affliction.

"Apologize? For what?"

He shook his head.

"It is rare grace that would ask such, my old friend, and more kindness than I deserve. More rightly, you might ask what I have *not* to apologize for. If there is a sin I have not been guilty of, it was not for lack of trying. I have realized, of late, that I have many amends to make in this town, and I owe more of them to you than anyone."

"I do not understand."

"Charming innocence. Abishag, I have mistreated you—dreadfully. I presumed of you, as of everything else, that you existed only to be my pleasing possession. I believed that I deserved to have you, when the truth of the matter was as opposite as day is from night. I never deserved you, Abishag; you are more righteous than I. My sins against you are many—sins both in word and in deed. Since my conversion, I have been engaged in a circuit of restoration, appealing to those I have wronged to learn if there is anything I might do to atone for my many offenses. In our case, my wrongs may be beyond repair, but I can at least extend my apology, and leave the forgiveness in your honorable hands. I hope I will be as well received by Jehovah."

"Repent? You are apologizing to me?"

"I am."

She smoothed the side of her veil with her hand.

"Well. News of your reform has reached me."

He shook his head humbly.

"Of all of the religions to which a man can convert, I can think of none more painful to a grown man than yours, but what choice have I? A religion is chosen for its truth, not its convenience."

She continued to regard him carefully, quite unsure what to say to the humble and pitiable creature that sat on the rock before her, behaving as little like the Hamon she had come to know as a frog is like a bird.

"You despise me no doubt," he said to her careful silence.

"Despise!? No, Hamon, I do not despise you—I never have despised you—truly."

He waved his hand.

"You are too kind, my friend. You were right to despise me—you would have been wrong to not. Besides, if I despise what I was, why should not you? No doubt forgivencss is far too much to ask of you."

"Hamon I . . . well, you have been . . . I have been perhaps disappointed at some of your actions in the past, but, I would not go so far to say that forgiveness is impossible. Forgiveness answers to repentance. As long as repentence is possible, forgiveness is possible."

Hamon teared up, attempted to speak, hesitated, then continued in a choked voice.

"I always believed it. I always believed it. You of all people, who have been offended the most, can now forgive the quickest. You, Abishag—bless the thought—are almost not human—an angel! Even when doubts assailed me—crying out that I surely had offended beyond the reach of the most forgiving of souls, I informed those doubts that they did not know my Abishag. Your well is deeper than most."

"Hamon, forever and always is forgiveness available to the truly repentant."

"Yes, yes, I had heard it was so, and allowed it as a charitable exaggeration, but now I see it is the truth. Your kindness is beyond measure. But enough of my suffering, what of yours? Surely I have too little respect for your own grief. After losing your beloved in such a dreadful way, one could wonder how you have coped."

She glanced up.

"Lose him? Why do you say I lost him?"

He looked at her in surprise, then shock, and quickly turned away shaking his head.

"Oh my lands, have I said too much? Oh wretched man that I am! How can I of all people be the one upon whom it falls to bring you this news, after all the pain I have already caused you! You truly do not know? Surely, I deserve this; it is my fitting penance. I am the most pitiable of all men!"

"But I did not lose him."

"Oh, and this is what you believe! This is dreadful beyond speaking! Of course you believe him alive—how could you know any different? Oh, that you could have chanced upon the news in the market—for it is well known. Why must I, at this moment when amends are my purpose, be the one who breaks your spirit with this terrible truth? And he was such an incomparable man too, a prince among us, and I, more than anyone, to blame for his demise. Truly the greater was destroyed by the lesser."

"Hamon, Jedidiah is alive—I don't know how or where you came to believe that he . . ."

Hamon was shaking his head and looking down.

"Hamon!"

He looked at her with compassion.

"I am so sorry Abishag. Perhaps I should leave now; I clearly have done enough. My best attempts to bring amends, and I blunder into this. And I so hoped that you would be able to marry happily, have the man who was worthy of you. One can wonder now if you will ever find another man of the same class."

Abishag had put her hand over her mouth and was staring at

him in disbelief. He noted it, and took on a paternal expression, which frustrated her.

"Hamon, Jedidiah lives."

He leaned in closer and spoke gently.

"Abishag. As unwelcome as it is, I have too much respect for you to deny you the truth. I would never presume to bring you such a painful truth without full knowledge. What I tell you, I know firsthand. When Jedidiah escaped, the elders demanded that he be chased and caught. I had no desire to participate, but since I had horses, they insisted that I was best fitted to catch up to him on that fateful day. My men—they set out west toward Tyre. It was a wet day, he was truly not hard to track. I warned my men to avoid conflict at all cost but then . . ." Hamon's voice trailed off as he appeared to choke up, and turned his head to the side. A moment later he looked back at her with tear filled eyes.

"He knew he was being chased, and he knew he could neither escape, nor overcome us. We wanted to take him peacefully, but when we caught up with him, well, there was a struggle. Some of the young men—they became overly zealous. I tried to hurry—to stop them—but it was too late. In the confusion, he was struck with a sword, and killed. I saw it with my own eyes. It was a terrible day, a tragedy I wish I had never witnessed. To this day I wish with all my soul I could forget it, but the whole scene is forever burned into my mind. I will be tortured with the memory of it all my days. As he lay dying before me, his last words . . . they were of you, Abishag. Do you want to know what he said?"

Abishag was staring at him, stunned speechless. He was choked up, earnest, sincere, humble, and entirely believable in manner and inflection.

"He said to tell you that he loved you. That you must go on . . . without him. You should marry, find a man to provide you the life and family you always wanted. He said—hard as it may be—you must forget him, and go on."

Abishag stared at him most quizzically, as he continued to look at her most earnestly. How to reply!?

"Hamon," she said in a carefully measured tone, "since you have shown me such respect, enlightening me as you have, and since you were present to see the place where the tragedy happened, perhaps I may ask of you a favor that would be supremely dear to me."

"Anything you ask. Just name it."

"I must see the body. If my beloved be truly dead, and you were there, you would know where it is."

Hamon hesitated ever so slightly.

"We buried it there."

"Then I must go at once and pay my respects. Please take me there."

He blinked at her.

"Well, it is a fair distance off and . . ."

"I don't care if it is the other side of the world! This is my beloved, I must go at once! You asked if there was anything you could do for me, to atone for the past. Well, this is that atonement. Take me to the body without delay!"

Hamon hesitated.

"Abishag! Surely you are in a great trauma—having been imprisoned all those cold nights, and now this."

"Cold? How do you know it was cold?"

"Abishag! Do you know how desperately I worked to get you released? How I risked my reputation? So much has happened to you—your brother repossessing your vineyard. And your beloved dead, it is too much for any maiden to face. Surely you are dizzy from it all. How will you support yourself and your mother? And now you would to return to the site of your greatest pain? I advise otherwise—for *your* sake. I would bring you forward, not back, to happier thoughts—the future. You are deserving of so much. In fact—I can and am willing to offer you a much more useful recompense than the thing you ask. Even this: I offer you security, honor, a place in a respectable household, that you might be safe from your reckless and unpredictable brother. Who knows what he will do next? So this I present as my amends—and for this I have come: I offer to buy your vineyard, outright, and give it to you. Your land should not be at the mercy of your brother's every mistake. Yes, I will do this for you, it is the least I can do. You are grieving painfully, but surely you can see that your beloved would want you to accept this generosity of me."

"Hamon, your kindness is great. But surely you would not deny a grieving girl the comfort of her foolish choice. Take me to the body. It does not prevent you from making these amends afterwards."

"Certainly not. But my reconciliation does not stop with a miserable patch of land. Beyond this—and I have longed for you to know it— that I have not ceased to love you Abishag, though I had released you to your chosen suitor. I of all men was most thrilled to learn of your being promised. But now that tragedy has rendered that union impossible, I—*I* will cover you!—how could I do less? If you will have me, and extend to me the forgiveness that you have assured me is available, I would yet have you, to live in my house, as wife."

"A true honor of which I am unworthy. Yet I cannot possibly accept an offer from any man, no matter how generous, until I pay my respects to the body of my beloved."

Hamon took a deep breath.

"Abishag. We are friends. Truly, I know what the objection really is. It is not grief over the death of your beloved. Tell me truly. Have you not vowed that you could never marry a non-Israelite, which you assume me to be? But you err. I have been consulting our most holy Law, and have been counseling with the elders over this matter. It so happens, that I am indeed an Israelite, and I can prove it by the very Law that you think alienates me."

Abishag looked at him curiously.

"But, a man must be *born* an Israelite."

"And this is where you err. You judge by a superficial

understanding of what an Israelite truly is. I would ask you, was Abraham an Israelite?"

"He was the father of them all."

"Indeed he was, but on what basis? Abraham has no portion in the lineage of Jacob; he was Jacob's father. Abraham was a wanderer and a heathen just as was my father. So how did Abraham become an Israelite? You once asked me what tribe would I be. I have an answer now. I ask you this: what tribe was Abraham? Surely none of the twelve—or all of the twelve—for all the tribes were yet in his loins. But through circumcision, Abraham became an Israelite and the father of them all. I am an Israelite by the same rule. I am of any and *all* the tribes. I certainly cannot be denied citizenship when my basis is the same as the father of them all. It is an Israelite brother who comes to you now with this offer."

She stared at him, thinking hard. He began to relax, and opened his palms consolingly.

"You see, Abishag, you no longer have anything to fear from me. I have repented, I have been circumcised, and I am, in truth, your Israelite brother. The elders have accepted me as such, and even now, a lineage is being drawn up for me. I am to be grafted into Isaachar, for it is in his allotted land we dwell. I have been informed by the elders, that a 'council of kinsmen' is a meaningless expression, unless we be kinsmen in truth. Thusly, the elders have adopted me into the covenant of Jacob, by the same means that Abraham himself was adopted, through circumcision."

Abishag had always known that Hamon was clever, and it was apparent that he had indeed been studying the Law, and had come up with a very intriguing argument. She suspected he was in fact telling the truth with respect to the declarations of the elders. His repentance, combined with the great goodwill that his restoration of lands had earned him, could well have motivated them to reward him with the highest of honors: naturalizing him as an Israelite brother. The only thing missing was a sensible biblical precedent, which he had cleverly supplied, likely hinting it into existence so as to allow the elders to think they had come up with it themselves.

Abishag's protracted silence was emboldening him. Hamon believed if his case was unassailable by her, it was unassailable by anyone.

Yet, Abishag slowly began to shake her head.

"You cannot claim the basis of Abraham."

"Certainly I can—I have been circumcised, just as was he."

"But . . . circumcision did not make Abraham an Israelite."

He snorted out a frustrated laugh.

"But how not? How can you say that?"

"Because it is true. Abraham did not become Israelite by circumcision; he became Israelite by the covenant of God. Circumcision was given afterwards, as a *sign* of a covenant already made. God spoke to Abraham and made him a promise, long before the circumcision. It is not so in your case. The outward sign without the prior covenant is meaningless. Where is the prior covenant with Amalek, of which circumcision is a sign?"

Hamon opened his mouth to reply, but then hesitated, his eyes shifting left then right. Then he began to shake his head.

"Abishag! I don't know where you come up with these silly arguments! Don't you see I am trying to help you? I am offering to redeem your land. I risked my reputation to secure your release from prison. I now offer to cover you. I do all of this for you, and all you can do is throw up these trivial ill-informed objections!"

"No biblical objection can rightly be called trivial, for the Law is the basis of all judgments. But as to your releasing me from prison, I am forced to wonder why I was in prison in the first place."

"Why could you wonder?—it was explained, was it not?"

"Until now. I was in prison for the expressed purpose of being interrogated to obtain information to apprehend Jedidiah. If you knew all along he was dead—and had buried the body yourself—why was I questioned so? And why did you have to prevail so to make your case to the elders? A display of the body would have secured my immediate release—as well as validate your offer now. So if you still contend that he is dead, where is the body?! I can accept no offers until I see it."

Hamon's face reddened. The humble manner that he had heretofore held with great consistency was giving way to something more sinister.

"Abishag! You are acting foolishly! You are about to make a grave mistake. Think it over—take a day, or two."

"I do not need a day to think it over. Until I see the body of my beloved, I believe he lives, and I proceed on that belief."

"What!—are you accusing me? Are you saying I lie about this? Surely the body is long gone. We made a temporary burial, so that we could return on a better day and honor it properly. But when we returned, it was gone!—stolen perhaps, or dragged off by some wild animal. Who knows what could have happened in the wilderness? He probably carried gold—any trail raider could have stolen the body and searched it!"

"Stolen a buried body?"

He blinked at her again.

"When I said buried, I did not mean *deep* in the ground! What tools would we have had to do that? We piled stones on it for respect, but it still could have been found."

"Then take me to that pile of stones—surely they are still there. Neither a thief nor a wild animal would be interested in a pile of stones."

"I—-I don't know if I can even find it now."

"You told me a moment ago the scene was forever burned into your mind."

"I . . . I . . ."

"And why was I questioned in prison? You never answered me that."

Hamon hesitated again, and with great effort rose to his feet, steadying himself on the rock with one hand, grinding his teeth.

"Abishag! I don't know how you come by all of these ignorant questions! I am the one who worked harder than anyone else to have you released! I staked my reputation! I resisted those who wanted you tried as an accomplice to his crimes! I knew you could not be guilty, even if he was! And now you insult me with attacks on my integrity? This is amazing!"

"I only asked a simple question. If your integrity can be jeopardized so easily, perhaps it is on frail ground to begin with."

"Frail ground! There is no more frail ground than the very ground you are standing on right now! This very land stands poised to be repossessed! Will you not allow me to redeem it for you?"

"I will not."

"You stupid fool!"

"A moment ago I was your gravely offended friend."

"I say this for love! For love!"

"Perhaps you should save these expressions of love for a maiden who can better appreciate them. I clearly am not worthy of you."

"Abishag! You . . . you . . . you are a . . . the stupidest, most beautiful girl I have ever seen. You are so dumb you don't even know how—how smart you are! Pathetic worthless creature! If you had a whit of sense about you, you would realize that you are *more* than worthy of me, and the fact that I would stoop to receive you ought to prove that to you!"

"I am in no way qualified to follow your mind."

"You are *over* qualified to follow my mind, you idiot!"

"I pray then that one day my idiocy will give way to the sense to appreciate your counsel. Until then, I can only hope that I might find pity from a lesser man."

"A lesser man!? You vastly underrate that dead friend of yours! If you could satisfy such a magnificent prince, you surely have more than enough virtue to satisfy me!"

"You think well of him?"

"I hated him! He was a great man, amazingly astute! By far the most princely man our little town has ever seen—a gallant, dignified, gracious, self-aggrandizing delusional fool. Dung!"

"Then that is all I am worthy of."

"But you will have nothing, don't you understand?— nothing! I would redeem your land! But you are too stupid to see that love is staring you in the face. I would cover and redeem, spare you this humiliation!"

The volume of his shouts echoed back from the canyon walls, fading to silence around them. Her reply was gentle.

"Perhaps I am not as afraid of humiliation as some."

Hamon almost growled and leaned in her direction. She took a step back, but he reached and balanced himself on the rock again.

"I have work to do," she said, turning back toward the row of vines.

"Yes, Oh! Of course! Work to do. You always have work to do! Enjoy your work child, for this will certainly be the *last* time you have the pleasure of having a *place* to work! Abishag!"

She was walking away. Suddenly she turned.

"I would have forgiven you, if you had truly repented."

Hamon pursed his lips together, and faltered to reply, suddenly smitten to the heart. She disappeared into the vines.

Chapter 19

The door upon which Dinah had knocked was tall and ornate, clever designs carved into its wood. It was a blustery day, the twisting wind was playing with her veil as she waited as an outsider before the door of her former home, finding it strange to wait for admittance where she had so long freely passed. The basket of fresh vegetables she was holding became heavy, and she put it down beside her on the step. Was she calling too early? Her father would normally be awake at this hour, though she knew he worked late. She heard faint noises and footsteps inside. Presently the latch turned, and the door cracked a short span, enough to admit a view, but not enough to allow any entrance. Upon recognizing her, Jalaam opened the door wider.

"Dinah. What are you doing here?"

Her father appeared fatigued, deep bags were under his eyes, and his expression revealed the dishevelment of insufficient sleep.

"Shalom father."

He scowled.

"I am not taking you back, Dinah. The new girl is working out quite well—I don't care what you might have heard. I'll have her trained before long."

"I am not returning to you father, I just . . . have something for you here, some vegetables from the garden on the hill farm. We have so many, I know you like fresh things, and I was coming down so I . . . I brought you some."

She lifted the basket. He frowned down at its contents.

"Produce?"

She nodded.

"Hm." he grunted, and stepped forward and moved the cloth cover, looking down into the basket. She held it up to him, and gave him a smile that was not returned.

"You . . . you're tired Father. Have you been working extra late?"

"No. No, cvcrything is quite on track Dinah, more prosperous than ever, why?"

"Oh, no reason. I was just . . . hoping you were not overburdened in my absence . . . well, not that I was much help to you, but . . . just concerned, I suppose."

"Don't waste your worry 'Din. Things are better than ever. But I suppose I might find a use for these fruits—since they're throwaways anyway," he said, pulling the basket inside.

"Yes, well, I have more that I could bring, from time to time, if you would like, and, while I am here, I had left a few things behind, my drawings and such—do you suppose I could come in and get them now?"

"Later, 'Din, I'm actually not up yet," he said, pulling the door back to a narrow slit.

"Alright—maybe I will visit the market and return?" she said quickly, as the door was closing.

Her father grunted an affirmation, and the door shut in front of her. After standing momentarily before the abruptly closed door, she sighed and turned toward her errands.

Dinah had planned to come to town with Abishag to get a

few supplies from the market, but when they passed the vineyard, Abishag decided to stay and tend to a few things. As Dinah moved down the street toward the market square, she glimpsed movement to her left. On a second glance, she ascertained that it was actually a group of guards transporting a prisoner. The street was narrow and they appeared to be coming in her direction, so she crossed to the other side.

The men were handling their charge roughly, shoving and jostling him, and as they drew closer she caught a few words out of the general din.

"Filthy Hittite" someone jabbed, and also "Pildash," which apparently, was his name. The prisoner was young, barely more than a boy, his face red with youth. He was easily intimidated by the guards, who seemed to be deriving sport from tormenting him as they ushered him along. After the group jostled by, she was about to continue on her way, when she suddenly stopped and looked back sharply. She had seen that face before, she was sure of it, but was not quite sure where. This boy, apparently, had been the one Hittite raider who had been captured after the attack on the harvest. She stood for a moment, looking back after them as they headed toward the old grain tower.

The face of the young Hittite prisoner continued to return to Dinah's memory as she moved among the tables and booths, finding her needed wares. Suddenly she blinked and stood erect, remembering exactly where she had seen that face before. She dropped the fabric she had been inspecting, and was about to hasten back to her father's house, when she heard her own name called out, high and sharp. She turned.

"Dinah!" the voice said again. She looked across the square, and a woman waved excitedly.

"Jemimah?"

Jemimah, waved again, but did not move in her direction. Dinah hurried across the square. After an animated greeting, Jemimah explained that she was here with her whole family, even her father, who had wanted to verify the truth of the rumor of Hamon's repentance, and was also attempting to locate his son

Benaiah, whom he had not seen nor heard from in some weeks.

"Where is your father now?" Dinah asked.

Jemimah pointed.

"He is in that building. He said to wait here, he will be out shortly."

While Jemimah was speaking, her sister Aijeleth, who had been browsing in a nearby booth quickly came over, slipping up close to her sister. Dinah and Aijeleth greeted each other coolly and courteously, falling into awkward silence. They turned at the approach of Jemimah's parents, Laban and Jael, who were speaking with each other lowly, not noticing Dinah until the last moment. Laban looked up curiously at the veiled maiden speaking with his daughters.

"Do I know you, daughter?" he asked, glancing at his wife, who shrugged.

"Father, this is Dinah! Surely you remember her, from when we lived on the farm—she used to go with us to Shammai's Torah readings," Jemimah exclaimed.

"Dinah? You mean the innkeeper's daughter—Jalaam's daughter?" he asked.

"Yes, yes, she is the one! Can you believe it? Look at her!"

"I don't work at the inn anymore," Dinah explained.

"No, I don't suppose you do," Laban mused, stroking his beard.

"No—Abishag has helped her," Jemimah explained.

Dinah smiled.

"She has a way with lost sheep. She even took me into her fold," Dinah explained.

"You live with Abishag now?" Jemimah asked.

Dinah nodded.

Laban looked quickly at his wife, and back.

"Abishag—you live with Abishag? Maiden, do you know where she is just now?—her booth is not in the square today. I am here on urgent business. I have come to understand that my farm may now be available for redemption, and if so my son, Benaiah, can begin working it. The former plantings will begin very soon, but I have not seen my son for some time." He shook his head, his expression growing somber. "My son—he has been making foolish choices. But I have learned that Abishag may have had some contact with him—she may even know where he is. I was hoping to speak with her, but, I have come to suspect that this maiden Abishag may not be forthright with me."

"Abishag? Not forthright? Surely you have her confused with another," Dinah replied.

Laban shook his head.

"It is not I who am confused, but she. She has been spreading dangerous rumors that my daughter and son have been infected with. I suppose it has all been discredited by now, but my son—-he may still be deceived."

Dinah opened her mouth in a silent "ohhh," giving a quick glance to Jemimah, who returned it knowingly.

"Well, my lord, I do understand your dilemma. But Abishag is not difficult to find, I know where she is just now. In fact, I will be returning there shortly. If you will allow me to make a quick trip back to my father's house, I will take you to her. I am sure she would be happy to answer your questions."

"Is she at the farm?" Laban asked quickly.

"Yes, she was in the vineyard this morning, I will . . ."

"Never mind, I know the way," Laban said, then looked around at his family, arranging by his expression for them to be prepared for a brisk march.

Dinah skipped quickly back to her father's house. From Laban's tone, it was quite clear that Jemimah had been in some distress recently, and could use her support. But Laban would abide no delay, and Dinah was compelled by sudden urgency to verify her suspicions about the Hittite boy. Coming to her father's house, she knocked urgently. Her father came to the door again, now dressed, and sucking on a fig from the basket of fruit. She moved through the door quickly when it opened, not allowing herself to be kept outside again.

"I will just be a minute, father," she called to him as she moved hastily down the hall toward her room, while he looked after her puzzled. She found the room nearly bare, except for rolls and piles of papers, which she had kept on high shelves. With all the furniture gone, she could not reach them. Hastening back to the hall, she dragged in a crate, and climbed up and started rummaging through some papers, pulling down several rolls. She shuffled briefly through them, then took a particular stack in her arms, left the rest, and hastened to the door.

"I will be back for the rest of these," she said on her way out, struggling to keep the awkward stack in her arms.

"No hurry 'Din," he replied, looking after her puzzled.

The door slammed. Then Dinah was immediately hurrying down the street, wrestling with her burden as she went, hoping to catch up with the family on the road to Abishag's vineyard.

****

The long ride down from Abishag's vineyard afforded Hamon less distraction than he might have hoped for. The peaceful hills and vines allowed his thoughts to play and replay the disastrous conversation with Abishag without interruption, as though accomplices to her insults. The trip was rendered even longer by the slow pace his recent circumcision demanded he maintain. The slightest bump brought stabs of pain that made his eyes water.

His anger gradually gave way to numb amazement. What a frustrating maiden! How did she so easily refute him? Hamon prided himself on his ability to sway people to his wishes. The proof of his skill was evident on every side. The whole valley was in his sway, but, somehow this maiden, hiding a dangerously clever mind behind maddening innocence, was able to not only see through his designs, but answer his arguments in ways that even he was not able to rejoin. His doctrinal case was well conceived—carefully researched—this he knew. Even the elders had found it plausible. Yet, she had brushed it aside in a moment. Where did an uneducated peasant girl get such sagacity?

He blushed, the memory of his ridiculous replies ringing embarrassingly silly in memory. How had she drawn him into making such a complete fool of himself? He once again felt the impression of being toyed with—though he doubted she would descend deliberately to such pubescence. Still, the sensation was the same.

Beautiful *and* smart! It was not fair. Why did such beauty have to be guarded by such cunning? Let her be beautiful, but why could she not be just a simple minded maiden, such as he was always able to bend to his wishes? And why did everything always turn out right for her? It was inexplicable. Put her in prison, and she comes out a hero. Even when going terribly wrong for her, every situation seemed to end up in her favor. He shook his head in frustration. She hovered maddeningly just beyond his reach. As untouchable by sickness and persecution as she was by attempts to woo her with kindness, she floated above every attempt to tame her, with seeming effortlessness.

Movement ahead stirred him from his reverie of frustration, and he looked up to see a group of travelers coming up the trail. He straightened on his mount, the habitual movement bringing a wince to his face. The travelers appeared to be a family. At this elevation, beyond most farms, it was likely that they were on some social mission. Though not in the mood for pleasantries, Hamon saw little chance of avoiding them on the trail. He expected that he would be recognized, as he was most everywhere, and would need to engage them in some way, his mood not withstanding. Being locally famous had its disadvantages. He sighed and spurred forward toward the coming travelers.

"Shalom friends," Hamon offered, as the parties met on the trail, projecting into his tone the quiet humility that had been his habit of late. Four sets of eyes peered up at him curiously, then widened in sudden recognition.

"Lord Hamon?" the father ventured, "Or am I mistaken?"

"No, you are correct, brother, it is I. You are out visiting on this fine day, I wager. I do not believe I have the privilege of your acquaintance."

Laban and his wife and daughters, surprised all to see such a person alone in such a place, searched beyond him as if expecting to see others in his company. He discerned their glances, and shrugged back over his shoulder.

"I happen to be out visiting myself, though to not much good, I am afraid."

"Lord Hamon," Laban said, "I am . . . most surprised to find you here. My family and I, we reside together in Jezreel . . . though we used to farm this area, some years ago. I . . . heard rumors, and was in Shunem today to discern the truth of them."

Hamon nodded amiably.

"Yes, news of my repentance has reached even to Jezreel, I am sure. And no report could do justice to the reality. Since the day I was converted, a happier man has never walked the earth. Little did I know the pleasure I used to take in confiscating lands would some day be far outweighed by the joy of restoring them. Such joys have been my wonderful privilege every day since that glorious vision—until this day, that is. I suppose some people just will not be helped, no matter how deserving of it. It is senseless, but each must choose for himself . . . or herself."

Laban looked at his wife puzzled, then back at Hamon.

Hamon had by now identified the family, and remembered which land had been theirs, and how and when it had been acquired. He knew that Laban's name had not been listed among the Brotherhood.

"Lord Hamon," Laban ventured, "If I may be so bold as to entreat you . . ."

"No boldness required, brother Laban," Hamon waved him off, "for the fields to the north and west of here are rightfully yours. As soon as the elders release them, they will be restored to you. I only hope you will receive them, and not deny this gift of God in favor of some childish fancy, as was the choice of the last person with whom I spoke."

Trembling with growing excitement, Laban stared speechless and mystified.

"My lands? . . . Restored?" he whispered.

"They are in the hands of your Israelite elders."

"They . . . who? The elders?"

"Yes, the elders have assumed responsibility for all the lands I used to control. As much as I yearn to restore all the land immediately, the elders have counseled that the restoration proceed in an orderly way, lest I be left with nothing for myself to live on. I have submitted myself to their authority. They have constrained me to only restore Brotherhood land, for the time being, with the rest to follow in the future. I only hope, that I find Israelites more willing to receive what is rightfully theirs than the last I encountered. Please do not fail to reclaim your land, when the time comes."

Even as Hamon spoke, Laban and his wife's eyes brimmed with tears, as the impact sank in, while Jemimah, trained to remain silent to allow her father to speak for the family, stood astonished and confused.

"Lord Hamon . . . this is most, unexpected, and incredible! For my family and I . . . this has been a dream, for many years, and to now find it a reality, I . . . I cannot express what this means to us. Surely I . . . how can I possibly thank you!"

Hamon matched the emotion with his own and appeared to tear up. Slowly, and carefully, he descended from his mount, the reason for his delicate movements evident to all. He stepped forward and reached out his hand consolingly toward the quivering couple, which was quickly taken by both Laban and his wife.

"My dear Israelite brother," he said, "There are no thanks to be offered on your side, only apologies on mine. But there is indeed a situation afoot in the land that has troubled me greatly, which you may be able to assist. I was up on this mountain today, for the purpose of addressing, and if possible, improving this sad state of affairs. It may not be told in Jezreel, but a strange and dangerous rumor plagues the land—one that prevents Israelites from accepting what is rightfully theirs. There is a maiden, on this very hill in fact, who is especially taken with this myth. I had hoped to dissuade her but . . ." he shook his head, his voice trailing off.

"Is the maiden called Abishag?" Laban asked.

Hamon's head snapped up.

"Why yes, yes as a matter of fact, it is she. Is she known to you?"

"Yes! Yes, the maiden Abishag is well known to us! In fact we were traveling these hills just now to call on her—though we have not been in contact for some time."

Hamon shook his head.

"This truly is the grace of God. This maiden, Abishag, who could not respect her? A finer maiden has truly never been seen in our village, but I fear she is a measure naive. It is tragic what has become of her—how she has been so taken in by that which is causing Israelites to not only reject the redemption of their lands, but is actually bringing sickness and death upon many. She means only good, I doubt not, but the lie has deafened her ear to my counsel. She will not hear me, nor would she receive redemption of her family land, when I offered it to her. Perhaps . . . *you* could undeceive her, if you find the opportunity. Anything you could do to enlighten her, I would take as your thanks to me."

Laban and his wife were staring wide eyed, while Jemimah's mouth had dropped open in disbelief.

"If I can possibly be of assistance, I will, my lord," Laban replied, almost reverently, "but I doubt my counsel could be better received than yours."

Hamon nodded, looking down at the ground.

"Yes, and I fear it so as well. But, if she will not be deterred, we can hope at least that the lie extends no further. This poor maiden may have drifted beyond the reach of reason."

"Yes . . ." Laban replied.

"Say," Hamon said, striking a different tone, "do you not have a son? One who was in fact, enlisted with the militia?"

Laban hesitated.

"Do not fear brother, my question is born of love. Our concern for him has been great, since his disappearance some weeks ago. He was very well liked, a promising soldier. I even recall that there is an unclaimed reward waiting for him."

"Lord Hamon, my son Benaiah—and this I say with great regret—I have not seen him for some weeks. This maiden Abishag, I have come to understand, may in fact know his whereabouts, which is the reason for my visit this day. I do not believe my son is injured or lost, but, perhaps, confused by recent events. Please understand that he meant no disrespect by failing to report, he is a very good man, at heart."

"Yes, that was my impression also—a very fine man. The reward that awaits him would go far toward reseeding your land, when it is restored to you. But it troubles me to learn that he has associated himself with this poor deceived maiden. I truly hope she has not beguiled him. If you do find him, please constrain him to report back to us. Even though his days as a soldier are soon to end, when your land is restored, we would like to honor him for his bravery."

This conversation, spoken in the full hearing of Jemimah, was unbearable to her in every way, and her silent vexation did not go unnoticed by her sister or mother, though her father was fully engaged with Hamon. Suddenly, Hamon turned and addressed her.

"And I have heard good reports of you as well, dear maiden. Your name is Jemimah, is it not? My nephew, in fact, has spoken highly of you. I do hope we can all keep in contact, once the whole family is back together again on your rightful land."

Jemimah, vexed speechless, and red in face, opened her mouth and then bit her lip, as she stared at him, unable to imagine the reply that would meet the circumstances.

"My youngest daughter is shy," Laban quickly explained.

"All the more endearing," Hamon replied. "Well, if you will allow me leave, I have more amends to make yet today. Would you be so kind as to assist me back onto my horse?"

"Of course, my lord." Laban said, and stepped forward to help Hamon mount.

Fond farewells exchanged, the parties continued on their way.

The counsel from her father, mother, and sister that Jemimah was forced to silently endure for the remainder of the trip to Abishag's farm tested to the breaking point her ability to answer meekly and submissively. If she had not known that her mentor Abishag was soon to be brought to her aid, she would not have been able to hold her peace. That and the little pipe that she gripped beneath her clothing, her fingernails almost digging into the wood. As her fingers passed over its fourth hole, the gentle melodic voice of the king came to her remembrance. It called out to her from the past, bringing to her remembrance a surreal and dreamlike evening that now seemed years ago, when he had cut the fourth hole in her pipe.

Be patient, little dove, and all will turn out well for you . . .

Her father, meanwhile, was charging her in the strongest terms, that if she truly had any love for her brother, for Abishag, and for her own family, for that matter, she would join them in persuading Abishag of her deception. And if she could not join them, she would by all means remain quiet, and allow no variance to pass her lips, now that the truth of the situation was so fully revealed.

For all of that, a measure of peace still found its way into Jemimah's soul, for the voice of the king, even in memory, had greater power than that of her own father.

I will be patient . . .

Abishag remained in her vineyard after Hamon left. The hillside vines, fluttering in the blustering wind, caressed the hands of their reflective caretaker, while her unanticipated visitors approached on the trail. The conversation with Hamon replayed in her thoughts, exciting a new awe at the darkness of his soul; his seemingly limitless ability to operate in the realm of deception and craftiness. His highly publicized conversion had been a cautious curiosity to her, one that she could not quite resolve in his favor, all outward evidence notwithstanding. Even when Hamon was freely dispossessing his lands into the hands of thankful and exuberant Israelites, asking for nothing in return, a little voice continued to whisper to her to beware. She had repeated its whispers to Dinah, and to her mother, and to Barkos and Jared, who had heeded her warnings out of respect for her insight, though not much was visible to justify them.

But Hemanah, though following her counsel on the treatment of his sickness, was not moved by her warnings about Hamon. For him, as for the rest of the population, no greater proof of Hamon's repentance could be imagined than the restoration of land. With the land restored, what else was there to amend? With that restoration openly under way, Hamon's conversion was received as a miraculous answer to prayer. But with the revelations of the day now justifying her doubts in full, Abishag was left with a new respect for his shrewdness and sinister power. Nor did it escape her notice that his newly acquired capital, a hold on the *hearts* of the people rather than their lands, strengthened his standing immeasurably.

At the same time, it rendered her own mission uncertain. Of what value was the seal of the king, if there was nothing to redeem? In spite of that, she trusted the wisdom of the king, for he would never have imparted his seal out of his own keeping and into hers, if not for certainty that she would need it.

For all the mystery of the situation, one fact stood above all others: Hamon was lying. If he was lying about the death of Jedidiah, he was operating in deception in general. And if so, then his conversion was false, and it was only a matter of time before he would use his new resource of popular trust to ill ends. How he would do it was a puzzling question, but that he would, was not in doubt. She shook away the tears that dripped from her eyes, tears of remorse for her childhood friend Hamon, and all he had become, wiping them on her sleeve.

Her desire to work in the vineyard faded, and in its place came a growing sense of urgency to relate what had just happened. The knowledge of Hamon's duplicity could not remain her own secret. She left the vines and turned toward home, knowing that there she would find the best of all audiences for her burdened heart, her mother.

Abelah and Abishag lingered on the porch where the daughter had related to her mother the whole conversation with Hamon. Though no answers to the situation were found, Abishag felt better for having told of it. Suddenly, voices were heard at the head of the yard where the two boulders sat, and Abishag and Abelah looked up. After a moment, Abishag recognized the party.

"Its . . . Jemimah, and her family," she mused softly, standing slowly to her feet for a better view. "I wonder why have they come?"

Suddenly duty overcame curiosity and Abelah hastened inside to prepare for guests, while Abishag went out to greet the visitors. A strange greeting it was, much warmer on Abishag's side than that of her visitors, though they were coolly cordial. A message of distress passed in a glance from Jemimah to Abishag, after Jemimah had greeted her with uncharacteristic reserve, and barely more than a word. Abishag was puzzled, but resisted the impulse to question why. After some awkward moments, Abishag invited them all inside.

The peculiar atmosphere continued in the house, the hostesses unable to draw much conversation out of their guests, and when Abelah left to retrieve a skin of goat milk from the animal hutch, Jael quickly got up and followed her.

"Abelah," she said urgently, catching up from behind. "Surely you know why we have come. You must be in great distress. You should know that we are willing to help, if there is anything we can do for Abishag, but also, we are searching for our son, Benaiah. Laban believes Abishag knows where he is. We must find this out from her, while we have her confidence, before we confront her."

Abelah stopped walking and looked at Jael oddly.

"Confront her?"

Inside the house, Laban had stood and paced, looking out the lattice, then turning to look at his daughters and Abishag, opening his mouth, then putting a finger over it.

Abishag glanced at the sisters, and back at Laban.

"Is there something you require, my lord?" she asked him.

Her question hung in the air, while he stared at her.

"Perhaps. Maiden, there is something that you . . . may be able to provide for me—if you will suffer me to speak plainly, for just a moment. My heart has been vexed these past weeks—terribly vexed. Before you sits a house in distress. For though my two daughters are with me today, the heir of my inheritance has neither been seen nor heard from for many days. I have only one son, and his absence has worried me exceedingly, though I do not suppose a maiden could understand the effect of such a thing upon a father."

Abishag glanced at Jemimah, back to Laban.

"My lord, do you mean to say that you are seeking your son, Benaiah?"

"That is it, in truth, maiden. He is gone from me many days."

"Let my lord set his heart at ease, for your son is not lost, but is employed on an estate near the city, living in a comfortable house. There is no need for distress," Abishag said.

"Is he?"

"I know it of a truth, my lord, for I have seen him there, more than once."

"Will you tell me where?" Laban asked, the tension in his tone detectable.

"It would be no less than my duty to not only tell you where your son can be found, but take you to him, if you so wish."

While this conversation was taking place in the house, Abelah and Jael were engaged in an interesting dialog of their own. The mother of Abishag, upon discerning the situation, hesitated not to give Jael a brief and direct overview of recent events, her mature tone and quiet confidence making an immediate impact upon her audience. It was one thing for Jael to hear such strange tales from her youngest daughter, but hearing them from a trusted and mature friend, the story sounded more credible, and Jael was suddenly uncertain.

When the women returned to the house, Laban looked poignantly at his wife, who returned the look with a mystified expression of her own.

"The maiden has agreed to take us to Benaiah," he declared, barely restraining his excitement.

"It may be . . . that the maiden has nothing to hide," Jael replied carefully.

Laban looked puzzled.

"What is your meaning, wife?"

"Abelah has just told me that it is all true . . . what Jemimah has been saying about Abishag."

Laban's eyes narrowed.

"What? All true?"

Then the reason of the awed expression on his wife's face became clear to him.

"Jael," he whispered, his expression darkening. "What is this strange speech? Have you forgotten everything we learned, even this very day?"

Jael put her hand over her mouth, looking uncertain again, glancing worriedly from Abelah back to her husband.

"No, but . . . there may be more to be known . . . more to

speak of."

"What more can there be to speak of?" Laban asked, his anger rising. "You well know the many dangers we have been advised of, dangers to life, health, and inheritance. Need I remind you of these things now?—in this room? Jael, this maiden has agreed to take us to our *son*," he said with a warning glance.

A soft voice cut into the awkward silence.

"My lord, if I may, the very thing you speak of should be tended to without delay. Your son awaits you. Surely the importance of reuniting with him outweighs that of resolving something that cannot be settled in a short time here. I beg that you not delay my desire to take you to Benaiah now, for he is most eager to see you."

The eyes of Laban flitted from his wife back to the maiden whose gentle entreaty lay before him, her tone free of guile, honest and gentle. She appeared the very picture of empathy and sincerity, and every whit sane in both manner and tone.

"Yes . . ." he replied, after studying her curiously for a moment. "That is, after all, why we have come."

Jemimah noticed the sudden change in her father, and glanced at Abishag in private awe.

Aijeleth remained silent, under the sway of many conflicting thoughts, as was her mother.

"You speak truly, my daughter," Abelah said, walking over to put her hands on Abishag's shoulders. "As you do . . . of all things."

Abelah looked up and met Laban's eyes, holding them in confident sincerity, while he studied both her and her daughter, puzzled. Seeing the two of them together, so serenely convinced of their outrageous deception, feeling himself the pull of their persuasion, it occurred to Laban that the women were even more dangerous than he had supposed. He understood now how his son had become so deceived. That in such a short time this maiden and her mother could rattle the clear sense of both his wife and his eldest daughter, whose silent expression he well understood, even after they had been so recently warned, was telling. It was a subtle and dangerous deception, seemingly harmless, yet strong enough to prevent Israelites from accepting their rightful inheritances from Hamon, and convincing them to partake of deadly medicines. For all of its unlikelihood, the lie somehow carried a power so strong that once believed, all sense could be swept aside in favor of a wild speculation. Into such had his son and daughter fallen.

He suddenly felt compelled to get his family out from under the influence of such bewitchment as soon as possible. Yet, he could not separate from the women at once, for he had not yet been reunited with his son.

"Maiden, it is not necessary that you go. Can you not just *tell* me where Benaiah is?" Laban asked.

"I can," Abishag replied, "but it is unlikely that you will see him if I do not go. You must understand that he is wary. He may see your approach, and not knowing the meaning of it, will flee from you, though he very much wants to see you. I must go in first, to assure him that you have come alone, that his superiors have not sent you to draw him out. Surely he has told you that he believes he is being sought."

Jael blinked.

"Laban—she speaks the truth! Benaiah said as much himself. He said he thought they would be looking for him."

Laban looked back and forth between Abishag and his wife.

"And he will believe . . . *you?*"

"He will, for it was I who arranged his current situation. I am known to the lady of the estate," Abishag replied.

Laban hesitated, finding no argument equal to her point. She was relating the sweep of Benaiah's mind in a way consistent with his own understanding of it, predicting his son's actions most probably.

"How do I know *you* will not warn him to flee from me?"

"My lord, you have my solemn promise. I appeal to your own

daughters to confirm me. Ask Aijeleth. Have I ever broken my word?" Abishag looked over at Aijeleth, who cast her eyes to the ground, ashen. When she looked up, her eyes were moist.

"No," Aijeleth whispered.

"Laban, what choice have we?" Jael interjected. "Abishag is our best and only hope."

"Yes, it seems she has bewitched both my daughter, *and* my son," Laban muttered.

"No!" Jemimah blurted suddenly, breaking her long silence. "No father that is *not* true. She has *given* you both your daughter and your son. It is true. When I was in Shunem, I had intended to not come home at all! It was Abishag who urged me to come home to you—against my own wishes I am ashamed to say. And now she is taking you to your son. If anyone is to blame it is me, not she!"

Abishag reached out quickly and stilled Jemimah.

"*You* sent Jemimah home?" Jael asked Abishag.

"It was only proper. She is of your house. I could do no other," Abishag replied.

Jael was looking at Abishag with growing wonder.

"Then why did you not send Benaiah home as well?" Laban asked.

"Certainly my lord understands that unlike your daughter, Benaiah is a grown man who has quitted your house of his own choice. I can no more place someone under your authority than I can take someone out. Benaiah made his own rightful choice. But if you wish, we may go to him, and you may put these questions to him personally."

Laban hesitated again under the sense of her argument. The maiden was difficult to contend with, her every offering being sensible beyond refutation. He perceived that every moment in her presence strengthened her influence on his family, yet, without her, he could not get to Benaiah.

“Very well, let us go,” he finally conceded. “But you must leave us alone when we are with him.”

Abishag agreed to this without protest.

Hamon, keenly aware that the one guard who might be able to contradict his version of the escape and subsequent death of the prisoner was still at large, wheeled his horse as soon as the party passed over the next hill, looking after them, his eye glinting intently. It was the break he had been waiting for. He stealthily followed them from a distance. Having acquired the strange intelligence that the missing guard was associated with Abishag—of all people!—it occurred to him that she may just lead the missing guard’s family right to him!

Hamon was familiar with the area above the home of Abishag from his days on the mountain as a boy shepherd, and knew from what vantage points the house could be watched. He cut through the brush and made his way to a bluff overlooking the farmyard, wincing from the bumpy ride. After watching patiently, he was rewarded with the sight of the party leaving the house, and Abishag was with them. His heart pounded in vexation at the sight of her, but he remained hidden. After the group topped the rise onto the trail beyond, he followed, cutting across the hill to keep them in view from above. He saw them take the less common trail to the east, which wound steeply down the opposite side of mountain emerging at the far side of the village.

****

Dinah hurried up the trail to the house. Having not overtaken the family of Jemimah on the trail, nor seen Abishag in her vineyard, she expected everyone would be found at the house. She topped the rise to the yard sweaty and out of breath, carrying her bundle of drawings awkwardly. Some of them had slipped out of her grip and fallen more than once in her journey.

Abelah looked up at Dinah's appearance in the door, and Dinah quickly glanced around the room.

"Is Abishag—has anyone been here?" she asked.

Abelah noted her urgent expression, and then the strange rolls she carried.

"Dinah. Are you well? What is the matter? Yes, Laban and Jael and the whole family were here, they left some time ago with Abishag, to go see Benaiah."

Dinah let out a big sigh, and entered the room, letting the bundles tumble onto the table.

"I missed them! Oh Abelah, there is something strange going on, and I think I know what it is, but I must speak to Abishag."

She crumpled into a seat and wiped a strand of black hair from her face, putting her face in her hands, then quickly straightening and looking back up at the ceiling, her eyes shifting in thought.

"My daughter seems to be in demand this day. Dinah—certainly you understand that what is spoken to her, will not remain unheard by me," Abelah said, handing Dinah a mug of water.

Dinah's eyes flicked over to it.

"Oh, I am sorry Abelah. Of course I can tell you. I was so hoping to catch up with them. I knew they were coming, but I had to go back to my father's house, and then, I couldn't go fast enough on the trail. How did it go? With Jemimah's parents?" she asked, then took a long gulp of water, peering up at Abelah over the rim of the cup.

Abelah smiled just a trace.

"Differently than they expected, I am sure. Truth can be suppressed, but it cannot be extinguished. It remains as a seed in the earth, to sprout again, sooner or later. For them, it may be sooner."

Dinah nodded, then her eyes drifted to her drawings on the

table, and widened again. She looked back at Abishag's mother again, growing serious.

"Abelah . . . I *saw* something today," she said ominously.

Abelah looked back and forth from the papers to Dinah curiously.

"I . . ." Dinah began, but was interrupted by a knock on the door.

The timing of the knock as both women were growing serious caused them to start. Abelah went over.

"Who is there?" she called through the door.

"It is I," said a clear male voice.

Abelah and Dinah's eyes met in a moment of recognition.

"Huram!" they exclaimed in unison, and Abelah hastened to throw the door open.

There he stood. Confident, dignified, well dressed, exuding the easy air they were quickly coming to appreciate. Curiously, he was holding under his arm a large bundle of official looking rolled scrolls.

Without delay, Huram, the born son of Abelah was welcomed into the house, made to sit, and offered every service that the humble farmhouse could manage, while his mother duly gushed and fussed. When allowed enough time to answer the succession of questions that were piled upon him, Huram explained that he had returned with a party of workmen to begin work on the mountain, and after assigning them duties, would be traveling on to Jerusalem. He was also curious to know what had transpired in his absence, and Dinah and Abelah gave him a full briefing of the wild string of events, the incarceration of Abishag, the attack on the harvest, and the apparent conversion of Hamon. Huram revealed little by his expression, listening carefully, and stopping to clarify some small detail now and again. His artisan mind would not suffer unclear details.

"Understand that I must be prepared to answer what the king will undoubtedly ask me," he explained. "He has no small interest in affairs here," he said to Abelah with a wink.

"Huram," Abelah said, putting hand on his sleeve, "Abishag is quite certain that the conversion of Hamon is not authentic. Even today, Hamon spoke to her, and he revealed many inconsistencies."

Dinah looked over curiously, not yet aware of this.

"Hamon was here?" she asked.

"He met her in the vineyard earlier. He—well, perhaps I ought to let her explain it to you."

Huram let out a thoughtful sigh, causing the women to look at him expectantly. He glanced up.

"Were any of the Hittite raiders, those who attacked the harvest, captured?" he asked.

Dinah's eyes widened again.

"Yes! In fact, I was just about to tell Abelah something about this when you came. I saw one of them today . . . the one who was captured."

"Only one?" Huram asked.

"Yes, and hardly more than a boy. They were taking him to the tower today, and passed by me as I was going to the market. Lord Huram, I have occasionally been able to draw a likeness of people . . ."

"And a very good likeness, I am aware," Huram said.

"You—how do you know I draw?"

"I saw your drawings, in the fire room that day, you had some with you, did you not?" he explained, surprising Dinah with his keen observation.

"Why yes, I suppose I did," Dinah replied.

"Dinah, you ought to see what Huram has drawn," Abelah said proudly, remembering the drawings she had seen of Huram's upcoming project.

Huram glanced at Abelah.

"Mother. You are most kind. But I draw easy things, buildings and such. I could never approach the talent of this maiden, who accurately renders the more difficult subject of people and faces. I am a craftsman, but *she*, an artist," Huram declared.

Dinah had never been prone to blush at a compliment, but this one found a place in her seldom touched.

"Have you not yet seen Dinah's work?" Huram asked.

Abelah admitted that she had not.

"Well then, Dinah, please continue with your story, you were about to tell us about a certain Hittite that you saw today."

"Yes. Yes! I saw him, and, I remembered that face from somewhere! So I went and got these." She pointed to the papers on the table, then reached in and shuffled through them, briefly, pulling one out.

"And I found this one."

She rolled it out on the table before them, while Huram and Abelah leaned forward to look. Abelah's eyes widened as she scanned the artwork.

"This . . . must have taken some time to do, dear," she whispered.

"No . . . no, not really, but this . . . look at this person here." She pointed. "This—this is that Hittite boy, I am *sure* of it."

The room was silent for a moment. Huram sat perfectly still as his eyes danced over the scene on the paper, but when he spoke his voice was low, and had an urgent timbre.

"Do you have more of these drawings Dinah?"

"A number of them."

"And you say this man is incarcerated now?"

"I saw them taking him to the old tower."

"Oh my soul," Huram said, leaning back thoughtfully, putting his fingertips together. "And you have also informed me that Hamon has been given charge of all prisoners in his new station as Defender of the City. This prisoner—this boy is in great danger. He is . . . a dead man."

Dinah and Abelah were stunned.

Huram looked over.

"Truly he is. Unless this boy escapes that prison, innocent or guilty, he will never leave this town alive."

"Yes . . ." Dinah whispered.

"But he *must* leave this town alive. He must live to stand before . . . the king," Huram concluded.

"Yes," Dinah agreed, catching up to his thought quickly.

"But how to get him out . . ." Huram mused.

Dinah and Abelah exchanged a glance, in which something passed.

"I think I know . . . a way," Dinah said thoughtfully.

****

Simeon and his wife Hildah looked up from their evening meal at a sound from the doorway.

"Your porch plants, my lady, I believe they ought to be inside tonight, it may grow cold."

"Put them on the veranda, Benaiah," she said.

Benaiah passed through the room and out the other door.

"I do not know where you got that boy, but a few more of his ilk and we could cut our household staff by half," Simeon commented.

Hildah studied her husband thoughtfully. She had already informed him that she had taken no treatment other than

Abishag's for her sickness, and now being several weeks in full health, he had little choice but to agree that it had been the cause of her cure. But she had hesitated to reveal the full testimony of Benaiah to him. She had, in fact, tried to limit her husband's exposure to Benaiah, aware of his forthright habit of speech. But his excellence in service was impossible to hide.

"Benaiah is an associate of Abishag," she tossed, baitingly.

"Abishag? The maiden with the medicine? What relation has he with her?"

"They are two of similar character, little surprise that they should be associates."

"If that be the case, if she is ever for hire, we may find a place for her here," he answered. "Though that she could actually match the service of Benaiah, I question. Despite the success of her medicine, the greatest fool in the world is not immune to an occasional stroke of luck. Such it may be with her and her medicine."

She glared at him.

"Not that she is a fool," he added, "I just find it unlikely that an uneducated peasant girl could be as sage as her success in this one thing portends. Her deficiencies have been noted by the wise."

"I find it unlikely that the ability to recognize a sage could be found in a town of fools," she muttered.

He stopped chewing and looked up sharply.

"What is your meaning, wife?"

Hildah looked at him and sighed.

"Wisdom itself is foolishness to a fool. If a town of fools calls one a fool, that one may be proved wise by the very accusation."

Simeon blinked, and then frowned.

"Do you mean to imply that I—we, are a town of fools? Is that your verdict or Abishag's? If hers, perhaps this maiden's medicine may be showing some unsavory side effects after all. I advise you to tame your tongue. The lucky success of a home remedy does not turn a whole town into fools—or a peasant girl into a sage."

"Simeon. The maiden has implied nothing of the sort. It is my own observation that now stings you. But I offer it not for that, but to give air to my thoughts, which I have held private for too long. Cast not my blame upon her, for she is unfairly accused enough."

Simeon stared at her uncertainly.

"This maiden has had some strange effect on you wife, I perceive."

"Again I say, cast not my failings upon her. For if you should question her yourself, I am sure you will find no fault, neither in manner nor substance, which makes it all the more curious why she is so disparaged."

He was silent.

"If so, then so," he finally conceded. "But I have no cause to question her, making the point moot."

"Is not my cure, and the sickness and approaching death of many, sufficient grounds to inquire?"

"That is not a matter for the elders, but for physicians. It is Jockshan who should render judgment on such matters."

Hildah almost cackled.

"As the serpent renders judgment on the leg it strikes! Is it not Jockshan who is most implicated, if it is found that health is being withheld in favor of death? It would mean the admission of much wrong for him to admit the presence of another and better cure."

"It is not that Jockshan's treatment does not cure. It is that, in this one case, hers has also," Simeon replied. "Jockshan has nothing to lose in this, but on the contrary, to gain. If it is deemed safe, he may try this treatment on those cases where he has not had success."

"I believe you will find such cases . . . replete," she replied, lowly. "And upon that fact, the need for inquiry rests."

Benaiah, who had hesitated in his return from the veranda upon hearing the tone of the conversation, was now near enough to discern its content as well, and deliberately made an inordinate noise as he entered the room the second time, so as to announce his entrance.

The couple looked up, their sudden silence awkward in the room.

"Excuse me lords," he said briefly, and moved to pass through the room.

"Benaiah," Simeon called out suddenly. Benaiah stopped walking.

"Yes my lord."

"I have been informed that you know, or are known of, the maiden Abishag."

"I do . . . and am, my lord."

"Good. Son, I find you a trustworthy person. Would you be willing to offer some judgment of her character?"

Benaiah turned to face them.

"A woman of more noble character I have never encountered, my lord."

"Ahh. I perceive these to be the words of a young man with a particular interest in a maiden," he replied.

Benaiah blushed.

"No my lord. Though the maiden would be prized by any young man of sense, she is already spoken for. My answer speaks only of her, not my desires toward her."

"I see."

He paused.

"Well then, of her intelligence, general knowledge of things, can you offer any insight? For she is understood to be nothing more than a peasant."

"It is only her great humility that allows this impression to stand uncontested, my lord. In the areas that you mention, I know not an educated man in the valley who could match her, though you will never find it openly displayed in her."

Simeon chuckled skeptically.

"Truly. And where did such as she acquire such graces?"

Benaiah sighed.

"My lord, I believe questions of this nature would be better placed to her directly, for I cannot answer the how of it."

Hildah was looking at Benaiah glowingly, thankful that he had answered with more sagacity than bluntness this time.

"Thank you son," Simeon said finally. "You are dismissed."

Benaiah bowed and left.

Simeon was aware of his wife's stare. He was not as uncomfortable with her argument as he was with the strange change in his wife's demeanor and responses, since partaking of the new cure. That she was cured was welcome. That she was distant and amiss as if carrying some inscrutable secret, he found unpleasant. It was as if a spirit had come over her, a spirit that wedged itself between them. Whatever its source, Simeon wanted it resolved.

"Hildah. I do not dismiss your declarations of this maiden Abishag's virtues, and the testimony of Benaiah cannot be discounted—if that were the end of it. But it seems this maiden has cast some kind of spell over you, causing you to place more confidence in her council than can be sensibly supported. You are cured, I will speak to the council about the cure; can that not be the end of it?"

"I am not certain that the end of a matter can be arbitrarily determined in advance. The end of the matter may well be what it declares itself to be."

Simeon looked at his wife puzzled.

"Perhaps, the end of the matter will not come until you are satisfied that I myself have interviewed the maiden. That is what you want, is it not?"

When she looked up, there was softness in her eyes.

"Would you?"

Simeon sighed.

If that is what it takes.

Chapter 20

Hamon was puzzled. After carefully watching the progress of the party down the rarely traveled easterly trail on that blustery day, he saw them approach the estate of Simeon, of the chief elders. What business would they have there? He stayed far back from the ridge, so his horse would not cast a silhouette against the sky beyond. He viewed the scene below as the stiff wind played with his garments and beard. He found himself staring straight into the gusty draft, and his eyes watered. He sighed, disappointed. He appeared to have been led to a dead end. Perhaps Abishag did not know the location of the missing guard, and was simply on an errand. A fugitive would surely not be found in the house of such a prominent person. For one thing, he would have no business there, and for another, a man running from authority would stay as far from the centers of power as possible.

Hamon was tired. The fatigue of his circumcision, the vexing conversation with Abishag, and the painful ride through the rough country all combined to make him wholly undesirous of remaining on a windy hill for hours on the remote chance that he might glimpse his missing guard. He wanted a drink. He reached down to his skin of wine and found it empty. He looked down and cursed. Shaking his head in disgust, he turned his horse away from the ridge and began the difficult and painful ride back to the main trail.

Scarcely had the conversation between Hildah and her husband concluded, when Abishag herself showed up at his gates, escorting Benaiah's family. It was Benaiah, who being on the porch saw them first. He recognized Abishag, then his father and his whole family. He was both apprehensive and eager at the sight of them. He knew his father trusted the authorities, and he may, in his desperation, deliver him to them, thinking he was helping him. If his father had come without Abishag, Benaiah would have felt compelled to hide, but seeing Abishag with them, he determined she must have judged it safe.

Benaiah himself went out to meet them at the gate. The greeting was quick but urgent, and it became clear to Benaiah that his father had much to say, but was hesitant to say it in the hearing of Abishag. When Abishag confirmed his hint with a poignant glance and a plain declaration, "Your father wishes to speak with you," Benaiah arranged a solution.

"I believe Hildah would like to see you Abishag. Shall I tell her you are here?" Benaiah said.

"Please."

Benaiah went to make the arrangements, and soon, Abishag was ushered inside the house, while Benaiah went outside the gate to speak with his father and family.

Simeon was surprised to find in his house at that moment the very person of whom he and his wife had been speaking, and might have suspected some clever arranging by his wife, if not for the fact that it was clearly impossible. It was truly a coincidence, though a strange one. Abishag explained her presence honestly: she had escorted Benaiah's family here to visit, since she knew the way.

Abishag sat humbly before the chief elder for the second time, not presuming to speak first. The first time she had been here, it was to receive blame for his wife's sickness, this time, to receive credit for her cure. She became aware of his puzzling stare, as though he were trying to discern the right opening.

"My apologies for my behavior when I was last in your house, my lord."

He remembered the moment.

"Perhaps I dismissed you too swiftly, maiden. Please accept my apologies. My wife is now cured, for which I suppose you are due some thanks. My wife has testified to me of you, and your medicine."

"The medicine that has cured your wife is not mine, my lord. I take no credit for its creation, only its distribution."

"There is something in that that troubles me, maiden. Though the success of the medicine is certainly welcome, I know something of its source. Some time ago, a stranger, with no credentials, was examined in our village. Since he was discredited in general, I would wonder why you presumed to give his potion to others. Surely this was a dangerous risk."

"If it was a risk, it was one which I first applied to myself, my lord. I also was sick, but was cured by this medicine. Since I had already partaken of it myself, as had dozens of others, I had good knowledge that it was safe."

"But you may not know the whole effect of it. A good woman named Orpha died under the influence of this concoction. How do you explain that?"

"I can in no wise explain the death of Orpha, for I do not know its cause. But I do know that she was dying, before she partook of this treatment, then she recovered. Your wife can attest to this," Abishag said.

Simeon glanced at Hildah.

"Orpha and I did have conversations," Hildah told him. "I observed her recovery."

He glanced back at Abishag.

"Maiden, I am not a doctor. But we do have a well-credentialed doctor in this village. If you supplied a list of names, perhaps he would examine them, and render an official opinion. Until then, I find it unwise to distribute something with mixed results."

Abishag sighed.

"I can supply a list of names, my lord, but I cannot guarantee they will admit to it. Many have come to me secretly, or by night."

Simeon huffed.

"Why would anyone do such a thing?"

"That is a question you may need to explore in your own house, my lord," she replied.

Simeon hesitated, and glanced at his wife.

Meanwhile out at the gate, a much different conversation was under way. Benaiah and his father's disagreement seemed irreconcilable. Laban spoke to his son of the reward waiting for him, of Hamon's conversion, of the restoration of lands, of the danger of his avoiding his duty, and of the miraculous reformations that were being received joyfully by all. To all of this, Benaiah remained resolute, a response his father found senseless and frustrating. The conversation, though difficult, remained cordial, until the subject of Abishag came up, and the seal of the king. Laban finally lost his restraint.

"Son, Abishag is a fool! A deceived, ignorant, little fool! Deceived and deceptive, and convincing only because she is so deceived she truly believes her own claims. I have spoken to her—heard her story. Even her mother is being swayed by this. But it is bewitchment. You may not know, but she has even been spreading a deadly poison among the population. If that does not convince you, what will?"

Benaiah bristled, but kept his calm.

"So when are we moving back in?"

"What do you mean?"

"To our family land. With all of these glorious reforms, surely our land is ours again, when do we move back?"

Laban hesitated.

"It is only Brotherhood land that is being restored at this time. But you ought to claim the reward that awaits you now, so there will be seed money when our land is restored."

"Father, the reward is a trick to bring me back into Hamon's power, and I doubt very much Hamon will ever relinquish that land. You know where I am staying father. Come to me when the land is back in your possession."

"And then you will come?"

"If we are in truth moving back to our estate, I will be there. But our land will never be secure, until the king's seal is applied."

When it was clear no more could be said, Benaiah embraced his tearful mother, gave his father a formal nod, and departed from them.

After a few more comments, Abishag was dismissed from Simeon's house again, though more cordially than the first time.

Simeon glanced at his wife, who stared back at him poignantly. The atmosphere of the humble peasant girl lingered in the room.

"I have done what you asked wife, and yes, she is a respectable person, pleasant and sensible. But that does not make her correct. When we find that she is not quite correct, will we quit with these lectures about the wisdom of a peasant girl and foolishness of everyone else?"

"We will, provided that if we find that she is quite correct, the counsel of the girl will be given greater respect."

Chapter 21

Abishag, traveling alone toward her home while the family of Laban returned to Jezreel, encountered Dinah and Huram on the trail. After a warm greeting, Huram informed her of the reason for his visit.

"I am to report shortly to the king, and he will want to know your state, but when I go to him, I am also to deliver these."

Huram opened a travel sack and lowered it where she could peek in. She saw a large number of rolled scrolls.

"What are they?"

"They are documents, royal documents. The business of the kingdom must go on. Solomon sent them to me that you might seal them, and I will return them to Jerusalem."

Abishag inhaled sharply, while Dinah absolutely gasped.

"Seal them . . . with the royal seal?" Abishag asked, amazed.

"As I said, the business of the kingdom must go on. These edicts will travel to different parts of the kingdom, carrying the king's orders, but unless they bear his Seal, they have no authority."

"Should I . . . should I do it right now?" Abishag asked.

Huram glanced around.

"It is a good time and place. We are alone. Some of these documents are urgent. Some are even to be delivered to this province, this village. I will leave them with your local authorities yet today, if you will seal them now."

Abishag looked up and down the trail. Not another soul was present. The three stepped to the side, and Abishag sat on a rock.

Dinah watched Abishag's hand travel into her garment, and return holding a small object. Reverently and methodically, Abishag sealed each of the documents, and returned them to Huram's sack, while Dinah watched wide-eyed.

"Thank you," Huram was saying. "I may have more for you to seal from time to time. In any case, the elders in the village cannot claim to not know the Seal of Solomon. These very documents will be posted in their halls."

Huram then explained the need to free the prisoner Pildash, and that it was believed that Benaiah could accomplish a breakout. Abishag added her voice in agreement, and the three proceeded to the gate of Simeon's estate. They applied for Benaiah, who was summoned and met them at the gate. Benaiah was thrilled to see again those with whom he had not a chance to speak when his family was present.

"We need your help, Benaiah," Abishag said. "There is a Hittite boy in prison. Huram believes he is in great danger there."

Benaiah glanced at her, then at Huram.

"This man needs to be broken out of prison, so I can conduct him to the king in Jerusalem. Your friends have recommended you for this job. Are you confident you can do this?" Huram asked him.

Benaiah's eyes widened.

"He can do it," Abishag testified. "He broke me out."

"Abishag! When I broke *you* out, you would not go. In fact, you rebuked me for it, but now you are instructing me to break someone else out?"

"It was a different situation, Benaiah. It was the will of the king for me to remain in, but it is his will for this prisoner to escape out."

Benaiah shook his head.

"The will of the king is hard to understand sometimes."

"Understanding is not necessary for obedience," Abishag said sagely.

Benaiah sighed.

"We will have horsemen waiting on the east side of the tower," Huram explained. "After you have the prisoner, take him around to the opposite side, and I will have him on a horse and gone in moments. With the help of the Lord, the key-keeper may not even know he is absent until morning."

"Will you do it?" Abishag asked.

Benaiah looked at her pointedly, almost disgustedly.

"Abishag, I have been dying to do something, *anything,* for weeks! You name the time, and consider it done."

She smiled at him.

"It must be done soon, the prisoner is in mortal danger," Huram said. "I intend to deliver him to the king myself, and I must be on my way as soon as possible."

"I can do it this very night," Benaiah said.

That night, while the key-keeper slept, Benaiah accomplished the breakout, and much more quietly than he had when he attempted to free Abishag.

As planned, Huram spirited Pildash, the utterly confused Hittite prisoner off to safer keeping. Benaiah was not aware, however, as he quickly left the prison in the other direction, that he was observed by other travelers on the road.

Chapter 22

Huram was not gone to Jerusalem long when once again the valley was shocked with alarming news. The Hittite raiders had struck again. This time, a remote farm east of town was the target. Word of the attack traveled like a lightning bolt through the valley, the ruthlessness of the raiders raising hair on necks, causing women to tremble, and children to weep in fear. The attack seemed calculated to terrorize as much as to spoil. The raiders had come by night, and that on a Sabbath, surrounding the farm stealthily by torchlight, just as the family was beginning their Sabbath prayers.

Suddenly, the blood curdling war-cry of the Hittite savages sounded, as the attackers surrounded the home on all sides, causing the terrified family to bar the door and windows and huddle together. The raiders sacked their barns, and spoiled their provisions. Every scrap of winter sustenance and seed grain was stolen. Not content merely with goods, the raiders then spilled the winter oil on the provender and set it aflame in the barns, chasing the terrified farm animals away. While galloping away with their spoil, the marauders had showered the house itself with flaming arrows. The terrified family fled the burning house. Minutes later the entire roof was consumed in flames, and its burning timbers fell inside destroying all the possessions contained therein. Only charred stone walls remained where once a peaceful provincial home had stood mere minutes before. The trembling and horrified family was left standing outside beholding a smoking ruin, their lives the only thing salvaged of all of their possessions, as the wild hoots of the receding attackers echoed eerily from the darkening hills.

An emergency meeting of the Council of Kinsmen was called in response, and Hamon, who had been charged with the protection of the village, was visibly furious to the point of lividity as the attack was reported. An intense discussion ensued, with varied responses proposed, including appealing to the king's royal forces for aid, doubling the size of the militia and putting them on regular patrols, and even employing the militia on a recompense strike back into Hittite territory. Hamon, visibly sullen, listened silently to the debate, not offering much in the way of strategy, his lack of participation gradually being noted by some. Finally, a question was put directly to him, as the village defender.

"The question is, Lord Hamon," asked Jezelel, the elected representative from the Brotherhood, "how can your militia, as strong as it is, protect us against these random and unpredictable attacks?"

Hamon let the silence linger as the question hung in the air.

"Brothers, I loathe to inform you of this, but the forces of the king himself could not provide security against random attacks such as these. No matter how large and how well trained an army, it simply cannot be in all places at all times. A clever enemy that shuns direct combat, though smaller in number, will always be able to find strategically chosen locations where it can bring an attacking force larger than those posted in defense. And when the defending army maneuvers to protect that location, the next attack will take place in the area it has vacated. The answer to this crisis is not to be found in any army, be it our own, or the army of the king. Being that our town is situated in these northern reaches of the kingdom, we will always be within striking distance of the Hittite lands beyond. And though the king has annexed those lands, the original occupants remain there, and will not cease to seek opportunities to avenge the injustice they believe the king has done to them. These strikes, I am afraid, will continue."

To the intently listening Council, Hamon's unassailable logic descended like a death sentence.

"But is there nothing then we can do, to assure our security?" asked Jezelel.

Hamon looked over at him, and then at the others.

"The defense against such threats is both simple and proven. Terrorist attacks, since time immemorial, have always been repelled by city walls."

The members of the Council regarded Hamon thoughtfully, exchanging glances with one another. Hamon, in his past manifestations, was famous for urging the surrounding of Shunem with a city wall. His plans in times past had been met with a range of objections, skepticism that it was necessary, and more so that it was possible. Since his conversion, no mention of it had crossed his lips, but the current crisis seemed to suddenly prove the strategic wisdom of a physical wall of defense.

Hamon looked around at their thoughtful faces.

"I understand, of course, that this has been proposed before, and am not unaware of the magnitude and difficulty of the undertaking. Nor do I despise the well-founded distrust that many had of my past proposals. But I am no longer motivated by vain ambition, to make myself something great, or to raise the symbolic status of our city. In fact, I no longer posess any land of my own to defend. It is in *your* interest that I now revisit this proposal. I have been solemnly charged in the office of Defender of the City. In that, it is incumbent upon me to offer fitting advice for our collective defense, my past sins not withstanding. Under the circumstances, I find no choice but to recommend that which I have urged before, that we begin in earnest the necessary task of defending ourselves, through the building of a wall."

"Lord Hamon . . . a wall would be quite expensive."

"And large, and labor intensive," added another.

"If one considers the many losses if these raids continue—the lost harvests together with all the labor to grow them, the expense of this protection may be much less than the loss without it," Hamon replied.

"Perhaps so, but how can such a project possibly be funded? It would take years of labor at great expense to ever complete."

"The magnitude of the challenge needs no telling. But it is a challenge that many cities of our size have matched on countless occasions in history. Our resources are no less than theirs. If other cities could do it, we can also. But we can only succeed with a collective effort over time. No single person has the time and resources to bring it to pass. No—our challenge is not the lack of resources, but the lack of will, and a unified plan."

"In ancient city-states where a city wall was constructed, the resources of the entire region were in the hand of the king of the city, who allocated them as required to achieve long term security, and each man had to be content with what was left to him. Such is not the case in Israel, for this nation's resources are scattered through private land ownership into many hands. This makes a combined effort more difficult to accomplish, though the same resources are present. But we have, at this moment, one advantage that has not been ours until recently."

"What is that?"

"This very body. For the first time in our city's history, governorship has been placed in the hands of an elected few: the seven of us. Truly it would have been impossible to achieve enough consensus in our former scattered form of government to do anything large. But the seven of us have been chosen to represent the whole, and charged with the solemn responsibility of making decisions that benefit the whole. If we, this body, agree that a city wall is necessary to assure our security, we can also make it possible by decree."

The lucidity of Hamon's proposal was stunning, and tingled in the ears of every member of the Council of Kinsmen, though each maintained his private reservations. The meeting was adjourned, and the members were dismissed with much to think about. Despite the ambitious nature of Hamon's proposal, it was generally noted that no other realistic defense against the Hittite raids had been proposed. It was also noted that the population would be expecting the Council to supply some kind of solution. If it did not, the usefulness of the Council itself could be rightly questioned.

Following a week during which council members consulted with their countrymen and neighbors, the body met again, anxious to revisit the discussion, for indeed the population had declared loudly that *something* must be done in response to the Hittite raids. If the Council would not take action, private parties were threatening to take matters into their own hands. After hurried preliminaries, representatives from the Brotherhood and the Elders brought the topic of the city wall to the table again, and various members spoke. Though the strategic benefit of the plan was little questioned, a recurring theme was the question of its expense. How could such a thing be paid for? And would the population have the will to follow through with it when the full cost was set before them?

Hamon echoed these same concerns, but also warned that if the venture were to begin, it must indeed be finished, lest a partially finished wall become an embarrassment to the town, and source of encouragement to its enemies.

"It would be better to not begin a wall than to start and fail," he warned.

"But you have yourself begun a wall. It even now stretches over the hills surrounding even the nearer farms," noted an elder.

"Begun yes, and this was done at my own expense, utilizing resources that I then had at my disposal. I no longer have the means to finish what I began. But the planning was well conceived. This much is in our favor. If the wall that my estate began were to be continued, we would be a step ahead in the work of design and placement. The Council could simply pick up construction where I left off, for its design was well conceived, and the workmen who began its construction could be reemployed. This already saves us perhaps one third of the cost."

"What of the other two thirds?"

"I have been considering that. It goes without saying that the fields within the wall would benefit most from its protection. Is it not right then, that those very fields should bear some of the cost? A percentage could be taken from each harvest, to pay for the wall's stones, and the workmen who place them. The cost burden could be spread out over a number of years. But . . ." he broke off.

The full attention of the Council was now upon him. He returned from apparent thought to meet their gazes.

"I fear it still will not work," he finished.

The six listening members were so fascinated with the prospect he was proposing that it was some moments before one of them asked the obligatory question.

"Why is that?"

"Because, though the plan is feasible financially, its weakness lies in the newness of this body itself. I am not certain that we have sufficient confidence with the population to overcome the hostility that will surely come when expense of the wall is subtracted from their profits from the fields. Men who consent to contribute their means while feeling freshly the sting of a recent raid may find it less important, when the hard earned profits of a harvest must be sacrificed. In that case, the wall project could in fact mean the end of this body, rather than the end of the raids. Our new form of government is young and experimental at best, and its legal status is tenuous."

Hamon looked thoughtful again.

The elder sighed.

"If only the ancients had already encircled our city," he mused.

Suddenly Hamon's eyes widened and he looked up, as if struck with an idea.

"Yes . . ."

All heads turned to him.

"What if . . ." Hamon began, his eyes wandering in thought. "What if our wall were *already* completed?"

"What is your meaning?"

"Only this. It occurs to me, that it would not be the wealthy who would object to the expense of the wall, but the poor. Those with less harvest would see in its taxation a threat to their sustenance. But the wealthy, with their personal needs not so intimately threatened, would rather see in the wall security for their holdings. If only wealthy were required to pay, the objection would be much less shrill."

"But the wealthy will surely object to bearing the whole burden themselves, when the poor also benefit from the wall."

"Doubtless. And there is something that has not occurred to me until this moment, but the mere existence of a city wall changes something very fundamental about our economy. If I am not mistaken, lands within a city wall are not subject to inheritance laws, but may be bought and sold freely and permanently. Is this not correct?"

Hamon looked over at the representative from the elders, who cocked his head and searched his memory.

"I believe you are correct, come to think of it," he said, stroking his beard. "We would have to search the Law for the exact language, but, yes, only lands outside of a city wall are subject to the laws of inheritance, redemption, and Jubilee. Lands inside a city wall may be bought and sold at any time. This much is true, but how will this help us finish our wall?"

"Only by this," Hamon replied. "If our wall were *already,* finished, the lands inside it could be legally and rightly purchased. And who would be in a position to make these purchases? The wealthy, of course, those who would be most favorable to our having a city wall."

A room full of thoughtful faces pondered the creative idea.

"And the poor would receive a fair recompense for their sold lands," the elder added, thoughtfully.

"But there are some who would never agree to vacate their long held lands," someone objected.

"Nor would they be required to," replied Hamon. "The same families could secure leases to farm the same land, and partake of their own harvests as they always had, but they would do so with both the means and the option to buy other lands, if they so wish, with the proceeds from their sold estates. There are always lands available for purchase, if not here, in other cities. Some may stay, some may go, but each would be treated fairly."

"And entirely according to law," added an elder.

"But the wall is not finished," objected a representative from the Brotherhood, "making the point moot."

"Is it not finished?" Hamon asked. "I am wondering, just now, at exactly what point in the process of construction a wall is declared complete. For even after it encircles, it is constantly maintained. Work never truly ends on a city wall."

The room was silent as new unforeseen possibilities seemed to float down around them like snow.

"Hamon, does the wall you began . . . encircle?" one of the elders asked.

"In fact, it does. As of one month ago, the ends were connected. Though it is not at full height, it does fully encircle the city."

The members of the council exchanged thoughtful glances, pondering the implications.

Suddenly the silence was broken by shrill screams from outside the building, and the sound of galloping horsemen, and shattering pottery.

The men started, and looked at one another urgently.

"It couldn't be . . ." one whispered.

"Right inside the village?!"

The council members hastened to the window of their upstairs meeting room and looked out to see a blur of horsemen on the street below, dressed in Hittite battle armor, racing through the center of town, breaking doors and windows with battle axes, and shooting flaming arrows. The invaders headed for the city square, where from the vantage point of the window, the council could see them terrorizing the booths of the merchants and knocking over their wares with long sticks as they galloped, circling the city square in a train.

"Hamon! Where is the militia?!" someone cried.

"Most of them are at the east farm, where the last raid took place, assisting in the reconstruction. I can dispatch a messenger to muster them, but they surely will not arrive here in time to intervene!"

The screaming and terrorizing continued for some minutes while the powerless council watched helplessly. Finally, the raiders peeled off down a side street and disappeared out of town, leaving havoc and distress in their wake.

"This must end," an elder whispered, seething.

"And now," another agreed. "We must offer the population a solution . . . today!"

A vote was hastily called. The livid council agreed to declare the city wall that Hamon had begun "complete" and resume construction upon it without delay. There was not a single dissenting vote.

Chapter 23

Abishag looked curiously ahead at the crowd of men that had formed around the Stone of Testimony, near the Hall of Records, where legal decrees were posted. The men were looking at a newly posted document, gesturing and speaking animatedly. The buzz of the crowd and their earnest expressions told her that no ordinary news was posted on the stone. She caught a glimpse of a tall gangly man standing near the post engaged in animated conversation with another man. Hemanah.

Someone brushed by her.

"Excuse me, my lord, can you tell me what everyone is speaking of?"

The man scowled and looked back at her.

"Men's business maiden. You would not understand. But if you want to know, there is a major shakeup about to happen. I hope your family has some funds put away, for much inheritance land is about to go up for public auction, according to what the Council of Kinsmen has posted."

Her eyes widened.

"Public auction?" she repeated, astonished.

The man continued on his way, with a shrug.

Back at her home, Abishag explained to her companions what she had learned that day, while Barkos, Jared, Dinah, and her mother listened with rapt attention.

"So everyone's land is to be sold, right from under them?" Barkos asked, amazed. "How can this be?"

"It is being done according to a clause in the Law. By the Law of Moses, lands within a city wall must be redeemed within one year. If they are not redeemed, they become salable property, no longer protected by inheritance laws and Jubilee. The Council has declared Hamon's wall complete, which means, everyone who owns land within it, if they wish to keep it, must redeem it at the highest price in a public auction. If they do not redeem it, it will go to the highest bidder, and the original owner will be reimbursed for it in silver."

"But that wall is nothing more than a pile of stones!" Jared objected.

"That is not how the Council has ruled. They have declared that the wall must be 'heightened' to protect against these raids that have been terrorizing us. All farms within the wall will be taxed to pay for it."

"But Abishag, *our* farm is within that . . . wall," Abelah noted.

"It is," she agreed. "As is Barko's vineyard."

"But what of the original value of the land?" Dinah asked. "The families who already own it should have a claim to it at that value."

"Yes, and they do. The original owners are granted an opening bid amount equal to the current value of their land, based on its most recent valuation. Anyone who wants to bid must match that amount. Bidding starts on top of that, and the original owner must then add silver to arrive at a total sum higher than any other bid in order to keep his land."

"They have to bid to keep their own land?" Jared asked.

"The Law says the land must be redeemed within one year. This is how the Council has interpreted that injunction," she replied. "The original owners will be reimbursed their land's value in silver. Silver pledged above that amount will go into city funds, and be applied to the building of the wall."

"But most of the people have no silver. Most of the people have nothing but land, especially Brotherhood families who profited nothing from this year's harvest due to the raid," Barkos objected.

"Then they are at the mercy of the wealthy who have liquid funds available," Jared observed.

"Are you sure this is legal?" Barkos asked Abishag.

She sighed.

"According to the letter of the Law, I suppose it is. But that Hamon's pile of stones could actually be what the Law of Moses meant by a city wall—that is doubtful."

"How are the people reacting?" Abelah asked.

"Well, strangely, some are welcoming it. They are saying it is the only way to protect against the Hittite raids. Others, I don't know. I suppose many are doubting, such as we are. I heard some men saying that, though the plan is not perfect, the population agreed to accept the authority of the Council of Kinsmen. They are glad that some action is being taken, even if it seems extreme."

"I am quite sure some families I know will not be favorable to this," Jared said. "They will fight it, they will perhaps reestablish the Brotherhood to raise the funds to keep their estates, for if they do not, the wealthy will buy out the poor, and they will be left with silver, but no land. They will have to move away, or take up careers as merchants. After finally getting their inheritance land back after all of these years, many will want to keep it."

"I am sure Hemanah will want to hold on to our estate," Abelah noted.

The occupants of the room exchanged glances.

"But he has no silver either," Barkos observed, voicing the common thought.

Abishag shook her head.

"Poor Hemanah. He must be in an absolute panic. He does not yet know of the resources we have available."

"Are you going to enlighten him then, dear?" Abelah asked her daughter.

Dinah snorted in laughter, and the group looked at her.

"I have not observed in Hemanah the ability to receive truth by the mere telling of it," Dinah explained. "Not that I hold that against him," she quickly added.

Abishag smiled.

"Yes, my brother, it seems, must sometimes be shown truth rather than told it. But in this case, I do not know if I am the one to show him. He may have to find out for himself, when the time comes."

****

Two desperate men, former leaders of the Brotherhood, sat before Jockshan, the physician, for the second time in two months.

"We, and many former members of the Brotherhood, are quite concerned that we will not be able to match and surpass all bidders when the day of the redemption of our land arrives."

The man leaned forward as he spoke, his brow deeply furrowed.

"We know you helped us in the past, that is why we now come to you right away while there is still time to raise additional funds," the other man added.

"You believe there is yet a mission for the Brotherhood?"

Jockshan replied. "Everything is different now—the Brotherhood, such as it was, has been disbanded. It is now represented in the Council of Kinsmen."

The two men exchanged a glance.

"Jockshan. With no disrespect meant to our representation—they are certainly acting according to what they believe is best for the whole population—it is just that the result of their decision is that we could lose our land again, and that so shortly after it has been restored to us. We have no silver with which to redeem our land if others step forward to bid on it. All of our harvest profits were lost when we invested with you in the Brotherhood. Other families, who shunned joining us—they may have some silver—but we of the Brotherhood have nothing. We who risked the most are now the most vulnerable. Everything we had prior to the harvest was pledged to Hamon to make the payments to continue the buyout. We have no silver, nothing at all, other than our land. Jockshan, you have to help us."

"How do you propose I help you? I matched from my personal funds every piece of silver that the Brotherhood raised. You at least regained your land. If you lost in this venture, I lost much more. I simply do not have funds to pledge to you, even if I do understand the risk that you face."

"But you have skill. You have the trust of the people. You have leadership. You arranged it before. Out of the very dust, it seemed, you pulled together a force that was on the verge of toppling Hamon's monopoly. It was an absolute marvel. If you could do it once, you could surely do it again. The amount needed to secure our land is much less than you raised to redeem it the first time. Jockshan, we need your help," the man pleaded.

Jockshan hesitated, observing the worry on the man's face. The risk of losing his land permanently was real, though he would be paid for it.

"What happens in that public auction is *permanent,* Jockshan. There will be no Jubilee redemption for it. If the land is not redeemed in one year, it never will be. But if it is redeemed, it can never again be taken from us."

"But without a harvest with which to raise funds, it is difficult to redeem anything," Jockshan objected.

"But there is a whole year within which the land can be redeemed, Jockshan. Thus saith the Law of Moses. If at any time during that year we can top the highest bid, we keep the land. That means, the next harvest could provide the funds we need, for it is now less than a year away—though barely."

"But if the deeds are transferred now, you will only be operating on a lease, at best, at the time of harvest," Jockshan derived.

"Yes. Only part of the profits will be ours, if we are under a lease. And if the new owner, whoever it is, knows the difference we must make up, he can make sure that our take of the harvest is less than that, to make sure we can't outbid him. We need another source."

"I see," Jockshan said. "So the Brotherhood could add to your bid before the year runs out and . . ." Suddenly his voice trailed off, and he looked up sharply in thought.

The two men exchanged a puzzled glance.

"Hamon . . ." Jockshan whispered, looking up in wonder, suddenly lost in inscrutable deliberation.

"My lord?" the man asked.

Jockshan looked back down, hesitating.

"Hamon . . . has a contract, we signed a covenant with him—the Brotherhood did—just before harvest, promising that we would not bid on any more land, for . . . a year and six months, in exchange for extending the terms. Remember?"

The two men stared at him, stunned.

"But Hamon is converted now," one of them stammered. "He surely would not bind us to a contract signed in his former state . . . would he?"

"Yes, he has restored all of our lands. He does not want them," said the other, looking back at Jockshan.

Jockshan did not answer right away.

"If he does not void the covenant we signed with him, the Brotherhood cannot help you in any way," Jockshan stated. "Nor can I, for the language of the covenant binds both me personally, and the Brotherhood, in whole or in part, from involvement in any land purchases for a year and six months. It is quite specific."

"Well then you must speak to Hamon first. I am sure he will be cooperative. He has been nothing but cooperative for some time now."

"Yes . . ." Jockshan mused, still distant. "Yes, very well, I will speak to him. That will be the first step. Then, we can explore ways that perhaps the Brotherhood can assist in this matter."

After the two men left, Jockshan sat in his chair for a long time, pondering with a new appreciation the strange covenant that Hamon had required the Brotherhood to sign, just prior to the harvest. Strange, how it extended for a year and six months, just long enough to prevent the Brotherhood from participating in any of the upcoming bidding. Strange how it would disqualify the entire Brotherhood, potentially the largest bidder in the area, from participating in any land purchases, just when the most extensive transactions in the history of the valley would be taking place. Strange . . .

****

Huram sat before Solomon. The urgent intensity with which the king listened to Huram's recounting of affairs in the town of Shunem, Huram found almost frightening. The king was known to possess singular powers of concentration, but this particular topic seemed to provoke him to levels of intensity previously unknown. The somber silence that stretched for mere seconds seemed hours, after Huram concluded.

"And she is fully unharmed, despite all," the king observed, finally.

"Yes, my lord," Huram replied, the tingling sensation in his spine making him thankful to be able to utter those three words truthfully. For all their cherished friendship, moments such as these reminded Huram that his friend was more than merely that, he was the king, and could rise to the plane of his office with blinding speed.

"I am, my brother, thankful for your careful attention in this matter, for though I am constrained by distance, few concerns are nearer to my heart," Solomon declared.

Huram shivered again.

"I am aware of that, my lord," he replied. "And your restraint in this matter is surely a credit to your great trust in the Shulamite. It is for that only, and in respect to your wise instructions, that I have allowed events to proceed with so little intervention."

Solomon nodded, the compliment bestowed upon his beloved not escaping his notice.

"Your confidence is not misplaced, my brother. It was, after all, she who chose this course, with my blessing. But the time of non-intervention is racing to an end. This space of repentance was graciously granted to her people by the Shulamite herself. Those of her village know not the opportunity that she has purchased them. They know not her great value. They know not . . . my love for her. She is my beloved bride, the fairest of ten thousand."

"And for all of that, she is my sister, as well," Huram replied. "I had not the opportunity to observe her as did you, but over the past months I have come to know firsthand she is well worthy of the confidence you place in her. If, God forbid, the king should perish, the Shulamite would be protected by my own hand, for it is not the king's orders alone that binds me to her, but my own soul as well."

At that, the king seemed to relax a small measure. He took a deep thoughtful breath.

"The proceedings in this village are nothing if not interesting, even without the presence there of my beloved. It appears there is much that must yet transpire before the time of our intervention. And though at present things proceed without our intrusion, they do not proceed outside of our watchful eye. My beloved knows this."

Huram perceived the last sentence was laced with a question.

"Could she have endured what she has without such knowledge? Surely she knows this well, my king. Yet, a single word from you, no matter how small, would carve into stone those sentiments that she carries in wood."

Solomon smiled at the craftsman's tradecraft simile. He lifted a finger.

"You may tell my beloved, that she has run well, that I am most pleased, that there are trials yet to be overcome, and that I am coming quickly. As for the other things that are in my heart, suffice to let her know that they are such things that another will never be able to convey. But this you may say, that I am preparing a place for her, and that it will never be complete until she abides with me permanently. And tell her that the vine, which is planted in my house is begun to thrive, and reminds me daily of the one who nourished it and gave it its strength and fiber. She is like that vine, for though her branches are in Shunem, her roots are wrapped around my throne in Jerusalem. Drawing virtue from here, her branches bear fruits afar. Together, and soon, we shall eat these pleasant fruits."

Huram nodded.

"She will hear all of these things."

"And send my strength to your mother as well," Solomon added. "Do you expect to return to them soon?"

"My travels will take me to the village and beyond again, for the project on the mountain is now begun, and I must manage the work force as it progresses, replacing laborers with craftsmen. I am come here only to deliver this report to you, and also bring this Hittite prisoner. If my lord permits, I will depart in the morning."

"Very well," Solomon replied. "Have you yet questioned the

prisoner?"

"The boy is young," Huram replied. "Though it would have been possible to derive confessions from him, I saved that honor in full for the king. For I do not want that he would find space to reconsider between giving testimony to me and to you also. At this time, he knows not why he is brought here. But once in your hand, he will surely speak, and his first and every word will be recorded in your hearing."

"Wisely done," Solomon replied.

The two friends regarded each other with warmth, both on the verge of smiling.

"This is proceeding well, despite all, is it not?" Huram observed.

Solomon shook his head knowingly.

"A most marvelous venture in the whole! The thing is surely of the Lord, for how else could things so work in our favor of their own? This prisoner is a mark of confirmation to us. We must have confidence in He who delivered him to us, and thusly arranged it all."

Huram found himself, once again, in nothing but agreement with the king.

****

Hamon was well satisfied with the progress of his plan, and the city wall project. Confirmed by the Council of Kinsmen in their last meeting, it put him, he believed, in the exact position he wanted to be. He called a meeting with his closest associates: his brother Caleh, his nephew Lotan, and in this case, even his father. Lotan showed up to the meeting early and tense.

Hamon looked up curiously at his nephew's taut expression.

"You will be less apprehensive after you learn the windfall that awaits you, Lotan."

"Ah," Lotan replied. "And I am sure it will afford all the enjoyments that money can buy."

Hamon studied him.

"You are too transparent, nephew, and too smitten. Did I not counsel you that it is foolish to let yourself become too attached to any one maiden? But, I have been improving your chances on that score also. You may end up with your little meadow flower yet."

Lotan reddened.

"Be that as it may," Lotan said. "I have news, with respect to that maiden's family."

He suddenly had Hamon's attention in full.

"Is the boy guard returned?"

"More than that. Benaiah is incarcerated."

"Incarcerated? That's the kind of news I like. How?"

"The news is not as good as you might suppose. The other prisoner is escaped," Lotan said.

Hamon grew tense.

"Escaped? Pildash, the Hittite?"

"I am afraid so."

After a moment of stillness, Hamon pounded the table.

"How can we gain one and lose another? Sometimes I feel our net is more a sieve! What else have you to tell me—good news I hope."

"Strange news would be more accurate. The boy guard by the name of Benaiah was seen at the east end of town. He was moving quickly, running almost, trying to avoid being seen. If I had not happened to be passing that way, he would have escaped without notice, but he was coming from the direction of the tower."

"From the tower?"

Lotan nodded.

"Yes. And after taking him there, we discovered that the other prisoner had recently escaped."

"How recently?"

Lotan paused.

"Very recently. Within mere minutes."

"Was he seen, chased?—was there any attempt to track him?"

"It is being organized now, my lord. It took some time to get a contingent together . . ."

Hamon suddenly cursed loudly, kicking the wall, causing Lotan to start.

"We tried to organize a search but . . ."

"But you did not find him! You lost him! Did I not charge you to make that prison more secure? Do you know what this means?! That boy knows the identity of ALL of the other Hittites! We needed him dead, not escaped! And now you wait until his trail is hopelessly cold to inform me?"

Lotan hesitated to respond, perspiration forming on his forehead, while Hamon paced the room angrily.

Lotan glanced at the door.

"Your brother will be here shortly . . ."

"Yes, and my father is expecting us also. Caleh must know everything you have told me, but there is no need of my father knowing of the escaped prisoner. Is that clear?"

"Quite."

"So you let your little Hittite slip away, eh?" Baal Hamon the elder rasped.

Hamon gasped exasperated, and looked over at Lotan and Caleh, but realized they would have had no chance to inform him of that.

"Ah. I wasn't sure of that until your reaction just proved it to me," Hamon's father said to him.

Hamon pursed his lips together hard and shook his head bitterly. How did the old man always do it?

"Oh you already hinted at it, with all your good news about the captured guard, your dealings with the Council, your chance to legally acquire all the land—with such a string of glowing reports, I knew you must be hiding *something* from me."

"Alright," Hamon replied. "Alright!" He stood up. "Tell us what to *do* about it!"

"Ahh—My counsel is finally sought. Unfortunate that I had to suffer through all your braggadocio to get to this point, but if you truly want my advice, I require something in exchange."

"And what is that?"

"I have witnesses before me here and now, and the right to distribute my inheritance as I will. You have assumed that all the gold would be yours, of course. But before these witnesses, I am inclined to pass a fair share of it to them, depending on how you answer me."

Hamon was silent, while Caleh and Lotan suddenly became interested.

"What do you want?" Hamon muttered.

"My people," his father replied. "Have you yet contacted them? When we last spoke you agreed to deliver a message to them. And don't lie to me, because I will know it!"

Hamon did not doubt it.

"There has been . . . *much* to attend to recently father."

"Ah. And that on the heels of informing me how splendidly your plan has been succeeding, how effortlessly, how perfectly, and yet no time to dispatch so much as a message to . . ."

"Enough!" Hamon bellowed. "I will contact them! What do you want me to say?"

"Oh splendid. Once again you reply with the all the grace of an ox in a dove's nest," the elder said, casting a wearisome look at the other two men. "How your associates must suffer under the clumsy club of your bumbling leadership. But to the point at hand, you have kindly informed me of the windfall of land you are about to inherit permanently, provided I assist you with a bit of gold. Well then. Here is my requirement: my gold will be available for this purchase, but only if estates are also secured for the Amalekites that I name to you."

"But Amalekites cannot own Israelite land," Hamon objected.

"Have you not just proudly informed me that Amalekites can now become naturalized Israelites, through circumcision?" his father replied.

Hamon opened his mouth but then hesitated, brooding silently for a long moment, while his brother and nephew watched, silently enjoying seeing their superior in a subservient position. The elder Baal Hamon cast a wink at his younger son and Lotan.

"He'll come to the sense of it by and by," he said to them, loud enough for Hamon to hear. Hamon fumed.

"And your counsel?" Hamon asked, through clenched teeth.

"We have an agreement then, witnessed by these?" his father asked, indicating Caleh and Lotan with his hand.

"Yes."

"Good, then let us prepare the document now, and I will dispatch a servant to get it on its way."

"Now?"

"It must leave this room today, impressed with your seal. And it must go by the hand of my servant not yours. Then, and only then, we will speak of my gold, and of my counsel."

The room fell silent.

"Do it, Hamon," Caleh urged.

Hamon shot him an irritated look.

"Very well," Hamon agreed. "Bring in the ready-writer."

The four of them witnessed while Hamon dourly dictated a letter to his father's relatives in the homeland, submitting to numerous corrections in language that his father insisted upon, then sealed it with his own seal, and the writer was dispatched to send it out with the daily messengers.

"Now," Hamon the elder said. "We may speak of my gold, and my counsel."

"The gold alone would be sufficient," Hamon muttered.

For the first time, the elder seemed to lose a measure of control, his voice rising as much as his infirmity would allow.

"Fool! One cannot be *had* without the other! Do you think I would enjoy seeing all I have acquired here lost to the wind by your bumbling gaffes?! Without my counsel, my gold will profit you nothing, for you will surely lose every last shekel of it before the next harvest! Now then, you *will* hear my counsel. This boy guard, Benaiah, who has just been captured. He is guilty of aiding and abetting the Hittite enemies, is he not? He may even be a Hittite himself for all I know."

"He is not. His sister is an Israelite," Lotan piped in, then blushed.

"And you have long been more interested in *her* than him," the elder said to him darkly.

Caleh snickered under his sleeve, while Lotan held silence.

"But what you are all missing is that he is manifestly a Hittite in his allegiance, if not in his blood. For who but a Hittite sympathizer would free a Hittite prisoner?—which means more to you than you know."

He stopped speaking.

The three younger men looked at each other curiously. Hamon the elder almost grew angry.

"It means that the escaped prisoner of last summer, whom this guard is protecting with his false story, is *also* a Hittite, you fools! You not only have something to discredit this boy, you have something to discredit the man you tried to convict, and could not convict."

"And if Jedidiah returns . . ." Hamon pondered.

"Yes. If he returns, this boy is proof he is an enemy of Israel. For all I know, this escaped man is *responsible* for the Hittite raids that have been occurring."

"But we have been publishing that Jedidiah is dead," Hamon objected.

"Yes. And if he is dead, these raiders are avenging that. If he is not, this boy guard, a Hittite sympathizer has been providing protection for an enemy of Israel. None of the words of such a traitor could be believed. If he starts blabbering about some miraculous escape, he will be dismissed as a traitorous fool. Whether the man you tried to convict lives or not, both he and the boy guard are now discredited. *Work* with that story. Try the boy and convict him. Put the blame for every evil of these Hittite raids upon him—and all of his associates. Your position will be much stronger if the man who outfoxed you last summer, ever returns."

"What if the *actual* Hittite raider, who was incarcerated until now, returns?" Hamon asked.

His father looked at him most disapprovingly.

"You insult me. I well know that your prisoner was *not* an actual Hittite. But if I must stoop to such a foolish question, I would ask why he would come back? To return to the prison from which he escaped?"

"Right. He is . . . surely gone," Hamon agreed.

"And you . . ." the elder said to Lotan. "If that boy Benaiah is put in prison and made to suffer, you could gain a bit of leverage on that maiden you worship by making yourself the one who smuggles him the odd extra crust of bread, at her request."

"Right . . ." Lotan replied, pondering.

"In any case, you will have a better chance of picking the lily of your eye, than my son does of his. He doesn't stand a chance with Abishag," he added with a smirk that blended into a rasping cough.

Hamon raged inwardly, but remained silent.

"And you . . ." the elder's sharp tongue turned toward his younger son, Caleh. "It would do you *good* to find some respectable maiden, and marry her. Your brother's shadow has allowed you to play at life without any real responsibility, but you will be left quite exposed when one of his insidious gaffes leaves him hanging from the gallows one of these days. Stop playing around like some school-boy and start building respect for yourself among the local population—you may need it one day. Leave your carousing for other cities."

Caleh blinked at the sudden penetrating attack.

"And now. I tire. The gold will be available when you need it. Be gone from me," Hamon the elder said with a sweeping gesture of his fingers, leaning back on his couch, removing both his eyes and his full attention from his three visitors.

Hamon glanced up at Caleh and Lotan slowly. There was nothing more to be said, and the three left the room, each astonished for his own reason.

Chapter 24

It was a cold morning in the month of Tibet. The fields lay dark and quiet, scattered with bare dirt and stubble from the now complete harvest, to all appearances, dead. But beneath the gray upper layer, millions of tiny seeds glowed with the spark of life, awaiting only the warmth of the spring sun and the soft caress of the latter rains to awaken them. Harvest had past and so had the traditional fall sowing, and the residents of the valley for the first time in many months were enjoying a long awaited rest. Blue-gray smoke rose from the tops of each of the little provincial hamlets that scattered the valley floor, blending into the morning mist.

But despite the serene appearance, a low current of anxiety flowed through each farmhouse that fell within the boundaries of the planned city wall, which was almost all of them. The reason for this unseasonable angst was the knowledge that on this day, the results of the first round of silent bidding would be revealed—bidding that could cause lands that had for generations been the untouchable birthright of the descendants of the Israelites who first settled them, to be acquired by others, permanently. More deeply did this anxiety flow among former members of the Brotherhood, for not only were they more attached to their lands, but were most without means to add a single shekel of silver to the assessed price of their lands, if a purchaser should match that amount with a bid. The secrecy of the proceedings intensified the anxiety even more, for with all bidders secret, even neighbors who had long lived together in peace found themselves looking upon one another with suspicion, searching their memories for any small conflict that might provide motivation for another to buy them out.

For all the reforms the valley had seen in recent months, an eerie discomfort had settled over the population, like a blanket of fog. How had such promise turned to such gloom so quickly? For many, the unspoken hope was that the event would pass quietly, that not many bidders would come forward, and that, except for the recording of some legal technicalities, everything would remain as it was.

The lone figure that walked the trail from the hillside toward the village, a single young woman named Abishag, resolute in her assurance, gentle in her demeanor, seemingly alone, yet carrying the seal of the highest authority in the known world closely over her heart, moved small and shadowy in the dim of pre-dawn, unnoticed by all. None knew that the answer to every man's worries and dreams was borne about her neck, and less would have believed it if told. Yet the Seal of Solomon was passing through their midst unawares, present for the very purpose of restoring the equity so longed for. It passed not openly, but not unduly hidden either, for any with a spirit to learn, would of it learn. Such were few.

The purpose of the maiden's travel this morning was to observe the proceedings in the Hall of Records, where the Book of Records would be opened, and bids placed upon the lands described therein would be read publicly. Well aware was she that the land on which her own home stood was also slotted for purchase, and any bids made upon it would be revealed this day. But her interest in the proceedings extended far beyond her own little vineyard, for she already suspected what was widely dreaded: that many, many estates would be found challenged, when the bids were opened.

Necks craned forward in the crowded room as the presiding officials unsealed the first of many documents to follow. Abishag also watched attentively, from a corner in the back, her presence unnoted. The Book of Names was opened, and the legal description of a plot of land, together with its ancient landmarks was read aloud. The rustling of a party in one quarter revealed the presence of that land's owner. The voice of the village recorder cut into the room, a voice so cold and precise, so without emotion, that the disturbing meaning of his words failed to register at first.

"The said land has been matched by bid, plus one-hundred shekels of silver."

The stunned silence that followed the announcement was nowhere more deeply found than in the quarter from which the previous rustling had occurred. The moment passed too quickly, and even before it was fully absorbed, the voice of the recorder again echoed in the chamber, as the legal description of the next plot of land was read. Again the fateful words were heard.

"The said land has been matched by bid, plus one-hundred shekels of silver."

Again it happened. And then again. The amounts varied, from fifty shekels up to one-hundred-fifty, but in each case, without exception, lands were found challenged by bid, in amounts that strangely appeared to be just beyond the reach of each owning party.

Abishag watched and listened intently, while her own estate, together with its lands, which were in the care of her brother Hemanah, was described.

"The said land has been matched by bid, plus thirty shekels of silver."

She heard the gasp of her elder brother, somewhere in the crowd ahead, followed by murmurings and whimpering, such as had followed the previous readings.

Thirty shekels of silver! A frightening amount for a poor family under the best of circumstances. She knew that Hemanah did not have it. Indeed, she herself had hardly ever seen that much money, aside from glimpsing gold pass between merchants during her time in Jerusalem. Such sums were unknown to her family, even following bounteous harvests. The amount revealed shrewd perception in the unknown bidder, as one intimately aware of the means of the estate, and its likely resources, just as had all the previous bids. That Hemanah would be unable to raise thirty shekels of silver after a lost harvest was an astute observation, putting redemption just beyond his reach, but not far beyond. This unknown bidder did not want to overextend unnecessarily. But who were these shrewd and calculating bidders, who with surgical precision were able to cut the lines so accurately? The secrecy of the proceedings rendered this impossible to know, yet for Abishag, it was impossible not to know. She marveled at how the identity of the unknown bidder could be a secret to anyone, yet, based on the conversations that she overheard following the adjournment of proceedings, general bewilderment was the consensus.

The pertinent legal paragraphs were read aloud at the meeting's close.

"Any land owner who wishes to redeem his land must do so within one year, by matching and exceeding the bid amounts read today. Any bidder may continue to post increases during that time. The bidder with the highest posting at year end will assume permanent ownership of the said estate."

The stunned and demoralized crowd dissipated with a sobriety that would make a funeral procession seem a celebration by comparison. Abishag, however, did not leave with the rest of the crowd. She waited until all had departed, and then entered the Hall of Records alone, with her hidden weapon. Putting it to use for the first time, she returned to her home, unnoticed. Back at the farm, Abishag related her morning's fateful activities to her carefully listening friends.

"So it begins," Abelah observed.

"You used it? You really applied the king's Seal?" Dinah

asked.

"I did. It had to be done. My only regret is not being able to consult with my brother first."

"Hemanah?" Jared asked.

"No. Huram," she replied.

There was a universal nod of understanding, as the occupants of the room exchanged glances.

"But I dared not delay any longer. The time for action has come."

"What did the officials say when they saw the seal?" Dinah asked.

"They did not see it. I prepared the document elsewhere, and delivered it to them rolled," Abishag explained.

Dinah repressed a smile in the silence that followed.

"I wish I could see their faces when they open that! This is going to . . . make some waves!"

"Hmf. Waves. Like an ocean swell on a mud puddle!" Barkos chimed in.

The others chuckled.

"Abishag. You *have* informed Hemanah?" Abelah queried.

Abishag shrugged meekly.

"I have tried for months to inform him. He departed quickly after the morning session—I did not get the chance to speak to him."

The occupants of the room exchanged amused glances.

"Well. He may find himself facing some . . . questions," Jared noted.

"Let him come here for answers then. He's not going to find them anywhere else. Maybe now he will listen," Barkos grunted.

****

Hamon and his associates were carefully examining a return letter from his father's Amalekite associates in Philistia when the interruption came. Being quite engaged in the letter, Hamon was not favorably disposed to the interruption, and if not for the urgency of the messenger, would have ignored it entirely.

"Excuse me," he said angrily while rising to step outside the room to engage the messenger.

"What is it?!" he demanded.

"There has been another bid, my lord," Sylva replied, "on one of the lands."

"Which land? Just go top it."

"It is uniquely worded, my lord. I believe you should see it for yourself."

She handed him a document, which he stared at and then frowned, mouthing the words as he read. Then he looked back at her.

"Highest bid plus one tithe?" he asked.

She shrugged meekly.

"Is this some kind of joke?"

"It was formally recorded, my lord."

"Who? Who would bid highest plus ten percent? That is absurd. Which estate?"

"It is the estate of Hemanah, my lord."

Hamon's eyes narrowed, as he looked away in thought.

"Hemanah!"

He continued to ponder.

"Hemanah you idiot," he muttered. "Sylva, Hemanah does not have any money. This is a farce, he's trying to . . . I don't know what he's trying to do, but he can't raise ten percent over what I can bid. He can't even raise thirty shekels!"

"What are your instructions, my lord?"

Hamon's eyes darted around, then he snapped his fingers suddenly.

"Alright," he declared. "My instructions? Here are my instructions. Go down and record a bid for five-hundred shekels of gold."

Sylva blinked, stunned.

"Gold, my lord? A shekel of gold is worth twelve times a shekel of silver . . ."

"Are my instructions unclear? Go do it!"

"Yes my lord, but do you really want to pay . . ."

"I am not going to pay! We will call for a Display of Means. We will bring down our five-hundred shekels of gold, he won't, and *both* of these bids will be thrown out. It will revert to thirty shekels of silver."

"Ahh. But, my lord, five-hundred is nearly all we have. Would it not be wiser to just deposit one-hundred?"

Hamon looked at her with irritation.

"You miss the point. We are not just refuting Hemanah, we are sending a message to anyone else who might want to muster a bid, and drive up the prices. When they see we have this kind of means, they will lose heart, and we will take the land for no more than our original bid."

Her mouth twisted into a thin smile.

"Clever, my lord."

"It is not difficult for a man to appear clever when surrounded with stupidity," he replied.

She blushed, and departed.

Hamon's associates looked back at him curiously as he re-entered the room.

"Someone entered a false bid," he explained. "I had to call for a Display of Means to get it thrown out."

****

A trio of elders had been appointed to oversee the bidding process. An emergency meeting of this trio was hastily arranged, after the receipt of a stunning report from the town recorders of an odd and unexpected bid. The elder Simeon was a member of this trio, and hastened to the Hall of Records for the second time that morning.

Messengers were immediately dispatched to locate Hemanah, the owner of the estate upon which the strange bid had appeared. And a message from the prior high bidder, "bidder number thirteen" as he was anonymously called, was received at the Hall of Records demanding an official "Display of Means," all before the sun had crowned noon.

The elders demanded of the recorders to know the identity of the latest bidder, and the recorders were at a loss to tell exactly who had delivered it. In frustration the elders upbraided them for recording this outrageous bid where any and all could read it, before the elders were even informed of it.

"What else was I supposed to do!?" the town clerk had angrily retorted. "It was a legally composed document. I do not render judgments on documents I record them! Besides, did you not strictly charge me that this is *secret* bidding? I am not *supposed* to know the identity of the bidders!"

For two hours, Hemanah, in increasing confusion and frustration, testified before a panel of questioners that he had no knowledge of a second bid being placed on his property, and no knowledge of who placed it. The elders cross examination of him yielded no results other than increased frustration on the part of all.

The demand for a Display of Means from "bidder number thirteen," was temporarily shelved while the elders deliberated, and Hamon was becoming increasingly irritated with the delay. A second messenger from his estate was dispatched to the Hall of Records, this time with a certificate of gold of certified weight from the Changers of Money, to be held in deposit, along with a repeated demand for a "Display of Means," by the other bidding party. This second message, to Hamon's great frustration, was answered with a vague and unsatisfying appeal to an unexplained "delay."

After the emergency meeting was adjourned with no satisfying result, Simeon returned home.

Hildah observed the uncharacteristic silence with which her husband Simeon entered the house, moving without comment to his favorite chair, where he sat down, removed his turban, and began rubbing his eyes, leaning forward with his elbows on his knees.

"There is so much tension in this valley," he lamented softly. "Sometimes I think the very earth is about to burst into pieces. And now . . ." he broke off.

Hildah studied him, curiously.

"And now?"

"If I had had any idea when I agreed to this appointment what a vexation it would become, I would never have accepted it."

"Your appointment is a sign of trust. The elders have shown you the great honor of entrusting you with the wise management of . . ."

"The wise management of insanity!" he suddenly blurted.

Hildah blinked.

He looked at her, then softened.

"Hildah. We could only hope that this bidding procedure would pass without incident. A hope that was, it seems, terribly naive. Why is this valley so cursed?! Everything we attempt, no matter how carefully conceived, somehow turns into some wild unpredictable debacle. When news of what happened today reaches the population—and it will, for it is public information—it will throw this whole wretched process into confusion. We may never recover the peace. A crazy bid was entered, this morning. A wild, ridiculous hoax! Something that in normal circumstances would be laughable, but in this environment can only stir up confusion, embolden forces barely restrained, tempting desperate men to act on their rasher passions."

"A legal bid?" she asked.

"Legal, yes, legitimate, no."

"How can a legal bid not be legitimate?"

He sighed and looked at her wearily.

"Hildah. The bid was entered in the name of . . . King Solomon!"

Hildah's mouth dropped open, and she covered it with her hand. In the silence that followed, Hildah's eyes darted over the carpet in front of them. Simeon sighed heavily.

"Well. Solomon certainly would have the means to afford . . ." her voice trailed off.

Simeon glanced up at her, first with surprise, then angry frustration.

"Hildah. You do not think . . . Hildah! Even you? Solomon is not here! The bid was sealed with the king's royal seal, dated this morning, but the king is not here. Do you not understand? The royal seal is never removed from the king himself. And the king is *not* in our village. It is a counterfeit!"

"Has the seal been . . . examined?" she asked carefully.

Simeon grimaced.

"That is just what I was afraid of. If *you* have such thoughts, how much more the rest of the population, who are desperate for any hope, no matter how wild? To go through the whole process of examining the seal would require weeks, maybe months, messages to and from Jerusalem, meanwhile tension mounts, patience wears thin—undoubtedly the whole procedure wrecks in a chaos of discontent. What was a simple matter is now a mish mash of uncertainty. This may even topple our newly formed government, which has been operating so efficiently. We were on the verge of having a city wall, a city wall! And now, we are on the verge of . . . complete chaos."

Hildah pursed her lips, nervously rubbing her fingers together in the tense silence.

"Who delivered the bid?" she asked.

"It was left on the desk. The clerks did not see, or cannot remember."

Hildah, who had thus far in life enjoyed a forthright relationship with her husband uncommon to the era in which she lived, found herself in a rare moment of uncertainty. She treasured the privilege of speaking freely with her husband, a privilege earned over many years of offering sensible replies. That she ought to say something to him was becoming increasingly clear by the moment, but that what she had to say would be received was doubtful, and portended only an unsavory and unproductive argument.

"What about the owner of the property?" she asked carefully.

He shook his head.

"It is the estate of Hemanah, of the north hill. He insists he knows nothing of it, and it certainly appears he does not."

"Do the rules of bidding mandate that only the male heir of the property deliver bids upon it?" she asked.

"What are you talking about?"

"Did not the daughters of Zelophehad act in a proprietary role concerning the redemption of their estates, when the male heirs had died?"

Simeon looked at his wife curiously.

"Of what import is that?"

"Only this: It appears that the elders have questioned the most likely candidate, the male heir, but in terms of redemption, it is the family land that is being redeemed. Any member of that family could pay the redemption price, could they not?"

"Well . . . yes, but in this case, it is not a member of the family that is . . . proposing a redemption, it is the . . . purported . . . King Solomon."

"I understand, my lord. I only mean to point out, that just because Hemanah does not have knowledge of this bid, does not mean no other member of the family does. Such a thing could be within the knowledge of one of the other brothers, or the mother, or . . . the sister."

Simeon glanced at her, then his eyes narrowed.

"Sister."

"Yes."

"You mean Abishag. That little peasant girl you have been worshiping lately. Well, if so, this should certainly break the spell she has had over you. To promote a sometimes successful home remedy is forgivable. But to deliberately throw a spark on the dry pile of tinder this valley has become is downright criminal. If that little urchin is responsible for this, even *you* ought to have sufficient grounds to doubt her."

"Or, if that little 'urchin' is responsible for something done in truth, even *you* ought to have grounds to accept her as credible," Hildah replied.

"Hildah!" Simeon shouted, surging to his feet.

****

Jockshan received news of the latest bid with the same stunned confusion as the rest of the population.

"King Solomon?"

The two senior members of the Brotherhood glanced at one another and back at the doctor.

Jockshan scratched his head, bewildered, then he blew out a tension-relieving laugh.

"This must be a joke."

"Or an act of desperation," replied one of the men.

Moments ticked by in silence.

"Or . . . the direct intervention of God, through the office of the king," the other man replied.

The heads of both Jockshan and the man's companion shot around to look at him.

"Surely, you are not *that* naïve," Jockshan said darkly.

The man blushed, and looked down, in silence.

"Who's estate was bid on?" the doctor asked.

"It was the estate of Hemanah."

"Ahh," Jockshan replied knowingly, then looked up sharply as if an unexpected thought had just occurred to him.

The Brotherhood elders glanced at each other curiously.

One of them cleared his throat.

"Jockshan. *Every* estate was bid upon, without exception. It has since been learned, that twenty-five out of the thirty bids entered were placed by one party—bidder number thirteen. But who is it?"

The doctor's eyes narrowed.

"Who indeed."

****

News reached even to Jezreel, before the sun had crossed the third watch of the day. Laban, the father of Jemimah, returned stunned to his booth of metal wares, after having witnessed a bid entered on his estate beyond what he could dream of challenging.

In awkward silence, the family went about their morning work, each tracing and retracing the wandering stream of their own private thoughts, absorbing the implications of their inheritance land being permanently bought out for money. But before long, their thoughts were interrupted by strange reports circulating among the merchants, reports which were confirmed by passing shoppers.

Jemimah could barely hold her peace, as the news was spoken in the hearing of, and then directly to, her father.

"One of the bids is already being challenged—by one of the poorest families in the valley, in fact, though I would not give a shekel for its chances of success," the fat man said to his companion, as he absently ran his hands over Laban's metal goods.

"They are poor for a reason," replied his companion. "Foolishness does not engender wealth. We always knew that oldest brother was a bit dull. After the father passed on, it's amazing he kept the estate together this long. But *this*—this is absurd!"

"More than absurd. It's criminal. He could be tried and convicted for this. Not only will he lose his land, he could lose his life."

"He did at least secure some good artwork—I hear. Probably put his last five shekels into that. The royal seal imprint is a respectable likeness."

The two men moved on, muttering to each other.

Gradually, Laban became aware of his youngest daughter's brooding stare. He looked over then frowned at her. Jemimah shrugged but kept her lips tight together.

"You hold your peace, daughter. Just because this came from the estate of Abishag, does not mean there is anything to it. She may have convinced her worthless brother of her wild tale, but not me. Maybe that's where he got the thing—from her."

Laban went back to his work, his brow furrowed in thought as his hands moved over their craft.

"It is a strange coincidence, though," she heard him mutter lowly.

Jemimah saw her sister Aijeleth approaching with a pot of water.

"I am going to go help Aijeleth," Jemimah said.

Her father nodded, and she hurried to meet her sister. Laban saw his youngest daughter approach and begin speaking animatedly to her sister, who listened for a moment, then lowered her pot to the ground while the conversation continued.

She is lobbying Aijeleth again. That stubborn daughter just will not relent!

Laban knew that his youngest daughter, through her constant insistence and a collection of circumstantial evidence, had made inroads into convincing his wife and eldest daughter of her strange tale, though none of them would contradict him openly.

It is all strangely coincidental, his lurking thought reminded him. He shook his head and tried to concentrate on his work. *Even Abelah confirms it,* the voice continued. *And your own son, Benaiah.*

The persistent little voice continued to plague Laban throughout the day. It did not respond to reasonable replies, nor would it quiet itself.

You only want to believe it for the sake of your land, you old fool! He scolded himself. *But its foolishness! There's nothing to it!*

****

The official word reached the ears of Baal Hamon, and just barely before the unofficial word, the elders having discerned that the rumor on the street was beyond containment. The message he read was plain, yet bewildering.

"Bidder number thirteen. The Display of Means, that you requested, came with the bid itself. The document bears the purported Seal of King Solomon. Until officially challenged, this

Display of Means will be treated as authentic."

Hamon's scowl deepened as he read the strange message, his associates exchanging uncertain glances as they attempted to discern the expression of their young lord.

"Bad news, I presume," Lotan queried.

"Bad is not the word for it—insane, is more like it. Our call for Display of Means has been met," Hamon replied.

"What?!"

"The bid carries the seal of King Solomon."

The stunned silence that followed this was deep and dark as a well.

"But, Solomon is not here," Caleh stammered. "He is not in the village—-it can't be."

"No . . ." Hamon agreed. "It is an attempt to . . . derail the process with nonsense."

"Well then let them try. It will backfire," Caleh said.

"No—it will work," Hamon replied.

"What?"

"I said, it will work!" he bellowed.

His audience was stunned into silence.

"You obviously do not understand so allow me to enlighten you. The battle we are engaged in does not take place in these ranging fields and vineyards. It takes place in the seven inches between the ears. Every inch we have gained on the ground, we have first gained by winning a battle in the minds of the people. And we have made gains, but they are fragile gains; they could evaporate in a moment. This false bid—its *real* purpose is to distract, confuse, throw the process into uncertainty, and then a protest will swell in the delay that follows. We needed a quick, clean conclusion, before anyone could mount a resistance. Whether it is a real seal or not, this bid is dangerous!"

"But what can we do? The elders say the bid must be

respected, until challenged. The next highest bidder must enter the challenge, if we think it is not legitimate. We have to challenge it."

Hamon sighed deeply.

"What if we don't challenge it?" he replied.

They looked at him curiously.

"That is obviously what they are trying to provoke—an official challenge. So, at least officially we allow the bid to stand. It's a small vineyard, a small estate. We will win anyway—after the false seal is discredited. What if we accept it for now, and dispatch a messenger to Jerusalem to render an official ruling later? Move on—let it lie—for now. We still win, in the end."

"But if we give the impression of accepting it, the perception—others may be encouraged to . . ."

"Perception!" Hamon exclaimed. "Now finally you are talking sense. And no, we do *not* give the perception of *accepting* it. We give the perception of discrediting it—but we do not challenge it *officially*."

"But how can we give *any* kind of perception, when the population does not know who we are?" Lotan objected.

"I am reconsidering that," Hamon replied.

"Really. Reconsidering it? Why?"

"Several reasons. You don't know the briefing I received earlier today. A rumor is being circulated, especially among the former members of the Brotherhood that we are attempting to monopolize the land. It is gaining strength. I know Jockshan is behind it. We may have to respond to these charges openly, show that our intentions are honorable—and coming forward, showing that we are not committed to secrecy would give us that opportunity, and also buy us some credibility."

"But what will you tell the people?" Caleh asked.

Hamon shot him a glance.

"I am working on that. But as to the other question—this

challenge on the vineyard, I am asking for your forthright opinion. Challenge it, or leave it be?"

The occupants of the room glanced at one another. Caleh fidgeted.

"I say, leave it," Lotan replied. "As long as we get a messenger on the way to Jerusalem right away, to bring us an official ruling."

Hamon looked at his brother.

"What do you say?" he asked.

"If . . . ," he began, "if you are attempting to show that we are not land hungry, letting the challenge stand would help that case."

"That's the smartest thing I have heard you say in a long time," Hamon said to his brother.

Calch accepted the barbed compliment.

"Alright, we leave the bid and get the messenger off to Jerusalem. Let's do it."

A message was drafted, and a messenger dispatched. Scarcely had he departed when there was a knock on the door.

"What is it?" Hamon called.

"A message, my Lord, from your father."

Hamon let out a wearied groan and went to retrieve the message, unrolling it before them. Then he gasped, and threw his hands into the air, then rubbed his head vigorously.

"How does he know these things?"

"What does it say?" queried Lotan.

"It says, 'don't do it.'"

Hamon sat before his father ungreeted. Unlike the last time, he came alone, staring at the lump of blankets into which his father was curled up facing the wall. To all appearances, asleep—or dead.

"By the gods of Siris, you are slow to learn!" the hoarse voice of his father suddenly muttered.

Hamon fumed.

"It is a false bid, father—-a false bid! Let that be proven, and we move ahead undeterred!"

"You know nothing at all. The intention of this bid is not to obtain land—it never was."

"I know that. The intention is to mire the whole process in nonsense," Hamon said.

"If you see no farther than that, you deserve to lose the land," said his father. "The intention, is to draw the king into the situation. You challenge that bid, you will have the king on your hands."

"But the king will refute them," Hamon protested.

"The king will refute YOU!" his father roared, with an intensity Hamon did not know the sick old man was capable of, rolling over to thrust a crooked finger into Hamon's face, then went into a wheezing fit. After it subsided, he continued on.

"You call that king on the scene, and in one hour he will have discerned everything, and by noon, YOU will be hanging from the gallows!—and probably me as well. Did I not counsel you strictly, do *nothing* to attract his attention?! That king is dangerous! And you in your stupidity were about to invite the axeman to come measure your neck! Oh, beautiful son, your discernment is stunning. You are the most imbecilic pig of a son that ever a man was cursed with! It would serve you right to find your feet dangling five cubits above the ground, but I have outfoxed the executioner for forty years, and I intend to pass naturally, so you will do as I say! And don't think you're going to ignore my counsel this time. You will have not a single shekel more of my gold if you do. After I am gone you can destroy yourself as often as you please."

Hamon's heart pounded under the impact of his father's diatribe, but he resisted, as he had hundreds of times, the urge to retort.

"But how will I refute the seal?" he managed, trying to keep his tone flat.

The elder gave him a disgusted look.

"How indeed? First I provide all of your gold, now I have to do all of your thinking. *You* figure it out. It's a false seal, you are many days journey from Jerusalem, way out in this far corner of the kingdom. The signs of its forgery must be everywhere. If you can't even manage a simple thing like that—well, don't get me started. It should be a simple matter to refute a false seal without getting the real king involved. Just DO NOT get him involved!"

"Father—it's too late, we dispatched the messenger already."

Hamon the elder's eyes widened, then his face turned deeply red. When he spoke, his voice husked low and cold.

"Send your fastest horse, and stop that messenger!"

Hamon collapsed into the chair in his private quarters, after having issued the order to catch and stop the messenger. He opened a flask of wine, poured a large mug, and sat staring at it. Caleh walked by, glanced in the open door.

"How did it go with father?"

"I hate him."

Chapter 25

In the next several days following the delivery of the bid bearing the purported seal of Solomon, the attention of the population was riveted on the proceedings. All were surprised to find that not only did the surprise bid go unchallenged, it went completely without comment from the authorities, for good or for bad. That such an astonishing thing could pass without provoking any official activity at all was the one result that no one had predicted. The silence was deafening. People began to wonder. Had the Council concluded that the seal was genuine? When pressed for details, the recording clerk simply repeated the law.

"If a bid is to be challenged, said challenge must be initiated by the previous high bidder."

Bidder number thirteen entered no such challenge.

The surprise extended even to the occupants of the north hill farm, where Abishag and her associates puzzled over the quiet acceptance of the bid she had entered. Hemanah responded first with shock, then denial, then a stream of disorganized arguments peppered with insults. But as days passed with none of the ill effects that he predicted coming to pass, his objections became less shrill. He was sorely outnumbered on his own estate, and every party there continued to insist that Abishag was wielding a genuine seal. His arguments eventually descended into a dark muttering sulk. A gleam of hope was spotted in his eye, however, when it was mentioned that his estate was, at least at present, no longer marked for transfer of ownership.

After several days of consideration, Barkos found it impossible to keep from hinting that his estate had also received a bid, and was scheduled to pass to a new owner if something did not intervene. Abishag responded to his hints directly.

"Do you want me to seal it?" she asked him.

"Are you willing?"

"The Seal of Solomon was not entrusted to me for my own benefit alone, but to redeem everything that is in need of it. This seal is for you—and all. Whosoever will be redeemed by this seal, I cannot deny. It is my duty to redeem your inheritance for you, if you so wish it."

"I wish it!" Barkos exclaimed.

The next day, the silence was broken with new and stunning news. One can only imagine with what shock the report was received that five more estates had been claimed by the king's seal. Five estates! And nowhere was the impact of that report greater received, but in the ears of "bidder number thirteen."

"Which estates?!" Hamon demanded, as he walked briskly down the street, angry to have been roused early after a night spent late in the drinking rooms. He hastened down to his tower adjacent to the Hall of Records, the scurrying, and worrying, messenger skipping along to keep pace. Hamon did not like to begin business before his morning meal, even less, bad business.

"They say it was some estates near to the first one. An estate belonging to Barkos, then one that many years ago used to be farmed by the family of Jared, the beggar. Even a family in Jezreel, now has an estate under claim."

"Jezreel? Who?"

"There is family there that used to live near the north hill, the estate of Laban, son of Rhuel, son of . . ."

"I know the lineage!" Hamon barked.

Sylva, Hamon's half sister, daughter of one of his father's concubines, was standing near the entrance to his building, and hastened inside when she saw him coming. He relaxed just a bit when he saw her. There were few people in the valley who Hamon trusted completely, but Sylva, fully foreign and without much natural beauty had not attracted the interest of any Israelite suitors. Thusly, her survival depended on her commitment to Hamon and his holdings, something which she well knew, and he knew that she knew.

"I want you in the meeting this time," he said to her gruffly, as he brushed by her.

"Yes, my lord."

****

"I did no such thing!" Laban exclaimed to the group of curious farmers that gathered around his metal shop.

"Then who did Laban? A bid appears on your own estate, and you say you know nothing of it? Tell us—who? Who is submitting these bids with the king's seal? Real or not, if it is being accepted—if there is even a *chance* it will hold, some of us may want to apply for it also. We are losing our land anyway, so why not?" a man demanded.

"Yes—you have no right to keep this a secret!" demanded another. The group chorused agreement.

"It is early in the morning!" Laban objected. "My whole family is yet here with me, and we have been here since before dawn—as any who work on this street can attest—as my family can attest!" He waved an arm toward his wife and two daughters who were watching the spectacle wide-eyed. "When would we have had time to travel to Shunem?"

"Your *whole* family?" a man asked. "Where then is your son?"

Laban froze, then looked over at his wife, then at his older daughter, then his younger.

"Benaiah," he whispered.

****

The elder Simeon, this time, met the town recorder privately, in a back room, well aware that many decisions would turn on the outcome of this conversation, and a forthright answer from the recorder would render those decisions much easier.

"Dakenath," he began, drawing close, "I understand that you have been instructed to protect the policy of private bidding. But that policy is enforced at the discretion of the Council, which under extreme circumstances, may call for an exception. This is one such case. I am the senior member of the Council charged with overseeing this process, and under the authority of that office I adjure you to tell me, if you know, who is delivering these bids?"

"I am free to tell you, of course, even without all of that, for the private bidding pertains to the bidder only, not the person who delivers the document. In this case, the purported bidder makes no attempt at anonymity, but presents himself, at least by seal, as Solomon. As for the delivery of the bid, the party, in this case, made no attempt at secrecy, but quite forthrightly delivered the documents to us. It was, the maiden, Abishag."

Simeon, though keenly attentive, did not appear surprised.

"I see. And you are quite certain of this?"

"She identified herself, even by name, my lord."

"I see. Does anyone else know this?"

"Certainly. My whole staff knows it, and, I would presume, other members of the population who were present on their own business when she delivered it could have identified her.

"I see."

****

Instead of a group meeting, this time, Hamon spoke to his advisors individually in his private quarters, with Sylva present recording every conversation. He seemed unusually coy in his communications, she noticed, as though he were not quite sure who he trusted any more. About mid-day, the rumor that was in the street reached Hamon's ears. He seemed to fade into a dark brooding sulk before Sylva's eyes.

"So it is Abishag," he commented to her, when they were alone between interviews.

Sylva nodded. Was that a hint of fear in his eyes?

"It appears so, my lord."

"And she bears, 'the Seal of Solomon,'" he said with mock reverence, looking up at her almost wildly.

Sylva did not know what to reply.

"What do you know about her?" Hamon demanded.

"Hardly anything. The time she was here recently was perhaps the most contact I have had with her in—well, ever."

Hamon flushed remembering the scene where Abishag had rebuffed his proposals of marriage. Sylva kept carefully quiet.

"She is . . . misguided, of course."

"Of course."

Hamon sat still for a long time, stroking his beard, while Sylva waited in the uncomfortable silence.

"Abishag . . ." he mused softly, as if to himself, then, "what is going on here?"

"Perhaps you should . . ." Sylva began, then reconsidered.

Hamon's focus returned.

"Should what?"

"Nothing. My lord."

"Nothing? No, that was not nothing. That was something. Perhaps I should what?"

"Well, I only thought, perhaps it may help if you consulted . . . father."

Hamon stared at her, then turned deep red as his lips curled into a snarl.

"Not this time. She wants a war? She is going to get it. And father has nothing to do with this."

Sylva observed while her half-brother seemed to descend into his own dark impenetrable thoughts, far away from the present time and place.

"Not this time . . ." he repeated into the air, as though Sylva were no longer present. "This time, it's personal . . ."

****

The steady stream of citizens that visited the Hall of Records that morning had all come for the same purpose: to determine directly from the town clerk the truth of the rumor they were hearing, that the purported bids of King Solomon were being delivered by the peasant girl, Abishag. This boiling pot did not go unnoticed by the trio of elders who were present in the building, watching the spectacle from an upper window, themselves considering the impact of the new knowledge. It was not long before they concluded that they must question the maiden themselves, and that soon, before large numbers of the population got to her first. Knowing nothing of the mind or intentions of the one who was stirring up such a tumult was unsettling to those charged with keeping the peace. They dispatched messengers to summon Abishag without delay.

"We must question her." The conclusion was repeated, and agreed upon, several times.

While they were in waiting, they were joined in session by a number of other elders, who having been pressed themselves by various members of the population for an explanation of the strange events, came to see what answers could be found. Before long, almost every elder known to sit in the gates was present, and when informed that Abishag herself had been summoned, none were disposed to leave.

****

Sylva returned to the door of the room where she had left Hamon alone.

"My lord?" she called.

"Yes."

"The maiden has been summoned. It is said she will be questioned by the elders, in the Hall of Records . . . today."

There was a momentary pause.

"Of course she has. Could anything else be expected?" Hamon's voice replied from behind the door.

Sylva waited, not sure how to reply.

"Which elders?"

"It is said that nearly all of them, are present," she replied.

"Is that so?"

"Yes."

"Sylva, step inside a moment."

Sylva obeyed.

The room was dark, the shutters were closed, and a lamp glowed low upon the face of Hamon, who was sharpening a blade on a stone in long slow methodical strokes. He spoke without looking up.

"It is only obvious that the maiden would be summoned, and I have already decided what to do. I am going to address the elders also, after her. But, I must know what she has said. I will arrive after she has departed—very shortly after. But . . . I must not see her, nor be seen by her."

He raised his eyes, causing reverse shadows to cast upon his face from the low lamp. She saw a glint in his eyes, unlike she had ever observed before.

"You will attend, Sylva, you will record for me the sense of her responses, and when she is about to leave, come get me. Dress like a virgin."

Sylva blushed.

"I . . . I am a virgin, my lord."

He looked up, then snorted, looking up and down her form with unhidden loathing.

"Ah. Doubtless. There is no fiercer guardian of a woman's virtue than gross ugliness."

Sylva's lip quivered, but she remained silent.

"What I mean is, wear the veil. It allows you to be present without being identified. Don't worry, you should fit right in."

"Yes, my lord."

Hamon went back to sharpening the blade. When Sylva did not leave, he glanced up.

"There was something else, my lord, a summons, from your fa . . ."

"Tell him I am out!" Hamon roared.

Sylva hesitated.

"He . . . he will not believe it, my lord."

Hamon snorted.

"Naturally, he won't."

Sylva backed out of the door and closed it gently.

****

The excitement at the farm that attended the summons of Abishag was plainly visible on the face of every person except Abishag herself. To the stream of questions and counsel that was showered upon her by her friends, Abishag remained serene, and untalkative. She was nervous, to be sure, but not paralyzingly so.

Barkos was a complete wreck.

"You should have waited until Huram was back!" he kept saying to her, and to anyone else within earshot, as he paced the floor.

"It was you that requested me to redeem your land," Abishag finally replied, to which he fell silent.

The summoners, an imposing group of armed militia men on horseback, waited while Abishag took a few moments to prepare for a day away. Dinah shadowed her, insisting that she would not face this alone, she would be right there with her. Abishag, though preoccupied with many thoughts, was inwardly thankful for the support of her friend and drew more strength from her than perhaps Dinah knew.

"I would go too, but I would never keep up," Jared offered, indicating his lame leg with a tilt of his head.

"Me too!" agreed Barkos.

Abishag gave them a faint but courteous smile.

"It is not your affair," she told them. "It is me that they want. I will answer their questions, and surely be home by midday."

Neither she nor they were as confident of her declaration as they pretended to be.

Abelah remained nearly as quiet as her daughter but was quick to assist with any needed service as her daughter was preparing to leave. Mother and daughter parted with few words but exchanged a glance in which volumes passed.

"The storm just takes the eagle higher," Abelah whispered into her daughter's ear, just before the parting.

Abishag nodded, remembering.

Moments later, Abelah saw her daughter being conducted away on the donkey that was brought for her while Dinah walked beside. The humble maiden with her armed escorts disappeared over the rise on her way to face interrogation by the highest authorities in the area over a matter that was both absolutely true, and completely unbelievable.

****

Back in the royal palace, King Solomon seemed to suddenly grow distant, asking, for the first time anyone could remember, one of his advisors to repeat his last comment. Moments later, he excused himself. Feeling a strange sensation in his chest, he wandered out into the royal courtyard, and was about to pass on into the garden, when the voice of the prophet Nathan, who happened to be sitting serenely on a garden bench, startled him.

"She will be well."

The words registered on the mind of the king, even as the awareness caught up with him that it was the prophet who had just answered his thought.

"Although, you are justifiably proud of her," the prophet added.

Solomon let out a gushing sigh, and then turned to sit next to the twinkling old sage, removing his crown to run his fingers through his dark locks.

"You have no idea how much I love her," he commented.

The prophet smiled.

"Do I not?"

Solomon glanced back at him, then reconsidered his last comment.

"Very well," he conceded.

The prophet simply nodded.

****

The glances that the guards chanced at the maiden they were escorting to questioning revealed to them nothing of significance. In fact, the woman's face was so inattentive that it seemed, to them, she was either less than sane, unaware, or uncaring of what was happening to her. They could not know that deep behind the dark eyes of the veiled and quiet girl, a storm of memories was flowing, memories of her beloved.

She could not see him, but it was as if he were exceedingly present, more so than any physical presence could ever afford. He was walking with her, quietly exuding upon her the same sensation of peace that she remembered feeling the first day she met him, a sphere into which he ushered her every time he spoke to her. She remembered those first intriguing moments by the well that fateful morning, when he had whispered her name; and the time he rescued her in the street that dark night; and finally, the fateful day when he had chased down her caravan and delivered her from hell to heaven, his gentle voice oozing warmth to her soul. She felt that same warmth now, though his voice was not audibly heard. She knew he was with her.

Peace, my beloved . . . peace . . .

Two veiled maidens appeared in the far door of the Hall of Records, followed momentarily by a third.

The elders, who had been in sober discussion while awaiting the arrival of their subject, fell silent and looked toward the entrance. The guards stepped forward into the room, with the maiden between them. Simeon recognized Abishag.

"You are Abishag?" Simeon asked, after a momentary pause.

"Yes, my lord."

"You will approach."

The sound of his voice echoed in the high-ceilinged room.

Both Abishag and Dinah stepped forward.

"And you are?"

"Dinah, daughter of Jalaam."

"You will retract. You have not been summoned."

"Did not our ancestors, Rachael and Leah, have handmaids by their side?" Dinah protested.

"You are a handmaid to this maiden? If you are the handmaid, where is the maiden's husband? For a maid cannot be maid to a maid."

"If I retract from my charge, I prove you true. But if I remain, I testify that this woman does have a husband, whom you know not," Dinah said.

"Maiden. If she did have a husband, we would be questioning him, not her. You will step back!"

Abishag spoke softly to Dinah, after which she did take a modest step backward.

The veiled girl in the center of the room stood solitary before the great men of the city, who were arranged facing her in a half circle. Her face was veiled, her head was bowed, and there was little in her expression that could be discerned by the light of the torches that lined the high walls.

"Maiden, you do understand why you have been summoned here today?"

Abishag remained silent, but offered a slow nod.

"It has been reported, on verified authority, that you have

been delivering bids on property to the village recorder. Do you affirm this?"

"I do, my lord."

"And are you aware of the exceeding sobriety of this bidding process, and its importance to the residents of this valley?"

"I am, my lord."

"Then surely you must be aware that the documents you have been delivering have been the cause of much consternation in troublesome times. Are you aware of the impact of these documents?"

"I am, my lord."

The occupants of the room glanced at one another and whispered.

"So we are to understand that, with full knowledge of the potentially dangerous effects of your actions, and the precipice of chaos toward which you force innocent Israelites, you have yet acted?"

"I have acted with this knowledge, but for none of these reasons, my lord."

"Why then do you do this?"

"The man whose seal these documents display has directed that I deliver them. I act on his authority."

"And who is that man?"

"Surely my lord can discern the name upon the seal."

"Maiden. The name on the purported seal is Solomon, King of Israel."

Abishag remained silent.

"Have you nothing to say about this?"

"The seal of the king speaks for itself, my lord. To this, what can I add?"

"The seal of the king is in possession of the king! Where then, are you obtaining this likeness?"

"Likeness, my lord?"

"Yes! Likeness, child! Some instrument is creating a likeness of the king's seal. Where is this instrument?"

"Has the imprint been officially examined, my lord?"

"You have not been brought here to ask questions, but to answer them! Where, is the instrument?"

Abishag, very slowly, dropped to her knees before them, bowing low, with her face to the ground.

"My lords. Please forgive my state. I do not disrespect your question, but I am bound by orders higher than yours. The man whose seal these documents display, also charged me to not display the instrument openly. I am constrained to obey his command on this point."

"Who?! Whose command?!"

"The King of Israel, my lord."

"And you believe it to be so! Maiden! Surely you err exceedingly!"

Abishag remained prostrate while the moments ticked by in silence, the counsel staring exasperated at the maiden.

"Well then," said Simeon. "If you are not willing to reveal the instrument to us, you must take us to the man who wields it. Surely you cannot deny us that!"

"I would not deny you that, my lords."

"Is he at your farm?"

"He is in Jerusalem, my lord."

Two elders leaned together. "This is senseless. The woman is deranged."

"Woman. Would you kindly explain to us how a seal that exists only in Jerusalem can appear here in Shunem absent the king himself, on such short notice? Surely the imprints that are appearing here cannot have issued from the instrument that is there. Can you not concede this?"

"Have you firsthand knowledge that the instrument is in Jerusalem?"

"I have knowledge that the king is there! Would you have me believe the unthinkable?—that the king has somehow assigned his authority here?—yet the business of the kingdom goes on without it? Just recently we have received edicts bearing the king's seal. How do you suppose he signified them, if his seal is not with him?"

"I am sure my lord has compared the imprint on those documents, with the imprint on the bids I have been delivering. The existence of an imprint on a document does not reveal the location where the imprinting was done."

"What? Are you saying the seal upon these recently acquired documents is the same as that on the bids you are submitting?"

"If the seal is the same, my lord, it stands to reason, that the imprinting device is the same and could have been done at any location."

"But you are not saying it *could* have happened. You are intimating that it DID happen—that the instrument which sealed these royal edicts is present in this valley, and that they were sealed here. Is this not correct?"

"It is, my lord."

"And also that you, *you*, of all people, know where this instrument is but you will not reveal it. True?"

"You have spoken it."

"Maiden. I do not think you appreciate the seriousness of the case before you. Not only do you have no consideration for the tremendous strain you are placing on your countrymen by these insensible actions, you do not comprehend the danger to your own person. It is itself unforgivable that you would cause such chaos in desperate times, but in doing so you are also committing crimes worthy of death when you are found to be false. Do you truly want to stand before the king with this falsehood attached to your name?"

"I gladly place myself at the mercy of the king, and submit to his judgment on this matter. I only want it to be found on that day, that I do not stand before him in violation of his direct command. Therefore, I must seal as he has instructed me to seal."

"You? You seal? Are you making these imprints yourself? You are! A great judgment awaits you maiden!"

"And I it, my lord."

"Have you nothing else to say on the matter? No explanation? No rationale?"

"I do. But my lord has instructed me that I am not to pose questions of you, but to answer them."

The elders rustled irritatedly.

"*You* would pose questions to *us*?"

An elder leaned over to Simeon.

"Let her *ask*, then! We are getting nowhere this way," he said.

"Well then *you* question her!" Simeon retorted.

The second elder, a man named Jebuseth, a dark man with a wide nose, took the floor.

"Maiden. Please proceed with your . . . question. And please rise before us, that we might better hear you," Jebuseth said.

Abishag rose, but only to her knees.

"My lord. I am not a Rabbi. But I have been told that there is a protocol to be followed when examining a seal for truth or falsehood. My only question is: has that protocol been followed in this case?"

"Protocol?"

"For the identification of a seal, my lord."

"Ah. You would have us take these documents to Jerusalem, and have them discredited there. Truly that would be appropriate, in most cases—and to be sure, these documents will appear in

Jerusalem—and then the fruit of your way you will eat. But it would take months of time to render a judgment in that manner—most impractical at this delicate moment. Is that your purpose?—to throw this process into delay and chaos, while we chase after the refutation to your false seal? This would be most convenient for you, but most inconvenient for the cause of order and justice. You must cease with this nonsense now, at our command."

"Have I been convicted of a crime, my lord?"

"You will be!"

"But at present, I have done nothing but deliver bids on property according to the law. On what grounds do you order me to cease?"

"On the grounds of decency! On the grounds of order, justice! Respect for your countrymen! And the rights of all to live in peace and harmony and engage in transactions according to the Law! On these grounds maiden!"

"It is on these very same grounds, that I have acted, my lord."

"And for this you insist that you will continue to act—against our direct command?"

"If it is right for me to obey you more than the king—you decide. But I cannot but testify to what I have seen and heard. The king charged me to do this. If forced to choose, it is his command I must obey."

"You will hang."

Suddenly a loud voice echoed from the back of the chamber.

"She will NOT hang!"

Heads whipped around to see the form of a young man, marching into the room, red in face, and wild with emotion.

"If anyone is to hang, it will be YOU! You who would defy the laws of the king, and the highest seal that exists in the land!"

"Benaiah!" Abishag said urgently.

He ignored her.

"And I, who have been rotting in prison all these weeks, when I committed no crime, other than obeying my king! This maiden Abishag—she is more than just a messenger of the king. She is to be BRIDE of the king! She will sit with him on his very throne! And if you unjustly defy her now, there will be death to pay in Jerusalem!"

"Silence! Guards!" Jebuseth ordered.

Several guards stepped forward to take Benaiah and forcibly move him back.

"You are guilty of escaping from prison—at the very least! And much more than that if you . . ."

"I have been escaped from prison from the first day you put me in there! Here are the bolts." He dropped the iron bolts to the prison door on the floor with a clang, and looked back up at the elders. "And if my wish were to escape, would I have come here? I have stayed in your prison only out of respect to this maiden's counsel, and to there I will return, with or without your guards. You do not detain me, I stay of my own choice. But you no longer have her testimony alone. I saw the king as well, when he was here. I saw his guards. I saw his authority. I *saw* him escape! He is not dead, he escaped with the aid of his men, and is dwelling in Jerusalem!"

"Escaped?"

"Yes, when you questioned him—for the death of Orpha, among other things. I tell you he . . ."

"You are referring to that madman who defied us in the trial? He planned this? He was behind all this from the start?"

"Was? No, he IS behind this, for he is not dead but alive, and he is SOLOMON, the King of Israel!"

The room went into a general uproar. Benaiah then recognized Simeon among the elders.

"Lord Simeon!" Benaiah said urgently. "I served in your house. You know that I am a true man. Tell them!"

Simeon had grown quiet and pale when he recognized

Benaiah.

"Son," he replied. "You are a good man . . . don't . . . don't throw your life away for this."

Benaiah looked almost hurt.

"My Lord . . . Simeon. You know I would not lie. I speak the truth!"

"You know this lad?" Jebuseth asked Simeon.

"He served in my house. He served well—that I grant. He is a good man," Simeon replied. "But a good man can be deceived."

Benaiah stared at him.

"You have spoken my thoughts."

Simeon blinked when the impact of the reply hit him.

"I can testify also," another female voice suddenly sounded.

The occupants of the room looked to find its source.

"I want my name and my testimony recorded in this case also, this woman is true," Dinah said.

"You have not been questioned maiden."

"True! But does not your Law declare that every matter must be decided by two or three witnesses? Do you deny me my right under the law? I have the *right* to testify! And I want my name recorded on the side of truth! Abishag has done nothing wrong! She has told the truth! She IS to be bride of the king! And he DID charge her to redeem the land. You have seen the seal, and now you have heard three witnesses! You will see! You will all see!"

"You impudent, little child!" Jebuseth said, indignant.

Dinah began to glow red, took a step forward and inhaled deeply, when Abishag suddenly placed a hand on her shoulder.

"Dinah!" she called.

Dinah looked around.

"Remember what spirit we are of!" Abishag said urgently.

Having looked away from the audience she was about to unleash upon, Dinah found herself gazing upon the face of Abishag, the only sight that could stop her runaway temper.

"Be silent with me," Abishag said.

The face, the gaze of Abishag, filled her vision with a model of everything she wanted to be. She had almost brought dishonor upon the very one she was trying to defend! Dinah teared up, then broke down. Abishag took her by the shoulder and drew her close.

Abishag looked back at the council.

"My lords. I did not request these testimonies from my friends, they offered them of their own choosing. But if there is any charge to be laid upon them, please lay it upon me alone. Benaiah will return to prison, as he has said, and this maiden will be silent until called upon. Please forgive them. They meant no harm."

Simeon looked about the room, reading expressions. Was that softness he was seeing on some of their faces? The woman, with her humble manner, and calm self-sacrifice, was affecting them.

"She speaks like a queen," one commented to his neighbor.

"A queen yes, but a deranged queen," came the reply.

"I hope she is not deranged, but deceived only. Such a noble person—she would certainly not be above repentance, once enlightened to the truth."

Simeon motioned to several of his companions and they huddled together to discuss the situation. Then he returned to address Abishag.

"Maiden, the serious straight that you place us in seems beyond your grasp. The Council must now convene for a time, for all must be done according to the law. For all of your graciousness, I have observed in you a lack of respect for authority. Therefore I urge you—yea, I urge you in the strongest terms—cease from sealing any more documents, until we have rendered a judgment. If you do not, we may be forced to detain you in ways you find less than pleasant."

"You mean prison, my lord?"

"You do not want to find yourself there maiden."

"I have already been there, my lord."

Simeon hesitated, having momentarily forgotten that.

"In any case, I am sure you have no wish to return," Simeon counseled.

"What happens to me is of no concern, my lord. If I be in prison again, or free, of this I can assure you: that just as you have urged, I will respect all authority—and each authority precisely according to his rightful office."

The council eyed her suspiciously.

"May I speak?" asked another voice, older, more mature, female.

The eyes of the councilmen turned to behold the steady gaze of a dignified woman who had recently entered. For Simeon, the reaction was not curiosity, but shock.

"Hildah," he whispered.

"Woman, if you have something relevant to add, you may approach," answered Jehusel.

"Thank you, my lords. Though I cannot testify as a firsthand witness, as these others have, I would like to offer my opinion of the maiden you have before you. As you have now questioned her, so also have I, not just once, but over time, that I might learn the meaning behind her strange actions. I report to you that I have found her honest in all things. So this I say: be careful how you treat her, for she has shown herself to be true in unexpected ways. I was sick, desperately so, but this maiden, Abishag, secured for me medicine that cured me of the swamp fever. Even our doctor has since conceded the effectiveness of this cure."

Jehusel was recognizing the woman, and turned to Simeon.

"Is this not your wife?" he asked, perplexed.

"It is," Simeon answered reddening, "and I approved this not."

"The maiden did not speak of how she came to know of this healing agent, but when I pressed her," Hildah continued, "she confessed to me that the source of the medicinal cure was the king. Whether you accept that answer or not, you must at least admit that its effectiveness attests to a wisdom beyond what this maiden should posess. Again I say—be careful how you treat her."

"Hildah!" Simeon husked. "You have not been summoned! You will be silent!"

Hildah lowered her eyes.

"Yes, my lord."

Jehusel looked back and forth from Simeon to Hildah, then cleared his throat. He attempted to speak, then looked back at Simeon, bewildered.

"Return home, woman," Simeon ordered.

"Yes, my lord," Hildah turned to leave.

Simeon quickly huddled with those around him.

"My wife, you understand, has been cured by the medicine that she secured from this maiden. But Jockshan has informed me that not all who partake of it improve. In any case, my wife has since become enraptured with this maiden Abishag, as though some enchantment has come over her. I cannot dissuade her. She speaks as one not fully herself," he explained desperately.

"Nonetheless, lord Simeon, her testimony here must be recorded," said an elder to Simeon.

"So be it," Simeon conceded tensely, looking around at their faces.

Many in the group appeared thoughtful, as they continued to behold the gentle maiden Abishag, who stood in the center in gracious silence.

"This maiden, at the very least, has made an extraordinary

impact among her associates," observed one elder to his neighbor.

"Yes," was the thoughtful reply. "There appears to be more to her than meets the eye. Very convincing—if her tale were not so far-fetched . . ." he left the thought uncompleted.

Simeon haltingly and hastily adjourned the proceedings.

"Dismissed, maiden. Guards, escort the man back to his cell—and make it secure this time!"

At that moment, the third veiled maiden Sylva, who had been standing silently by the door, left quickly escaping notice.

The council found themselves under the sway of many unexpected thoughts, as they attempted to absorb the drama that had just unfolded before them. The aura that attended the maiden's presence lingered in the room, softening the atmosphere. But even so, the elders concluded that regardless of the gracious nobility of the maiden, and her honest conviction that she was sealing rightly, the seal she was wielding simply could not be authentic and must be challenged—for the sake of peace. The problem was that the council could not legally challenge it. Any challenge would have to proceed from the previous high bidder.

They were not to be long vexed with this riddle, for just when they were failing for an answer, they were rescued by the entrance of the very party in question. Hamon announced his presence humbly, from the threshold of the door, pleading entrance, and assuring them that he had information that would prove useful, if they would hear him. Being invited to step forth and let his intelligence be aired, he first praised the council for their justness, then voiced concern about their present challenge, admitting that he had heard in the streets that a maiden by the name of Abishag was responsible for the current crisis.

"I very much need to speak to you before she arrives. I have information concerning her—significant information."

"Before? You are too late, she has already come and gone!" Jebuseth replied.

"She has?" Hamon asked, "My most sincere apologies, lords, I could have saved you much confusion concerning this maiden. If only you had known . . ."

The curiosity of the council was pricked.

"Lord Hamon. If you have something of significance do not withhold it now. Perhaps it is not too late. Do tell us."

Hamon hesitated, appearing thoughtful, then addressed the council.

"I suppose the time has come," he began, with a deep sigh. "The time has finally come to inform you such things that I know that are not commonly known about this maiden. There are many matters concerning her that I have long held in silence, in order to protect her. But now, it appears that I have no choice but to let the truth be known—no matter how unpleasant."

"But first, I must confess something that I had hoped to withhold, in the interest of peace. As you know, no man has shown greater commitment to the erecting of a city wall than I, and no man has taken more zealous steps, whether in public or in private to see it accomplished. It is the threat to its completion that pries me from my silence against my will. I have long believed—as the astute council has certainly noted—that zeal for our city wall will certainly wane, as the cost and work it entails replaces the sharp memory of the attacks we have suffered as an undefended city. It is my great desire, as defender of this city, to see the project to completion, and this has provoked me to take steps to ensure it will indeed be finished."

"I have no ambitions in this valley—though my sincerity will forever be doubted by some. But regardless of their doubts, I must act in the benefit of my countrymen, even if misunderstood. A city wall is not built in a day. It is a long and expensive venture. After I had divested myself of my holdings, it became clear that I would not be able to personally finance such a venture, as I had begun in hope some years ago. Being fully without means, at just the hour when I was lamenting my lack of funds to contribute toward the cost of the wall, my father, seeing his end approaching, laid upon me gold that I knew not of until that moment. I was shocked to find such an unexpected resource in my hand, especially at such a crucial time. But seeing that two unlikely things came together at the same moment, I began to understand it to be a gift from God, and that I should do as I had aspired."

Hamon paused and attempted to read their scowling faces.

"When the opportunity came—quite unexpectedly—to secure estates through this bidding process, and also the profits therefrom for some time to come, I, with much personal reluctance, sacrificed my own desires to the obvious decision, that I must temporarily re-acquire land, for the purpose of using the future profits of those lands to ensure the completion of the wall. My only comfort was the knowledge that after the wall was completed, the land could be returned to Israelites, as is only proper."

"Brothers, I am bidder number thirteen. I humbly and willingly identify myself in this moment so that you might know and understand my current anguish, and be equipped by what I will shortly tell you to mitigate the danger brought on us all by a lovesick and ill-informed maiden. It falls upon me, as previous high bidder, to challenge the false bids that have been vexing our process, and though I would prefer to perform this in secret rather than openly, I have come to realize that any challenge to these false bids would more likely to succeed if I came fully forward. For this purpose I now declare myself, and also so that those who would accuse me later, may rather see my purpose now and understand."

"Brothers, though it disheartens me to learn that you have already called the maiden in for questioning—for my tardiness I can only plead wrestling with a difficult decision. There are some things that I can inform you concerning her that will shed tremendous light on the situation at hand, if you will yet hear me."

After a moment of hesitation, Jebuseth glanced at the men around him, then cleared his throat and responded.

"Lord Hamon. Your presence here, and your speech is . . . a surprise to us all. Suffice it to say, you have our full attention. And though no man has required that you identify yourself as a bidder, your forthrightness in doing so is honorable, and justifies hearing your full explanation. As for the maiden Abishag, the fact is, our questioning of her was to no good result. We are very concerned just now that she will continue to do things which hinder the cause of peace."

"Doubtless," Hamon replied, shaking his head, "for I have much experience with this particular maiden—*much.* I have observed the odd wanderings of her mind for many years, ever since my father employed me as a sheepherder on the hills above this maiden's estate. Early on I observed fault lines in her spirit that I had hoped would never break open. But alas, the pressure on her has proven more than she could bear, and though I attempted to counsel her, the mind of a female can descend to places unreachable by reason. Such has been the case with Abishag. There is nothing I wish to do less than add to her grief by challenging the bids in which her false hopes reside. But the peace of this valley is worth more than the comforts of a deceived maiden. And though it will break her spirit, as it will mine when I tell you what I must shortly tell you, I truly have no choice."

"This maiden, as we all well know, is poor. It was the desperation of poverty that drove her, in earlier days, to actions of which we need not speak, in her three year absence from this area, which was noted by all. Her ill-fame has followed her, though, to my understanding she has reformed a measure since that time. But prior to her departure, it was made clear to me, both by her family, and by the maiden herself, that she had seen in the wealth of my father the answer to her impoverished state. Since I was young and reckless and not of a mind to marry at the time, I refused her, perhaps more harshly, in retrospect, than I would find needful now. It was for this cause that she fled away with her Phoenician lover, a thing of which we have all heard. He took her to faraway lands, and taught her dark secrets of bewitchment—arts which she is able to wield to this day. When he treated her unkindly, she was forced to flee and return here, and found herself in greater desperation than when she first left. In increasing eagerness, she continued to present herself before me, for, with my full maturity and wealth now in my hand, and the failure of her previous blunders before her, she saw all the more plainly her salvation in me. And though I was then marriageable age and inclined even to marriage, I had firsthand knowledge that she was now a damaged woman. Not wanting to draw attention to that ugly fact, I declined her advances on the basis that I was a foreigner and not fit to marry an Israelite woman—for you understand, seeing in her a childhood friend, I still had some respect for her feelings. She then attempted bewitchments upon me, but being aware that she could wield these dark charms, I was able to resist—for it is well known that such enchantments work best on those who are ignorant of them. So I resisted, and hoped that would be the end of the matter. Sadly, it was not so."

"In the years that followed, I believed her spirit was on the slow course of recovery, even with all she had suffered. I prayed that she would one day find peace and solace for herself, but, alas, the man who had abused her before, suddenly returned. So cunning was he, and so knowledgeable of the weaknesses of her mind, that he was able to drive her beyond the realm of sanity, to the point of believing a desperate lie. The maiden, since then, has not been in her right mind—as is now openly manifest to all. Pitiful confused creature! Again she lost her lover!—and this time, to death."

"The sorry tale of what happened next is painful to tell. When she learned I had become a naturalized Israelite, removing—in her mind—the one obstacle to marriage with me, her desperation reached a climax. I again declined her, and this time was forced to declare the ugly reason why. Having done so, I saw something in her eye that almost frightened me. Her first reaction was silence, but in that moment, I perceived that her tortured spirit finally snapped. She threatened me, pronounced enchantments upon me, and informed me that she no longer had need for my resources. She declared that soon she would reveal a wealth greater than anything I could imagine, and cause me to regret forever not accepting her into my house. I suspected at the time that thing would be the false seal with which her lover had deceived her, but I hoped and prayed that she would display it to me only, win her symbolic victory, and be satisfied with that. Unfortunately, the worst possible outcome of this whole sad affair is upon us, as you well know, and have recently observed."

"But what is to be done? I tell you all of this, not to bring harm or dishonor upon the maiden, for she has already reached a state so pathetic that even pity cannot stoop deeply enough to reach her. Though she has committed crimes worthy of death, I have shunned, for the past weeks, to enter a legal challenge, for I knew she was the author of the thing, but I also knew she was more sick than guilty, and not worthy of death. She is but a lost little sheep, wandering in ignorance, adrift beyond the realm of sanity. Such would be harmless under most circumstances, but in this crucial time, represents a most serious danger. Since her first bid went unchallenged, she has now become emboldened to make claims beyond her own little estate. Had it been only hers, I was inclined to let her keep it. But for legal purposes, and the peace of the valley, these bids must be challenged, and I, Lord help me, am the one who must bring them."

"You will appreciate the impossible position this places upon me. I am now searching for a way to discredit her false seal without the involvement of the king or his subjects, and to protect the maiden from a most pitiful end. I inform you of all this with a most earnest plea for your help in this matter. Please, let not the woman's folly be brought before the king, and forgive my unworthy plea. I am in a most wretched position."

The council's reaction to Hamon's tale ranged in turns from surprise, to shock, to pity, to disgust, to resignation, and by the end of Hamon's speech, most were nodding sympathetically.

"You speak of many things that a man would rather not speak," Simeon observed.

"I have, but the hour has forced them from me," Hamon agreed. "And I am glad only for this: doubtless the council has observed the woman's strange enchanting power—though I am sure none of you have been deceived by it. But other more simple citizens perhaps could fall prey to it. It is needful to have disclosed this that ignorance might be dispelled, for do not underestimate her—she is dangerous! She is filled with enchantments, and the power to deceive many innocent Israelites is in her hand."

The council was nodding knowingly.

"Your forthrightness, lord Hamon, is most timely—and enlightening, and allows some sensible explanation, finally, of what was fully inexplicable before, of the woman, and of her motives, and of her powers. Thank you for your testimony. It is clear that you gave it at considerable personal cost. And your desire to protect the maiden from her own folly is noble, and—I believe the Council will agree—will be respected. I believe I can speak for the whole Council in saying, we will find a way to keep this ugly matter out of the king's courts, if possible, for your sake and hers," Jebuseth said.

"Your kindness is as appreciated as it is undeserved, my lord," Hamon replied.

"And we had already decided to take every available action to discredit this false seal—but certainly you understand the need for a quick solution, lest the process become mired in controversy. How to discredit it, while keeping the bulging barrel that this valley has become from breaking first, is a riddle we have not yet solved."

"I may be able to help in that matter also, my lords," Hamon said, "and if we cooperate together, we may prevent many undesirable outcomes. Would you be willing to assist me? For with your assistance, I believe we can gain just the space we need to deal with the false seal."

"How so?"

"With your support as to the matter of my bidding on estates—surely the council can appreciate the impact this will have in some quarters. Circumstances required that I disclose this to you, but my name will certainly be stained by the disclosure. I want nothing other than the peaceful transfer of property, and the completion of the wall, but with my past sins in recent memory, the population may doubt that. With our process challenged by this false seal, I chose the course of full disclosure, and that voluntarily, as you all can attest. I truly have nothing to hide. But the rumor is soon to go out that I am buying land. If that be so, let it be tempered with the truth that I am only acquiring it temporarily.

"So this I propose: the land will be returned to Israelites when the wall is completed. I am unable to match the bid language of the false seal—no man could, it is absurd. But I offer my own seal in response. If anyone will accept my seal with respect to his estate, I promise a return of his land after the wall is completed. This is my covenant with you. But if any accept the false seal—I can promise no such thing. Who knows what will become of those lands when the truth of the thing is sorted out? This should supply sufficient motivation to dissuade most from accepting the false seal, giving you the time you need to discredit it. In this way, I believe, the risk of chaos can be greatly mitigated."

"So you are declaring that you will enter a counter bid, on all properties claimed by the false seal?" Simeon asked.

"I counter bid with my own seal. And not only that, I offer a promise to return the land after the wall is completed—but only to those who accept my seal."

Simeon and the elders exchanged glances. Simeon motioned at Jebuseth to accept Hamon's offer.

"This could very well salvage our threatened process. An ingenious plan, lord Hamon. We will owe you much, once this is all over," Jebuseth said.

"I am yet in debt to you, my lords, as I will always be. But let this small service be my thanks for your gracious acceptance of me as an Israelite," Hamon replied.

Chapter 26

When the news reached the ears of Abishag that Hamon had followed up her session before the council with arguments of his own, the sense of which were repeated to her, she was once again showered with advice on how to respond. Meanwhile, the main points of Hamon's speech were repeated in homes and fields throughout the valley at the urging of the elders. Also spoken of, almost to the exclusion of all other conversation, was the flood of attending revelations that came out of the day of drama in the Hall of Records. Events had become so unpredictable, so riveting, that the population's attention upon the process, though keen to begin with, was now feverish. Such a concurrent breaking of unlikely mysteries! That Hamon had been bidding on land! That Abishag the peasant girl was wielding something she claimed was the king's seal! That it would soon, perhaps, be discredited. That Hamon pledged a return of land to all those who accepted his seal and shunned the other. Two seals in the land, and a choice to make!

Hamon's seamy version of Abishag's history excited as much gossip as it did useful conversation, inspiring by its titillating nature more talk than thought. But the high stakes were felt everywhere. It was not just drama, it was drama with life changing repercussions hanging in the balance. The two seals were set forth in complete opposition, forcing upon the little provincial world a dreadful choice, with such high stakes making the decision all the more fearful. As these newly released revelations filtered out among the varied and pressured population, a chorus of passionate discussions was ignited in every corner, and gut-wrenching decisions were guessed and second-guessed, and then guessed again.

Abishag was counseled by her friends toward silence, toward confronting Hamon, toward approaching Simeon—and Hildah—directly, and even toward leaving the area altogether to let the king deal with the situation himself. After politely enduring more advice than she hungered for, Abishag excused herself, and went alone to her vineyard.

It was there, while letting the peaceful vines remind her of her beloved—while finding in them some wisp of his wisdom and spirit, that she noted odd movement in the distance. From the vantage point of her hillside vineyard, it was possible in certain places to gain a view of the valley, the village, and the wall under construction that surrounded it. It was this wall that caught her attention. The methodical movements of workmen on the wall had been, heretofore, a familiar sight. But this time, those movements appeared somehow different, more disorganized. After pausing to watch for a few moments, she sighed deeply, and returned to the house.

"I must speak to them," she declared, when inside.

"To whom?" Barkos asked. "To Hamon? To Simeon?"

"To none of these. I must speak to the common people. They are giving their strength to Hamon's wall, when they need not, simply on his promise to return their lands when it is finished. It is the common people who must hear—first hand—and be able to ask their questions of me. It is only fair. The council—they have already heard."

"Where? Who are you going to approach?"

She smiled.

"I need approach no one at first, for the king has given them cause to approach me. I will speak first to those who come here for medicine."

****

"Why did you not come when I called for you?" Baal Hamon the elder demanded of his waiting son. Hamon stared at the wheezing lump of blankets from which the voice had emerged.

"There was no time, father. The maiden was coming to address the council. I had to respond immediately."

Silence.

"Besides, I knew your threat of withholding gold was a bluff. You don't have much left."

More silence.

"At least you knew better than to lie to me. Truth on both counts, I suppose. However, I hope you had the intelligence to discern the real truth of the seal. What did you say to them?"

"The council?"

"Yes."

Hamon noticed the bait in his father's question.

"What . . . is the real truth of the seal?" he queried.

The lump of blankets moved, and his father's face emerged, looking pale and gaunt.

"The truth is, son, the dark chariot is coming for me soon, and I am luckier for it than you. The gods will carry me beyond the reach of this king. Not so, for you."

His father lay back down, while Hamon brooded.

"And I am to find that enlightening?"

"You told me once this maiden would never lie, nor be fooled," the elder declared.

"No," Hamon agreed.

"Have you seen this seal? How good is the likeness?"

"It's a perfect likeness."

"Oh, gods."

Hamon was silent. His father cocked his head and studied his son curiously.

"You don't understand? You are going to have to flee, son. It's over. This seal . . . it is re-"

Hamon trembled, then exploded.

"I know! I know it's a real seal! Of course it's authentic! Do you think I am an idiot? Do you think I'm as stupid as that council of fools? The genuine king's seal is somehow in the hands of that wretched maiden—I don't know how or why, but it is! Abishag is not stupid! Disrespected, underestimated, wrongly accused—all these might describe her—but stupid? Oh no. She would not perpetrate some doltish ploy. Hemanah yes, but Abishag no! It *must* be the real seal . . . but . . . what to *do* about it?!"

He broke off shaking his head in frustration.

The elder noticed that his son's hands were visibly shaking.

"I told you already. You have to flee, son. It's the only way. The king has found you—take what you have left and escape with your life."

"But I have nothing left!"

"Nothing left? Of course you do. Take the gold . . ."

"The gold has been placed in deposit as my Display of Means! It cannot be retrieved until the question of the seal is settled!"

His father stared stunned.

"You bound the gold to that!?"

"I had no idea at the time that this was coming. How could I have foreseen this? No one did! Not even YOU!"

His father was still aghast.

"I don't believe this! You bound up all the gold? Are you insane?!"

"I had no choice! I was following YOUR counsel! Where was your famous foresight this time? Tell me! Where was it? You forced me to do it YOUR way and you led me into a trap! For all your posturing, you were just as blindsided as I was!—as everyone was! You did not warn me of this, you delirious old fool!"

"Old fool? Delirious old fool? Ha! Let me tell *you* something! At least I was not so stupid as to consign our entire means into the hands of foreigners who care not a whit for our interest! Without the gold, you have nothing! That royal seal has the power to redeem back everything it took me a lifetime to gain! You could at least have salvaged the value of the land in gold, but now you inform me the gold is all tangled up in this legal rats nest?! Fool! You have lost in one day what took me forty years to gain! Now you have to flee, and you will be left with nothing! Nothing!" his father wheezed bitterly.

"You're wrong father. I do not have to flee—not yet. The seal only has power if people believe it. Outside of that, it might as well be a clay spittoon! Just let me work the people for a while—I will have them *begging* to receive my seal! I can always flee later."

"Flee later? Oh, no you can't. Never! Not with this king on the hunt for you. If you don't start running now, you will *never* get far enough away Where could you flee on short notice? You can't go back to Philistia, all our people are straining under the king's stones there. North? He has ground the Hittite empire into powder—and has them *thanking* him for it! The Midianites to the south have toppled, even Egypt is paying tribute. East? Ammon and Moab have crumbled and become vassals, and the Amorites are next, and they hate us more than the Israelites. You wouldn't survive a week there, and with the sport those savages would make of you, you would *wish* for the quick death of a clean hanging!"

"You can't flee and leave a fresh trail. This 'gentle' king has the soul of a bloodhound! Anywhere you land his guards will already be there waiting with your wrist chains. He sniffed you out all the way from Jerusalem, and slipped in and put the noose around your neck while *you* bent down to help him do it! He is on a purging rampage! 'Prince of peace' they call him. Ha! His peace is a lie! He is engaged in a silent war—a vicious bloody war, yet so serene that women plant flowers and let their children play in the streets in the middle of it! Treacherous! He will have rooted out every foreigner in the land before he is done! You would have to flee to a different *world* to escape!—the far, far east, perhaps, or the north. It's your only chance."

"Father! I can't flee without a shekel to my name to a far away land of strange speech! What will I do? How will I survive? I *must* stay here—I must find a way to manage this. Listen to me! Abishag is clever, but the people are stupid. They still think the man is dead. They think I am an Israelite, and have repented. I can convince them. I can beat this! The people—they will believe me. They will even build my wall for me!"

"The people, yes, but the king, no. The king is not stupid! He is on to you already—he has been on to you for months. You are hemmed in, and the axe is on its way down."

"Not if the people do not accept his seal! He obeys his own laws! He is powerless outside of them!" Hamon retorted.

"But what of the ones who have already accepted his seal? THEY will force a judgment from Jerusalem!—even if you discredit it for everyone else. Can you refute the seal outside of the king's courts, even to the satisfaction of this maiden? She will *never* be deceived—she cannot be."

"She and her associates are a small number, and they are bound together in one location. They stay together. They could meet with an accident," Hamon said.

"Oh, beautiful son, just brilliant! So you will murder the king's bride. Have you gone insane? You think this is the path of safety?"

"She is NOT the king's bride! She is MY bride! I had her first!"

Baal Hamon looked at his son with a mixture of pity and

disdain.

"You *never* had her."

Hamon had stood to his feet and was standing red-faced with clenched fists, his heart pounding.

"I will not allow him to steal her from me," Hamon seethed lowly. "He has no right to take what is rightfully mine. She will *never* live to be his queen. I will show this king a higher level."

"That higher level, for you, son, will be the top of the gallows. For one thing, you put way too much value on a miserable maiden. Foolish! Stupid! Pubescent juvenile idiocy! It's going to be the death of you! For another thing, you greatly underestimate this king's savvy. You think you can outsmart him? He had you defeated from the moment he stepped foot in this town. Look at the rest of the world. From the wise to the fool, they are falling on every side—whole kingdoms full of wise men with trained armies! If they cannot stop his advance, what chance do you think you have?"

"They don't know what I do."

"And what is that?"

"I know his law. I have been studying his law—quite deeply. I can trap him in it. I know he will not act outside of it. Asa Barak escaped one time, though he was guilty, but the king allowed him to slip away, rather than violate his own law. I can do the same."

"He will have destroyed you before you find this unlikely way."

"Not if I can wipe out this cancer here," Hamon replied. "There will be no one to summon him."

His father shook his head.

"It's too risky! It will never work! It will be transparent!

"Not if it's managed correctly!"

"You are going to get yourself hung!"

"I would RATHER hang than flee destitute to a far away land!" Hamon screamed. "I would end up a slave, or worse! I will fight this—and WIN!"

Baal Hamon the elder was silent for a long moment. Then he savored a deep sigh.

"I suppose, if I were your age, in your position, I would do the same. Our relatives are en route here even now—it is too late to turn them. They had to first escape from the king's labor force to even begin. There will be nothing for them to return to once they arrive here. They will be desperate, and could make you a formidable ally. But promise me this—if in the end you do flee, come here first. If I am still breathing, slit my throat. I do not want to fall into the hands of the son of David."

"It would be my pleasure," Hamon replied.

"No doubt. I am sure you have dreamed of it for years. What is your plan, have you told me all of it?"

"Have you any more gold?" Hamon asked.

"Very little."

"Then I have very little to tell you."

"In that case you have very little to keep you alive. Tell me, or die. You very well know you cannot survive without my counsel, gold or not."

"Perhaps," Hamon replied.

"You have no plan," his father observed.

Hamon brooded.

"Do you?"

The elder paused, allowing his reply to punctuate a mature silence.

"I already gave you my counsel."

Chapter 27

. . .wisdom is better than strength: nevertheless the poor man's wisdom is despised, and his words are not heard. The words of wise spoken quietly should be heard more than the shout of a ruler of fools.

Ecclesiastes 9:16-17

Abishag studied the nearing farmhouse, a residence much like many in the area. It was a humble home surrounded by fields, small, well kept, and for one family—home and inheritance—for many generations. She was aware of Dinah's repeated glances in her direction as they approached. While traveling to this place, they had passed the wall under construction, and just as Abishag had reported, dozens of ordinary citizens were seen carrying stones to help the workmen. The young, the old, women, even children, all were engaged in backbreaking toil, convinced that the completion of the wall was the key to the redemption of their land.

"Why do you start here?" Dinah asked.

"Because this family—I saw none of them at work on the wall. This means they may not be captive to Hamon's lie."

"A respectable family would certainly help," Dinah replied. "So far we have nothing but lowly beggars."

The comment did not sit well with Abishag. Indeed, over the past months, many beggars had paid a visit to Abishag's farm, and believing her testimony and having no homes of their own, many had settled nearby. Living in fields and sleeping under trees, eating of the farm's produce, and placing their full hope in the return of the king, the beggars stretched Abishag's resources.

"Lowly beggars . . . of which I am the lowliest of all," Abishag replied. "Our king does not save the wealthy, for they have no need of salvation. It is the sick that need a doctor. We are fortunate to be lowly, or the king would have passed us by in search of greater need."

Dinah lowered her eyes.

"I only meant to say, there are so few others."

"There are few. But desperation is as a seed. When mixed with faith, it grows into belief. That is why the destitute were first to believe us. But now the situation has gotten more desperate for many. We may find more believers."

Abishag indicated the farmhouse ahead.

"This family—I also have reason to think—has been cleansed by the medicine. We have that in our favor."

The farmhouse was situated on flatland, sown with field crops such as wheat and barley, but around the house strung the vines of a small vineyard. Abishag observed it in passing.

"Some fox damage also," she noted.

Dinah looked at her curiously.

A noise ahead made them look up. A resident of the farmhouse had seen their approach. A young boy, perhaps ten years old, ran quickly and disappeared into the house. Moments later a woman was seen looking out the lattice and then standing in the doorway. The woman stepped forward to greet them, peering curiously at the approaching travelers, while the wide-eyed boy watched from behind her skirts.

"Shalom my friend," Abishag offered.

The woman studied the two maidens, looking them up and down. She was herself middle aged, tall and thin, with quick dark eyes, traits that the boy shared.

"May I be of some assistance?" she offered.

"You are most kind, dear lady, but it is I who come to offer assistance to you," Abishag replied, "I am . . ."

"Abishag!" The woman suddenly exclaimed, throwing her hand over her mouth. "You are Abishag—the one who is sealing land with . . . with . . ."

"Yes, it is I, and this is my friend, Dinah. We have something here for you." Abishag removed a bag from her shoulder and lowered it. "Fresh vegetables from my farm on the hill. We were told the gardens down here sustained some damage last season."

The woman peered into the bag, while the boy stepped timidly forward, and then his hand shot into it.

"Stop it, Joash! You don't know what's in there!"

"Yes I do. I saw an apple."

"We have an orchard on the hill," Abishag explained. "There are a few sweet fruits left, though the season is late."

The woman looked at the pair nervously and narrowly.

"My husband is in the field—if you have come on business. I am here alone, except for Joash, and my aging mother. There is much to do—to prepare for—and not much time."

"Oh, we do not intend to stay long. I only hoped to share with you some blessings that have recently befallen us—there is a new way to repel the foxes—for example. I noticed some fox damage to your vineyard—it does not have to recur next year."

"It matters not a bit to me maiden. We will not be here next season. We—my husband, he is trying to find a place in Jezreel, if my mother-in-law can move. She has lived here her whole life, you know—in this very house—on this same plot of land."

"A mother—and only one son," Abishag observed.

"Yes. One son, the only seed for my husband's inheritance."

Dinah had by now recognized the woman as one who had come for medicine, more than once.

"I am thankful that you took not only the medicine, but the treatment," Dinah offered. "It is well to see you in such good health."

The woman seemed to hesitate, staring at the two maidens.

"Yes, well, for that I must thank you . . . though my husband did not approve of my being gone to the heat those weeks. But he is thankful that I am quite whole now."

As she said the last, she glanced past Abishag and Dinah. They turned in the direction of her glance and saw a man coming down the path with cultivating implements over his shoulder. He was a stocky man, red of beard.

"My husband approaches."

The man was trudging along slowly, studying the ground. He did not notice the maidens until he was nearly upon them, and looked up surprised.

"Eli," said the woman. "We have . . . guests. The maiden . . . Abishag."

The man's eyes widened.

"Abishag? Why?"

Abishag smiled, and bowed toward him.

"Greetings my lord. We are visiting some farms in this area. It seems there are some strange rumors afoot, and we hoped, through making contact, we could perhaps shed some light on questions that have been confusing to many."

Eli exchanged a glance with his wife in which a silent warning passed. The maidens were ushered inside the house and made to sit in relative comfort while the wide-eyed boy watched and the aging mother reclined on a cot. It turned out, to Abishag's favor, that the man was quite willing to discuss the topic of the seal, listening carefully and not objecting as Abishag methodically and humbly tried to give an honest account of how it had come to be in her possession. The the man stroked his red beard thoughtfully, as Abishag assured him that his land could be redeemed, free of any cost, by the seal of the king. She also revealed that the medicine that had cured his wife, was of the wisdom of the king, as was a new way to repel foxes from vineyards, the evidence of which could be seen at her own farm. At this point, his wife interjected that in her travelings to the farm, she had indeed noted the strength of that vineyard.

"Abishag," Eli offered, when the conversation appeared to be coming to a conclusion. "You are an unusual person—that much is apparent—and of strange fame lately. I would perhaps like to hear more of these matters, and to see your vineyard for myself. But as for taking this seal—there is considerable risk involved, you must understand."

"I do understand," Abishag replied. "I would only request that my lord also consider the risk in not taking it."

The man nodded thoughtfully.

"You speak of Hamon's seal, I perceive. He promises restoration of the land, but only to those who take his seal, and deny . . . your seal."

"But yet you have not taken his."

"Not yet, no."

"May I ask why?"

"It has occurred to me, that there is nothing to force Hamon to perform his promise. He is bound by no law. We have nothing but . . . his word on the matter."

"And you find that unsatisfying."

"I do."

"Well then. I come to you on the same grounds. You have my

promise on the matter. Whether you accept my promise or his, this much is true: you must decide, my lord. If you take one seal or the other, you have a chance of regaining your land. If you take neither—you have no chance."

"Oh, my soul, what an impossible choice you offer me maiden! Why must it all hang on this? Why can I not just keep what I rightfully inherited and not have to risk everything on a matter that I cannot possibly discern? This decision has been unfairly forced upon me."

Abishag nodded empathetically.

"If it is any help, my lord, I have had to face just such a decision myself, but with much more than my own land hanging in the balance. My decision affects everyone in the valley, and all who place trust in this seal. I would never dream of doing such without complete assurance. If I am wrong, I am worthy of death. But I know that I act in truth."

"Even so, if I take your seal, I am a partner to all of your liabilities, and could be tried as an accomplice to a crime worthy of death," he replied.

"If I am wrong, I will plead the full blame—you have my promise."

Eli pondered the puzzling maiden who sat so humbly before him, speaking commonly and convincingly of claims outrageous. Either she was insane, or she was correct, and she did not appear to be insane. He was about to speak when his wife whispered something in his ear. The man nodded.

"Dear maiden. You are most believable—and I do not think it is by the art of some dark enchantment. But there is more to this matter than the redemption of land. The truth be known, our harvest was committed to the Brotherhood. It was fully lost—in the Hittite raid on departure day. We have our land, but we have scarcely anything to sustain us through the winter. Hamon has declared that his barns are open to provide grain, to any who accept his seal. But anyone who takes your seal must pay with money. We have no money—and I would not dream that your seal will be accepted for payment there. We will receive a fair sum, if and when our farm is purchased—but the completion of that transaction is a whole year away. Until then, we have not any money to live on."

Abishag was surprised.

"Hamon is withholding food?"

"*Providing* food, is his claim, but only on his conditions—accepting his seal and rejecting yours. The food will become more important as the winter stretches on. If we take your seal, on what will we survive?"

"I see your dilemma. But *still* you have not taken his seal."

The man stared at her, then rubbed his head vigorously.

"I don't know *what* to do," he replied, truly vexed.

"We have sustenance at our farm, my lord. We would surely not fail to share with you if you are truly in need."

The man looked at her with gratitude, but not quite belief.

"It is a small farm, maiden, and I understand there are a number of you to support. Can you truly promise that your stores will last longer than the season? Can you make this same promise to any and all who accept your seal? Surely your generous offers must include some reasonable limitations."

Abishag hesitated. The man did have a point.

"You are quite correct, my lord. I do not know where all of the necessary sustenance will come from, or even how much will be needed. But I do know that the king owns treasures sufficient to supply the needs of every family in the valley, if necessary. I place my faith in that, and that he will not allow us to starve in his will."

"And now you ask that same faith, of me."

"I do not ask you to trust any bridge on which I do not walk myself, my lord."

The boy, who had been watching closely and listening carefully, whispered something to his father.

"I don't know son," he replied. "As far as I can see, we are leaving this place. But we will acquire other land for you someday, somehow, if not here, somewhere else."

Abishag misted.

"Do you truly believe, my lord, even if my claims are false, that the king of Israel would approve of what is happening in this valley?"

The man studied the floor between his knees for a long moment.

"It's wrong," he whispered. "Something is wrong. I cannot prove it by the Law, but I feel it in my bones. How can I give my strength to Hamon's wall—to redeem land that is my birthright? It makes no sense. But this sealing you are offering is a hard thing. How can I bind my future gain or loss to something so improbable? Since the Brotherhood failed, I have learned that the Lord does not honor unnecessary risks. We nearly lost everything that way."

****

"The elders have hired an official examination of Abishag's seal?" Jared asked the beggars who stood before him, a circle of faces with whom he was well familiar.

The beggars at the farm, though burdensome to support, were sometimes a useful means of reconnaissance. Their many sets of eyes and ears traveled to and from town, reporting what they learned proudly, as indebted men offering what small recompense they could.

The hobbled, old man twinkled with the joy of private news and glowed under the gazes of his companions.

"The sage came from far away," he said excitedly, "a sage from the king's service—or so they say—at least from the former king's service, a sage from David's service! No, no—-Saul! Yes, even Saul! He may have come from Jezreel—or even farther!

Farther!—yes! Camels! Ohh. Draped with wealth. Ahh! Such a very wise man—to look at—very wise! I have not seen a wiser looking man in . . . well, I perhaps saw one once that might have equaled him in the appearance of wisdom, but not exceeded, and not in this area. No! Men of such wise appearance rarely sojourn here. They sojourn in places like Sheba, or Scythia or, several other places like that. Such a wise looking man! His beard was like a bundle of wheat! His clothes were as fine silk . . . his voice flowed like honey . . . his servant carried scrolls, fine scrolls, decorated scrolls, and as numerous as the olive trees on the hills of . . ."

"Eliphaz—please, just tell us what happened?" Jared interjected.

"It is just as I was telling you—he came to examine the seal of the maiden—bless her righteous soul! Aye! Here she is now!"

The group turned to see the approach of Abishag and Dinah.

The maidens joined the circle, as several at once began explaining to them the sense of the intelligence they were trying to draw from the little man in the center. Abishag turned to him.

"Did this sage examine the seal?" she asked.

"Examine! Oh! Did he examine! I have not seen such a terrifying examination in—well, I may have perhaps seen one equally terrifying, but not surpassing. It was the third hour when the seals were placed before him—and the sixth before he uttered a single word! He sat, he stared, he paced, he drew close, he touched, he filled the seal with dark sand, then slowly blew the dust away—then filled it again, then blew it again, then! Oh! He called his servant! He was exhausted! He stopped to drink wine. His servant fanned him as he sat. His servant was nearly as finely dressed as he!—His servant had walked while he rode the camels. His servant brought forth a bag of fine silk. Out of this bag, the sage displayed such a stunning collection of ancient seals—laid them all out on the table—I have never seen such a collection!—well, perhaps I did on one occasion, but, that was many years ago—many years, and far from here, to be sure. But then he called for a sample of the king's seal!—the one imprinted on documents recently received from Jerusalem. How they all watched him then! He laid it out on the table, then, side by side, the maiden's document, and the document from Jerusalem. Side by side. He drew close, then stepped back, then drew close again! He waved a lamp over them. He held them up in the light, side by side, he filled each seal with black sand, and slowly blew it out, first one, then the other, then the one again, then the other again, then the one . . ."

"Eliphaz! What did he rule?!" Jared demanded.

The expression of Eliphaz grew grave, and his listeners leaned in closer.

"What did he rule? Simply this. You understand—all the elders were there. It was they who summoned him, after all. Of course they would all be there—would they not? Of course they would! He told them this—and this is what he told them: he was such a wise sounding man—and wise appearing! His voice was like honey. He told them that in all his years—and how they were watching him! He told them that in all his years, he had never seen a better counterfeit. Indeed he did! Well, he did confess that perhaps on one occasion he had seen a counterfeit equally good, but none better. So good a counterfeit it was, he said, that only the best of the best-trained experts could ever hope to discern it. The difference would be impossible to detect, for the common man—but he was not a common man!—he said. So wise appearing. He even asked to see the instrument that made the impression, so that he could admire its quality! Ha! To the untrained eye—he said—this seal would certainly seem identical! Yes! Yes! He used the very word, 'identical!' "

"But did the elders believe this?" Abishag asked.

"Believe it? Aye! To a man! They thanked him! They paid him—I saw gold pass—I did not see the amount but I saw gold pass! The elders published his report—and sent it out with runners. Certainly they believed it—for who could doubt the testimony of one with such a wise appearance!? Even I would have believed it—and I do not believe very much. I have not met the man who believes less than I do—except, well, perhaps on one occasion I met a man who believed equally as little of what is there to be believed as I, but never less so, or more so, rather, or less so I do mean—but he was so wise in appearance! I have not seen a man with a wiser appearance in . . . well . . ."

Abishag had turned and was walking slowly down the trail. Dinah hurried after her.

"Abishag. The people—they will not believe this report. Not all of them."

"Perhaps not all. Some will still believe us. But, there is another matter to solve, now."

"What is that?"

"We are running low on sustenance. The medicine is nearly gone, as you are aware. But the silver, it is almost gone now too, from supporting everyone. I had spoken to some merchants who were perhaps willing to accept the seal as payment for goods, but now . . ." she shook her head.

Dinah was surprised.

"I did not know we were running low on silver. We could have been charging a modest fee for the medicine."

Abishag stopped and faced her.

"No Dinah. We could not have charged for it; what we were freely given, we must freely give. But now we must find some way to meet the needs of those who depend on us. My brother Huram has not returned in some time. Perhaps he will soon, and I can send a message by him to the king, but if he does not, we must find some other way."

"Abishag, do not worry. I can work. I can earn money still. We will get by."

Abishag gazed at her companion then slipped her arm around her waist. She knew that such a large number—the dozen or more beggars, plus the group in the house, could never be supported by Dinah's labor alone.

"I love you, Dinah."

Dinah blushed, and the two continued down the trail.

"The Lord will provide, some way. You are strong and kind, but even you could not do that much work."

The two friends, more like sisters now, continued to stroll and discuss the results of their first direct effort to enlighten some local residents. Both agreed that the effort had proved both worthwhile and promising, and they made plans to visit more homes over the next few days. But both were also aware that if messages had reached the population that the king's seal had been examined by an expert and determined to be a fake, their already difficult challenge would be even more daunting.

****

Hamon leaned forward motionless before the gaming board with his chin in his hands while the torchlight flickered on his deeply furrowed brow. The Arabians watched patiently, exchanging a knowing glance. Then suddenly he pounded the board with his fist, causing the pieces to fly in every direction.

"Lasting twenty moves is exceptional, for a novice. Most men fall before ten," Alakhi Beneshish said.

"Ah. And a third jewel in the bag is not a bad day's work for a man who has already earned ten shekels of gold. Is there anything else you wish to plunder me of, before you depart?"

"We came here on your invitation, my dear lord, and performed at your request," replied the master gamesman. "The gold was contingent upon a favorable result, and did we not achieve that for you? Our judgment on the seal was accepted by all. As for what happened here," he indicated the game board with a nod, "you did not have to accept my challenge."

"You swindler! Insidious scoundrels, that is what you are," Hamon grumbled.

"Which is why you hired us, my lord. What you asked today was not easy. I do not know where or how you obtained the imprint of those seals, but truth be known, I would not want to deny them in an official court."

Hamon brooded.

"Have you ever met him?" he asked.

"Met who?"

"King Solomon."

The gamesman and his crier looked at one another.

"Only once."

The room was so quiet that Hamon's angry breathing could be heard.

Alakhi Beneshish leaned back in his chair and sipped his wine.

"Have you . . . ever failed to win?" Hamon asked, flicking his fingers at the gaming board.

"Only once," replied the Arabian.

Hamon flushed deeply red. Then rose quickly, and stomped out of the room.

****

Several days later, Abishag and Dinah were joined by an unexpected guest—the woman, Hildah. Hildah had made the trip to the farm one morning, knowing that her husband would be away that day. Abishag explained their desire to go directly to the people, answer their questions, so they could make decisions about the seal with the benefit of having heard both sides. Hildah was ready to burst with passion to help in some way, but following her surprise testimony at Abishag's questioning, she was restrained by her husband more than ever. She desired to go with them, to add her voice and testimony to Abishag and Dinah's, but knew that she could not be away from home long. However, since on this day, Abishag and Dinah were to visit a nearby farm, Hildah agreed to come along. It was well to have her along after what befell them on that occasion.

Abishag, though proceeding with her usual friendliness, was soon perceptive of the walls of unbelief from which her appeals bounced. The family was large and had several grown sons who had been actively working on Hamon's wall. The father met the maidens in the yard, not offering any hospitality, and preventing any movement toward the house. Abishag soon found herself under the cold stares of three large sons as well as the father as she stood in the trail attempting to relate her testimony.

"This seal that I have been given to wield—I claim no worthiness of it. But it is as freely available to you as to anyone else. Your land can be claimed today."

"A meaningless claim maiden. And more than that, an illegal claim—a crime. It threatens to destroy us on many counts. Do you know how difficult it is to build a wall and still maintain a farm? My sons and I, we carry twice our normal load, but the more people agree to help with the wall, the lighter our load becomes. You are working against us by undermining our labor force with these lies. The sooner we finish the wall, the sooner we receive redemption. We are working not only to our own benefit, but to everyone who is in need of redemption, when we lend our strength to the wall."

"I so appreciate your sacrifice and your labor for your countrymen, my lord. I only wish to inform you, the price of redemption is already paid. It is a free gift. You could never work enough to earn it. Where is the end of all of this toil? You spin a rope from an endless wheel, for the wall was declared complete already. That is why the land is up for auction in the first place. At what point then does this redemption take place? There is nothing in the Law requiring it, and no clear point at which the wall is complete enough to require fulfillment of Hamon's promise. The whole thing rests on his word, and his opinion of when the wall is satisfactory. But the seal of the King, it is a finished work. All you need do is receive it," she replied.

"And for all that—you miss another exceedingly important point—the necessity of protection! Has it escaped your notice that the Hittites are bolder than ever, and dangerous to our peace? The more our nation prospers, the greater a target we become.

Without this protection, it is needless to own redeemed land—even if your unlikely seal could accomplish it—for the fruit of the land will be carried off as plunder as soon as it leaves the vine."

"My lord. The need for protection cannot be dismissed. But what greater protection could you wish for than the king's own eye on your property? If he seals it, he is obligated to defend it. He does not save it today to lose it tomorrow—no wise king would run his kingdom that way. He will defend it. He will provide a more sure covering than any wall farmers such as ourselves could build. A day of redemption is coming. He will *keep* that which you have committed unto him against that day," she replied.

"But where is he, maiden?!" the man demanded. "Where has the king been during all of this oppression? In all the years of Baal Hamon's foot on our necks, the king did nothing to protect us! Why should I think that he will defend us now? We have of our own found an answer, and Hamon, who was our enemy, is now our friend. But the king—he is as aloof now as he ever was. He is a silent king—silent and passive. And do not speak to me of his seal. The presence of his so-called seal without his personal presence is absurd. If his seal were here, *he* would be here. Have you not heard of the recent examination? The seal was proven by experts to be false."

Abishag was starting to form a response when Hildah broke in.

"My dear man. I understand your argument, and please allow me to respond. Do you know who I am? I am the wife of Simeon, of the chief elders. This maiden, strange as it may seem, speaks the truth. I can attest that she is an honest person, not a deceived person. The king IS present—he is present in his bride, and all of his authority is in her hand. She knows what he wants done. It is the elders who have been deceived, first by Baal Hamon, then by his son, and now, more recently, by one so-called expert on seals. Why was an amateur expert called? If the seal is false, why was not the appeal made to the courts of Solomon, as is legally proper? No, this testimony had to come from a self-proclaimed expert, with no legal authority. Does this not sound strange to you?"

"It sounds like grace to me, woman, undeserved and unappreciated grace. Hamon is giving this maiden space to repent of her folly, for if the appeal does go to Jerusalem, she will surely hang. What more evidence of Hamon's reformation does one need? In the past, he would have leaped at any opportunity to send one of his enemies to the gallows. But this woman who threatens to destroy his most noble efforts, he tries to save! Such kindness cannot continue indefinitely. If she persists in this foolishness, the space of grace will run out. Saving one person cannot justify destroying everyone else. If she does not repent soon, the people will *demand* a judgment from Jerusalem, and that day is approaching soon."

"But I have already requested a judgment from Jerusalem," Abishag replied.

"And to your splendid and undeserved good fortune it has been denied!" the man replied. "Do you not see that the entire valley is straining to save you, while you strain to destroy it?"

"It is the reverse, my dear lord," Hildah replied. "Abishag is straining to save the whole valley, while the whole valley strains to destroy her."

Suddenly, a sound was heard, and a horse-drawn wagon appeared, hastening into the yard. It came to a quick halt and two men jumped out.

"You see? This is what I told you!" one man said angrily. "These maidens have been visiting farms, pretending great humility, convincing people to give up our wall effort, casting our inheritance land into the abyss of permanent sale! Joriah! Do not believe them! They are enemies of Israel, and all that is right!"

"I do not believe them. And I and my sons are going to see the wall to completion, regardless of their lies."

"You maidens—woman!" the man shouted looking temporarily surprised at the sight of Hildah. "You have no right to deceive the people like this with your baseless and arrogant lies! Have you no shame? Have you no sense? Have you none of the virtues that made Israel great? To think—the seal of the king! The *bride* of the king—of all the ridiculous lies! And some people are wavering that it is actually true! Cease and desist at once, woman! For the sake of my family, my land, and everyone in the valley, I adjure you! If you continue, you will have me and all of the men on the wall to contend with, and I will not be as gentle as the Council! They have nothing to lose in this. But for me—this is my life and livelihood!"

"Now just a minute . . ." Dinah said, stepping forward, flushed.

Abishag quickly took her arm.

"My lord, I do mean no harm to your life and livelihood, in fact I . . ."

"Well then get out! Take your witchcraft and go back to your Phoenician lover and leave the people in peace! You are a stench in Israel! An abomination among us! I have a mind to silence you permanently myself!"

The maidens took a step back under the power of the man's rage, realizing that he had the ability to carry out his threat.

"My lord, I have come here in peace . . ."

"Joriah. Did you invite them here!?"

"No I did not. They have come of their own, and I have heard enough of their lies. However, this is still my land—at least for a few more months—and I will not suffer any blood to be spilled upon it, no matter how just the cause. Woman, I order you to leave my property at once—all of you!"

"Yes, my lord."

"And if you come back—to any of these farms, I will be there first! If I do not precede you there, I will follow you there! Your lies will go unrefuted no more! This is going to stop!" the man shouted after them. "And don't try any of your witchcraft on me because it will not work! I am on to you!"

Over the next few days, Abishag and Dinah did try to continue engaging the people, making themselves visible in the marketplace in hopes of sparking natural conversation as well as visiting selected farms. The man who threatened them was true to his word. He and several others organized an effort to warn the people, visiting residents before Abishag could get to them, setting their minds against her. Finding people even willing to listen was more difficult than ever before. Conversations fell quiet when Abishag passed by, cold stares met her, and whispers followed her. Possessing a giving spirit and so much to give, she found this a difficult burden to bear.

Dinah was quietly seething—not taking it well.

"This is *not* what I was expecting. I don't understand it. The king himself has commissioned us—the king! I thought we would be more successful. We can offer everything the people need, redemption of land, a solution for the foxes, medicine that truly heals, yet, we are hated. It makes no sense."

"I have been an outcast before, Dinah," Abishag told her. "One must learn to love, even when hated. The people are not evil, they are just deceived."

"Abishag! You amaze me—after how you are treated? You are called a harlot, an abomination, and a witch! Yet you continue to extend goodwill? You are too kind—to *everyone.* You could probably even say something good about Hamon himself!"

"I could."

"Dare I ask?"

"He is a good adversary."

Dinah gaped, then chuckled.

"Well *that,* and that *only,* I can allow."

The pair moved toward the square hoping to negotiate some purchases for the household. Most of the merchants were giving Abishag's seal a wide berth, not wanting to risk their goods in exchange for it. Abishag had in mind to try another place or two. She knew she dare not try the seal at Hamon's barns, it would be anathema there. But supplies were growing short, she needed to secure provisions, somehow—and soon.

As they rounded the corner, they suddenly found themselves facing Hamon himself who had been coming the other direction with Lotan. All four froze, recognizing each other instantly, and unable by virtue of the situation to avoid some kind of interaction. Hamon had apparently been discussing something with Lotan and had broken off in mid-sentence, his mouth remaining open as he saw Abishag, and then Dinah. The reaction upon seeing Abishag could rightly be called surprise, but upon seeing Dinah, a strange aspect came over his countenance. Abishag watched his face redden while a vein pulsed in his neck. Glancing over at Dinah, she discerned a similar reaction, though Dinah was more fully covered by her virgin's veil.

"Excuse us, please," Abishag said politely, stepping into the street to let the men pass, nudging Dinah to the side also.

The parties continued on their way.

"He still appears a bit angry at you," Abishag commented to Dinah.

"I am sorry Abishag. I did not dare say a word to him, lest I say what I really think of him . . . again."

Beyond the corner, Lotan was staring at Hamon curiously.

"What was that all about?" he asked him.

"That little wench of a barmaid. She's going to kiss my feet one day—you watch," Hamon replied lowly. "And it won't be a day too soon."

****

Hamon's plan to marginalize Abishag's seal and starve out the group at the farm by providing grain from his barns only to those who accepted his seal seemed to be working. He knew Abishag would never waver, but some of her less stable associates perhaps could be swayed. Perhaps even Dinah could be drawn to apply for sustenance at his barns, independently of Abishag. He had some choice responses already planned for her, if that should ever happen.

As the season wore on, the pressure for food would become acute among the population, particularly among those who had formerly been his most zealous enemies, the members of the failed Brotherhood. They had lost all their harvest and had little in savings to buy food, and that only increased his sway among them. Though Abishag was known to have some source of silver, her purchases—which were watched—were modest. Hamon doubted that her supply of silver was especially great, and may run out—perhaps soon.

His estimation of her means was correct, a situation that Abishag was watching closely. She was also aware of the dwindling of the medicine on which so many depended. She assured them that supplies would soon be replenished, even as she lowered the doses. She was soon to find out that the patience of those who were taking it would not endure much longer. Upon entering the market square that day, her attention was drawn to a new merchant, working a booth she had not seen before, and he seemed to have drawn quite a crowd. Drawing closer to investigate, she found herself recognizing many in the crowd as those who had been to her farm for medicine. The man working the booth was selling fine looking flasks, artfully decorated, of which Abishag chanced to get a whiff when someone passed nearby. It smelled a bit like Solomon's remedy for the swamp fever. The man in the booth had prepared a supply of these flasks, displayed in neat rows. They were small, and after watching for a moment, Abishag realized he was charging a high price for them.

A woman passed closely by, carrying a flask.

"Excuse me," Abishag said.

The woman turned.

"May I ask what you have there?"

"Abishag! Oh, you will surely thank the Lord for this—you were right!—there is another supply! This man has discerned the recipe for your medicine!"

"Another supply? For the medicine? It cannot be."

"But it is. It is very close if not the same. I get the same feeling from it as I did from yours."

"Will you allow me to smell it?"

"Certainly!"

The woman handed Abishag her flask. She smelled it, then dabbed a drop on her finger, putting it to her tongue. It did seem similar.

"I would like to examine this potion, my lady," she said.

"Well you can get some of your own, right here. It's four shekels for a flask."

Abishag blinked.

"Four shekels? That is sixteen days wages! The medicine I give you is free."

"But you have no medicine dear," the woman said, then took her flask and walked away.

Abishag waited until the crowd died down, then approached the merchant.

"Medicine for the swamp fever maiden?" he asked.

"Where did you get this, my lord?"

"Where? I made it. I am an alchemist. This medicine is known in the area. I discerned the recipe and mixed it."

"Has it been tested?"

"Of course! Of course—many have partaken of it. It is very soothing, just try some once, you will see."

"I am sure it is soothing, my lord, but I have no need of it myself. I was just wondering if its long term effects have been determined."

"Absolutely. People who take this medicine get well. It has been distributed in this area for some time now. Many can testify."

Abishag was not recognizing the man, and he, apparently, not her. He was not a local.

"Would you be willing to share your recipe with me, my lord?"

"Ah. Now maiden. It took me many years of practicing alchemy to gain my skill. It is my livelihood, you understand. If you wish to buy some of my potion, you may, but I cannot give you for free what cost me so much, you understand."

"I see. Well, perhaps I could purchase a tiny sample then, if you will allow me."

He eyed the two of them suspiciously.

"Are you a potion mixer maiden?"

"Me? Oh, no, I am a vine tender. I know nothing of such things. But I am curious about your medicine—if it is as soothing as you say."

"One taste will convince you maiden."

She paid him and the man gave her small sample. She wandered down the street, sniffing it and pondering. Dinah touched a dab to her tongue also. They puzzled over it for a while, agreeing that they must examine it more closely later.

****

The LORD will not suffer the soul of the righteous to famish: but he casteth away the substance of the wicked.

Proverbs 10:3

When Abishag returned home, her mother had been watching for her. She went out to meet her daughter in the yard. Abishag saw on the face of her mother evidence of ill news, and became immediately attentive. Abelah drew in close.

"I need to speak to you. You are aware we have been running

low on basic necessities—though the others do not know this. Abishag, everything is gone now. We can perhaps salvage some unharvested produce that hangs dry on the trees and vines, but the cruse is nearly empty, and we have no flour. The farm animals are thin, from relying on winter grazing, for we have not been feeding them properly. There is nothing to set out, even tonight."

"Have you spoken to Hemanah?"

"No, he has believed your testimony—that you had plenty to sustain us for the winter."

"We did have plenty, but we are supporting more people now. Even the medicine has run out. I learned today that someone is selling a similar potion in the market to the sick and desperate. Still, I cannot doubt that the king knows our need. He will not allow us to suffer lack," Abishag said.

"True enough. But the beggars—they have a keener sense of these things. They know when supplies are dwindling. Some of them have been speaking of returning to the beggar's wall to catch what they can from the people."

"Understandable, for they have no pride to hurt, but I do wish they would not go, for it creates the appearance of lack on our part among the people. They will not be able to reconcile this with our testimony that we are under the care of the king. They are saying he is a silent king, either unaware or uncaring toward the needs of our area."

"It could appear that way," replied Abelah. "But we know that the king, for his own wise purposes, leaves some things to their own course. He may allow us to endure for a time, but that does not mean he has forgotten us. The whole nation is prospering under Solomon's leadership; the high prices our produce received at this year's trade fair are an example. How his kindness hides behind his humility! He secretly bestows upon people benefits that they never credit back to his actions. But you and I know. No doubt the king is very aware of our need, however it may appear. Even though we have nothing at the moment, he will not let us come to great want."

Abishag nodded.

"But the beggars will be the first to leave. I must speak to them before they go."

"Then what will you do?"

"Pray—the same as you."

Abelah regarded her daughter knowingly, then mother and daughter returned to the house. Abishag went out onto the porch and leaned on the rail, gazing up at the hills. Many months until harvest, no food, and no money. The king afar off, it seemed, and the residents of the farm resorting to begging. In just an hour or less, it would become apparent to all that there was no food.

She sighed and breathed a prayer. *Lord, what do you wish me to do?*

The day was cool, though the sun was high and the sky was clear. Movement suddenly caught her attention. She looked down. A little bird was feeding on the porch, picking for tiny seeds. She smiled at the creature, remembering Solomon's way with animals. Then suddenly she noticed something. What was on the bird's leg? She caught her breath, and stooped down toward him. The bird was tame! He hopped up onto her finger.

This is exactly like the bird that Jedidiah showed me that morning. Then the revelation hit her. It was not exactly like that bird, it *was* that bird—and something was attached to its leg. She carefully detached it, and found it to be paper. She unrolled it and held a tiny note, no bigger than the palm of her hand, very fine and containing a tiny picture and some text, scribed in ink by a very sharp stylus. She quickly moved out into the full sun and squinted at the writing. After a few moments of examination, she realized the picture was a tiny map of her own farm. Beneath the map was written a few lines of perfect but small text. She read . . .

Beloved. Space is limited, love exceeds paper. Silver spent, and your bundle of myrrh despised? Gold will be found here. Do you know what day it is? Can you find east? Use the bent hoe. Will write more shortly. I am coming quickly. Jedidiah.

Abishag caught her breath. A message from Jedidiah—the king!—and clearly to her!

She studied the note again, with renewed interest. The map of her property was recognizable, but situated within it was a strange object, one that did not exist on her property. It appeared to be a tiny cube with horns. Suddenly she recognized it. The brazen altar! It was a tiny perfect drawing of the brazen altar that stood in the outer court of the temple that Solomon was building. But why did he draw it on her property? She strolled out into the yard, studying the ground.

The note had meaning. With such a small space available, every word was carefully chosen, she knew. *Myrrh despised* . . . the Seal, Solomon's Seal, he had joked of scenting it with myrrh, then actually done so. *Despised* . . . quite perceptive, for his seal was in fact no longer accepted for purchases. And this note, apparently, was a map to hidden gold—gold that Solomon would have hidden before he left the area, much before, in fact! Just how far ahead had he foreseen?!

She wandered toward the area of her farm where the image of the brazen altar appeared on the map. It was near her vineyard, but not in it, about a bow shot off the main trail. She found the place, and carefully examined the ground. It appeared completely undisturbed. She scuffed at the rock and dirt. It was hard and dry. She continued scuffing in an expanding circle, searching with her feet. There was no evidence of anything being buried there. She removed the note, and examined it again. Four strange words caught her attention: *use the bent hoe*. Her mouth whispered the unusual words.

Why? Why dig with the bent hoe? Would not any implement suffice? But he would not have given such odd instructions without a reason. With a sigh, she left the location, and wandered back to where the farm implements were kept behind the animal shed. Shuffling through them, she found the bent hoe that he had repaired. When she pulled it out of the shadows and into the sunlight, she suddenly froze. The bent hoe! He had also marked a temple cubit on it! With a rush of revelation, she looked closer and saw that there were many tiny lines scratched neatly into the blade—a calendar and compass for each day of the whole year! She hurried out into the yard, looking up at the sun. It was near midday. But which day? Winter Solstice! East would be easy to find on this day! She went back to the place where she had scuffed the ground, and dug a small hole in which to insert the hoe, pointing the handle of it directly toward the sun, so that it left no shadow.

She waited breathlessly, in the minutes that followed. The shadow formed to the east, as the sun moved west.

Gold! The brazen altar does not contain gold—it is brass! Gold is found—in the holy place, where the ark rests! And the ark rests exactly sixty temple cubits west of the brazen altar!

She looked down at the hoe, Solomon's mark of the temple cubit showing clear and exact on the handle. *Gold will be found exactly sixty cubits due west of here!*

She remembered the day when the two of them had planted the spice garden, using this very hoe. She had not even known he was king then, yet he was already planning for THIS day, accurately foreseeing that she would stay while he returned to Jerusalem, and that she would need gold!—on this day! Her own question echoed in her ears.

"What if I need to know east on another day?"

"Simple . . ."

Amazing man!

The shadow of the hoe stretched east, as the sun moved west. She stood behind the hoe and looked in the direction of the shadow, sighting down the line scratched on the blade for Solstice to find due west. Soon she noticed a very clear landmark, a boulder, with a sharp point at the top, exactly due west! She picked up the hoe and began carefully measuring the distance . . . fifty-seven . . . fifty-eight . . . fifty-nine cubits, fifty-nine appeared to be exactly under the boulder. She peeked around it. On the ground rested a small pile of straw. She moved the straw, and saw softened earth. Her hoe uncovered it easily, and she found the lid of an earthen jar, just inches beneath the surface. She pulled the lid, and instantly, the glint of gold shone in the sun. She knelt down. A rolled paper was also present. Her eyes widened. She quickly picked up the paper and unrolled it. The scent of myrrh wafted up as the page unfurled. She shivered, and not for cold.

My sister, my spouse,

Please accept my apology for my abbreviated greeting in my last message, you will appreciate the need to not burden our poor little friend with extra weight—I was quite concerned that he be able to get to you on this day. If you are indeed reading this on the Winter Solstice, no doubt you will find the contents of this jar useful at this time.

As I write it is now the fourth month. Shortly, I will tell you that I am the king, and that I love you, and that I have loved you from the morning you met me by the well just north of where you now stand.

She glanced over and did in fact see that very place, a dozen paces or so away.

I would have revealed myself sooner, but the Lord has prevented me. Please forgive me this delay, for the containment of this love threatens to burst the stitch of my spirit.

As I write, my only solace is in the knowledge that you will soon know, and if you are reading this, my proposal was accepted. I am no doubt jubilant in spirit; for our coming together in marriage is nigh at hand.

If I have predicted correctly, you have nobly chosen to remain in this area for a time. If I may guess again, your attempts to redeem your village have nearly run their course, as has the silver found in your house. Fret not if progress seems faint, and not many are convinced, for numbers are not the only measure of success. Your doings here will burn the coming judgment into permanent memory, and the story of what you have done will be retold for generations. Thanks to your sacrifice, never again will the residents of this valley fall prey to treachery.

Hamon is growing desperate. He is crafty, and may have identified me by now. Be cautious, the wounded animal is most dangerous. Let the jar of gold remain where you found it, it is safer than the house. The medicine will be replenished soon also.

And now, speaking of love—for it is your love I most desire—a wealth of it awaits you. If my love for you were turned to gold, it would make my natural wealth as debt. The world contains not the paper to record my love for you, nor the ink to write it, and if I attempted it, there would be no room left in the jar for the gold.

Take courage, my love, I am coming quickly.

Shalom, beloved, my dove, my sister, my spouse, my queen. Our reuniting is close at hand.

Your Jedidiah

Abishag collapsed to sit on a rock, tears streaming down her face, blurring the sweet scented paper before her eyes. It was a long cry, a love cry, a cry of courage, and she emerged from it with a feeling of euphoria. The wisdom of the king had reached far into the future, and foreseen accurately everything that was taking place. She was safely in the king's will—safe as she would have been had she gone with him to Jerusalem. She reached into the jar and removed a single shekel of gold worth many days' wages. She admired it for a moment, feeling its cool weight. She had never before held such a large piece of money. Then she carefully replaced the cover to the jar, and reburied it.

Abishag carried both the shekel of gold and the letter back to the house, but it was the letter that she carried closest to her heart.

Chapter 28

Two are better than one; because they have a good reward for their labour. For if they fall, the one will lift up his fellow: but woe to him that is alone when he falleth; for he hath not another to help him up.

Ecclesiastes 4:9-10

Hamon was vexed. Reports from the market had it that Abishag was making purchases with gold! If so, her sudden means threatened his case with the people instantly. If Abishag did indeed have gold, as the reports claimed, the foundation of his strategy to take the land was poised to be smashed in an instant. Thus far, he had relied on the fact that he had placed gold as a Display of Means in the sight of all, whereas his rival had only presented an unproven seal. Gold in sight, was more convincing for most than a seal uncertain. However, once informed that Abishag was purchasing goods with gold, it did not take him long to worry that she might also soon put forth a Display of Means behind her own claims upon land—in gold! That, of all things, would be most devastating to his case. How to respond?

The first thing he needed was information. He hastily assembled a group of men of the baser sort to assist him, and then dispatched one, a diminutive man by the name of Arphaxad to enter Abishag's farm posing as a beggar. His mission: to return with a report of where the gold was hidden, and also the amount, if possible.

Arphaxad, small and ragged with a prominent lisp on his tongue, was deemed quite suited to play the role of beggar, more so since he had been a beggar in truth, in occasional seasons of life, aided by his love of strong drink. Among his acquaintances, Arphaxad insisted on being called by his full name, an insistence which inevitably led to its being shortened to "Arph." The louder his insistence, the more the abbreviation was repeated. "Arph" was outfitted in rags and dispatched to his mission, after having been promised a handsome reward.

Hamon was not any too confident of this agent's ability to maintain the necessary guile, but being in a straight of time, he allowed him as the best that could be found on short notice. Therefore, he was pleasantly surprised by prompt success, for Arphaxad was welcomed among the beggars at the farm, and even had opportunity to enter the house itself early on. It was only days later that he returned to excitedly report that he had located the gold. With the lust for the reward that Hamon had promised him foremost in mind, he hastened to give an account of his intelligence.

"How much gold?" Hamon had asked him, narrowly.

With a lisp, Arphaxad reported, "I did not in fact shee the gold, my lord, but I am most schertain I know where it iszh."

"How can you be certain of something you did not see?" Hamon asked.

"I entered the maidensz room by shtealth, when the othersz were out, you shee. I thought perhapsh the gold might be hidden there. I found it not, but while there, I found thish!"

Arphaxad held proudly before him a tiny scrap of fine paper.

Hamon became immediately attentive, snatching up the scrap

and focusing his full attention on it.

"This is a map of the farm. I know these landmarks well. But what is this object here?"

"Yesh," said Arphaxad, knowingly.

Hamon continued to study the tiny map until printed letters at the bottom focused in his vision.

"Gold will be found here . . ." he whispered.

"Yesh—and, what will be my take, my lord?"

Hamon appeared lost in thought.

"My lord?" Arphaxad repeated.

"Yes—you, the gold, this gold, it is apparently buried. We must plan a search—by night. A share will be spread among all who help me retrieve it. Your take and theirs depends upon how much is there, of course."

Hamon wasted no time. He handpicked a team to help him recover the gold on the first dark night. He waited most impatiently for such a night, constantly afraid that the gold could appear at the hall of records as a Display of Means at any time. With nervous impatience he waited through the fourth quarter of the moon, which on successive clear nights filled the hillsides with light. The crew recruited for the actual digging was kept on the ready, and the longer so, the more bickering and unrest rose up among them concerning the amount and distribution of the expected reward.

Finally, a west wind granted an overcast day, and Hamon, expecting an especially dark night, roused his troops. His ragtag army, each member of which was included partially on the qualification of a ragged appearance with the rationale that they could pass as beggars if discovered, had more in common with petty criminals than noble beggars.

At the final briefing in which the strategy was rehearsed, Hamon found the atmosphere among his troops oddly stilted. After impressing upon them in the strongest terms the need for complete silence, followed by a strong injunction to vacate the site immediately on the first suspicion of discovery, the reason for the strange mood was revealed. The men were suspicious of each other, and some had become convinced that others among them were committed to cheating them of their share of the gold.

"On a dark night anything could happen!" one complained. "How are we to be certain the shares are fairly weighed?"

Some were threatening to quit the mission altogether.

Hamon, frustrated almost to the point of nausea, conceded to bring along an accountant equipped with scales to verify the amount of gold immediately following its discovery. Thusly Ono, the tall, clumsy and aging accountant for Baal Hamon's estate, was summoned from his house at a strange hour to a strange mission. Though Ono was meticulous in record keeping, he was rather unaware in most every other way, and a mission that would have raised suspicions in other men was received by Ono with more annoyance at the hour, than questions about its purpose. With the assurance that a professional would be responsible for weighing the shares, the hodgepodge squad agreed to proceed, dressed themselves in rags, and took up their digging implements for a late night hike.

Like a train of limping camels, the group struggled up the trail with difficulty in the darkness (torches were disallowed on the trail) with Hamon and Ono bringing up the rear. For himself, Hamon intended to stay a distance away during the actual digging. He was much too famous locally to pass as a beggar if discovered, no matter how dark the night. He planned to come near only when the container was discovered.

Thus Hamon and Ono traveled together both carrying digging implements, which Ono carried awkwardly with his scales, having never been employed in manual labor. Hamon was forced by this to divide his attention between the path ahead and the gangling man next to him, whose wandering path and swinging hoe threatened to do unintended damage. Meanwhile Arphaxad, who had left with the former group, being both shorter of leg than the rest of the travelers, and not without his trusty flask of wine, began to lag behind his cohorts.

Ono walked with his head down and eyes locked upon his barely visible feet that flashed out in front of his long dark robe. Traveling thus, he was wholly unaware that he was quickly overtaking the lagging crewmember, Arphaxad. Hamon, whose eyes were carefully scanning the scene ahead, noticed the shortening gap between himself and the straggler, but did not register Ono's failure to perceive it.

Hamon was straining into the dark to identify the man while bearing to the right to allow Ono trail berth should they overtake the straggler, when Ono stepped cleanly upon the robe of the slightly inebriated Arphaxad causing them both to trip. The tall accountant lunged forward falling headlong upon the back of the shorter man, who yelped as if attacked. When Hamon perceived what had happened and stepped forward to both hush and assist, Ono, struggling to his feet, stepped hard upon the blade of his hoe, causing it to spring up and whack him a full blow in the face. Certain that such a blow would be followed by an outcry inharmonious with the need for stealth, Hamon stepped forward to try and clap his hand over the accountant's mouth. But Ono, now doubled over in pain with the hoe under his elbow, stumbled swiftly away, causing the back end of the handle to whack the quickly approaching Hamon in the eye.

Arphaxad, being fully engaged struggling to his feet, had not identified the other two in the darkness, and thought he had been attacked. He arose brandishing his spade as a weapon. He swung the handle vigorously at Ono and missed, but did connect with Hamon. In the general confusion that followed, Hamon, with the disadvantage of having received two unexpected blows, had difficulty bringing the mayhem to a quiet conclusion. He stood in the trail panting and angrily urging silence, while holding the right eye that had met the Ono's handle, and nursing the left cheek that had met Arph's.

Meanwhile, the rest of the troop, unaware of the goings on behind them, continued on ahead. After some furious but hushed scoldings of both of his subjects, Hamon discerned that his accountant was spent by the event. Ono was not able to stop weeping and was a miserable mess. Arphaxad, the only one of the three who was not nursing a throbbing head, was, with the aid of slight inebriation, struck with the humor in the event and was barely containing laughter. Though succeeding in swallowing the bulk of his chuckles, he could not maintain a completely straight face in the midst of Hamon's angry admonishments, which aroused even more anger on the part of the latter.

Perceiving anew the disadvantages of having one as ill suited as Ono along on such a mission, and becoming more nervous by the moment about the troop that was going on ahead without him, Hamon suggested that Ono remain here until he recovered. The other two hurried to catch up with the others.

"What about weighing the gold?" Arphaxad protested, struggling to keep pace.

"I will see to the gold!" Hamon angrily retorted.

By the time Hamon and Arphaxad resumed their trek, the party ahead had completely disappeared into the darkness.

Hamon had carefully explained the topography of the area to the entire band, and with the help of a larger map, pointed out the landmarks from which the place to dig could be identified. These landmarks Hamon deliberately rendered with slight inaccuracy, a precaution intended to prevent anyone finding the gold without his presence. Still, he was uncomfortable being so far behind, lest the group ahead overshoot their target and wander right into the farmyard.

He and Arphaxad struggled up the trail. The night had become almost completely black, except for the receding torchlights that glowed from the town below like faint orange sparks. Hamon and his companion could hardly see each other. The sound of their stumbling up the trail became the only assurance of each other's near presence.

For Arphaxad, such darkness was a convenient development since he had not failed to bring along his flask from which he sneaked sips. Between these, his muffled chuckles, and his concentration to stay centered on the dark and rugged trail, he was fully occupied.

Finally, the two topped a rise and saw a dark patch to the

right of the trail, which Hamon understood to be a vineyard. Upon locating this, he knew their destination was in the rough unfarmed hillside to the left of the trail. Having located the predetermined point at which to break in that direction, he led the struggling Arphaxad up a rocky incline. Soon the slope leveled into an area of flat scrub brush. Somewhere on that brushy plain, the buried gold was waiting.

A moist wind whipped up from the valley, and the sky smelled of rain. Hamon glanced up at the darkened sky, no stars or moon were visible.

"We need to hurry along," he informed his companion, "rain may be in the making."

By sighting with some difficulty certain markers on the ridgelines, Hamon was able to find the north south plane, and then follow it, sighting other landmarks for the east west plane. A large pointed boulder was passed, which assured Hamon he was on the right track. Upon arriving at the site, he lit a torch and held it low to examine the ground. His heart pounded upon discerning evidence of recent disturbance to the surface of the ground, but to his dismay, none of the earlier arriving party was anywhere to be seen.

"They have run off with the gold already!" Arphaxad exclaimed.

Hamon snorted.

"Without digging?"

"Oh, right."

"But where are they?" Hamon wondered.

He strained into the dark night in various directions without success until a momentary pause in the wind allowed the sound of the other party. Hamon turned in the direction of the sound and, listening again, became quite sure he had located them. The clink of a shovel confirmed it.

"Why are they digging over there?" Hamon asked, irritated.

In response, Arphaxad merely hiccupped. Hamon looked

around.

“Arph, are you drunk?”

“No my lord. Although, I am surrsty from the hike. Do you have a flask?”

Hamon pursed his lips angrily.

“No, Arph, I do not have a flask—I am not up here on recreation! And you’re drunk. Admit it!”

“You—you won’t think lessh of me?”

“I couldn’t possibly think any less of you!”

Arph sniffed.

“You flatter me my lord. I am not worthy of it.”

Hamon stared at him.

“You’re more worthy of it than you know,” he muttered.

A distant shovel clinked again. Hamon turned toward the sound.

“They are digging much too close to the farmhouse. We must stop them at once.”

When Hamon started in that direction, Arphaxad took a step to follow and then stumbled, dropping his implement in front of Hamon who tripped on it. Hamon also got a clean whiff of alcohol. He stood up and cursed at his companion.

“Arph!”

“I am shorry, my lord!”

“Arph! Stay here. I can’t have you down there digging in your condition, you will kill someone! Go sit by that rock up there and keep an eye on the farmhouse. They hang a lamp on the porch that you will be able to see. If anyone starts this direction, whistle. Can you do that?”

Arph put his pinkies in his mouth and inhaled.

“Not now, you idiot!” Hamon said, clapping his hand over the little man’s mouth. “Now—up to that rock!”

"Yesh, my lord."

Hamon hurried down toward the others, while Arph scrambled up a bank to sit and lean against a rock, taking out his trusty flask.

When Hamon arrived at the other party, they had already made a healthy scratch in the ground, which extended partially onto the main trail. He surprised them with his quick approach.

"Not here! You are digging in the wrong place! Look what you have done to the trail!—anyone will know someone was here now! The site is up there!" he pointed.

The men looked at him sheepishly, leaning on their spades.

"But—but the landmarks . . ."

"You read them wrong! Trust me—the site is up there! Now let's go!"

One of them noticed that Hamon was alone.

"Where is the counter?"

"He's coming. Now come, we haven't much time."

Grumbling, the men followed Hamon to the other site.

Upon arriving at the place, Hamon angrily pointed out the landmarks again, rebuking them for their mistake, and urging them to get started.

"Not until the counter gets here," one of them protested.

"Fine! He's just down the trail. I will go and get him. Stay right here—and be quiet!" Hamon conceded.

After Hamon departed, the men squatted on the ground to wait, and soon took to entertaining themselves with an argument over just who had misread the landmarks. After several minutes of this, it occurred to them almost simultaneously, that they were now certainly very near the gold, and if found quickly, some portion of it might be distributed before the official count was made. With sudden vigor, they threw themselves into the task of unearthing it.

Hamon, suspicious of this very thing, was traveling downhill on a dark trail faster than normally would be prudent, when suddenly the trail dipped and vanished beneath his step causing him to plunge forward and scuff his knees and palms on the sharp rocks. Cursing and slapping the dust off of his garment, he hastened down to where Ono had been left, only to find that his accountant was not there. After peering urgently in all directions and calling as loudly as he dared and getting no response, the urgency to return to the party on the hill overcame him. With a groan of disgust, he scrambled back up the trail.

Meanwhile, the men, with the vigor of gold lust, unearthed a large and deep hole in a rather short time. When Hamon came upon them, he was not surprised to find they had been digging but was surprised at how deeply they had gotten.

"Get any of it in your pockets yet?"

The men froze, looking startled, but not guilty. Hamon knew they would not still be throwing dirt if they had found it.

"Where is the counter?"

"Tell me this," Hamon replied. "Would you prefer to have no gold and no counter, or some gold and no counter? I couldn't find him."

The men looked at one another.

Hamon peered down into the hole.

"I can't imagine it would be that deep," he said, changing the subject. "Dig a little more, I'm going to circle around. We may be off location by just a little."

He turned and walked off. The men stared after him for a few moments. After a brief and heated argument, they conceded that there was nothing to be gained unless they found the gold, counter or no, and grudgingly returned to their task.

Hamon spent some time realigning himself to the landmarks, moving up and down the trail and sighting carefully as the men continued to dig. After checking and rechecking, he was fully convinced that they were in fact digging at the place shown on the map. When he returned to the site, the men had opened a hole deeper than a man could climb out of, and were taking turns going down to toss up dirt.

Hamon pursed his lips, frustrated.

"It's not here," one of the men said angrily. "This whole thing is a waste. I'm breaking my back over an empty hole!"

Hamon scratched his head, baffled.

"Did you find any evidence that something *had* been buried here?" he asked.

"The surface was scuffed, but, down under, it did not seem to be disturbed."

The man in the hole, covered with sweat, threw his spade down in frustration. It clanked against something hard. His head snapped back around.

"Wait!"

Everyone hastened to peer down the hole. The man poked his spade around where the sound was heard.

"Something is down there!"

"Ok, come on up, I'll go down with a torch," Hamon said.

A rope was tossed down, the man scrambled out of the hole, and Hamon descended down. He bent down poking and scratching the ground with his spade. The men crowded around the hole watching excitedly from above. After scraping down to the object, Hamon straightened and sighed.

"It's just a rock."

"Are you sure?"

"Look for yourself."

He held the torch down low and stepped to the side. The men groaned in disappointment. Hamon looked up at them. Suddenly all heads jerked to the left at a sound.

"Someone's coming!" one of them exclaimed.

"Wait!" Hamon cried.

Too late. The men scattered, leaving him staring up at a patch of dark sky. In the silence that followed, he waited for their momentary return. Then he remembered his strong admonition to leave the site at the first sign of discovery, which as the minutes ticked by, became apparent had been obeyed. Such careful obedience would not have disturbed him so much had it not been for the fact that in the scramble to flee, someone had kicked the rope, causing it to fall down the hole.

It was sometime in the next half hour, during which full realization of his predicament descended upon Hamon, that the cloudy sky made good on its threat, and served up one of the downpours that the area was famous for that time of year. He had attempted, up until that point, to carve out some hand and footholds with his spade from which to make his escape, but the sheeting rain quickly turned the bank into a slippery mess and erased his efforts, while the bottom of the hole turned into a deepening puddle. Shelter from the rain that showered into the open hole was impossible.

Becoming aware of the fruitlessness of trying to climb out in such conditions, he changed strategies, and tied his spade to the end of the rope, hoping to toss it up and snag something solid enough to bear his weight. After several attempts, he found the rope behaving cooperatively, and attempted to climb. He was perhaps halfway to his goal when the spade broke its promise to hold, and Hamon landed on his back in the puddle. The rope snaked back down thereafter, followed by the spade itself, which, as luck would have it, managed to make contact with his eye that had already been bruised.

He groaned, grabbing his tender eye, while the rain lovingly caressed the mud on his face. He enjoyed the comfort of this repose for several minutes amazed that he could actually be in such a predicament, until it became apparent that he ought to get up before the water level in the bottom of the hole rose above his nose. Not quite prepared for death by drowning, he scrambled to rise, slipping, while the showering rain crescendoed into an almost deafening roar.

He tried to look up at the opening, shielding his eyes with his arm. He had no desire to repeat the painful sequence, so this time he chose instead to tie a loop in the end of the rope, and toss it out that per chance it could snag a bush or rock sturdy enough to support him. Not finding success at one angle, he began adjusting his tosses to land in different places on the surface.

Meanwhile, Arphaxad, being awakened by the rain from his drunken slumber, began making his way back down to where he understood the rest of the party to be, wondering if the mission was to continue in such stormy conditions. Upon looking up from his careful steps, his eyes beheld the strange site of a rope repeatedly flying up out of the ground, and disappearing back down to the surface. Not quite understanding what he was seeing and being more than a little superstitious, he beheld the phenomenon from a safe distance for some time, before curiosity overcame his fears and he proceeded to the edge of the hole.

Hamon recognized the silhouette of a man against the sky.

"Arph! Is that you?"

"My lord? What are you doing down there? Did you find the gold?"

"Never mind the gold! Arph, secure this rope! I need help out of here!"

Arphaxad's eyes widened.

"Yesh, my lord!"

Arphaxad picked up the end of the rope and looked quickly around. Not finding anything solid, and propelled into haste by the urgency of Hamon's appeal, he placed the loop around his waste and leaned back, digging his heels into the mud.

"Is it ready?" Hamon called.

"Yesh! Come on up!"

With a vigor heightened by frustration, Hamon jumped up to hang on the rope, intending to climb out on arm strength alone. The vigor and the weight of Hamon quickly exceeded the grip of Arphaxad's feet on the muddy soil, and unable to extricate himself from the loop around his waist, which Hamon had cleverly formed into a slipknot so as to help it grip securely whatever it chanced to encompass, Arphaxad soon found his person passing beyond the circle of the bank, and proceeding down the hole at a fair speed. He landed like a sack of wet grain on top of Hamon who once again found himself lying face up in the bottom of the muddy hole, this time with a drunk man on his chest.

"Arph! You fool! You did not tie it down!?" Hamon screamed, holding the already tender spot on his head, which had chanced to impact Arph's knee or elbow.

"I shaw nothing to tie it to, my lord!"

What Hamon spoke to his companion next, he spent a full minute in the saying, and the details of his expressions are not fit to repeat. Suffice that a string of revelations about Arph's intelligence, character, and parenthood were detailed, while the two of them reclined in the driving rain in the puddle at the bottom of the hole. When Hamon's diatribe wound down, Arphaxad, in one of his moments of keener perception, was struck with a question.

"How are we going to get out of here, my lord?"

This question, uttered as it was in such blissful innocence inappropriate to the problem at hand, excited in Hamon a rage rarely found among the sons of men, and he proceeded to shower upon his companion another string of invectives, achieving in it a degree of eloquence and creativity that soared to heights seldom reached in the fine art of personal disparagement. Realizing somewhere along the way that his companion was either too drunk or too ignorant to appreciate the artistic excellence of his torrent, and that his pearls of wit were being wasted on an unappreciative audience, Hamon eventually descended from his crescendo, and was left with grumbling to himself under his breath, punctuating his indiscernible comments with kicks and stomps that splattered mud.

Arphaxad was staring at him with eyes as wide as saucers.

"What!?" Hamon demanded.

“They told me you had converted, my lord,” Arph said, solemnly.

Hamon looked at him with the expression of a man who had just swallowed a mouthful of sour vinegar.. Arph sat down in the mud and leaned back against the dirt wall. Hamon rubbed his head vigorously, and shook the rain from it, glancing up at the opening.

“Hapsh I could boosht you out, I am considered quite shtrong,” Arph suggested.

“As if you could lift me,” Hamon replied bitterly, looking down at the smaller man, then noticed the rope lying tangled in the mud on the ground.

“Wait. Arph, I can’t see what’s up there. That’s why I couldn’t lasso anything. But if I lifted you up, perhaps you could see enough to toss the rope around something . . . solid.”

“Eh? You are a clever man, my lord,” Arph, said wagging a finger at him.

“Shut up you drunken fool.”

Hamon bent to retrieve the rope, the end of which disappeared into the mud. He gave it a pull, soon learning from Arph’s yelp that the smaller man had been sitting on it.

“Hey! That burnsh!” Arph exclaimed, rubbing his backside.

“Never mind that! Here, get up, Arph.”

It took several attempts from several angles and positions, but Hamon was finally able to get the not too stable Arph to sit on his shoulders, with the rope in his hand.

“I cannot shee anysthing,” Arph informed him, leaning forward to balance his upper body against the muddy bank.

“Then stand on my shoulders.”

Arph tried to find an angle to step up higher, while Hamon tried to get a hand under his foot. Upon doing so, and attempting to lift Arph higher, it became apparent that Hamon was standing on the other end of the rope that Arph was holding. It pulled tight, and the top-heavy arrangement toppled sideways and crashed into the sidewall. It was only by Hamon's extreme effort that they were prevented from collapsing into a pile at the bottom of the hole again. Eventually Hamon got his foot off the rope and leaned against the muddy sidewall, while Arph tried to coil up the rope. In the second attempt, Arph did get his feet positioned on Hamon's shoulders, but was too wobbly to keep his balance, forcing Hamon to steady him with a strong grip on his calves. It also required Hamon to lean forward with his face into the muddy bank.

"Can you see anything?!" Hamon grunted.

"I shink so. I can perhaps shcircle a rock over here."

"Is it a big rock?"

"I shink so. I'm going to try."

"Well, hurry up about it!"

Arph leaned down and made an underhand swing which caught the bank on way up and went nowhere, causing a shower of mud to fall on Hamon.

"I have to stry again!"

Arph pulled the loop back over his shoulder this time and threw overhand.

"I shink I got it!" he reported triumphantly.

"Good, now, I'm putting you down, Arph!"

Hamon leaned back from the bank to allow Arph to sit back down onto his shoulders. The change in weight almost toppled them again, and Hamon was forced to bear-hug Arph back down to the ground.

"You are a schmart man!" Arph praised him.

"Shut up, Arph, let's just get out of here. You go first, you are lighter, so you can make sure it's secure up there before I try it."

"Right."

Hamon looked around.

"Arph."

"Yesh."

"Where is the rope?"

Arph looked around, then up slowly.

"I shuppose it is posshible, it flew out when I threw it . . . my lord . . . like a bird," Arph said, making a fluttering motion with his hand.

If it had been light enough to see, Arph would have seen Hamon's face grow redder faster than he had ever seen a man flush before.

"I do whishh you would no more cursh at me, my lord," pleaded Arph.

Hamon responded by informing his companion that murder would be more appropriate than cursing. He reared to deliver a backhand, but his footing slipped, and the blow was only glancing. Still, the intention hurt Arph more than the actual impact would have, and he began to whimper.

"I am shorry, my lord! Don't worry, a schmart man like you will find another way to get ush out. I know you will!"

With all the traveling, digging, and time spent in the hole, the night was getting well along, and from the surface, the glow of approaching dawn was showing in the east. Hamon put his hands to his temples and leaned over to think.

"We have to get out of here—and soon!"

"My lord?" Arph ventured.

"What!"

"It has been shum time schince I obeyed a call of nature."

Hamon glanced at his companion as at a vile insect worthy of smashing. Then began offering such an exceedingly polite response to the request that his real opinion of it would have been betrayed, had not his voice raised sharply in volume at the end to deliver another string of invectives that are not fit to print. Arph reconsidered the urgency of his need.

Hamon then suggested that they repeat the previous maneuver, except that this time Arph would be supplied with a spade, with which he might be able to hook the rope, which certainly might be very near the mouth of the hole. The awkward maneuver of getting Arph onto Hamon's shoulders was repeated. Arph's eyes could barely peak over the edge.

"Can you see the rope?" Hamon grimaced.

"I shink sho."

"Ok, pull the rope closer with the spade . . . carefully!"

Arph lifted the spade over his head, and let it fall over a loop in the rope. It sunk into the mud.

"I have it!"

"Pull it carefully."

Arph tried to pull. The end of the spade was sunk into the mud, and would not move.

"I cannot pull the shpade."

"Why not?"

"It's shunk into the mud, I will have to go up to get it out."

Hamon patiently explained to Arph, that if he *could* get out, he would not *need* to reach the rope. This clever comment seemed to inspire in Arphaxad a bit of thought. It was in this moment of inactivity, that Hamon was struck with another idea.

"Wait . . . Arph, can you pull yourself up on that spade?"

"But what about the rope?"

"Forget the rope! Pull yourself up on the handle of the spade!"

"Oh! Yesh!"

Arph tried, but his arm strength was not sufficient.

"I cannot do it, my lord, though I am conshidered quite shtrong."

Hamon quickly concluded that his motivation to leave this

dreadful hole was sufficient to propel a man twice the size of Arph out. He wrestled around until he got his hands under Arph's feet, and then commanded him to pull. With all the power of his well-developed rage in his hands, Hamon forced Arph's feet upward, while the latter both kicked and pulled. A shower of mud kicked from the bank flew from Arph's thrashing feet into Hamon's face, and Arph's heel contacted Hamon's tender eye more than once. At last, as Hamon grunted loudly under the strain of maximum effort, Arph was propelled upward and over the edge, while Hamon fell backward to land on his back in the puddle again.

"I am out!" Arph exulted.

Hamon sat up, and inhaled a deep breath of relief. He wiped a mud soaked lock of hair from his eyes with his sleeve. Then he removed his sopping upper garment, and tried to wipe his face with it. Arph peered over the edge. Hamon looked up.

"I am out, my lord," he repeated.

Hamon replied that he was aware of that, and made every attempt at clarity in directing Arph to make secure the end of the rope to the boulder, before tossing it down.

"There is one other thing to mention, my lord, I do musht have told you not to call me 'Arph.' "

Hamon trembled, but with great effort, contained himself.

"All right. *Arphaxad*, lower the rope!"

"In jusht one moment, my lord, I really mussht go tend to a call of nature firsht."

Arph disappeared from sight, while Hamon screamed after him, to no avail. Staring up at the open hole in stunned disbelief, Hamon realized that the sky was getting lighter. He squatted down in the mud, and resigned to wait, rubbing the back of his neck. His soaked tunic lay in the mud beside him, as he waited in the rain.

Arph scrambled up the hill toward some scrub brush, in hopes of finding a safe place for his errand. There was not much cover, but his urgent need to tend to the situation forced him to accept it as sufficient. It did not escape his notice that the sky was becoming light, accentuating his worry at the lack of cover, and so hurried to get it over with. He was just in the state where a man would most not want to be seen, when he became aware of a dark figure, coming down the trail from the direction of the farmhouse. He sunk deeper into the low bush, and watched. The form became a woman carrying a pot, apparently traveling to the well for morning water. He tried to remain still, and waited. She passed by without looking up. Judging that she would pass by again the other way shortly, he thought it wiser to wait before going back to the pit to extract Hamon.

Hamon, meanwhile was growing restless, thinking that his deliverer should certainly have returned by now. He wavered on the possibility that the little fool had actually abandoned him. After pacing angrily the two steps available to him, he decided he would have to chance calling out.

"Arph!" he said urgently, in a loud whisper.

Silence.

He began repeating this call, to no avail, becoming more angry and desperate by the minute.

As Dinah returned toward the house with her full pot of morning water, the brightening morning revealed markings on the trail that she had not noticed before, markings that did not seem fully accountable to the night's rainstorm. She paused to examine strange scuffings, seemingly made with tools.

While she was thus engaged, she heard a faint but strange sound, and looked around, stopping to listen. She heard it again. It appeared to be coming from a short distance off the trail. Curious, she moved in the direction of the sound and shortly recognized it to be the bark of a dog. Surprised to find such a sound coming from an unexpected direction, she followed it, until she stopped short, noticing a strange pile of freshly placed dirt. From near that pile of dirt, the sound of the dog's urgent cry seemed to be emanating. It was quite clear to her then what must have happened. Some poor pet had fallen into a pit in the night and could not get out. She hurried forward and saw the edge of the pit, and then bent to look down into it.

Hamon saw the silhouette.

"Arph!" he said, more urgently than ever.

Dinah blinked down into the darkness.

"Oh—you poor doggie! It's ok, I will get you out of there."

"What?" Hamon blurted, surprised at the female voice.

"Is someone there?" Dinah asked, startled.

Hamon stepped forward to look closer, and the light crossed his face. To Dinah's surprise, she found herself staring down at a shirtless man, sopping wet, covered with mud, at the bottom of a pit.

They recognized each other at the same time.

"Hamon?"

"Dinah!"

"What on earth are you doing down there?"

"That is none of your concern, woman. I need a rope!"

"Why do you have a black eye? How did your robe get all torn? And, what are you *doing* down there?"

"I said that is none of your concern! I need a rope! Get me one! Now!"

"Oh, none of my concern is it? Well. In that case I suppose my imagination will have to satisfy my curiosity. I always heard you had canine tendencies, but I did not know you had the habit of spending your nights in muddy pits barking at the moon."

"Dinah! You miserable wench! This is no time for your insidious jokes, can't you see my predicament? Get me a rope, will you?!"

"Your predicament is quite clear. But if I were in it, I might find a little courtesy a better strategy than insults. Are you not even going to ask nicely? Say please?"

"Dinah!"

"Say it."

Hamon growled, and kicked the mud.

"Oh, bad doggie! Are you going to bite me?"

"Dinah—that is *not* funny."

"It's at least as funny as all those nights you left the inn leaving no gratuity, neither in word nor in silver."

"When did I ever do that? For all the money I spent in that wretched hole, you should be thanking me!"

"Wretched hole? Have you an attraction to such places?"

"Dinah! I meant that miserable inn of yours—that new girl they've got—you pay for full mugs of wine and get half!"

"Oh, I am so sorry, are you thirsty?—doggie needs water."

She tipped her water pot and let a small amount splash down on him.

"Dinah! You miserable tramp! I will make you pay for this, you worthless washmaiden!"

"You look like you could use a good wash. Shall I send you some more water down?"

She started to tip her pot again.

"No! Stop! I need a rope—that's all!—you filthy, little harlot!" Hamon spat, adding a string of curses.

"Ah. Very heartwarming. Pearls of kindness straight from the heart of a converted soul. If that's your attitude, I should just go away and leave you to your barking, you flea-bitten mongrel."

"Well you are just standing there tormenting me! What do you want, woman!? I'm trapped down here! I've got two shekels of silver with me—if that's what you want!"

"You can keep your filthy silver. I don't need it. But an explanation wouldn't hurt, unless you prefer to let my imagination run wild. It's the crack of dawn, I find you here half naked, covered with mud, at the bottom of a pit, barking like a dog. Does this not justify a certain curiosity?"

Hamon sulked, flushing with humiliation.

"Oh you are so righteous aren't you. Look at you, Dinah the sweet little virgin standing there with your nice little veil. Bahh! I don't believe it. Not for a minute—if I had any doubt I don't now. Torment me down here like I'm a plaything for your amusement. You are a filthy little barmaid, and that is all you will *ever* be!"

Dinah reddened.

"You slimy snake!"

She picked up a glob of mud and threw it down at him.

"Oh no—not me!" he replied, pulling a chunk of mud of the wall to fling back up at her. "*You* are the slime of this town. I could find ten men to testify to your ill-fame in less than an hour! You stand up there and condemn me? You will never be righteous, I don't care how many veils you wear. A pig in a silk suit is still a pig!"

Dinah had heard enough. She inhaled deeply and let loose with a torrent of insults, but Hamon, this time, was not to be outdone. The insults flew both ways, as well as the mud, but Hamon out-shouted her, taking advantage of a greater capacity for volume, if not quickness of speech. Soon Dinah could not hear her own voice for his bellows.

"*You* question *my* conversion?!" he shouted. "You? Oh, that's rich. Look at yourself, for once, you sassy, little prig! You're no better than me. You think you are so holy, so righteous—all your vain little prancing around in that stupid veil, condemning me, but you are spring loaded to sling poison—and mud—in an instant, without the slightest twinge of conscience! You have shown your colors. You have all the resistance of a vulture smelling carrion! Oh sure, see the nice little Jewish girl, paling around with a truly righteous virgin as if it could rub off on you!—but get away from her for one minute and you turn into the cocky little rat that you are! So, go ahead and condemn me, call me a sinner, and a hypocrite but I will tell you one thing, Abishag would *never* do what you are doing right now! She would have had me out of here in under a minute, and would be washing my feet right now. You *know* that's the truth. But not you. You were born a roach, you have lived your life in dung, and you will always have the smell of it. Give it up!—Who are you kidding? You could wear that veil for a million years and you would never be half the queen Abishag is. You are proving it, right now! You will never be like her, NEVER!"

Dinah fell to silence, smitten. Hamon saw an expression come over her face unlike he had ever seen—while her sharp tongue hesitated in a longer silence than he had known it capable of.

"You are right," she finally said, cracking.

"Oh, funny. Now you are going to offer restitution and penance, I suppose. I can't wait to see what you come up with for that."

"No, I mean it. You are right. I am wrong. Terribly wrong. I am so sorry."

"Of course."

"I'm getting you a rope. Right away. I was wrong to say what I said, now—and ever. I'm through with this. I am ashamed of myself, I hate being like this—and I'm stopping now. I never should have treated anyone like this—even you."

"Oh, even me. How sweet. You lace your apologies with barbs, and then wonder why they ring hollow."

"That's not what I meant! Ugh! Why can't I say anything right? I'm sorry—I really mean it!"

"Sure Dinah. I can see what you really mean. You're so full of poison you can't open your mouth without it spouting out. You don't fool me with your little righteous girl game. It's a thin whitewash on a pile of dung."

"Look, I said that wrong, I said a lot of things wrong, but on this, I am agreeing with you: I am not righteous—I will never be.

The only thing I can do is *support* the righteous, and that is what I do now. If you can find it in your heart to forgive me, very well. If not, I remain in your debt for my inexcusable rudeness."

Hamon gazed up at her blankly. Then he shook his head.

"Whatever, woman. Are going to get the rope, or not?"

"Right away. But what am I going to tell everyone what you were doing up here?"

He hesitated.

"I fell in this pit last night—I was up here hunting," he grumbled.

Dinah noticed the spade in the ground nearby.

"Mmmm. Hunting eh? What for?"

"You said you wanted an explanation! I gave it to you, now get me that rope!"

"I will. But it would be easier, if you asked politely."

Hamon sulked in silence. Finally, Dinah sighed.

"I have no rope, but I will be back shortly. Stay right there—or need I say that?"

With a burning urgency to report her find, Dinah hurried back to the farm. To get a rope, yes, but more importantly, to inform Abishag, and to recruit men to return with her, lest the creature in the pit become violent once released.

Wait until they hear about this!

Trembling both from the cool morning breeze on his wet clothing, and from fear of discovery, Arph waited with more panic than stealth for the maiden to leave the edge of the pit. Finally, she disappeared, and he hurried down to peer into the hole. Hamon, flushed with humiliation, saw the shadow on the ground before looking up at the form above who made it.

"Now what?!" he demanded. "Are you going to get it or not?"

"Get what, my lord?"

Hamon shot a glance upward.

"Arph!"

"Yesh—I could not come while the maiden wasz here."

"YOU should have not gone away in the first place, you idiot! But in any case she is returning any minute. And I would rather eat dung than accept help from that filthy little whore! When she returns, I will be GONE! Arph! Get that rope down here NOW!"

Arph quickly and tremblingly tied the rope around a nearby boulder, and tossed the end down to Hamon. Then he returned back to the edge.

"Itsh ready."

"Are you clear of it?" Hamon asked.

"Yesh."

"Show me your hands!"

Arph raised his hands.

"Step back away from the hole."

Arph did so.

Soon Hamon, with the aid of a few grunts, exhumed himself for the first time in hours and triumphantly stomped to his feet next to the pit. Then he threw his head back, and spit viciously into it. He looked over at Arph. The little man took a frightened step backward. Suddenly, noises were heard on the trail.

Hamon quickly picked up the spade and the rope.

"Let's go!"

The odd pair fled the site, running into the high brushy country, disappearing over a rise, and not stopping to look back.

After Dinah returned with help to the empty pit, she recounted again for them what she had discovered there early in the morning, insisting that she was telling the truth.

"I thought I heard something last night, and I even came this way to investigate, as far as the well, but saw nothing. But—his story—it makes no sense, no sense at all," Jared commented.

Abishag sent Dinah a silent message, and the two of them departed together. While walking down the trail, Abishag explained to Dinah about the pigeon and the map, and the gold, and also the map being recently missing from her room.

"So, he was looking for the gold," Dinah concluded, sitting next to Abishag on the edge of the well.

Abishag nodded. "The map could not be understood without understanding the Temple of the king."

"But how did you know the measurements of the Temple?"

"He told me of it. Short of that, I would be just as lost as Hamon. One must be told of things one has never seen. It was so for me, not so for Hamon."

Dinah glanced up toward the open pit.

"It must have been quite an ordeal," she commented.

"It certainly appears so."

The maidens stared at the ground for a moment, until the humor of it reached them, and they both chuckled then grabbed their bellies in laughter.

"It's amazing," Dinah exclaimed. "Months ago, before any of this happened, the king pre-placed gold for you—a gift on time release—but at the same time, hid it from Hamon. He could not even touch it."

"You understand that Hamon will be even angrier now," Abishag warned.

Dinah's expression went flat, and her eyes lowered.

"I was not exactly kind to him, I am afraid."

Dinah then recounted the sense of her conversation with Hamon, looking shamefully at the ground. "Sometimes I fear I will never be righteous."

"It sounds to me like you showed some fine restraint, under the circumstances," Abishag said.

"Not enough restraint. When will I ever gain control over myself? Sometimes I think . . ." she paused, while Abishag waited. "Sometimes I think, he was right. I will never be more than a . . . a filthy barmaid. This veil. What is it anyway? A piece of cloth. It doesn't change the inside of a person. No matter how hard I try, I just . . . my past habits are too strong."

Abishag sighed.

"Just because you are not at the destination, doesn't mean you are not on the journey."

"Yes, well, it's a long journey."

"It is a lifelong journey, and long I have traveled it. The only ones who fail to arrive arc the ones who cease traveling. But you are not a quitter, Dinah. If you were, you would have quit the inn long ago. But your strength is now directed to a better cause. And it serves a better purpose—I am depending on you too. Since you have joined me, this road has been much easier for me."

"Truly?"

"Without a doubt. For so long, I have walked alone. You can never know how thankful I am that you have taken this journey with me."

Dinah glanced at her friend, seeing on her face a wistful expression.

Too bad *he* will never . . ." Abishag began, letting the rest of the thought fade unexpressed.

Dinah blinked.

"You mean Hamon!"

"I said that wrong. Forgive me. This is the day of grace. I meant to say—there is time for him yet," Abishag corrected.

"You have more faith than me."

Hamon plodded down the street toward his building, his eyes focused only ahead. Passing through the hills, he had chosen a path that avoided the main trail, but after entering the city gates, he could no longer hide. Curious stares and astonished pointing from morning travelers followed him.

Sylva gaped at the sight of him in the door of his building and inquired urgently the reason for his strange appearance, asking if she could provide any aid. She was silenced by a glare cold enough to instantly freeze the glowing coals of a furnace.

Hamon stumbled up to his private quarters without a word, leaving Sylva to clean up the muddy mess behind him.

Meanwhile Arphaxad, exhausted, cold, wet, hungry, destitute, and now homeless, stumbled, moaning, down the road to Jezreel in the cool dawn. Hamon, using the handle of his spade as a club, had repaid Arph seven-fold for his injuries and humiliations. When the spade handle splintered into pieces, Hamon finished the job with a rock. He sent Arph on his way minus several teeth, commanding him never again to return to Shunem on threat of death, which Arph believed.

Arph eventually failed on the road, and may have even perished, had it not been for the kind attentions of a maiden on her morning chores who found him groaning in the ditch. Jemimah and her sister tended to the injured man and took him home. Jemimah's father returned home at midday to examine the pitiable man whom his daughter was nursing and found his condition to be just as bad as his wife had reported.

"Can he speak?" Laban asked.

Jemimah nodded.

"A little."

Laban patted the little man's hand, whose eyes rolled over.

"Who did this to you, friend?"

The man closed his eyes, and rolled his head to the side, wincing.

Laban shot a glance at his wife.

"Are you afraid to say?"

The man murmured something unintelligible.

"Excuse me?" asked Laban.

Arphaxad turned and fastened his eyes directly on his benefactor.

"Baal Hamon," he replied, "Baal Hamon . . . the unconverted."

Laban's eyes widened. He glanced at his daughter and then his wife, who had placed her hand over her mouth.

Chapter 29

The medicine had been gone for several weeks. It was not long following the discovery of the gold which Abishag so needed that she found herself staring longingly at the empty pots, remembering the words of Solomon on the note, promising a soon replenishment. Unlike the gold, the replenishment of medicine did not come before the bottom of the pots was reached.

Having so recent an example of the king's timely care, Abishag did not doubt the promise for more medicine. But such confidence was not so easily maintained among the desperate souls who were depending upon her for medicine. Having discovered that Abishag had gold, they could not understand why she did not simply purchase the ingredients to make more medicine. Though Abishag did know the proper prescription for the remedy and had a rough idea of its ingredients, she did not have the exact recipe, and she knew that some of the ingredients could be dangerous, especially in the wrong doses. She informed the parties who made their way to her farm by night that more medicine was expected, but could not explain to their satisfaction just how or when it would show up.

The rumor of her gold, as it spread in the valley, also brought some new visitors to her farm from among families to whom she had recently testified. Hearing that she now was wielding resources that a peasant girl ought not to have, many who had rejected her story were now reconsidering. The fact that they were reconsidering was also noted by Hamon. However, as days passed, and no Display of Means was lodged behind Abishag's seal, his initial unease subsided.

The thought of making a Display of Means never occurred to Abishag. The king had left plenty enough gold for living expenses, but not enough to purchase all the land in the valley.

Hamon was carefully watching the battle of perceptions, and when he perceived it moving in Abishag's direction, he was urgent to find some sort of equally convincing response, lest the population escape the grip of his lie. He knew that the power of Abishag's seal was activated only by belief in it. As long as people did not believe the seal was authentic, it was powerless. If the seal was not applied, the king would have nothing to come and enforce, and Hamon would not have to flee the area. But owing to Abishag's newly acquired gold, some citizens were starting to question his lie. Hamon's apprehension intensified each time a family drifted in favor of Abishag, movements which he tracked with careful attention.

The fact that Abishag declined to place a Display of Means in gold was a puzzlement to some residents who were re-considering her testimony.

"Why would Solomon purchase with his Seal, and not with gold?" they asked.

She tried to explain to them that the gold was not sufficient to purchase land, nor was it sent for that purpose, but the Seal was.

"The gold that I have is only a deposit guaranteeing that which is to come. But the Seal—that is the word of the king, a sure promise, for the honor of the very throne stands behind that."

"But the king has no limit of gold. You should not be left short—if it is in fact the king's gold. Surely he would understand our need to see more evidence, to support such bold claims," they would reply.

Such arguments circulated, causing some to sway one way or the other, while Abishag, as best as she could, tried to simply hold to an accurate testimony, whether people found it satisfying or not.

The question of the medicine was also puzzling to some. If the medicine was truly a gift from the king, why did he leave a short supply? To this, Abishag could only respond that more medicine would be forthcoming soon—and remind them that not so much medicine would have been necessary, had more people followed her instructions to drink the hot air of the fire room. She explained this to Dinah as well, who had been puzzled by the shortage.

"Solomon left enough medicine to cure this valley several times over, if not for the fact that so many people became addicted to it, without taking the true cure," she reminded her.

****

Hamon brooded, eating little and sleeping less. His servants kept carefully quiet, tiptoeing around him and straining to anticipate his whims. He seemed distant, even to his closest associates. Having been asked his opinion of the gold which Abishag wielded, and not having been able to devise a fully satisfying response, he avoided questions by shunning public appearances. Still, he was able to fuel a few of the stronger objections with statements of his own.

"Her paramour could have left her a few token shekels of gold," he allowed. "But he apparently did not have very much—not enough to display means behind her false seal. A strange king who would be crippled by such a shortage."

Inwardly, he worried that she might indeed have enough gold to make a real showing, or that more gold might come into her possession at any time. Perhaps she was waiting for the right moment to step forward with it. He knew his frail explanation could be blown to bits in a moment, and he would be left with no argument. But beyond that, the fact that she had gold at all troubled him.

A soft knock sounded on his door. Hamon did not look up from the scroll he was studying.

"I'm busy," he informed the unknown messenger.

"My lord," Sylva said, "a sealed message has arrived. It is addressed to you . . . by name."

"From Philistia," he surmised.

"No, my lord, it is from Tyre."

He looked up, and frowned.

"Tyre?"

"Shall I take it back to the records room?"

"No, Sylva I will take it here."

Hamon closed the door, and sat down to unroll the document, pushing the crumbled clay from its broken seal into a small pile on his desk. The exterior of the document, unlike most, was devoid of any kind of writing, other than his own name and location. This message, whatever it was, was from a sender who wanted to remain anonymous. He noticed that the paper was of a fine, official quality, revealing the means and care of a wealthy sender.

The document spread before him revealing its most important secret instantly. Hamon's eyes widened, and he looked up in thought, suddenly alert.

"That queen . . ." he whispered.

Hamon had known that Chavah, following her visit to the area the prior summer, had planned to continue north, perhaps to Tyre. But the fact that she had remained there this long—that was surprising. Why did she not return to Jerusalem? His attention returned to the paper, quickly scanning the contents. Then he rose abruptly.

Sylva saw him approaching.

“I need twenty servants. Have them report to me at my private residence by noon,” he said abruptly, without explanation.

“What? Twenty?—your home?”

He shot her an irritated glance.

“Yes, I will arrange it, my lord,” she said quickly.

“And make sure two of them have the swamp fever.”

“The . . . the . . .”

“You heard me!”

“Yes, my lord.”

Hamon left, and hastened to his private residence on the east hill.

Hamon’s instructions for the staff that arrived were strict and blunt: finish all assigned tasks and then prepare to vacate the premises as of tomorrow—and plan not to return until further notice. Do what advance work is possible today.

The infected servants, two young foreigners, were assigned a particular room where they dwelt for two straight days. They were instructed to keep the room neat and to be ready to leave on a moment’s notice.

****

It was not by accident that queen Chavah arrived in Shunem by night, and unlike her previous visit, she was not attended by a royal caravan. She traveled quietly, with the modest aid of only two servants, whom she had acquired in Tyre. She wore a full-face veil for the first time in years. Upon arriving, she avoided the city and proceeded directly to the home of Baal Hamon on the east hill. Arriving late, she found the gates dark and quiet, no guards were visible. She peeked curiously into the yard beyond. There was no one visible to whom she could apply for entrance.

"I have been expecting you, my queen," came a voice from the shadows.

Baal Hamon stepped into the light.

"You received my message?"

"Yes. Please enter."

"What about these?" she indicated the servants standing by her.

Hamon gestured to his left.

"Let them proceed to the guest house."

Chavah nodded to the servants who proceeded as directed while Hamon picked up Chavah's parcels. Without further comment, he turned and began walking the stone path toward the high steps of the mansion. After hesitating, Chavah followed.

Inside the house, Hamon proceeded to a room down the hall leaving Chavah standing in the entry. She was still there when he returned. He passed by without a glance in her direction.

"Sit in there," he ordered, gesturing.

Chavah saw a sitting room ahead. The house was dark and quiet. She proceeded to enter and found a place to sit. She looked around at the large, quiet room with its expensive looking artwork. Several minutes later, Hamon returned, carrying a flask. He took a seat across from her.

She smiled faintly. He did not.

"Well. It has been some time, I suppose," she said.

He let the silence linger. She felt nervous.

"Have you informed him?" Hamon asked abruptly.

"Who?"

"Solomon."

"Well. No, of course. I should speak to you first, I thought."

Hamon nodded silently.

"It has been five months, by my reckoning," he said, glancing down at her form.

"Yes . . . five."

"You carry it well. It may have gone unnoticed . . . so far."

She blinked and nodded.

"Have you any idea who the father is?" he asked.

"I . . . beg your pardon?"

"Because I do not," Hamon finished.

"But it was . . . it was you. I am certain that . . ."

"Ah, the joys of being a woman, eh? A man can always deny the deed, but not so for a woman. It could have been any man, for all I know. How many others have there been, since then?"

"But . . . there were none . . . I am quite sure . . ."

"Yes, you would be quite sure, would you not? But I am not sure. How could I be sure? I am only sure of this: I was not the first, so why should I think I was the last?"

Chavah blushed.

"So, your problem is quite clear. You must find someone to take the child. Certainly, you cannot take him back to your king."

"Why do you speak to me this way? I thought you would help me," she said, trembling.

"Help you? Ahh, help you. Yes, of course. And by this help, I claim responsibility for the deed, and put myself in the path of a certain and unpleasant death."

"So . . . you . . ."

"And the sinful woman is to be burned with fire—I understand. And the husband who was sinned against—in this case—I have cause to think he has the ability to enforce the sentence. So why would I put myself in the path of such danger?"

Chavah stared at him, finding the Hamon she faced now a very different creature from the one she remembered. Was she in a dream? Was this truly the man who had been so kind to her just a few short months before? His hard stare bore down on her. She began to panic.

"I could simply tell him of you," she threatened lowly.

"And then we *both* die. No—you won't tell him," Hamon replied flatly.

"He will discern you! Solomon will discern you! He will find you out!"

"Are you under some illusion that he thought you a virgin? Do you think he failed to discern that? Bah! It could have been any man. I deny any part of this. Where are your witnesses? There must be two."

"Hamon! What has happened to you? You were so kind! I thought you were my friend. I thought surely you would understand, help me with this child. I am frightened."

"And well you should be. You are facing a fearful fate. I have no desire to jump into the flames with you, if I can avoid it. If I am to help you, there must be some recompense for my risk. Some . . . *great* recompense."

"What do you want?" she husked.

"Have you any gold?"

"Gold?"

"Gold!"

"Only a little. I already spent most of what I brought with me on this journey."

"How much do you have?"

She hesitated.

"Just a shekel or two . . . now."

He snorted.

"A shekel or two of gold, to put my neck under the axe. Do you think me as much a fool as you?"

"But what can I do!? What can I give you!? I cannot go back to Jerusalem and get more—I can't see anyone!"

"You cannot even be *seen* woman, at least not much longer. It appears you have little time left to save your neck!" he shouted, letting his voice rise.

Chavah began to sob.

"I don't understand why you are doing this to me! Where is your honor?"

"My honor? Oh, that is rich. A woman in your condition giving lectures about honor? You are wicked and dangerous. You trap innocent men with your charms and then try to make them pay the debts for your sins. I should just send an anonymous tip to the king and be done with you."

"You wouldn't dare!"

"How are *you* going to deny it?"

Chavah felt her heart pounding as the truth of his question rang in her soul.

"I will have the baby in secret—and *pay* someone to raise it. I thought you would be honor-bound to help me, but if not, no one will ever know. You can't blackmail me—where are *your* witnesses?"

"I am glad you asked that. Gentlemen?" Hamon turned toward a curtain, room divider. It rustled, then pulled back to reveal two men sitting in chairs. Chavah gasped.

"Lotan, Caleh, did you hear this woman admit to being with child five months now?"

The pair answered in the positive.

"Did you hear anyone admit to being the father?"

They replied that they did not.

He turned back to Chavah.

"You see, my queen. Your life is now in my hands. If you wish to keep it, I will expect you to do as I say from now on."

Chavah was stunned speechless, her gentle friend suddenly having morphed into a creature evil beyond her imagination.

"What kind of a devil are you?"

"A happy one. For there is something that I need you to do for me. And now that we understand each other, I believe you will be cooperative. It will not be difficult."

Chavah stared at him.

"And then, you will see to this child?" she stammered.

"I will."

Chavah studied the carpet.

"What would you have me to do?"

Hamon poured himself a mug of wine, offering her none. He leaned back in his chair and took a sip.

"A simple testimony is all I need. Have you any experience with the Seal of the king?"

"The Seal? The Seal of Solomon?"

"Yes, the Seal of Solomon, you miserable tramp!" he bellowed.

Chavah trembled.

"I—I have seen it many times. I was there, in fact, when it was first given to him, when he first took the throne. Why?"

"There is a false seal in the land. It is causing confusion among the people. I need you to testify that the seal of the king is with the king in Jerusalem."

"But the seal of the king is always with the king."

"Then your testimony should be an easy thing. You need only tell the truth. Can you do this?"

"This is all you ask?"

"It is all." Hamon let his eyes wander toward his witnesses. "It is all you need do, to save your life, and provide for your child."

"You could have merely requested this of me," she sulked.

"Forgive me. I have a great burden for the population here. I so wish them to be undeceived. I had to be sure of your cooperation," he said kindly.

She blinked studying him, amazed at the sudden transformation from anger to kindness.

"Testify. How and where will I?" she asked.

"I will arrange for some appearances, some places for you to make your statement. It should take no more than a week or two. You will also testify to the king's approval of our city wall. Then you must leave this area again. When the child is born, I will take charge of him here. And you will go back to your king, in peace. Agreed?"

Chavah looked at Hamon, at the watching men, and back at him. She was about to speak but her eyes suddenly brimmed and her throat went tight.

"Ah—none of that, woman. Get your crying done here, for I will expect a much better performance in public. Can you do this? Or shall I send you to the burning?"

Chavah sobbed and found her voice.

"I can do it!" she croaked. "I will—just leave me alone!"

"As you wish, my queen," he said with deep and unexpected tenderness.

After Chavah was shown to her room, Hamon reclined with wine with his brother and nephew.

"Do you suppose it will work?" Lotan asked.

"Do you suppose it will not?" Hamon replied. "Who could doubt the queen?"

Caleh was staring at his brother, then he snorted. The others looked at him.

"You have a lot of nerve, violating the king's promised like that."

Hamon shrugged.

"He tried to steal my queen, I got his first."

Caleh shook his head.

"If I were you, I'd make her lose the child. Better yet, finish them both while you have the chance. You are going to get caught."

"How?"

"She will tell him. Somehow, somewhere along the way, the truth will come out."

"Ah, my so prudent brother—always counseling caution—how touching that you would care for me so. But you miss the point. You see the danger, but not the opportunity. For one thing, she won't live that long. She is nervous, desperate, racked with guilt—such a person is susceptible to disease. She won't leave here without the swamp fever—I guarantee it. The wind is blowing cold in her room right now. In a few years, the disease will take her life. I can control her that long. As for the child, its existence affords a rare opportunity. Think of the benefit of having a string to pull in Jerusalem any time we want. Say we need inside information—say we need to be warned if the king is planning actions in this area. As long as that child lives, we call upon our loyal queen, and she dare not deny us. The child must live. I have a week to put the hooks in her for good—then she will pay recurring dividends from Jerusalem."

"I say it's dangerous."

Hamon surged forward.

"It's dangerous everywhere! If you have not noticed, we are on the brink of losing everything! These are fearful days—but cowardice will kill us! We have to meet the challenge of our times. If we do not match the iron with flint, we *will* lose to this king—just like the rest of the world. Don't you see how he operates? He bluffs. He gets people cowering, faltering under the spell of his aura, and then he has the advantage of them. But it won't work on me. You can't remain passive with this king, you have to attack him—stay ahead of him, it's the only way. He is clever, but he has not seen the likes of me before—I've even got his queen working for me, and with her help, I *will* outmaneuver him!"

****

Chavah, afraid, desperate, and realizing that there was little time left when she could be seen in public without broadcasting her pregnancy to the world, dressed carefully, and pursued diligently the tasks that Hamon charged her to do. When in front of a crowd, her instincts as a performer took over. She was able to make a convincing showing before her assigned audiences.

But inwardly, she was exhausted, both emotionally, and physically. Her emotions swirled between fear, depression, and the nervous terror of being hatefully abused. Cooperation was the only option—a fact that Hamon made sure she did not forget. Persistent nausea tormented her, which she attributed to the pregnancy. But something was added to it in the last few days, some sort of chest cold, which made it even worse. Her eagerness to satisfy Hamon's demands quickly grew, so she could leave the area, and him, behind forever. Well, not quite forever. Reality persistently refuted that dream, reminding her that there would always be a child—her child—living in this area for many years to come. Life had changed, permanently, and irreversibly. She was bound by the child to Hamon, and could never escape. She felt trapped, and the panic of it pressed in on her.

Being a very social spirit, living alone in a strange place with no friends to support her would have been hard enough for Chavah, without the crushing pressure of guilt and fear bearing down upon her. She felt as if her spirit were being squeezed and suffocated to death by a dark and powerful snake. Yet for all that, she smiled to the people.

Hamon had dismissed Chavah's servants from his property, telling her that they would be returned to her only when she had finished doing his bidding. The gruff care that she received hurt and puzzled her, and the long, still nights, during which she was left inexplicably chilled by a lack of adequate blankets, became the backdrop for many tears. Hamon himself was confusing and fearsome. He was alternately kind and cruel, leaving her confused and paralyzed. With the skill of a snake charmer, he could coax up in her a measure of trust, and then dash it in an instant. But even after having done so, he could find a hidden path by which it could be raised again. He could stir her emotions any direction he wished, on a whim, and she could not resist. She felt powerless before him, unable to deny his demands. On one occasion, he had her ready to receive his carnal attentions again, but then he turned cruel, laughed, and called her a wicked and filthy woman—sentiments which she found believable. In the dark of night, she was almost suicidal. In fitful dreams, she saw the face of Solomon and ran desperately to him, but he would turn away from her, and Hamon would step between them.

Never before had her impressions of a town—and a man—reversed themselves so fully. She had loved this place on her first visit, it was lively and positive. Now it seemed shadowed with the heavy dark spirit of death itself. She began to wonder if she would escape with her life.

****

When news of Chavah's return reached the hill farm, it was received with surprise and wonder. When it was reported that Chavah was speaking against the seal, Abishag listened quietly in private grief, though everyone was watching her closely for some reaction.

"Abishag, how are you going to respond to this?" Dinah finally asked her.

"It is understandable that the people would believe Chavah over me, for she is the queen, and it has long been believed that the seal of the king never leaves the king. But what is puzzling to me is this: why is she here in the first place? Her first visit, I can understand, but this is different. She seems to have come alone, for no known reason, and does nothing but speak the mind of Hamon, as if her own."

This insight inspired some puzzlement among the residents of the farm.

The queen's testimony was thoroughly convincing to the population. Who could doubt the claims of someone in such an unsurpassed position to know? If the queen herself denied the alleged king's seal, certainly only a fool would hold to it. What headway Abishag had made, now hit a seemingly insurmountable obstacle. Those who had been drifting in her direction suddenly fell distant. With no medicine to give to the people, and no testimony to equal Chavah's, Abishag became a name associated with foolishness, and those who had chanced confessions in her favor were made to feel foolish.

The queen was also quite vocal in her support of the city wall. She patiently reviewed, for various audiences, some of Solomon's building projects, assuring them that the king very much desired to see his kingdom strengthened through edifice. The evidence of this was obvious in Jerusalem, as those who had traveled there recently could attest. She also assured them that justice required each man's inheritance land be returned to him, and Hamon's plan to make it so, after the completion of the wall, was in line with everything noble and good.

"If one wishes to honor the king, he ought to support the man who supports his goals," she told them. "And no one here is more in harmony with the values of the king than this man, Hamon. Do not be distracted by this false seal with its false hopes of getting something undeserved. Solomon honors diligence and hard work and despises the slack hand that seeks only charity."

Many of the king's proverbs were quoted in support of this. She also issued ominous warnings.

"There are few of Solomon's many gifts greater than his kindness and grace—he is slow to anger and abounding in love and forgiveness. But there are some things a just king cannot forgive. I fear for the fate of those poor souls who have mocked his royal seal and gone on record in favor of this falsity. Solomon will be forced to deal with them as he must."

The power of the case was irresistible to all but Abishag's

closest associates. At the farm, some were growing despondent, and some of the beggars who had placed their hopes in Abishag's testimony wondered if they had only sealed their doom.

Once again, the response that Abishag ought to have to these things was a topic continually raised before her.

"Are you going to respond to these lies? Surely you must. Queen Chavah would recognize the true seal if she saw it, would she not? Can you not just show it to her?" Jared asked.

"It is not my place to refute the testimony of the queen. However, if I am allowed a private audience with her, it would be my duty to do and speak to her as the king would desire."

Abishag spoke this while standing near the boulder that sat near the entrance to the yard. Dinah, Jared, Barkos, and several of the beggars were present. It was while in this conversation that a voice sounded beyond the group.

"Well spoken, sister, as one queen respecting another."

Everyone turned.

"Brother Huram!" Abishag cried.

The royal brother of Abishag stepped forward elegantly to greet his sister, erect, composed, and kind in both voice and expression.

The general noise that accompanied the greetings showered upon Huram was loud enough to bring Abelah to the porch of her house, after which, she hastened out to join them.

"You have been gone so long, my son. We have been alone." Abelah said.

"You are less alone than it may appear, my dear ones. There are not many who travel in the hills this time of year, but if any chanced to hike beyond that ridge yonder, they would behold a larger work force than toils on that so-called city wall below us. We have been engaged up there for some months already, though you knew it not," Huram said.

"Have you been up there, all this time also?" Abishag asked.

"No, I have been in Tyre, and longer than I expected, for after I delivered your captured Hittite prisoner Pildash to Jerusalem, the king added to me another assignment. When queen Chavah did not return to Jerusalem, the king searched out and discerned that she had gone on to Tyre—where I frequently travel. He instructed me to locate her, and report on her doings, but not to return her to Jerusalem. The king knows more of her state than she is aware. This mission put two queens to my charge, Abishag and Chavah. The king is very interested in the affairs of both of his queens."

"It took no small amount of sleuthing, but I did locate Chavah, and fortunately for me, she has returned to this village where I now have both of the king's loves in the same view for a time. How long she will remain I do not know, and the king knows that I am needed here and cannot follow a wandering queen to the ends of the earth. I may be forced to attend to one or the other. Chavah has learned that the king is planning a wedding, and has, for reasons I dare not disclose, avoided returning to Jerusalem, for she believes this upcoming wedding is to be hers."

"Huram," Abishag said, "the presence of queen Chavah here has been puzzling to me, and to us all. She has done nothing but undermine my testimony and repudiate the seal that the king provided for redemption of the land. There are precious few who believe us, now that she has come."

Huram nodded with compassion.

"It is not unforgivable that the people believe the queen, well they should, for she represents—or ought to represent—the values of the king. They have no way of knowing otherwise. What is less honorable, is that they disbelieve *you.* Your every claim has been followed by vindication, from medicine that cures, to gold that weighs true, honesty in word and deed—even your remedy for the fox plague—all these things are undeniable. Evidences such as these ought to provoke some respect for you, regardless of the testimony of Chavah. Any who respect you and treat you with kindness, even if they do not join you, will not go unrewarded by the king."

"We have been discussing the medicine, lord Huram. There is another purported medicine—several actually, being distributed among the people. It is thought that our supply was left short," Abishag told him.

"As you well know, the medicine that Solomon left you was properly dosed and of able supply. An overabundance of that which cures the people leads not to health, but addiction. They will be ever taking it, but never able to come to health."

"And so I fear. I have obtained some of the purported medicine. It seems stronger dosed in the lily than Solomon's. That can only mean more opium, which I think dangerous. The only thing that restrains its consumption is the high cost that is charged for it."

"Truly this is death to the people rather than life. Do you know who the source of this potion is? For the king will not allow his subjects to be abused with this."

"I know not all who are making merchandise of this," Abishag said, "but I could perhaps try to find out next time I am in town."

"That would be pleasing to the king. Though he may allow it to be distributed here for a short season, the king will not let a plague of addiction spread in Israel."

The return of Huram resulted in an evening celebration among the residents of the hill farm, and a hastily arranged but merry feast. Those who had not had much exposure to the king's master craftsman were impressed with his manner and elegance as Huram patiently answered all of their questions, telling them of the king, and reminding them of things to come. He also inquired of Benaiah by name, and his sister, Jemimah, impressing them all with both his memory and concern.

"Benaiah has been imprisoned," Abishag told him. "After the Hittite prisoner was broken out, Benaiah was captured and blamed for it. He has responded nobly, but surely he must wonder why this has befallen him."

"It takes a man of exceptional character to walk the path that has been required of Benaiah. He will surely not be left here when the king returns."

"Left here? When the king returns, will not all be made right?" she asked.

"All will indeed be made right, but first, the king will return for you, and all your household, that you might be wed together in his house. Another chance for repentance will be given everyone, where one last time, the king will display his wisdom. Those who are wise will join you. I fear for what those who remain in your absence will face—in that dark time before the king's final return. Again I ask, how is it with Jemimah, the little dove?"

"She is yet in her father's house, but that was my doing. Left to her own choices, she would be living here, with us."

"She will have her desire—and in a far greater house than this. Such a one will surely not be left behind."

The words of Huram were both ominous and comforting to all.

When the evening grew late, Abishag and her brother left the house to walk in the orchard, enjoying some private conversation. Under the apple tree they communed, the bride and her assigned comforter, in a special relationship that never could be explained to another. Abishag was more at peace with her brother than any man, save her beloved, and drawing great strength from his presence and words, fell asleep on his shoulder. Huram carried his sister back to the house and placed her in her own bed. He then spent the night in the guest hut and arose early the next morning to return to where his men were at work on the mountain.

Later that morning, Abishag went to town to see what she could learn about those who were selling medicine. Since the first seller of it appeared, a number of merchants began offering their own versions of the medicine, each with a slightly different concoction, competing with one another on price and quality. Some tried to bolster interest in their product through the use of fancy and ornate flasks, decorated with mysterious foreign writing. Others claimed theirs was closest to the original medicine.

Others promised the lowest prices. A cottage industry was springing up in the absence of real medicine, and Abishag was worried for the health and welfare of the citizenry. As she made her way through the city, her thoughts swirling with the many unexpected events that brought her to this moment, her course so strange, yet so sure, the voice of her beloved beckoned again. He was now, as Huram assured her, the soon returning one, whose presence in her memory, nay, in her very being supplied her with the strength to meet her unique challenges. The return of Huram, afforded a new and welcome strength, and not a little comfort. Even so she was little prepared for what she would encounter over the next few days. She was about to enter the market square when a gruff little voice reached out to her.

"One filling many refillings, maiden."

Abishag started, and looked over to see a ragged old beggar with a straggly beard, tucked into a corner, squatting behind a small supply of plain leather flasks. He was holding one of them toward her, with a twinkling expression.

"Thank you, but I do not drink, my lord."

"Ahh, wise maiden, for wine is a mocker and strong drink a brawler, but this flask contains neither. I have here medicine for the swamp fever. Relief for the suffering."

Abishag flushed with anger.

"My lord. You do wrong. What you have here is death for the people, not life. I can assure you that the medicine for the swamp fever has run out some time ago. All who are selling this dishonor the king."

"Ah, yes they do. They do, they do, they do. But I am not selling. The only thing I ask for this medicine is the return of my empty flask. One filling many refillings, as I say."

She blinked and stared at him. He was still holding the flask toward her.

"Who are you, my lord?"

"Who am I? Who am I? No one of consequence! But were

the same question posed to you, such could never be said."

Suddenly, there was the sound of a commotion ahead. Abishag looked toward it. Someone brushed by her.

"Queen Chavah is in the city again!"

Abishag excused herself, and hastened toward the sound.

Chapter 30

Abishag observed that a crowd had gathered in the corner of the square, and one of the elders was making an address. Beyond them, she saw Chavah seated on a litter. Abishag observed the queen from a distance, sensing there was some great heaviness behind her smiling appearance.

"Queen Chavah is not to be here much longer," said the elder, "and lucky we are to have been blessed by her presence twice in the same year. She has helped us to discern a difficult situation, and find the path of truth and peace. For that, we can only thank our blessed God, and wish that we could reward her in some way. The queen is tired, and will need to rest soon, but she has agreed to respond to a few questions from among us this morning."

The elder looked over the crowd. A man raised his hand, and was bid to speak.

"Some declare that the king was here—last summer, though in disguise. Not many believe this, of course. Oh queen, what have you to say to this?" he asked.

Chavah smiled widely.

"The king? Here? Oh, and I missed it! I so love to travel with him to the villages of Israel—he will get a good scolding from me when I return!"

The audience chuckled. Chavah went on.

"The secret visits of the king—this is a tale I hear in many of the towns I visit—particularly those that are on the upswing. You can be proud that your city has risen to such a state to attract this rumor." The crowd laughed. "Seriously. The king—and his seal with him—is in Jerusalem almost all of the time. The demands of his office do not allow for extended absences, and when he does travel, there is no doubt of his presence. Most towns are a month or two just in preparation for his arrival. If the king was here, trust me, you would have known it."

Another man spoke.

"As you may know, oh queen, there is a plague among us—a swamp fever—that destroys the lungs. It is known that the king has medical knowledge. We have a doctor here, but there has been another treatment circulating that seems to cure also. Could the king have sent something here for us?"

Chavah conferred with the elder briefly. Then she turned back to the questioner.

"I am sorry, I was not aware that there was a sickness here. But I will inform the king when I return—he will want to know of this. He may well have something to help you. I urge you to not do anything hasty—wait for the king's medicine."

Several other questions were allowed, and then the elder dismissed the people with the advice that they not unduly tire the queen. The crowd disbursed, except for a couple of maidens, who remained to try and get some personal attention from Chavah.

Abishag remained where she was as though frozen, staring at the queen from a distance while the departing crowd brushed by her. Soon she was standing alone in the empty courtyard. The queen, who had been busy answering the attentions of her admiring maidens, happened to glance up and see the solitary woman, then looked again, intrigued by something in her expression. Not only was there an unusual stillness surrounding her unknown observer, but Chavah perceived a moistness about the staring woman's eyes, and found herself drawn in by an expression so exceedingly earnest it was disconcerting. The eyes of the queen locked with the eyes of the woman, her stare of fascination then blending into one of vague recognition. Chavah frowned slightly. The woman looked . . . familiar to her, in a dreamlike way. The maidens followed the queen's gaze curiously, and one of them mentioned the name of Abishag. The queen's head snapped around to look at the girl who had spoken, then back at Abishag, and a moment later mouthed the name in a question herself.

"Abishag?"

Abishag nodded ever so slightly, and then, began to move toward the queen. The maidens, sensing that the situation had suddenly changed irrecoverably, drew back from the queen who stood up to meet the approaching woman. The two, queen apparent and queen to be, stood face to face.

"Is it truly you? Are you Abishag?" Chavah asked.

"Yes, my queen, it is I," Abishag replied softly, "and I very much need to speak with you."

The queen blinked at her, looking her up and down satisfying herself that this was indeed the former nurse of King David, a person she had almost forgotten in the four years since his death.

"Abishag! Where have you been these past years—do you live here in this village?"

"I do, and I must speak to you, truly, without delay, and if I may be allowed the honor, alone."

The queen, mesmerized by the direct yet humble manner of the girl that stood before her, after pausing more in wonder than indecision, agreed, and suggested that they could retreat to her guest house for a private conversation.

"Where are you staying?" Abishag asked.

"At the estate of a local prince by the name of Hamon. I am sure you know of him."

"Hamon—you are in Hamon's house?"

"Why yes, why?"

"Is he . . . at home now?"

"He is out on business. Do you have some objection to meeting there?"

"No, no, my queen. Thank you, I will accompany you at once if you would be so kind as to have me."

The two departed together followed by the curious stares of the maidens.

Chavah was puzzled by the somber manner of the maiden Abishag, who after her strange and cryptic greeting, fell silent and offered nothing more. Chavah attempted some small talk with the girl she vaguely remembered, but Abishag offered only the vaguest of polite responses to Chavah and appeared under the sway of deep thoughts.

"Do you know why I am here?" Chavah asked at last after they had entered the house, all attempts at safe and meaningless conversation having faltered. To this, Abishag looked at the queen with an expression that revealed a frighteningly complete knowledge.

"I am here in service of the king—King Solomon, you . . . remember." Chavah continued. "Yes, of course you would know the king, who in the land does not?—but it seems, his seal has been dishonored in this land, by a counterfeit. I am here to testify that his seal is not here, but in Jerusalem, where he applies it in the business of his reign."

"The king sent you here for this purpose?" Abishag asked.

"Well, no he did not exactly send me, it is simply the duty of a queen to act in her king's behalf, wherever she finds occasion. In the case of his royal seal, I am qualified to testify."

Abishag nodded.

"You have seen his seal, my queen?"

Chavah looked at her curiously.

"Why yes I have seen his seal, I have seen it many times. It is quite familiar to me, why?"

Abishag took a deep breath.

"Because, my queen, if you are in truth in combat against a false seal, it would perhaps be more effective to discredit not only the documents that bear its imprint, but the instrument itself."

The queen stared at her.

"But we know not where the instrument is."

"We?"

"Lord Hamon and I, yes—you certainly know lord Hamon—he is the governor who has asked for my help with this matter."

"Yes, I do know lord Hamon, and I also know that he knows who keeps the instrument that you testify against—has he not told you of this?—where the instrument can be found?"

The queen looked at her with a curiosity that was drifting toward irritation.

"He has told me he does not know where it is, dear maiden, why should I not believe the word of one whom the elders have trusted as their governor?"

Abishag nodded slowly.

"The word of a trusted governor ought never be dismissed lightly, or without due cause; however, in this particular case, I have the great misfortune of being the one constrained to prove to you its falsehood. Hamon has not told you where this seal is, or who is applying it, but he does know, as do I. My queen, if you will allow me to assist in your service to the king, I can let you see this seal that you oppose for yourself, that you might better discredit it. If it were possible to see the seal, would you not have a duty to examine it?"

Chavah hesitated, weighing the implications of Abishag's question.

"Of course, if it were possible, I would be duty bound to see it for myself, but can you truly take me there?" she asked carefully.

Abishag's eyes were now deeply watering.

"I can, my queen," she whispered.

Then, as Chavah watched, Abishag reached into her clothing, and slowly and ceremoniously pulled out the small cylindrical object hanging about her neck that had thus far been seen by no one, save Huram and Dinah. She turned her hand and opened it in the vision of the queen, looking up at her knowingly.

Chavah's eyes became wide as she stared at the object, wide with wonder, then with fear, as though she were staring at a ghost. She caught her breath and looked up at Abishag's tear-filled eyes, and then back down at the seal. Abishag nodded slowly, wordlessly inviting the queen to step closer. Timidly, Chavah did so and stared at the seal for a long moment, and she began to shake her head from side to side, as the most unexpected object blurred before her in her vision.

"How did you come to have this?" she demanded.

"You recognize this to be the true seal of Solomon?" Abishag asked.

Chavah continued to stare, shaking her head.

"How can this be? How can this be!?"

"My mission, my queen, is as you have stated yours to be, to serve the king and to replace the purchases of a false seal, with this true one. For it is the duty of every Israelite maiden to serve her king, wherever she finds an occasion."

Chavah was shaking her head.

"I . . . madness! Solomon gives his seal to no one! You prideful little creature! I don't know how you came to have this, but how can you think he would charge the likes of you to apply his seal? That the king of Israel would so disgrace himself to entrust his royal signet to the care of a miserable little peasant! You are insulting!—to me and him!"

"But this is his true seal."

"Yes! Well, it certainly appears to be his true seal in every respect, I mean it IS his true seal, it is one of a kind, surely and inexplicably lost by him on some journey and picked up and found by you, perhaps, for such a thing could never be copied to such perfection. It is his seal, but . . . but . . ." her voice trailed off.

"My most honorable queen. Your maidservant cannot begin to explain to you the events that have led me to the unlikely position in which I find myself, nor am I in any sense worthy to bear this royal seal. I objected to his entrusting me with it in the first place, but I am not equal to the disobeying of my king's word, no matter how great my unworthiness. You have called me a miserable peasant, but you flatter me—I am much worse. A poor person might at least be righteous, but not only have I no wealth, I have no goodness. Be that as it may, you are aware, oh queen, that the authority in the king's seal is not dependent upon any person's merit. The authority of the seal resides in the king himself. It is by that same authority that this seal is in my possession today. It is by his choosing that I have it. The king was present here, in this very valley, months ago. He is executing justice here even now. Hamon, you must know, is a foreigner, and an enemy to Israel, to the king, and to all that is right. I have been charged to assist the cause of justice. I have no value, no authority, no wealth, no goodness. But as little as I have of these, I have even less choice. The king has directly charged me, and I am constrained to obey his wishes, and seal back what Hamon is wrongly attempting to obtain through guile."

Chavah was gaping at her. Of the many questions that flooded her mind in response to such a speech, she could only blurt, "Solomon was here?!"

"He was, my queen. Surely you know of his sudden departure from Jerusalem last summer, and that he told very few where he intended to go. He was traveling north toward Tyre, but sojourned here for a time, living among us secretly, revealing his true identity to none. While here, the injustice in this area could not escape his vision, nor would his anointing allow him to remain passive. After he revealed himself to me, he enlisted me to . . . ," she broke off. Chavah was shaking her head in vigorous disbelief.

"This is impossible! I do not know how you came to have this seal, but it simply cannot be as you say!"

"But it is! You of all people know what inspired his sudden departure. He told me of it. It was your own doing that drove him to it, when you displayed your artwork in his worship chamber, in the house of vines!"

Chavah gasped and threw her hands to her face.

"How do you know of that? No one knows of that!"

"Solomon does."

Chavah hesitated, staring at Abishag as at a ghost.

Suddenly there was a noise at the door. After a timeless moment of stunned stillness, Chavah finally broke away from Abishag's gaze and went to look out the shutter. Abishag watched her go, wrenching inside and tearful, quickly hiding the seal back inside her garment.

Chavah opened the door, and Hamon's voice was heard! He entered briskly into the house. Chavah turned and walked numbly back into the room as Hamon followed. When he entered the room, he froze and ceased speaking. There he beheld, to his great surprise, standing side by side, queen Chavah and Abishag.

Read the conclusion of Solomon's Bride in Book 5

THE BRIDEGROOM COMETH!

Order books from secretwineonline.com

To leave a comment about *Solomon's Bride,* call

(352) 474-8636

To send a message to the author directly, send email to
solomonsbride@gmail.com

Made in the USA
Charleston, SC
05 August 2016